Between Cases

BETWEEN CASES

ANNIE DYER

Copyright © 2021 by Annie Dyer

All rights reserved.

Apart from any permitted use under UK copyright law, no part of this publication may be reproduced or transmitted in any former by any means, electronic or mechanical, including photocopying, recording or any information storage or retrieval system, without permission in writing from the author.

Between Cases is a work of fiction. Names, places, characters and incidents are a product of the author's imagination and are fictitious. Any resemblance to actual persons, living or dead, events or establishments is solely coincidental.

Please note this book contains material aimed at an adult audience.

Editing by Eliza Ames

Cover design by Qamber Designs

Cover image copyright ©2023

Imprint: Independently published

❦ Created with Vellum

ABOUT THE AUTHOR

Annie Dyer lives in Manchester, England. She spends her time finding ways to procrastinate from tidying up, usually through creating characters. Staple foods include chocolate, Pad Thai and whatever hasn't gone off in the fridge.

You can find out more about Annie's upcoming books and the inspiration behind them through her newsletter and Facebook group, Annie's London Lovers.

https://www.facebook.com/groups/AnniesLondonLovers

Visit her website to sign up for the newsletter and received access to bonus epilogues!

https://www.writeranniedyer.com

ALSO BY ANNIE DYER

The Callaghan Green Series
In Suggested Reading order (can be read as stand-alones)

Engagement Rate

What happens when a hook up leaves you hooked? Jackson Callaghan is the broody workaholic who isn't looking for love until he meets his new marketing executive? Meet the Callaghans in this first-in-series, steamy office romance.

White Knight

If you're in the mood for a second chance romance with an older brother's best friend twist, then look no further. Claire Callaghan guards her heart as well as her secrets, but Killian O'Hara may just be the man to take her heart for himself.

Compromising Agreements

Grumpy, bossy Maxwell Callaghan meets his match in this steamy enemies-lovers story. Mistaking Victoria Davies as being a quiet secretary is only Max's first mistake, but can she be the one to make this brooding Callaghan brother smile?

Between Cases

Could there be anything better than a book boyfriend who owns a bookstore? Payton Callaghan isn't sure; although giving up relationships when she might've just met The One is a dilemma she's facing in BETWEEN CASES, a meet-cute that'll have you swooning over Owen Anders.

Changing Spaces

Love a best friend's younger sister romance? Meet Eli, partner in the Callaghan Green law firm and Ava's Callaghan's steamy one-night stand that she just can't seem to keep as just one night. Independent, strong-willed and intelligent, can Eli be the man Ava wants?

Heat

Feeling hungry? Get a taste of this single dad, hot chef romance in HEAT. Simone Wood is a restaurant owner who loves to dance, she's just never found the right partner until her head chef Jack starts to teach her his rhythm. Problem is, someone's not happy with Simone, and their dance could be over before they've learned the steps.

Mythical Creatures

The enigmatic Callum Callaghan heads to Africa with the only woman who came close to taming his heart, in this steamy second-chance romance. Contains a beautifully broken alpha and some divinely gorgeous scenery in this tale that will make you both cry and laugh. HEA guaranteed.

Melted Hearts

Hot rock star? Enemies to lovers? Fake engagement? All of these ingredients are in this Callaghan Green novel. Sophie Slater is a businesswoman through and through but makes a pact with the devil – also known as Liam Rossi, newly retired Rockstar – to get the property she wants - one that just happens to be in Iceland. Northern lights, a Callaghan bachelor party, and a quickly picked engagement ring are key notes in this hot springs heated romance.

Evergreen

Christmas wouldn't be Christmas without any presents, and that's what's going to happen if Seph Callaghan doesn't get his act together. The Callaghan clan are together for Christmas, along with a positive pregnancy test from someone and several more surprises!

The Partnership

Seph Callaghan finally gets his HEA in this office romance. Babies, exes and a whole lot of smoulder!

The English Gent Romances

The Wedding Agreement

Imogen Green doesn't do anything without thinking it through, and that includes offering to marry her old - very attractive - school friend, Noah Soames, who needs a wedding. The only problem is, their fauxmance might not be so fake, after all…

The Atelier Assignment

Dealing with musty paintings is Catrin Green's job. Dealing with a hot Lord who happens to be grumpy AF isn't. But that's what she's stuck with for three months. Zeke's daughter is the only light in her days, until she finds a way to make Zeke smile. Only this wasn't part of the assignment.

The Romance Rehearsal

Maven Green has managed to avoid her childhood sweetheart for more than a decade, but now he's cast as her leading man in the play she's directing. Anthony was the boy who had all her firsts; will he be her last as well?

The Imperfect Proposal

Shay Green doesn't expect his new colleague to walk in on him when he's mid-kiss in a stockroom. He also doesn't expect his new colleague to be his wife. The wife he married over a decade ago in Vegas and hasn't seen since

Puffin Bay Series

Puffin Bay

Amelie started a new life on a small Welsh island, finding peace and new beginnings. What wasn't in the plan was the man buying the building over the road. She was used to dealing with arrogant tourists, but this city boy was enough to have her want to put her hands around his neck, on his chest, and maybe somewhere else too...

Wild Tides

Being a runaway bride and escaping her wedding wasn't what Fleur intended when she said yes to the dress. That dress is now sodden in the water of the Menai Strait and she needs saving - by none other than lighthouse keeper Thane. She needs a man to get under to get over the one she left at the altar - but that might come with a little surprise in a few months time…

Lovers Heights

Serious gin distiller Finn Holland needs a distraction from what he's trying to leave behind in the city. That distraction comes in the form of Ruby, who's moved to the island to escape drama of her own.

Neither planned on a fake relationship, especially one that led to a marriage that might not be that fake at all…

Manchester Athletic FC

Penalty Kiss

Manchester Athletic's bad boy needs taming, else his football career could be on the line. Pitched with women's football's role model pin up, he has pre-season to sort out his game - on and off the field.

Hollywood Ball

One night. It didn't matter who she was, or who he was, because tomorrow they'd both go back to their lives. Only hers wasn't that ordinary.

What she didn't know, was neither was his.

Heart Keeper

Single dad. Recent widow. Star goal keeper.

Manchester Athletic's physio should keep her hands to herself outside of her treatment room, but that's proving tough. What else is tough is finding two lines on that pregnancy test…

Target Man

Jesse Sullivan is Manchester Athletic's Captain Marvel. He keeps his private life handcuffed to his bed, locked behind a non-disclosure agreement. Jesse doesn't do relationships – not until he meets his teammate's – and best friend's – sister.

Red Heart Card

She wants a baby. He's offering. The trouble is, he's soccer's golden boy and he's ten years younger. The last time they tried this, she broke is heart. Will hearts be left intact this time around?

Severton Search and Rescue

Sleighed

Have a change of scenery and take a trip to a small town. Visit Severton, in Sleighed; this friends-to-lovers romantic suspense will capture your heart as much as Sorrell Slater steals Zack Maynard's.

Stirred

If enemies-to-lovers is your manna, then you'll want to stay in Severton for Stirred. Keren Leigh and Scott Maynard have been at daggers drawn for years, until their one-night ceasefire changes the course of their lives forever.

Smoldered

Want to be saved by a hot firefighter? Rayah Maynard's lusted over Jonny Graham ever since she came back to town. Jonny's prioritised his three children over his own love life since his wife died, but now Rayah's teaching more than just his daughter – she's teaching him just how hot their flames can burn.

Shaken

Abby Walker doesn't exist. Hiding from a gang she suspects is involved in the disappearance of her sister, Severton is where she's taken refuge. Along with her secrets, she's hiding her huge crush on local cop, Alex Maynard. But she isn't the only one with secrets. Alex can keep her safe, but can he also take care of her heart?

Sweetened

Enemies? Friends? Could be lovers? All Jake Maynard knows is that Lainey Green is driving him mad, and he really doesn't like that she managed to buy the farm he coveted from under his nose. All's fair in love and war, until events in Severton take a sinister turn.

Standalone Romance

Love Rises

Two broken souls, one hot summer. Anya returns to her childhood island home after experiencing a painful loss. Gabe escapes to the same place, needing to leave his life behind, drowning in guilt. Neither are planning on meeting the other, but when they do, from their grief, love rises. Only can it be more than a summer long?

Bartender

The White Island, home of hedonism, heat and holidays. Jameson returns to her family's holiday home on Ibiza, but doesn't expect to charmed by a a bartender, a man with an agenda other than just seduction.

Tarnished Crowns Trilogy

Lovers. Liars. Traitors. Thieves. We were all of these. Political intrigue, suspense and seduction mingle together in this intricate and steamy royal romance trilogy.

Chandelier

Grenade

Emeralds

Crime Fiction

We Were Never Alone

How Far Away the Stars (Novella)

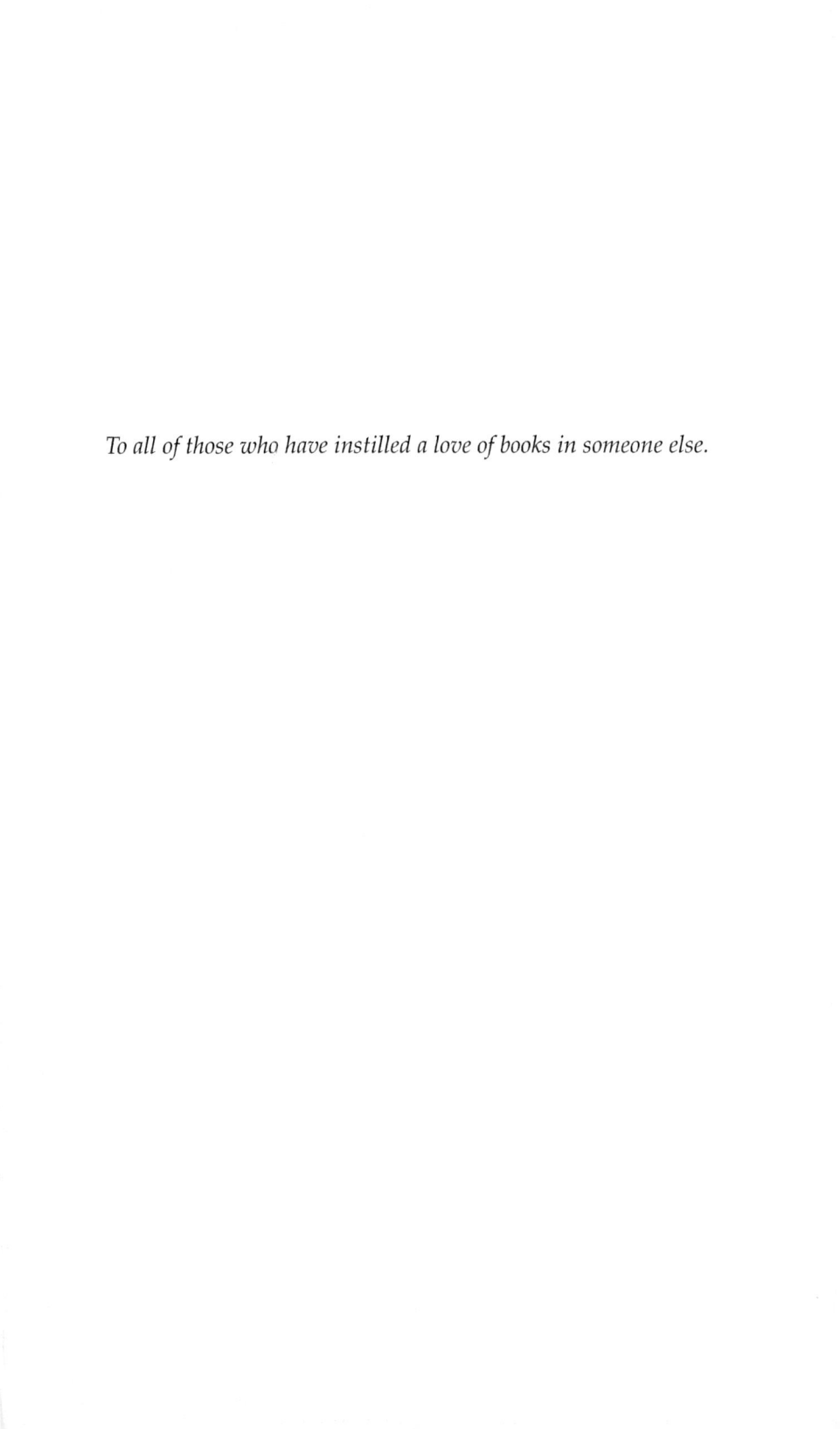

To all of those who have instilled a love of books in someone else.

BETWEEN CASES

Case law or common law is the body of decisions of the high court and appeal courts forming the binding legal principles of the English Legal System. The decisions of the higher courts are binding on the lower courts and the decisions set a precedent for future cases to include their interpretation of the statutory provisions. This is to be contrasted with statutes themselves which are binding as drafted.

CHAPTER 1
PAYTON

If he didn't take at least two steps backwards he was going to find his balls spewing out of his throat and his penis retracting into his bladder. I was officially done with this shit.

"Excuse me," I said, trying to slip past him even though he was mid-sentence on some topic that was 'All About Him'. I had no idea why I was being polite.

"Shall I come with you?"

He grabbed my arm. He grabbed my fucking arm. I resisted the temptation to knee him hard in the testicles and make all my fantasies come true.

The bar was loud enough to make me raise my voice. "No thanks. I'm going to find my friends." Who were at the bar. Together. Drinking margaritas. Together. While yet again, I was being hit on by a totally douche.

"But I thought we had a thing going here. You know, I've bought you a drink and we were mid-conversation about the choices I'm having to make about my career and…"

I exhaled deeply and tried to seek my inner calm. Unfortunately, the bitch that was my inner calm had decided she was taking a vacation in Hawaii and had left her cousins Tired and Stressed in her place. "Actually, I put my drink and your drink on my tab. You're telling me about you, and haven't asked me a single thing about me yet and you're way too close into my personal space considering you've known me all of twenty minutes." I could've been worse. To be fair, that was pretty tame for me.

He looked shocked, his overly large mouth gaping slightly open and his eyes wide. "I thought—"

"Look, Ed, I think this was never going anywhere. If you want to score here on a Friday evening you need to get a bit more creative. You know, ask a few questions, listen to her answers, at least pretend you're interested in what she has to say and you never know, she might be drunk enough to go home with you," I said, almost applying the cruelty filter. "Good luck in your search."

He started to speak but I managed to find enough room to turn around and walk towards the door where my sister, Ava, was waiting for me, along with two of the girls I worked with at my law firm, Callaghan Green, where I was a commercial litigator—a commercial litigator who had endured an incredibly stressful and busy week ending in a huge win for my client.

The end of a case always depressed me somewhat. I liked the busyness of a big case with a lot at stake. I enjoyed the adrenaline rush and the deadlines, the battle of wits with the opposition. But when it was over I felt a huge sense of loss and something my counsellor had equated to grief. I wasn't quite sure it went that far, but I would always get a little bit more tense than usual until the next client came along. I was aware I wasn't quite sane.

"Do we need to let the bar staff know where you're leaving his balls?" Ava said, her long blonde hair hanging in a curly mess. She was my youngest sibling, the baby of the seven of us, and looked the part of princess, a role she had always been given by our four older brothers, although Seph, my twin, was only just older than me.

I shook my head. "I left them attached. It was too much effort." We headed outside into the spring London night. It was just about warm enough to be able to wear a jacket rather than a coat and I was dreaming of evenings sitting by the Thames with a cool beer and the warm sun on my shoulders. Those sorts of evenings were still a couple of months away, which made me feel even more like going home and burying myself in a good book and having a hot bath. "Where are we heading?"

Ava gestured to a side street. "Silvia's. Unless you want to go pick up another mansplaining arsehole to insult for the evening."

My sister was surprisingly sober. "I'm giving up on men," I said, feeling better now the confession had met the air. "I'm done. I'm all about the job and my family and my friends."

Ava raised her brows disbelievingly. "You said this about ten years ago and decided you were into girls instead."

This was true. I had an experimental phase around the start of university as my boyfriend had been a cheat and an idiot. It had lasted about nine months, during which time my parents hadn't raised a single eyebrow and had welcomed the single girlfriend I'd brought home with the same open arms they'd shown everyone else. "No. No relationships. No dating apps. No men. I've had enough with picking up wankers in bars."

"Stop picking up wankers in bars then. Other places are available as are other sorts of men. Join a book club or go to the gym with someone who isn't one of our brothers and therefore doesn't look like a bodyguard. Ask Callum to set you up with one of his colleagues at the zoo." Callum was our brother who wasn't a lawyer. Instead he was a vet, one with his own YouTube channel and a very popular Instagram feed.

"Callum would probably try to set me up with a gorilla and video it to get a few thousand likes," I said as we entered Silvia's. "Besides, I don't see you setting the dating world on fire." Ava had been dateless for at least four weeks; I hadn't even seen her on-again, off-again bed warmer Antonio about.

"The gorilla would probably have better grooming techniques than most of the men you've dated in the past twelve months, Payts. Regroup, consider what you want and then set about it the right way; not picking up dicks in bars when you're both half-drunk. But joining the nearest nunnery is not going to make you happy. Decent sex and a few good orgasms should be mandatory," Ava said, heading straight to the bar and ordering two margaritas.

Silvia's was a small, very boutique-style, cocktail and bottled beer bar that was most popular straight after work or for a liquid lunch. It was quieter as it was later on and we perched on the barstools, accepting the small plate of stuffed vine leaves and a bowl of olives. It had a Greek theme and we knew the owner—who wasn't called Silvia—well enough to be fed whatever bar snacks she hadn't sold at lunch.

I stared at my sister, my two colleagues and a friend of Ava's now in the bar with us. "Since when did you become an expert on decent sex and few good orgasms? I thought Antonio was yesterday's headline?"

"He wasn't much of a headline," she said. "He had a good-enough sized cock that filled a hole but he really didn't know what else to do with it."

"Don't let our brothers hear you say that," I said, taking a sip from my margarita. "Else they'll fill his hole. With cement."

Ava laughed. "They've heard much worse from Claire. Have you heard from her today?"

Claire was our other sister, a few years older and currently very pregnant, which meant she was more argumentative than normal. The only person able to handle her was her soon-to-be-husband, Killian, and even he was looking slightly fraught. "A text this morning wishing me luck for when we received judgement and another letting me know that sex does not induce labour. I didn't ask for details."

"We should go see her tomorrow. At least try to be supportive while she has the world's longest pregnancy. And it'll give Killian a break from trying not to kill her," I said, biting into a stuffed vine leaf. It tasted divine: all glorious carbs and flavour.

Ava groaned. "I need to go shopping for a house warming gift for Max tomorrow. Fuck knows what to get the couple who have everything." Max was our eldest sibling and had just moved into a newly renovated house with his girlfriend, Victoria. "Let's not have too many of these and we can go early."

I raised an eyebrow. "Why do you want an early start on a Saturday morning?" My sister was a notorious late riser on the weekends. She flipped houses for a living and spent Monday to Friday on job sites, bossing about construction workers which meant starts earlier than seven am a lot of the time.

"I'm viewing a few houses tomorrow afternoon," she said, knocking back the margarita and gesturing to the bartender for another two. "Time for a few new projects."

I finished my own drink and felt slightly less cranky. Ava felt the same way I did when a project was finished. "Why can neither of us accept when we're between jobs and just relax like normal people?"

"Because we're not normal people," Ava said. "We're Callaghans."

. . .

Despite having invested in the biggest bed I could find, I woke up each morning tucked onto one side, as if leaving room for an imaginary boyfriend. It had been a long time since anyone had been on that side on a regular basis: my last boyfriend had been booted nearly three years ago, and although I'd had a few casual relationships since then, no one had been under my sheets for more than three separate occasions. I'd been burnt, and not just when I was a teenager, but since. There had been Matt, who was an investment banker: charming, intelligent and charismatic, he'd treated me like a princess and in my head I'd picked out the names of our children and where we'd hold our wedding reception. In his head, he already had a wife and a piece on the side, which happened to be me. I'd found out when I'd met Claire for a meal in an upmarket restaurant and he'd been gazing into his wife's eyes instead of mine. Somehow, I'd not lost the plot. Instead, I'd taken a photograph and sent it to him and then watched him finish his meal absolutely petrified that I was about to come over and cause a scene.

Then there'd been Gary. He'd healed my heart and promised me the world for two years. For a few months we'd even lived together. He was a teacher and played soccer every Saturday afternoon, taking me out for lunch on a Sunday and tolerating my twin brother, Seph. One evening I'd come home from work to an apartment empty of all his belongings and a note apologising, telling me he'd met someone else and wanted to end it before anything physical happened. And that had been three years ago and there had only been men worthy of up to three nights since.

I stretched out across the mattress, enjoying the coolness of the sheets and the space. We'd left Silvia's early last night, avoiding any more wankers and I'd strolled home to a hot chocolate with a dash of whisky and my book, the latest in a series set in an interesting club in Seattle. It was making me wonder if such clubs existed in London and how to discover one without alerting my siblings. Lazily, I checked my phone, knowing there would be a couple of messages from Seph at least. My twin was still struggling to find himself since splitting from his very long-term girlfriend and needed frequent mollycoddled. He had managed to move in with Max and his girlfriend, Victoria, but given that they had six bedrooms and countless reception rooms I didn't feel too sorry for them.

> Callum: Is it tonight Max is having this house party?
>
> Claire: Yes. I sent an invite that you should've accepted and it should be in your calendar on your phone. I say should because you keep ignoring me.
>
> Callum: Shouldn't you be giving birth to my niece or nephew round about now?
>
> Claire: Yes, but I'm not. He or she has inherited your DNA for being late, clearly.
>
> Callum: Does the diary entry have something in it about bringing a gift?
>
> Claire: This is a lot of questions for Friday evening. Shouldn't you be getting laid?
>
> Callum: Who says I'm not?
>
> Seph: You're messaging us about a house warming party. If you're anywhere in the process of getting laid you definitely won't be seeing her again. If it is a her.

There was a break in the timeline while Callum clearly went back to whatever he was, or rather who, he was doing and Claire no doubt continued pacing around the house in the hope it would induce labour. I skimmed down the rest of the messages, enjoying not having to rush out of bed to get to work or a meeting, or god forbid, a gym class.

> Callum: What sort of gift am I meant to get for a fucking house warming present? This sort of shit needs to come with instructions.
>
> Claire: For fuck's sake, Callum. A plant? A bottle of wine or Champagne? You could go with something more personal but not, and if I could underline NOT I would, a pet or any form of animal.
>
> Callum: But what if we all turn up with the same present?
>
> Seph: If we all turn up with whisky Max'll probably have a freaking orgasm.
>
> Me: And what about your future sister-in-law? Do you think she'll appreciate the whisky?
>
> Seph: Get her a bottle of really decent merlot or malbec. Then they'll both be happy. Did they get engaged too?
>
> Claire: No, but it's only a matter of time. Like this baby making an appearance. Hopefully. I think it wants me to be pregnant forever.
>
> Seph: None of us want that. Seriously. You were bad tempered before, now you're just unpleasant. We've nominated Killian for a sainthood.

Me: Claire, what've you bought them?

Claire: A set of red wine glasses and a bottle of merlot. Hopefully to be used later for wetting the baby's head.

> Me: Keep wishing. Ava was nearly three weeks late. Anyone heard from her this morning?

Seph: Weren't you with her last night?

> Me: Only till about 9. It wasn't a late one.

Seph: Maybe she's just sleeping in.

> Me: Apparently she's checking out some houses this afternoon so she wanted to go shopping early on. Although it is only 8.30. I wish I could sleep in longer.

Callum: Back to presents, people.

Claire: How about passes to the zoo? Or an adopt an animal thing—as in one you get newsletters about, not an actual animal. I don't see Max homing a friendly alligator or something.

Callum: That's me sorted. Cheers.

Claire: And you couldn't have come up with that yourself. Lazy.

Seph: I have no idea either.

Claire: Which is ridiculous seeing as you live with them. How about a voucher for a meal out so they can get away from you?

Seph: Somewhat harsh but I'll take that and run with it. See you later.

. . .

I hit the home button and left the conversation, wondering what Ava's plans were given that she wanted to be done early afternoon. She answered her phone just as I was about to hang up, sounding predictably groggy.

"What time is it?" she said, muffling a groan.

"Quarter to nine. What time are we meeting?" I said, still sprawled out in bed.

There was a low groan and a muffled voice that sounded distinctively male and familiar, but I couldn't place it.

"Eleven?"

"I thought you were busy this afternoon?" I said, now highly suspicious that my little sister wasn't alone and when she said she was going home yesterday, she had lied.

"I can push the viewings back till later. Meet me at eleven at Walsingham's on Thayer Street. I think I'm going to get them this set of cushions and throws I've seen that'll be perfect in the snug," she said, still sounding half asleep. "Actually, make it midday." There was definitely stifled laughter in her voice.

"That's fine," I said. "But when we meet, you're going to tell me who you're with and you're not going to lie to me."

"Gotcha," she said, and hung up, leaving me feeling more than a little bit lonely in my bed on my own.

It was just after midday by the time Ava showed up at Walsingham's. She was freshly pressed and tidied, radiating something that made people look at her as she walked down the street. I didn't remember life before Ava: there were only eighteen months between us so she'd always been a fixture. Where I had been the determined and stubborn sister, she'd been the gracious and ethereal one, the girl who just naturally charmed with her smile but had the brains to follow it up. I'd had the brains, but the charm had to be worked at. If I didn't love her so much, I'd hate her.

London buzzed around us, Saturday shoppers out in full force along with the tourists who were a continual trail of ants leading a parade around the sights. "How was your morning?" I said, obviously fishing.

She shrugged, stepping into the shop. "It was a hook up. Nothing to talk about. An itch got scratched. You should try it some time."

"I've tried it plenty. I'm not usually as evasive," I said. My sister was typically all too happy to analyse and score whichever hook up she'd been entertained the night before. That she wasn't saying anything was something to dig into next time she'd had a few too many glasses of wine.

"What are you going to get them?"

"I was thinking of some books. Classics—the really nice editions you can get. There's that book store next door I thought we could try; plus, they have a lunch menu and a licence in the coffee shop inside," I said. I had been stumped for ideas as between Max and Victoria, they were richer than God and more alcohol or a house plant just seemed thoughtless. Books were something they both loved and the house had been renovated with several built-in bookcases.

Ava walked straight over to a set of shelves where material and cushions were displayed, including a tropical print that looked suitably historic in design. It turned out I was right; the print was a replication of one from the nineteenth century and matched the wallpaper in the snug.

"I'll pick them up after we've been to this bookstore," Ava said, putting her card back in her wallet. "No point dragging huge bags everywhere. Besides, I know how long you'll spend in there."

I decided not to respond, because she was unfortunately right. I liked big books and I could not lie and the bookshop next door was drool worthy, possibly better than the prospect of a night with most men.

Cases, as it had been named, was an independent, although it had three or four other premises across London and one in Bristol. Like a lot of bookstores, there was a licenced café, but unlike most others the spaces were also used as live music venues.

This one, next to Ava's favourite home store, was the flagship and it was huge. I hadn't been in this particular branch before so I allowed myself the time to walk in slowly and savour the dark wood bookcases that bordered a wide aisle leading to what used to be a ballroom. Again, the same mahogany bookcases ran around the room, smaller ones dividing it into sections, the tiled centre dotted with leather Chesterfields and tables, perfect for lounging on with a book and a glass of red. Above was a mezzanine floor where the bar and café were situated, and above that was another floor of books.

"This was some vision," Ava said, taking in the surroundings. "Pretty much everything that could've been restored has been. Even the original fireplaces are dotted about."

"And so many books," I said, hoping I hadn't drooled when I spoke.

"But you only read electronically these days. Mainly because the covers are too embarrassing to be seen with," she said, raising an eyebrow.

I shrugged. "God gave us book boyfriends to make up for how fecking shit other men are. Actually, it's not the covers, it's just easier to read on my phone or my Kindle or my iPad. I still buy books though."

"I know; I've seen the mess that is your lounge. I wish you'd move; let me find a nice townhouse for you where you could have your own snug. I'll meet you in the bar—I've got a birthday present to buy," she said wandering away in her own world.

I left her to it and started to browse the shelves, looking for some pretty classics for Max and Victoria—and something for myself. The shop had an immense collection of unusual books: editions of *Alice in Wonderland* and Ted Hughes' poetry that I hadn't come across before and I soon had a basket full of treats that meant getting them home would be a workout in itself.

Popping the basket on the floor, I took out my phone and took a step back, wanting to get a really good shelfie for my collection on Instagram. The different bindings and colours were far too pretty to ignore and it was a good bit of inspiration for when I finally did move and got that big bookcase I'd always dreamed of.

"Shit!"

I wasn't sure who said the word first but my phone bounced on the floor and my ass was about to follow. The brick of a person I'd backed into caught me from behind which allowed me to rearrange my legs into a stable position.

"Why is the world obsessed with taking photos?"

I swung around, my mother's Irish temper raising its very ugly head. "Why is the world not? There's nothing wrong with trying to capture something beautiful and if you can't appreciate that," I gestured to the shelf, "then go and find the nearest sports shop. I'm sure that'll be more to your taste!" He was wearing a T-shirt that was tight over his chest and biceps. One arm was tattooed which did not match the round glasses that were perched on a strong nose. His light brown hair was neatly cut and he needed a shave. And a sense of humour.

His arms crossed over his chest and he glared at me, his

biceps bulging. I folded my own arms and matched his expression.

"If I wanted to own a sports shop then that's what I would've invested in, instead of a bookshop, princess."

I laughed with feigned hysteria, aware that a few people were looking our way. "Nice try, Thor wannabe. Now crawl back under your nearest weight stack and pin yourself down if you will."

A suited security guard had glided towards us. He had my phone in his hand. I breathed a sigh of relief. "See, it's clearly obvious you're only in here to cause trouble and insult people. Behaviour much better suited to elsewhere."

"Mr Anders is this lady causing you trouble?"

I stared at the security guard.

"She's nothing I can't handle. Thanks, Reece." He pushed his glasses further up his nose and accepted my phone from the guard.

"Nothing you can't handle?"

"Trust me, princess, you aren't anywhere near the top of the shit storm I'm dealing with. Now, are you in my store to buy books or just take pretty pictures for your social media accounts?"

He actually owned the store? This was the owner of Cases? I'd thought it was some old guy who had bought the premises?

"No way are you the owner."

He eyed me, arms still folded. He was tall, taller than any of my brothers which was why I'd thought I'd stepped back into a brick wall. "I'd show you the legal documents but I'm sure they're not something you'd be interested in."

My laugh was pure genuine pleasure. "Actually, dealing with legal documents is my job, you pretentious arsehole. I'm a lawyer, one who specialises in business, so if you want to put your stereotypical judgements back in that Neanderthal mouth of yours, you might not lose business." I pointed to the basket overflowing with books on the floor. "That is what I was going to buy from you. But you know, maybe I should go to one of your competitors. They might be more understanding of someone who really likes books and just wanted a picture to help model their own bookcase." I left out the part about Instagram. That was not in my best interests at present.

He pulled off his glasses and rubbed his nose. "Shit, I'm sorry. I don't spend much time on the shop floor and today is not good for me trying to be a people person." He rolled his shoulders and holy fuck the man was built. "Owen Anders, not an asshole most of the time." He held out the hand that didn't contain my phone.

I debated not taking it, because I could be a dick like that, but the look on his face was one of genuine sorrow. "Payton Callaghan, book lover and present buyer."

"And lawyer."

"And lawyer," I repeated.

"Can I have your business card?"

I frowned, puzzled.

"I'm in need of someone who specialises in commercial litigation. Hence I'm unable to people properly today."

I rummaged around in my purse for a card. He shifted and picked up my basket of books. "Here," I said. "I'm good at what I do if you do need someone."

He accepted it, the basket looking like it weighed the same as a bag of popcorn in his hand. "Thank you, Payton. I'll take these to the till over there. I'll make sure everything's discounted—just add any more to it that you want."

I fought the urge to touch the stubble thing he had going on and find out if it was soft or rough. "I appreciate that. I'll make sure I tag you in the photo when I Instagram them later."

His mouth cracked out into a broad smile. "The publicity

never hurts." Then his eyes caught mine and I took a step back.

"I best get moving. My sister is waiting for me in the bar."

He nodded. "Your phone. It seems to have survived the fall."

I took my phone and inspected the screen: not a single crack. "That's one bonus," I said. "I think that would've been my third screen this year." I was notorious for dropping it when I became distracted.

"Maybe you should get a camera." His own phone started to ring. "Excuse me, I know who this is. I'll leave these at the till."

I watched him walk away, jeans well-fitted enough to show off the arse underneath as well as strong muscular legs. He was clearly an attractive man. Just a shame he was yet another tosser.

CHAPTER 2
OWEN

It was the worst of times. Forget the other part of Dickens' prose when it was also the best of times; the best of times had been sacrificially slaughtered on receipt of the letter I'd had in the post on Friday. This was just after I'd managed to get home from sorting some sort of staffing disaster at the Westminster store. My bad mood had lingered, a little like the stench of the Thames on a really hot day, and unfortunately the person who had just received the worst part of that stench happened to be some hot shot lawyer who I massively insulted. And she also happened to be as sexy as hell, which wasn't something I needed to notice right now.

When I'd managed to calm down my mother, who happened to be on the other end of that phone call, I'd done a quick internet search on one Payton Callaghan and found both the answer to my prayers and my worst nightmare.

I needed a lawyer and fast. I needed a good lawyer too, and she would certainly tick that box. However, if I was to get her on side, I'd have to do more than apologise and give her a fat discount on some books.

"You know, Owen. I could try to reason with him," my

mother, Dot, said, sitting with her feet up on the small window seat in my office, clutching a mug of coffee, one I suspected was laced with whisky.

I tapped my pen against the desk. "I don't think reasoning with him is going to work. He wants me to buy him out, but the price he's suggesting is…"

"Extortion," she finished my sentence. "He's doing it on purpose. This isn't to do with the business. It's about me."

I'd figured as much. When I'd started Cases five years ago, my mum's boyfriend, Dave, had gone into business with me as a silent partner in my first store. It had been a success from the word go and his shares made him a tidy profit, without him actually having to do any work. He was fairly successful songwriter and musician on the side to being a bit of an entrepreneur; he and my mum had met at one of his gigs and had enjoyed a peaceful and happy relationship up until about four months ago, when my mother suddenly ended it, saying he'd 'changed'.

A mid-life crisis was my suspicion but I'd stayed silent in the hope that they'd work it out. So far, they hadn't and now it seemed he wanted to make their ending more permanent.

"It doesn't matter what it's about, I need to take legal advice because ignoring it won't make it go away." I had the funds to buy him out, but what he was asking for was ridiculous and I'd be a fool to pay it.

"Tim will be able to advise you…"

"Tim's acting for Dave. He can't represent me as well," I said to her. Tim was the lawyer I usually used; however, Dave had commandeered him first. "I think I've found someone though."

"You know someone?"

"They kind of walked into me today."

My mother eyeballed me. "That doesn't sound very professional."

"I wasn't. I insulted her and insinuated she didn't know what a book was until she told me she was a lawyer who specialised in business. This is her," I said, spinning my monitor around so my mother could read Payton's bio.

"Callaghan Green. I've heard of that firm. They're very reputable. Do you think she'll take the case? Especially if you've been your usual charmless self," she said, that eyeball becoming hairier.

I groaned and sank back in my chair. "She's a business woman. She'll take the case because she'll be getting a fee from it, that's if she has time."

"What exactly did you do?"

I gave my mother an evaluatory stare. She had always been my biggest critic: through college, through starting up the online dating company, through buying a bookshop, she had always had an opinion as to whether I was doing her parenting skills justice. The same when I had a girlfriend. She told me she brought me up to be a perfect gentleman, never once saying *I brought you up to not be like your father,* although that was clearly what she meant. I've never been sure whether or not I made it to perfect level, but I liked to think I was nearer to that than complete arse.

Today could quite easily send me down to that level.

"I was presumptuous and insulting," I confessed and then told her the rest of the sorry encounter.

"What did she look like?"

"You've seen her picture. That."

My mother shook her head. "No. What did she look like on a Saturday afternoon in a book shop? Not when she's dressed up being lawyerly."

I stifled a groan. I knew exactly what my mother was doing and it wasn't fair; I wasn't falling for it. "She looked like her picture just not dressed for the office. I was more concerned with the fact she was obsessing over taking a photo of my bookcases without checking if she was treading on anyone." She hadn't. She'd looked like a fiery pixie with a blonde bob and the biggest blue eyes I'd never drowned in.

"Okay, fine." She didn't believe me. "Forget about the letter from Dave's lawyer and your encounter with the pretty book-buying lawyer and focus on getting tonight organised. That needs your attention."

The first shop I'd started was small. It still existed— in fact it was the ones Dave was part owner of—and had its own speciality of genre books along with an upstairs dedicated to crime. Given its size, no one had believed me when I said I was going to turn it into a live music venue, but people believing in me had never been a prerequisite to actually getting stuff done. It held thirty people, plus a band and we sold out each time. Cases had a reputation almost immediately for atmospheric music, jazz or country acoustic sets, in an intimate venue and it wasn't long before my contacts from my own music days started bringing in fairly well-known names who were keen to play somewhere smaller that was just about the tunes.

Tonight we had an acoustic set from a band I'd been following for some time, the lead guitarist was a guy I'd known briefly when I was at college. Tickets had sold out some weeks ago, so we had a full house in the largest bookstore in my group and I needed to boss some staff about, given that my manager had broken his arm playing five-a-side-football last weekend and had just undergone surgery to re-pin it.

We had closed at six, an hour earlier than usual for a Saturday, giving us ninety minutes to put the leather Chesterfields and tables in the storage rooms down the sides and clear the centre to make a stage area. This store was the perfect venue: big without being huge—it maxed out at one hundred and fifty—and people could watch from the mezzanine floor above where the bar was as well as downstairs.

"Owen, there's a woman asking for you," Mick, my assistant manager and resident muso shouted above the din of furniture being shifted.

I looked up to the last remaining soft seat where a woman with long auburn hair was lounging, a broad smile on her face. Immediately, my stomach sank. I didn't need this today, not today of all days when everything else had been such a shitter.

"Win," I said, taking a few footsteps towards her with the faint hope she'd keep her voice quiet so my employees didn't have to hear about my private life, or current lack of. "What can I do for you?"

Her eyes grew larger, as if she was hoping they'd turn into black holes and she could swallow me with them. "I was hoping to hang out tonight."

"It's sold out so we're at capacity," I said. "I'm sorry. I can put reservations on a couple of tickets for you for the next gig. Ricky Whisky is here next Saturday. I'll make sure you get a decent discount." I was aware that my words would be nowhere near my mother's required standards for how to treat someone you've fucked a few times, but I had no intention of leading Win on. She'd wanted more. I'd wanted away.

She let loose a loud sigh and stood up, then took the remaining few steps so she could put her arms around me and pull herself close. "I'm sorry, baby, I didn't want to hurt you by making you come back to me so I thought I'd make the first move. I missed you." She pushed her tits onto my chest and thankfully my cock received the message from my brain that getting anywhere near hard right now would result in blue balls and absolutely no jacking off material.

Untangling myself from her limbs, I edged a step back, aware that Mick was watching us closely. "Win, I'm sorry if

I've given out the wrong signals but I'm really not interested in anything else happening between us. We had a good few nights together, but I don't want anything more."

"Are you sleeping with someone else?" she said, horror striking her face. "I'm not into sloppy seconds."

And she totally had the wrong idea about that phrase.

"No, I'm really not but it wouldn't matter if I was because we ended a couple of weeks ago and I haven't been in touch, so I assumed you'd understood that we were through." I rubbed my brow. I wanted to go home, have a shower, kick some computer-based asses and have a beer before sleeping in really late in the morning. Then maybe I'd hit the gym and run a good twenty-k before Ash, my best mate, turned up hungover and in need of a Sunday lunch—also getting out of his apartment while his Saturday night hook up cleared off. However, I had a business and this was it, so I was here. And in a moment Win wouldn't be.

"How very fucking shitty of you," she said, blinking so hard one of her false eyelashes started to dislodge. "I thought you were this gentleman businessman. With biceps." She gave one a slight squeeze and I wondered if this was how women felt when someone grabbed their arse.

"I'm really trying to be gentleman like, but it's hard when I'm not talking to a lady. So if you'd kindly take a hint before I'm really not a gentleman and have security help you out of here..."

She shot daggers at me from her eyes and strutted out, her heels clicking on the tiled floor.

I rubbed my eyes, only opening them when I heard Mick laughing. "Sorry, O. It's good to see you're human and make mistakes like the rest of us," he said, shifting the last chair like it weighed the same as a bag of cotton.

"I think the last fortnight has just been a murder of mistakes," I said, butchering the English language and its collective nouns for my purpose. I really could do with a fairy godmother right now."

Or even a pixie-sized one in a suit. I shook the thought out of my head. I did not need to make life any more complicated right now.

CHAPTER 3
PAYTON

"I'm sorry you got stuck with Ava on Saturday," I said, scooping the foam off my latte with a spoon. "Why she had to choose to go back to that friend's and make you give her a lift, I don't know."

Elijah Wilder, friend and litigator extraordinaire, eyed me from over his black coffee. We'd worked together for nearly two years, except when I'd spent six months in Manchester helping to get the office there set up. He was the head of department, having a good six years more experience than me, and, as I'd admit to anyone, had been a great mentor and rock when I needed it.

He was also the firm's eye candy along with my brothers, something I really didn't get about any of them, although I could understand it more with Eli. "It was no problem. And it meant she got there safe."

I shrugged. Saturday's housewarming had been a good night. There had been a barbecue that Victoria had taken charge of; Max's job solely that of keeping her wine glass full. Ava had also bought them a karaoke machine, which wasn't one of her best ideas and one she'd kept from me, else it never would've seen the light of day. Victoria's colleagues from the history department at King's University had loved it though and some of them could actually hold a tune. At some point, my twin, Seph, thought he could sing as well and had proceeded to butcher a Kings of Leon classic until Max had threatened to batter him over the head with the other mic. "Ava takes advantage of people. Be warned. She finds someone she thinks is kind and sucks them in for as many favours as they're willing to give."

Eli smiled, draining his coffee. "Except I'm not that kind. Come on, Payton, you know me better than that."

I grinned. I did know him better than that. He was a devil with clients and a beast with opposing lawyers and sometimes would put the fear of God into me when I heard him on the phone in our shared office, tearing someone a new hole. "I was just worried your recent break up would've turned you soft."

He sighed and gestured to the wait staff for another couple of coffees. This was our Monday morning ritual: seven o'clock meet up for caffeine, breakfast and a preview of the week's cases and court appearances. It was also an occasional post-match analysis of weekend events too and there had been many times I'd spouted to Eli about how fecking stupid men were and he'd attempted to rationalise my thoughts, usually after a one-night stand or a third date with a dick who I realised was an idiot after wasting too much time. "I know it was just a few weeks ago, but it had been over way before that. When was the last time you saw her in Borough or me go up there?"

He had a point. "I get that. Still, you now have the whole big bad world of dating to investigate again."

The waiter brought over our coffees. My latte came with a chocolate dusted heart on top which I decided was worth a picture.

"I have dated before, Payts," he said. "Are you getting me in on the photo?"

"Of course. The world of Instagram needs to see my sexy colleague."

He flipped me the bird.

I took the photo.

"You've got a quiet week for you," Eli said, studying me. "A chance to get your time recording up to date and get on top of a few files."

"Hmmm," I said, adding a filter and popping it on Instagram. I hated time recording—logging the number of hours you spend on a case so the client is billed correctly. It had to be done monthly and those figures showed whether or not we were on track to meet our target. Just because I was an equity partner didn't mean I got out of having a target, because essentially, I took home a share of the profits. That didn't mean I had to enjoy the admin side though. "I deserve a week of calm and quiet after the last couple. I have the Kingston case going to court in three weeks, so that'll be fecking hellish."

Eli shrugged. "All the more reason to get on top of everything while you can. I've got court and a mediation this week and a three-day court case next. Which leaves me with no time to be going on any of those stupid dating apps you keep advertising."

He was growly this morning. Probably not enough coffee. Or still getting over the fifteen minutes he had to spend with my sister.

"Excuses, excuses. I will get up to date on the crap through. Maybe spend today wading through it and then find something more productive to do. I do have three meetings this week. One's on that horrendous case from Wilmott Masons and I need to do a bit of reading on precedents on that." I scooped off the foam again, making sure to break the heart in two.

Eli watched what I was doing through narrowed eyes. "Why don't you get back on those dating apps? Maybe you'll meet a decent man this time. We're not all complete fuckwits. Not that I'm offering my services." He looked slightly uncomfortable, something which I enjoyed the sight of.

We had never gone there, even during the brief period when we were both single. As much as Eli was gorgeous, all dark hair and brooding stubble, we were too similar in temperament to do anything but be buddies or bicker. Seph had brought it up once when we were out for drinks after work in his unsubtle, unfiltered way and suggested that we'd have successful, genius children, to which we'd looked at each other in horror and then vilely abused my twin.

"They still wouldn't be accepted," I said. "As much as you're desperate for me to lavish my loving on you."

His phone rang before he could respond and he grabbed it before I could see who was calling. It was too early to be a client and he cancelled the call, so my curiosity was left unsatisfied.

I was buried deep in files with a calculator before nine o'clock, a playlist from my music library on low to fill the too-quiet air. I'd heard Jackson and Maxwell clatter into the office from the gym they maintained in the basement just after eight and then the usual incoming noise of the office staff and other fee earners shortly after. Seph had popped his head around the door and dropped off a coffee and a bagel without saying anything, which was very much appreciated and I seriously felt that the day, despite it being Monday, was getting off to a good start.

"Payton? Are you alive in there?"

I lifted my head from the files, recognising the non-dulcet tones of Phillip, one of our receptionists. "Sorry, Phil, I was buried arse deep in billing crap. Come in."

He stuck his head around the door and frowned at the mess across my office. I'd even taken over Eli's area and he'd escaped to use one of the bigger conference rooms. "There's someone here who wants to see you as soon as possible. He's come in to make an appointment but as your diary's clear, would you see him today?"

I pulled a face at the files. Anything to escape time recording. "I can see him now if he has time. This isn't urgent."

Phil looked at me judgmentally. "Well, it kind of is, but if that's what you want to tell yourself. I'll see if wants now. Are you able to clear space in here or shall I see if a meeting room's free?"

"No offense taken, mother Phil. Yes, I'll clear in here. Bring him through, with a pot of coffee maybe and those Danishes I saw Clara appear with." I'd been ransacking Seph's office for stationary when I'd seen one of the fee earners trot by with a box of pastries.

Phil rolled his eyes dramatically and sighed hard enough to extinguish a forest fire. "I'll see what I can do. By the way, this potential client is hot. You may need a cold drink to stop yourself burning up."

"Professional, Phillip. That's all we ask. Be professional." I shook my head. He gave a knowing snort and exited, leaving me ankle deep in files.

Two minutes later and the knock at the door was followed immediately with it being opened. I'd just cleared about enough space when a familiar face and equally familiar mountain of body entered. I looked up: glasses, light brown hair with flecks of blonde, rough stubble and a tight, fitted shirt that did all kinds of good for those biceps.

"Payton, this is Owen Anders." I shot him a look of distress. He started to close the door. "I'll bring you coffee. And pastries."

I didn't thank him. "Good morning, Mr Anders," I said, holding out my hand across my fairly cleared desk. "It's nice to meet you."

He accepted and shook my hand with a firm grip. "It's good to meet you. I assume we're pretending Saturday didn't happen?"

I sat down. "It depends. If you admit you were an arse then I may try to forget about it."

He folded his arms, not sitting down. I'd grown up with four older brothers, all of whom were much taller than me. I did not get intimidated by height. Nor was I intimidated by attractive men who had just the right amount of facial hair. "If I were an ass, what were you?"

"A woman you misjudged," I said, tempted to fold my arms and mirror him. Instead, I looked down at the notepad on my desk and picked up my pen. "If you want legal advice then I'm more than happy to help. If not, skip on out of here and quit wasting my time."

"Is that how you speak to all your potential clients?"

His arms were still bloody folded.

I sighed, more at the point he'd made than the arms, and stood up, offering my hand. "Good to meet you, Mr Anders. How can I help?"

His grin included fecking dimples. "Pleasure to meet you, Ms Callaghan. I have a legal issue I'm hoping you can assist me with."

"Take a seat and go ahead."

We both sat and I focused on his mouth, avoiding the biceps and dimples and the hair. I wasn't in the market for a fling or relationship or having any sense of attraction to a potential client, but given that I had only just stopped my hand from playing with my hair, I knew I was automatically entering flirt mode.

"You've been in Cases," he began and I nodded. "I started the first Cases six years ago, partly funded by my mother's partner, David Melville. It's grown since then and each shop is run as a separate business, so it is just the first store he has an interest in."

His hand flicked through his hair making it look boyishly messy. I pulled my eyes back to his mouth, which was also a mistake. "Understood."

"He wants me to buy him out. He's split up from my mother and I figure he's trying to sever all ties. I had this letter from his lawyer. He's suggested a figure that is far more than I know he's entitled to." He passed me the letter.

I glanced through it, recognising it as a standard notice of dissolution, meaning that the partnership had to be wound up. The amount he suggested was eye watering considering this was a bookshop in a world of eBooks. "Okay. Was there an original partnership agreement?"

Owen shook his head. "No. While I wouldn't say Dave's been like a stepfather to me, he's been a good role model and father figure to large extent."

"Why did he and your mum split up?" I wasn't sure it was an appropriate question to ask, but I asked it any way.

Owen looked up to the ceiling. "My mother decided that she was destined at this point in her life to be free and single. I have no idea why. She's said very little about it. Dave probably deserves to be pissed off."

I rolled back my shoulders, trying to loosen them up as discretely as I could. Three weeks of what felt like being permanently stationed at a desk and then the days in court meant that I should've invested in a few days off on a masseur's table at some remote spa.

"Hot bath," Owen said, looking at me curiously. "Himalayan bath salts. Then strong thumbs to unknot you."

Visions of his hands navigating their way across my back and lower flashed in front of me and I sank a little deeper into my chair. "The bath sounds like a good idea."

"Not the thumbs?" If my man sense was working properly he was flirting with me. But it wasn't, and hadn't been for some time.

"My thumbs won't reach that far."

Those dimples appeared, deepening as if to say 'we know you're single' and I let my resting bitch face dominate. "Partnership Act eighteen ninety. There's a partnership with no agreement. We need to start with getting Cases One valued. No doubt Mr Melville will want to do the same thing as he's unlikely to trust the accountants you will use."

Owen's jaw clenched. "Fuck. I didn't want this to get messy. Is there any other way to resolve this?"

I shrugged. "You can make him an offer you think is reasonable and see if he accepts."

He raised his arms and put his hands behind his head. His T-shirt raised slightly and I saw abs, not obsessively overcooked abs, but ones that looked like they were gained from sport as opposed to the gym. I bit my bottom lip.

"I can try that. I'm not sure he's looking for a quick fix though."

"Does he need the money?"

Owen shook his head. "Not really. He receives drawings from Cases and he has other cash besides that. He buys businesses that are struggling and turns them around then sells them on. He's also a bit of hippy, which is a bit of a fucking contradiction. That's how he and my mother met."

"She's a hippy too? Or did she own a business?"

His eyes shone, dancing with amusement. "She manages

one of my bookstores now, but before that she was a hippy, as in Stonehenge and New Age. She ran a business selling healing crystals and is a Reiki master and that was how they met—she realigned his chakras. If you end up meeting her, she'll probably try to realign yours—they're clearly out of synch."

I didn't have to try to muster a glare. "There's nothing wrong with my chakras, whatever the hell they are. Leave them be." My door swung open and Phillip entered with the coffee and pastries. "You're officially my favourite person," I said to his quickly retreating back.

"Let's see about that during your next crisis," Phillip said.

If Owen hadn't been there I'd have lobbed my stapler at the door as he shut it. However, I was trying to demonstrate some degree of professionalism.

I poured the coffee and picked the apple Danish before he could as there was only one and it had been calling my name since it had been brought through the door. If it had been a normal potential client, I'd have been far more gracious and probably not even eaten in front of them, but for some reason my brain wouldn't associate him as being that.

"Hungry much?"

I nodded, my mouth too full to reply.

He smirked annoyingly and picked up the cherry Danish. I had half expected him to skip the pastries given that he had the body of someone who spent time exercising and was therefore irritatingly healthy. "I like it when a woman has an appetite."

I was pretty sure he was flirting. "If I ever tried to curb my appetite there would probably be a petition and trucks delivering cakes. I get ridiculously hangry. Hence I get my money's worth from my gym membership."

He chewed thoughtfully. "That's balance. You don't look like you have a cake addiction."

"Is that a compliment or are you just creeping to get back

in my good books after Saturday and because you need some legal work doing?"

"And I thought I was being subtle." He polished off the rest of the pastry. "I'm sorry for being a dick. It was a bad day, not that it's a good excuse. How long are you free for?"

I thanked the gods of coffee and the patron saint of caffeine for all things holy, as I was starting to grasp some clarity. "You're forgiven. I wasn't exactly polite back."

"Be honest though: you wanted a picture for your Instagram, didn't you?" he said, his tone like liquid chocolate: smooth and morish. "I understand. My shops are pretty fucking amazing."

Then I laughed, almost choking on my coffee and the tension that had been building for the past few weeks started to leave my body.

"What did I say?" he said, his palms upwards, questioning.

"You didn't. Well, you kind of did. I've never thought of bookshops as being "fucking amazing"." I studied him, trying to read his eyes to find out how much praise I could give him without his ego exploding. "Although the two I've been are fecking spectacular."

His smile was genuine, like a child who had just been told he'd won a colouring competition. "You think so? What do you like about them?"

"They make me feel like I'm stepping into another world. They could be from a book themselves, like Harry Potter or something else fantastical. It's the dark wood and the high ceilings. I could spend a day in one," I confessed. I'd loved books since childhood. My big brothers and sister used to read to me, sometimes fighting about whose turn is was to read a bedtime story to me and Seph but my favourite had been when our father read to me. At first I remember his voice being stilted, as if he was reading a case file—although that wasn't how I described it back then. I'd complained to my mother that he wasn't as good as her or even Max at reading and he'd overheard me. Years later, he told me he started to listen to Max reading and Jackson, then he practiced reading to Ava using different voices and then he became my favourite.

Books had been my escape and there was nothing I wouldn't try reading. Spending a day in a bookstore was as much of a relaxing fantasy as spending a day at the spa. "I don't see you as a bookstore mogul though."

He leaned further across the desk towards me. "Why's that?"

"Because you don't look like a bookstore owner. Even with the Harry Potter glasses."

"I take it you're a fan of all things Hogwarts?"

I nodded. "Actually, that's a good idea for a present." He looked confused. "Sorry, my sister's due to have her first child any moment and I didn't know what to get as a present—a set of Potter hardbacks would be perfect."

"When's your next meeting?"

I glanced at my clock out of habit. "I haven't today. I should've had a trial this week but it finished early, so I have a clear diary.'

"Will you come and see my first bookstore? Then I can prove that appearances are deceptive and you can buy your niece or nephew a gift."

There was no way I could say no, even if I wanted to. His face was alight with enthusiasm and hope; telling him no would've been like kicking a puppy and I was kind to animals. "Yes. It'll give me chance to see what your business partner is happy to leave—that's if you want me to act for you on this?"

Broad shoulders relaxed and I saw tendons release their tension. "Please. What do you need from me?"

"Your accounts to start; I'll have a forensic accountant look through them. And you'll need to sign our contract and agree on fees. If you can come in tomorrow to do that, I'll get everything drawn up," I said, almost knocking over my coffee as I stood up and reached for my jacket.

"That's fine. How long can you spare me to look round?"

My smile couldn't be stopped. "As long as you'll have me." The words sounded almost as if they had a different meaning altogether.

CHAPTER 4
OWEN

We walked to Cases even though the tube would've been quicker. I bought coffee to go for us from a café Payton knew well and we walked by the Thames and over the Millennium bridge towards St Paul's Cathedral. I teased her and found out quickly what buttons I needed to press to get a heated response or a smile. I liked both. I liked her. She was petite and bubbly, wavy blonde hair almost hitting her shoulders and big blue eyes that widened when she was enthusiastic.

"The Pullman trilogy was better than *Harry Potter*," I said, knowing what response I'd elicit.

"If you're thinking of the *Northern Lights*, then you have a point in some ways. But in terms of enjoyment and the having the whole universe to buy in to then you're overwhelmingly wrong," she said, taking three steps to my two. She was short: I was possibly a foot taller than her when she wasn't wearing heels and even with me walking slowly she was still having to try keep up. "Lyra is an incredible character, but she just doesn't stand up against Hermione."

"What's your favourite book of all time?" I asked her. I

had no intention of been driven into an argument: I just liked seeing her fiery.

"You of all people should know that's an impossible question," she said. "Favourite for what purpose? Favourite as in most admired, or childhood book, or genre specific? Classic or the book I read in the bath when I've had a shit day and want to read the literary equivalent of a chocolate bar? Are you actually a book lover or do you just sell books to make money?"

"All of them and both," I said, opening the door into the first ever Cases. At the front of the store were the freshly published, the top ten in various genres and gift books. Beyond that, the book store specialised in classics and literary fiction, while upstairs was dedicated solely to children's and young adult books. This was the smallest venue for music, as we didn't use the upstairs at all. That was solely reserved for children's authors and story time, plus various other events that were kid-focused. It hadn't always been that way; when it first opened we stocked everything, but as I opened more premises I decided to give each store a specialism.

"I haven't been in here," she said. "And I wish I had."

"Now you have," I replied. "And you have a free pass to come here whenever you need to escape. You haven't told me your favourites."

"I like lattes. Large ones. And those comfy chairs. And you telling me how you ended up owning several bookstores," she said and headed to the chairs she'd pointed to, the ones that were near the hardback classics.

Surprisingly, I did as I was told and brought her a coffee, myself a green tea and sat down next to her. She was already immersed in a book: *Written on the Body* by Jeanette Winterson, and rather than interrupt her, I found something myself to read—the new Jack Reacher—and for about half an hour neither of us spoke.

She intrigued me. Everything I'd read about her told me she was a successful lawyer, listing her achievements and significant wins, yet she was only twenty-seven. I knew she was from a family of lawyers and the firm she worked for was hers, along with her siblings. Yet the tiny woman curled up in the chair nursing a book and a coffee, her hair mussed from the breeze outside, looked anything but. There were layers there and some were tired and exhausted.

Blue eyes pierced me from over her book. "My favourite classic is *Jane Eyre*. My favourite children's book is *What Katy Did*. Best series—*Harry Potter*. Favourite modern book would be *The Travelling Hornplayer* by Barbara Trapido. The fluffy chocolately book for when I need to forget the day is *Pretend You're Mine* by Lucy Score. Yours?"

I put my book down, remembering the page number. "*Norwegian Wood* by Haruki Murakami for modern; *Hard Times* for classic; series is the Jack Reacher books; *The Weirdstone of Brisingamen* for kids and I don't have a comfort book. All of those are subject to change at any point."

Her book was down now, her focus on me which made me want to preen or discreetly flex my biceps that I had caught her checking out before.

"How did you end up with this? I mean, you don't look like a bookstore owner. You're not wearing a tank top or tweed and books are too light for you to bench press, so what's the story there?"

She was trying not to look too interested and kept shifting her eyes so she did not look directly at one part of my anatomy.

I stretched up, managing to flex my arm and hoping she couldn't tell it was intentional as I'd look a complete dick. "I loved to read growing up. We moved quite a bit, my mum would follow one good cause or another and I'd change schools every so often. Before I made friends in whatever area we were in, I'd read, or sometimes we'd live somewhere fairly remote, so books were something to do. At college I studied computer engineering and learned coding, but took a few modules in literature."

"That doesn't explain how you ended up with the finances to invest in this." She was blunt and to the point.

"While I was taking my Master's, me and a friend developed a dating app for students and professionals. We sold it eighteen months later for a considerable sum. Don't judge," I said, raising my eyebrows. My ex had frowned over the idea of me inventing a dating app, especially as we had tested it out considerably ourselves.

Payton tipped her head to one side and looked at me, clearly assessing. "From dating to bookstores."

"To maybe dating again?" I looked up at the ceiling as soon as the words came out. There were probably laws against dating clients and I really wanted her to sort out the mess David and my mum had put me in.

She laughed and her cheeks pinked. "I'm not dating anyone at the moment. I need a man-free few months."

"Why?"

"Too many idiots. I need to recalibrate. But thank you. I'm flattered. How about a non-date?"

"I'll take a non-date. If you change your mind and want to make it an actual date, let me know. Shall I show you the Potter books?"

She swung her legs down and picked up what she'd been reading. "I just need to check my phone. It's been so nice to be away from the office… holy shit."

Her body stiffened and her face changed to petrified.

"What? What's the matter?" I moved next to her, my hand automatically touching her shoulder.

Her eyes were wet when she looked up at me and I saw fear. "My sister's pregnant, really overdue, and she's just been rushed into hospital for an emergency caesarean. Maxwell and Seph have been trying to phone me—they're already on their way."

"What can I do?"

She shook her head. "I don't know. I don't have a car and there's a train strike on. She's at a hospital in Oxfordshire near my parents. Maybe I can hire a car."

It took just over an hour and a half to get to the hospital, then a further fifteen minutes to find out where Payton's sister was. I'd driven like The Rock in a Fast and the Furious movie and I suspected I'd possibly picked up a speeding ticket, but Payton's confident front had melted like an ice cream cone in a toddler's hands as she'd started to panic over her sister. She'd spent most of the journey on the phone to her twin, who kept ending the call to get more updates from their mother, who I knew was called Marie.

I'd grown up an only child, but we'd always had people round us, and my mother had been the person who took in the waifs and strays who didn't have family or were on their own for whatever reason, so I had no idea what shyness was. Walking into the waiting room with Payton's parents, non-pregnant sister and four brothers (two with their partners or wives), didn't faze me, although Payton, given the speed at which she forewarned me about her family, clearly thought it would do.

From what she'd described, they were a little bit crazy with more than a slice of oddness and I'd probably be interrogated without knowing it, given the stealth skills of her lawyer brothers. Again, I wasn't worried. I'd been in too many rooms with completely new people to be so and I doubted that I would be even acknowledged, given the severity of what was happening.

"Payton!" A tall man wearing glasses grabbed her as she dashed into the waiting room. Three other dark haired men looked in our direction. "Where were you when I was calling? I wanted to wait but we needed to get here."

She had her arms wrapped round his waist. "In Owen's bookstore, reading. I had my phone on silent. Sorry, Seph." She pushed him away gently and turned to me. "Owen, these are my family."

I looked at each person as she named them and gave a slight nod.

"How do you two know each other?" the one called Max asked. He was the biggest although Seph was the tallest.

"We bumped into each other on Saturday and I'm now one of Payton's clients."

"What's the case?" her father asked, his expression changing from worry to interest. "I was commercial lit like Payton is now."

I looked to Payton. They were waiting to hear how her sister Claire and her baby were. The last we had heard was that she'd been taken in for an emergency c-section about twenty minutes ago.

"They'll all be interested. And it'll give them something else to think about," Payton said, managing to give me a smile.

The brief version was still a good fifteen minutes in the telling, taking questions into account. Then Ava, Payton's younger sister, started to ask questions about the renovations and décor of the buildings and the conversation turned to issues I had around the leases of the premises.

"Thanks, Owen," Marie, Payton's mother said.

I answered another question around expansion and a

property I had been looking at in Bristol. "You've distracted us nicely. My husband won't think of it as a distraction though: he'll consider it a good use of his time. If he tries to bill you for it, let me know." She cracked a wry smile. "I'm going to get coffee for us all and see if I can accost a nurse on the way." Her gaze turned to her husband. "Come help, Grant." There were the faintest traces of an American accent still there.

I sat down next to Payton and felt five pairs of eyes land on me. Looking around, I caught each pair until they stood down, knowing I was being assessed.

"How did you manage to get Payton out of work and into a bookstore during daylight hours?" Max said, his arms around the waist of a dark haired woman who was standing in front of him.

I shrugged. "She didn't take much persuasion and I wanted her to see the Cases that my mum's partner is part of."

Max glanced at Jackson. "Can you persuade her to spend more time there this week rather than at work? She refuses to take time off."

"No I don't!" She'd been quiet for longer than I'd anticipated. "I have no reason to take time off at the moment. I've plenty to sort out."

"Which will take you no more than a day if you're thinking of your time recording and file management," Jackson, who Payton had said was the second oldest and the managing partner, said.

Before she could argue back the door opened and Marie and Grant came in with a nurse who was smiling. "Is everybody here?" the nurse said.

I looked at Payton and mouthed to her to ask if I should go. She shook her head.

"Mother and baby are doing well. There were no complications and everything went as well as we could've hoped. I believe Dad will be out soon to let you know the name."

"Do I have a niece or a nephew?" Payton said and I wondered if she was about to pin the nurse down until he told her.

He shook his head. "I'm sorry, Dad asked me not to say. He said you deserved to wait a bit longer after he had to put up with your sister's verbal aggression. Those are his words."

"Joy. Freaking joy," Payton said. "Killian used to be so pleasant until he ended up with Claire."

"Seph, have you got the spreadsheet with the guesses for weight and gender?" Jackson said. "Owen, care to join in the bet?"

Seph pulled out his phone. "It's unfair if you don't know that Killian is as tall as you and all males in our family were over nine pounds."

"Apart from you," Max said. "Because you were born needing to catch up."

"Fuck off, Max. I was big for a twin."

"Yeah, you always did try to get my share of the food," Payton said.

"Because he had to work extra hard to catch up," Max added, his girlfriend still in his arms.

"I'd respond but we've company. Want to have a guess, Owen? It's a straightforward twenty," Seph said, glancing at his phone.

I dug out my wallet and passed him a note. "Eight pounds five and a girl," I said.

"Done." Seph pocketed the cash. There was no resemblance between him and Payton apart from the eyes.

It was another five minutes of arguing and debating about names and weights before a fair-haired man walked in, blocking the doorway until everyone noticed him. A loud cheer broke out and I figured this was the baby's father. Hugs and handshakes and slaps on the back happened, and he hugged me without blinking twice.

"Well?" Marie said. "Do I have a granddaughter or a grandson?"

There was a laugh, almost of disbelief. "You have a granddaughter. The rest of you have a niece." His words sounded choked. "Both she and Claire are doing amazing—both are fine. The doctors did what they needed to in time."

"Does she have a name?" Marie asked. Everyone else looked shocked. I put a hand on Payton's back, noticing she'd lost colour.

"Elizabeth Rose," he said. "And I know about the bet. She weighed eight pounds three and if Seph's won it, Claire's demanding it be spent on a bottle of Champagne."

There was more noise, except from Payton who was still quiet.

"Not me," Seph said. "We shouldn't have asked Owen to join in. He was the closest with the right gender. Well done." He dug in his wallet and handed a wad of notes over to me.

I shook my head. "Use it for wetting the baby's head. Are you the best person to keep hold of it though?" There was a laugh from the room, including Payton which made me feel stupidly proud.

There was more noise in the room, most of it from Marie who was asking Killian multiple questions and Ava who was chirping in. Payton was still quiet. "You want to get some air then come back when it's your turn to see your niece?"

Large blue eyes fixed onto mine. "That'd be great. You sure you don't mind? I can get a lift back from one of my brothers—you don't need to hang around."

"I don't need to get back soon," I said, following her out of the waiting room. "There are no gigs tonight and I haven't had any messages about staffing crises so I'm good for a few more hours, but I don't want to be in the way."

She laughed and shook her head. "My family are used to having people around other than us. My niece will have a photo of you holding her in her baby photo album by the end of the day. I think Marie brought a polaroid camera and there's no way you'll get out of that."

"Is your family obsessed with photos?"

We headed outdoors into the rain that was now falling, fine drops rather than a chuck-it-down. We'd left our coats in the waiting room, but although it was wet and April, it wasn't cold. "My mum is. Callum too."

"I've seen him on social media," I said about the brother who was just a bit older than her and Seph. "Is he a vet?"

Payton tipped her head up to the sky, letting rain fall on her with her eyes closed. "He is. He's at London Zoo now, but he travelled the world before and put stuff on YouTube and Instagram. I think he's at the point where he's received used panties in the post but we ignore all of that because he's an ass."

I realised there were tears mixed in with the raindrops. "Payton, are you okay?" I was fairly good with people but I wasn't a mind reader. I saw she needed to get out of the waiting room and needed some space but I wasn't sure why.

Her laugh was choked. "Yeah, I'm just relieved. I don't cope well when I'm not in control and when I got the message that it was an emergency..." Her face scrunched up slightly as she tried to hold back the tears.

I stepped towards her and pulled her into me, the top of her head barely up to my shoulder. "She's fine. Your niece is fine. All's well and you don't need to think about what could've happened, because it didn't."

Her hands wrapped around my back, warming my skin. "I know. I'm sorry you had to see me like this. I'm not a wuss, really."

"Why would crying make you a wuss? Why would being

worried make you anything other than strong? I don't get it," I said quietly, holding her a little tighter. She felt good in my arms. She was soft and warm and smelled of cinnamon and spices. But I'd asked her out on a date and she'd said no, and I wasn't one to keep asking a woman. Whatever I felt had to be platonic.

She nuzzled into me. "I don't know. Please don't tell my family I got upset. They'd worry."

Now I understood. She was protecting them, or she thought she was. "They might guess anyway. Let's get something to drink before you go back to see your niece."

"Thank you," she said. "And I am sorry for calling you an ass. You're turning out not to be."

I laughed quietly, still holding her. "I can be sometimes. I'm male. It's part of our genetic programming. You good for us to head to the café?"

I felt her nod against me but ignored it. I'd spent only a few hours with her but I could tell she needed more time to hide so I pulled her closer and started to feel her shoulders relax. I inhaled her scent and wondered why this didn't feel awkward: me holding a woman I barely knew.

One of her hands came up to my shoulder and she held on, resting her head against my chest. Looking down I could see her eyelids opening and closing slowly as if she was just waking up.

"I don't want to say thank you again," she said.

"Then don't," I murmured. "And there's no need to move any time soon. Especially now the rain's stopped." There was even a glimmer of blue sky.

"Are you being a creeper and enjoying having a woman pressed up close to you?"

The humour in her voice told me that she was starting to feel better, happier.

"You've said no to a date, so I'm taking what I can get," I said, keeping my voice light.

She head-butted my chest lightly. "I need to sort my shit out before I go on any dates, Owen."

"That's fine. Just tell me when you're ready to dip a toe back in the dating pond and I'll lend you a hand. Let's just get a drink now and you can go meet your niece," I said, starting to release my hold.

"I forgot her present," she said, sounding sad. "I know; no one else will have remembered but..."

"They're in my car."

She looked up at me. "What?"

"When you were on the phone to your brother I grabbed a set and got them bagged up. They're in the car."

She continued to look blankly at me.

"The *Harry Potter* series—you wanted it for the baby. If you don't like the editions I picked then that's fine, I can change them..." I wondered if I'd hugely cocked up. "Or if you changed your mind about what to get—"

I was silenced by her lips pressing onto mine, her arms thrown around my neck. For about a second and half I was still, my brain trying to process what had just happened, then sense kicked in and my hands grasped her waist and my mouth took control of the kiss. She tasted of coffee and cinnamon and her lips were soft and gentle and responded so easily to mine. She felt like a life buoy in a deep sea.

Then the rain started, this time harder and wetter and those were words I wanted to use to describe something else. We broke apart, her hand immediately going to her face to touch her lips.

"Don't apologise," I said. "Don't."

"Okay. It's raining. Should we get that drink? Then maybe go to the shop to see if they have wrapping paper and tape?" I saw her swallow her anxiety.

"Yes," I said and deliberately put my hand on the small of her back as we walked inside. I would've taken her hand but that would've been too much; but I needed to keep contact with her so it wasn't just a kiss, otherwise neither of us would've been able hold our heads above water. "Let's get the books from the car and then we can wrap them while we get a drink."

We didn't say anything on the way to car, or on the way to the shop. I tried to look interested while Payton picked out wrapping paper and ribbon from the limited choice, keeping hold of the books instead. I saw her keep glancing at me, her lips pursed as if she wanted to say something, although I thought I knew what that something was.

"I'll get the drinks," she said when we got to the café. It was filled with a mix of doctors and nurses, some patients and family, all with a mixture of expressions. "Coffee?"

"Please," I said. "And water."

I watched her as she queued up with a tray, her head up again, her eyes brighter. By the time she'd returned I'd taken the books from the bag and inspected each copy. They were gift editions, illustrated and cloth covered. I'd had just about enough time to make sure they were perfect copies.

"These are gorgeous," Payton said, placing the drinks well away from the books. "I might need to get them for myself. You need to let me know how much I owe you."

"We'll sort it out later," I said. I had no intention of letting her pay, but that argument could be saved for after. "Please don't tell me you're one of those Potterheads who has to have every edition?"

"Not quite," she said, looking through Chamber of Secrets. "This is divine. She's a lucky girl." I saw her blink back tears.

I cleared my throat. "Are you upset?"

She shook her head. "No. I'm relieved and a little bit

amazed that my big sister has a baby. I don't know how to handle it."

I took one of the sheets of wrapping paper and started to wrap the first book. "It's okay to feel everything, you know. Just stop trying to analyse it and enjoy the feeling."

"What if I cry all over her when I hold her? Will I be able to hold her? What if she cries and I don't know what to do?" She started to wrap too, her hands busying themselves.

"I don't think you'll be the only one crying. I don't know if you'll be able to hold her and I don't know the first thing about babies so if she cries I guess you give her back to your sister or Killian," I said. "Have you checked your phone?"

"Weirdly, no. I usually have it glued to my hand." She reached into her purse and pulled it out, the screen filled with messages. "Photos. Fuck, she's gorgeous." She showed me a picture of the baby, who looked like most babies I'd seen already. "She has Claire's eyes."

I carried on wrapping, pushing a tag and a pen towards her, while she looked at the photos.

"She's tiny. Max has held her and she looks so small. I need to see her." She put her phone down and watched as I finished wrapping the last book. "Shit, I'm sorry. You've done everything again. I'm not doing well with adulting today."

This time I did laugh. "Payton, it's fine. There will be a day when maybe you can adult for me. Write out the tag and let's get you to see your niece."

We headed to the ward and the room where Claire was, Payton now telling me stories about her brothers and Killian, Claire's fiancé. I could see anticipation and nerves and excitement all bubbling under a pre-prepared persona.

"Here's your gift," I said as we reached the door. Voices tumbled through, Seph's and Ava's. "I'll wait for you in the room we were in before."

Her smile faded. "I know it's been a weird day and you've

kind of jumped in at a very deep end here with having to give me a lift, but it'll feel weird if you don't come in and meet her. Unless you don't want to, I get if that's too weird."

"I'm happy to, but won't it be strange for your family if I come in?"

She tipped her head to one side. "Yes, but it'll be stranger if you don't."

"Okay," I said as she pushed the door open.

I wasn't sure what to expect. I'd held a newborn before, a couple of times actually, but neither had been born in a hospital, or after an emergency caesarean.

Claire was lying propped up in bed, an IV next to her and the baby snuggled to her chest. Killian was sitting beside her, his focus flitting between his new daughter and fiancée. Seph and Ava were standing at the side, two of the three wise men on a visit.

"Hey," Payton said, heading straight to her sister. "You look better than I thought you would." She kissed her cheek. "How are you?"

Claire smiled. "Better now she's here. Sore and uncomfortable but that doesn't matter. Who's your friend?" Claire's eyes fell on me, assessing.

"This is Owen Anders—"

"The bookstore owner," Claire interrupted. "I read about you a few months ago. How do you know my sister?"

So this was the interrogation I hadn't received from her brothers. "We bumped into each other on Saturday. And I need a lawyer."

"I was in one of Owen's stores when I checked my phone and saw five thousand missed calls from the brothers. Owen drove me here and stopped the meltdown from happening. And kept his head enough to make sure I brought Elizabeth's gift," Payton said, handing a bag across the bed to Killian who laughed.

"This could've waited. You've even managed to wrap it," he said, pulling one of the books out of the bag.

"Elizabeth says thank you and she'll let you indoctrinate her when she's old enough for them to be suitable," Claire said, looking at the tiny baby.

"How do you know what they are?" Payton said, disbelief in her voice. "Can you see through paper now? Is that a pregnancy superpower?"

Killian snorted. "Her only pregnancy superpowers were being as bitchy as fuck and more demanding than normal, which I didn't think was humanly possible."

"I've just been cut open so your spawn could be delivered safely. You could at least be complementary about my superpowers," she said, shifting in the bed and holding the baby out to Payton. "If you hadn't bought her the *Harry Potter* series I'd have been worried. Hold your niece."

Payton took her as if she was made of glass, her face lighting up with pure adoration. I hoped there would be someone to reign in what she bought Elizabeth for birthdays and Christmas, else there'd be one hugely spoilt girl at some point.

"She's so tiny and pink."

"You should've seen her straight after," Claire said. "I've never heard anyone say newborns were cute and she illustrated exactly why. She also screamed the place down, a bit like you do when you're not allowed any more margaritas. Her screaming was the most wonderful sound in the world. Killian's sobbing was not."

Killian was clearly a wise man as he simply smiled and shook his head, looking at the books. "These are gorgeous. Thank you Payton and Owen."

I raised my brows at him and he passed me the tag. She'd put my name on there too.

CHAPTER 5
PAYTON

During the journey back the city I tried not to think about the state I'd left my apartment in or the clothes that were strewn everywhere. My swearing off men equated in my mind to not having to tidy up the hurricane that I left behind wherever I went.

I decided on the way home Owen clearly had magical powers as he'd managed to charm all of my family, my brothers included. He was easy going, intelligent and seemed to know what to say at the right time—completely the opposite to my usual foot-in-mouth haphazard manner.

"Do you want to stop and get dinner from somewhere?" he said as my stomach rumbled for the ninth time. "I'm not inviting myself back to yours—I have a frozen meal in at home courtesy of my mother who's not realised that I'm thirty-two and can cook for myself yet."

"Don't turn it down. Parental meals aren't something that should cease. When I moved back here from Manchester my mum came over with about sixteen frozen containers for me and Seph, with a list of instructions how to heat each one up," I said, fighting fatigue. I was still on the verge of tears which was not a place I wanted to remain in, especially in front of Owen again. He was going to think I was a complete weakling and not the strong woman I thought I was most of the time.

He switched lanes, avoiding an idiot who was trying to race through London. "What were you doing in Manchester?"

"We had a satellite office there that we decided to expand. I went up there for six months to help it get off the ground. It should've been longer but Seph split from his girlfriend and started to go off the rails, so I came back as soon as everything was pretty much sorted," I said, remembering the state my twin had been in when I returned. He was drinking too much, not sleeping enough and fucking anything with tits and long hair, usually female. He'd turned into a party-addicted manwhore and refused to listen to anyone.

I saw Owen's arm muscle tense as he changed gears and felt a forgotten clench between my legs. I was attracted to him, but then most straight females would be as he was gorgeous in a gym-geek kind of way, but he was also a good guy and that had thrown me. I wasn't usually the girl who went for the decent men; I had a tendency to target the overly groomed metrosexuals who haunted the city in search of a personality. So Owen, with his gorgeousness and charisma and charm was sending me completely off-kilter. Because I wasn't dating anyone.

"You and Seph are close?" he said, glancing at me, interest in his eyes.

I pulled my hair back from my face, yearning for a shower to get rid of the hospital smell. "We all are, I suppose. But I'm close to Seph in a different way. He's never been cross with me or blamed me, other than for wrecking his bike when we were kids. We've never fallen out and I know that's weird. How about you? Do you have brothers and sisters?"

"No. I'm an only child," he said. "So your family seems huge to me. What are your thoughts on food?"

"You're hungry, aren't you?" I cast my eyes over him and laughed. He was a big man and we hadn't eaten since the pastries in my office. "There's a pizza place near my apartment if you want to join me and don't mind ignoring the complete disaster of a mess that is my home."

He laughed. "I'm used to messes. And pizza sounds good. I could eat anything right now. How about your other siblings? Do you all get along?"

"We're tight, but we do argue sometimes. Maxwell is stubborn and bossy pretty much all of the time. Jackson was a workaholic until he met Vanessa; he's a bit calmer and more of a planner. Claire's always been really together and focused while Ava's a charmer and flirts through life. Callum's been away for years and has his own issues. Marie's mine, Seph's and Ava's mum. The other four lost their mother when they were young—I think Cal was only about two. What's being an only child like?" I said.

My family was usually a subject of conversation for someone who was new to us. Big families were rare and the closeness of us was unusual to everyone else. To me, it was normal. I loved my siblings and they were my best friends. The message from Seph about Claire had rocked me this morning and I wasn't sure how to recover from it, other than staring at the million photos I'd taken of her and Elizabeth.

Owen grinned and skipped a track. He'd picked the music and we'd listened to acoustic sets for most of the way back. It had been relaxing and more chilled out than I was used to. "I had a weird childhood. My mum's a hippy for want of a better description and liked to move to where she felt she was called. We lived by ourselves sometimes, but always near to friends and people she'd met over the years. Sometimes we lived in shared houses and communes. I was home schooled for a lot of it until I hit fourteen and then my mum managed to stay in one place while I did my exams and then got into university. Different from having the same family all the time," he said. I watched his face as he spoke and saw no sign of sadness or regret at how his childhood had been.

"You sound like you were happy," I said.

He nodded. "It was normal to me and I was resilient as a child. From being little I knew how to make friends and suss people out, so I could generally tell who was a nice person and who to avoid."

"You weren't especially good with me on Saturday," I said. "According to you I was only interested in taking pretty pictures and would know nothing about legal documents." I enjoyed the blank expression he pasted on his face that was broken by a smile.

"Yeah, well, nobody's perfect all of the time. Is this your apartment?" He slowed the car in front of the nineteen-thirties detached houses that had been converted into apartments. I was renting at the moment, unsure of where or what to buy, and work had been too busy to actually think too much about it. The lull in my diary would give me chance to see a few properties or at least look online at what the market was like at the moment.

"I'm on the second floor. You can park outside—I have a permit on me," I said, gesturing to a space that was conveniently empty. He did a bit of reverse parking that would've been beyond my skills even if I could drive and I felt my legs wobble as I got out of the car. The overwhelming urge to sob hit me again and I forced it back, plastering that smile back on my face.

"Okay princess, let's get you inside." An arm wrapped around my waist and guided me to the door. I fumbled for my keys and then struggled to find the fine motor skills to get the key in the lock. Owen's other hand took them from me and he opened the door. "You're exhausted," he said. "You keep trying to stop from crying because you're too fucking tired."

I reached the bottom of the stairs and clung onto the rail. "I just need a good night's sleep…" Words ceased to exist as large arms scooped me up and I found myself nestled into Owen's large chest as he took the narrow stairs two at a time. "And I could've managed to get up the stairs myself. I don't need looking after."

He placed me down carefully and unlocked the door with the keys he still held. "Let's talk about that when your legs are a bit steadier."

I let out a frustrated growl. My legs weren't steady and I couldn't attribute their spaghetti status to the day I'd had, or the last few weeks. I was kidding myself if I thought it had nothing to do with the man who was holding open the door to my apartment.

"Let me order pizza for both of us. Then I'll let you rest. Max says you're not allowed in work tomorrow and the only case you have at the moment is mine," Owen said.

My feet froze into the ground. "What the fuck? Max can't do that! I need to do my time recording and shit, just get on top of things. And how come you ended up being the messenger?"

Owen shrugged, using a hand to steer me into my apartment. I headed straight for the fridge where I knew I had a bottle of prosecco. He followed me, taking a glass from next to the sink and filling it with water. "Drink. Before you hit the booze, have water."

I glared at him but took the glass. "Messenger?"

"I offered. While you were in with Claire and the baby I sat in the waiting room with your brothers—except Callum. They were talking about how you were burning out and they were worried about you. Max said you needed to take time off but if he suggested it, you'd probably yell at him and ignore him anyway," Owen said, digging around in my cupboards and finding a glass for himself. "I said I'd mention it when I brought you home. Do you still want pizza or Chinese? I noticed a takeaway around the corner."

I dragged my ass to my sofa and sat down, watching him move around the small kitchen as if he had always been there. "Pizza. Please." I wanted to rage against my brothers and Owen and shout at how embarrassing they were to bring a stranger into all of this—all of what? I didn't need time off work unless it had a purpose and there was something to gain such as a trip abroad or a visit to see friends. I was tired, but that was understandable.

Then the broad bespectacled beast of a man came and sat down next to me, his warmth radiating from him and surrounding me like a plush blanket. He didn't touch me and I figured that was killing him as I'd seen how tactile he naturally was.

"I hate that they see me as being weak," I said, my stare resolutely fixed on the glass of water both my hands clutched. "And I shouldn't be having this conversation with you."

"Why not me?"

"Because I hardly know you. You're a client. You've been dragged into enough shit today to probably last you at least the next six months without watching soap operas or reality TV."

"I can't say I watch either and you dragged me along to see your new born niece which isn't a fucking issue, Payton. Everyone needs more moments like that, when it's just pure happiness, even if it's just as a stranger," he said. "I'm going to get the pizza. While I'm gone, don't wallow in your self-pity. Straighten your apartment up; get changed; play some decent music really loud. I'll take the keys so if you don't hear me knock, I won't wake up the neighbours."

My head wanted to pick holes in his words and tell him was being cruel and that he was wrong, but instead of needing to hit out, I felt relief rip a hole in me. "Thin crust. Ham and peppers on a barbecue base. Lots of onions." I stood, my legs no longer soggy noodles.

He hit me with a broad smile. "Got it, princess. Back in a bit."

For the first time in recent memory I followed someone else's instructions. I put music on loud, thankful for the thick walls that separated me from my neighbours and started to tidy, chucking clothes in the laundry, old post in the recycling bin and pots into the dishwasher. I needed to clean properly, but not this evening. By the time I'd finished tidying and quickly showered, tying my hair up in a messy bun and finding a pair of skinny jeans and baggy jumper that had once been Ava's, there was the sound of footsteps in my entrance hall and a loud call of "pizza" ringing above the music.

"Feel any better?" Owen said. "It looks better in here."

"It was bad. I'm sorry you had to see it," I said. Tidying wasn't my forte. I was always presentable and my work was impeccable; I could organise the fuck out of a case and someone else's life but I struggled with my own.

He shrugged, putting down three large pizza boxes on my coffee table that I had given a quick wipe. "I've seen a lot worse. Feel better now you've done it?"

"When did therapy become your second profession?"

Those dimples appeared as he smiled. "I sell books. That's like selling therapy."

"About the kiss," I said, knowing I needed to bring it up else I'd be thinking about what to say until the next time I saw him.

"It was good, wasn't it?" he said, opening one of the pizza boxes and taking a slice.

It had been good. I'd acted impulsively, which I did frequently outside of work, but how he'd felt against me was something I wanted to feel again and again. It had been like throwing myself against a brick wall that was warm and safe and exciting all in one. "But it can't happen again."

"Because you're not dating," he said, taking another slice of pizza, the first one demolished. "I get it. That's fine."

"And you're my client," I said.

"And friend." He looked straight at me and my bullshit meter was working hard to detect any. "There's no reason why we can't be friends, right?"

No, no bullshit was being detected. "No reason. Will you be the type of friend who helps get me home safely on Friday after we've wet the baby's head or the type who shakes their head in judgemental disgust?"

"I'll be the type who stumbles home with you, carries you half way up the stairs before dropping you on your arse and then falls asleep in your bath. Eat some of this pizza," he said, pointing to one of the boxes. "That's your weird shit one."

"It's delicious," I said. "Want to watch something on Netflix?"

He grinned, this one suggesting something naughty was flicking through his mind. "You're the first woman who's suggested actually watching Netflix and meaning it. I must be losing my touch."

"Or maybe you never had it to begin with?"

He shifted closer on my worn sofa and kicked me gently in the leg. "I have it in spades. Whatever 'it' is. What are you going to do tomorrow?"

I turned to look at him, my mouth completely devoid of words with which to answer. "Work."

He shook his head. "No."

"Yes. I have stuff to do. Nothing's urgent, except starting to sort your file out, but I still have things to clear," I said.

"Jackson was disabling your fob. You won't be able to get in the building." There was no heat or power to his words, they were said in the same tone as he might tell me what the weather forecast was. He picked up another slice.

"They can't do that. I'm an equity partner."

"And if they don't do it, you're going to be ill. If you won't do it for yourself, do it for your family who think you've been working too hard and worrying about everyone apart from yourself."

I bit my bottom lip. Other people worrying about me was my least favourite thing. Having a few days where the only thing I worked on was Owen's case I could cope with, if it helped my siblings. I especially didn't want Claire worrying. "Did anyone ever tell you that you're blunt?"

He considered my words for a moment. "No. They didn't have to. I just don't see the point in not being honest. Is having a few days off too much for you to handle?"

The TV came on, the speakers doing their usual thing of being a hundred decibels too loud. "No. I have things to do. And it'll give me chance to see Elizabeth and clean up here and maybe look for somewhere to buy."

"And maybe just chill out and hang around a bookstore for a day, reading and drinking coffee?" His words were like honey.

"That would depend on whether I can find a decent bookstore."

The remote control was wrangled from my hand. "Okay. Ignoring that. What are we watching?"

Sleep was fitful. I had a series of dreams, some involving babies locked in filing cabinets and another where I was locked in a bookstore but none of the books would come off the shelves so I couldn't read while waiting to be rescued. Analysing the dreams seemed pointless and waking up without an alarm ringing on a Tuesday was strange enough to have me out of bed and making a coffee before even checking Instagram and my bank account.

I'd wiped down the kitchen after Owen had left, and put the dishwasher on its second cycle of the day. While my coffee machine did its thing, I started to plump cushions and dug out the vacuum cleaner, cringing at the state of the carpet. By the time my second coffee had filtered into my bloodstream I felt awake and that I'd achieved something productive.

And then I was hit by a sense of emptiness. It was eight am. I should be at work like any other day. My colleagues would be in the office now, or on their way to meetings or grabbing an espresso. Eli would be getting ready for a meeting with a QC; Seph was at a breakfast network meeting near Euston and I was in my pyjama shorts and tank top, and I didn't know what to do with myself.

Don't wallow in your self-pity.

I heard Owen's words. They didn't make me feel the anger I'd expected, instead they calmed me, maybe because it gave me a focus. I went into my bedroom and stripped the sheets off the bed; chucked the old magazines—most of which I'd never got around to reading—in the recycling; spluttered madly when I delved under the bed to retrieve old underwear and sleep shorts that were going in the bin and then I decontaminated the bathroom.

By ten o'clock I was sweating, had The Killers on loud and had an apartment that was cleaner than it had been when I first moved in.

And I felt as if I had achieved something other than a legal victory.

I searched around for my phone, finding it on my dresser,

still on charge. A list of messages filled the lock screen but I ignored them and went straight for the camera, taking photos of my now tidy and rather pretty home, including the bookcase ordered by colour as opposed to anything as boring as author name.

My phone rang in my hand, Seph's name flashing on the screen with a picture of him holding Elizabeth.

"Is everything okay?" I said, panic having filled up my chest. Yesterday's stream of missed calls about Claire's emergency section had upped my anxiety level somewhat and I was now conditioned to be jumpy whenever my phone rang.

Seph's voice was calm; he sounded happy. This was good. "Everything is fine. My morning meeting went well—two potential new clients, one's already booked in for an initial meeting. Eliza is doing fine. There was a stream of photos on the group chat but I don't think you've checked them yet."

He was checking up on me. "I've been busy."

"Doing what? Or doing who? Just to note: no details please, else I'll have to kill him." I heard Seph's fingers drumming on his desk.

"I've told you: I'm not dating at the moment. I've been cleaning."

"Why? Are you expecting a visit from Mum?" That would be the only reason Seph would even think of cleaning although he was tidier than me.

"I think she's preoccupied with the baby, thank God. Have you shortened her name to Eliza or has than come from Claire and Killian?" I said, thankful for the gossip.

"Check your freaking messages, Payts. How's your bookseller today?"

He was out for gossip of his own. "I don't know. He left about nine yesterday evening. He dropped me off, told me I was banned from work and then got pizza. We watched the start of a series on Netflix."

"Did you chill?"

I growled down the phone at him. "No. I told you, I'm not getting involved. Besides he's a client and we have rules around that."

"Yeah, I've sometimes thought we should get rid of those. They've cockblocked me on a couple of occasions."

"Please don't tell Jackson that, else you won't have a cock left."

"That's probably a good idea. What are you doing for the rest of the day? What's your plan?"

I thought for a moment. "Shower and head out somewhere. I don't know. It's the first time in forever I don't know what to do and it's weird."

"Go away for a few days? Or go check out the exhibitions at the V&A museum. You've always said you wanted to do that but never have time. Or see Callum at the zoo?" Seph had clearly pre-planned his ideas.

"You've had a meeting this morning about me, haven't you?"

"Not this morning. Yesterday. So what are you going to do?"

"Take a gap week. In London. I'm going to buy a couple of guides and go sightseeing with a new camera. Try eating out in different places and new bars. See some bands." It felt right. I had a plan, a flexible one, but a plan. "I'm going to be a tourist."

"Let me guess where you're buying your guidebooks from?"

"For fuck's sake, Seph. Do you ever stop? Yes, I'll probably buy them from Cases and support my client. I need to see Owen anyway to get his accounts from him, but there's nothing else to it. He's a friend." I snapped at him and then heard laughter which riled me even more.

"If it helps, we liked him. He's coming out Friday to wet

Eliza's head. Please be nice to him. He plays rugby too and we could do with someone else who can play wing."

My firm had just started their own rugby team and were constantly prowling for additional players, or as my sister-in-law Vanessa put it, additional drinking buddies.

"I'll be nice. Don't you have work to do? Because if you haven't I have time recording you can finish for me."

"Eli's done it. I saw him having coffee with Ava this morning. Do you find that strange?"

"Why would it be strange? He's really good friends with you lot and was at Jackson and Vanessa's wedding where Ava was too. She's probably trying to get him to invest in a house," I said, wondering why Seph was reading into something that was as invisible as air.

"Yeah, you're probably right. Enjoy your book shopping—got to go!" He hung up on me, the sound of Jackson in the background suggesting he was about to get an ear bashing for something.

I showered and dried my hair, using my flat iron to do something that Ava called 'beach waves'. If anyone asked, I would tell them that my make-up usually looked this subtle and I was only spending extra time on doing it because I had the extra time, but in reality I knew I was going to see Owen. Given that he had seen me at my worst, he deserved to see me at my almost best. Not that I was interested. I wasn't getting involved. And that was going to have to be my mantra.

I checked my phone after forcing myself to get dressed first. I knew I'd get distracted with social media and baby photos. It was all there: Elizabeth Rose was now Eliza and she was dressed in her first outfit. My sister looked healthier and had more colour to her cheeks and Killian couldn't stop smiling. There had been multiple selfies sent, including one of my mum, Claire and Eliza that almost had me ruining my mascara. It became my lock screen saver.

Then there was another message.

> Unknown: Got your number from Max. Hope that's okay. I'm at the Covent Garden store today as I have a couple of new members of staff to interview but the coffee's hot and I have a whole new delivery of pretty hardbacks. Owen.
>
> Unknown: I have a pen drive with my accounts on too to give you.
>
> Unknown: If you do come over, my mother is in the store today and she will interrogate you and try to realign your chakras. I'll try to stop her but she doesn't listen to me.
>
> Unknown: Hope you slept well. I'll stop messaging you now because you probably think I'm a creeper. It's Owen by the way.

I read the messages again, knowing I was smiling. I debated responding but then decided turning up would be better, so I stayed silent, instead posting a couple of photos of my now tidy home and the bookcase to Instagram. I had a feeling Owen would be checking my updates.

———

As a small girl I got lost in a bookstore. My mother nicknamed me Alice once she found me as I'd been tucked in the children's section with an illustrated copy of *Alice in Wonderland*. I was completely unaware I was 'missing' and that my mother had the shop shut down and everybody looking for me. She'd been relieved and furious at the same time and I'd looked up at her with wide eyes and responded by telling her I'd fallen down the rabbit hole. This had made her laugh, although there were tears at the same time which had worried me.

The bookstore in Covent Garden with its street entertainers outside reminded me of that day. Inside was a maze of aisles and comfy Chesterfield sofas and tables, which I realised were part of the Cases brand. There was a small café and an area filled with seating that had been cleared for a book signing later in the day. The signs outside told me that it was a crime writer, one I had read previously and if I was still here later on, I'd listen in.

I found coffee first, paying my usual homage to the god of all things caffeine and grabbed a pastry, which were becoming a second addiction and would mean I had to go train with my brothers at some point. Then I found a nook down an aisle where the modern classics were and discovered an E. M. Forster I hadn't read. I slipped my shoes off and curled up, feeling like the little girl I'd been when I dropped down that rabbit hole years before. I took a quick selfie and messaged it to Owen, no comment, just the photo.

And then I lost myself studying Giotto in *A Room With a View*.

CHAPTER 6
OWEN

My mother saw the photo on Instagram before me because she'd managed to uncover who Payton was and where she could stalk her. Her time as a nomad had ceased once I graduated and she'd discovered the internet as a travelling medium. Social media was her wagon.

"Owen, I think Payton's in the store," she said, elbows deep in a box of books in the storeroom. "She's just posted a new picture. Why don't you go say hello?"

I paused and studied my mother, her hair long but tidy without the beads and plaits of my childhood. "Because she'll think I'm stalking her."

"But you need to pass the accounts on to her and then all this business with you and Dave can come to an end," my mother said, admiring a new edition of *The Secret Garden*. "And we can all move on."

I shook my head. "I don't need to move on from anything. I'm perfectly happy with him earning his cut each month and lending his business advice every so often. I'm not the reason he wants out, Dot." I knew calling her by her name instead of Mum would irritate her.

"You should understand, Owen. When you and Amber split you wanted to cut all ties and move on. You wouldn't even tolerate the idea of having one of the bands here if there was a chance she'd be supporting. Sometimes we need to wash ourselves clean of someone…"

I exhaled deeply. "It's okay, Dot, you can stop now. For the record, I avoided Amber for two months. We're now friends and I realise that being divorced and friends doesn't really go together but we managed. You and Dave—I have no idea what's happened. Amber slept with someone else; as far as I'm aware, Dave hasn't even looked at another woman, so unless you've looked at another man?"

She shook her head. "That's not my scene. You know that."

I did. She and my father had been in a fairly long relationship before I'd been born although they hadn't lived together. He'd taken up a job opportunity in Germany and they'd agreed to split before she found out she was pregnant with me. I'd had two parents who'd loved me and strong values built even though they weren't together. You didn't play with people's feelings.

"Fair enough. I still don't get why you ended it with Dave."

She sighed and shook her head and I knew I wasn't getting any more from her. I'd almost given up in the last few days; she'd been reticent to say anything about him, other than passing comment on the amount he'd asked for to buy him out. My take was that he didn't want to be bought out; he wanted another chance with Dot because since I first met him when I was fifteen, he'd only had eyes for her. "Go take your lawyer a coffee. I believe it's a soya latte."

I eyed her and decided to take a walk around the store, checking stock and staffing levels and that everything had been set up for the author night. If I happened to see Payton on the way, then that would be a bonus. We could catch up and I could give her the accounts documents. I'd already been into the Callaghan Green offices to sign the contract for them to represent me.

There were a couple of understocked shelves and displays that needed addressing, but other than that my staff were on top of things, so I browsed behind bookcases, ignoring the continual chirp of my phone as emails came in. I broke deals with publishers, as all bookstores did and made negotiations over volume. When I'd first started I had very little wriggle room: now was a different matter as I'd made a name for my stores. We were influencers and trendsetters and as much as I'd berated Payton for using Instagram, I had a social media mogul who knew what he was doing and how to set trends for people's reading. That side, that business side, was all about manipulation and I understood that, as much as it differed from how I was personally. I'd learned to keep the two things separate.

A blonde head was bowed over a book in one of the modern authors aisles, her legs curled up under her, hands caressing the book as if it was made of some precious metal. I stopped and watched, not quite understanding the montage. She was petite and slight and so large with her personality that she eclipsed whatever else was happening around her, even when she was nose deep in a book.

"Hey," I said as Payton looked up, probably aware that eyes were watching her. "How's your book?"

She put it face down on the arm of her chair and looked at me with glazed eyes, clearly wrapped up in the story. "Good. I can't believe I haven't read it before. I will pay for this one, I promise." She smiled, looking sated—an expression I associate more with a woman who'd just orgasmed than one who'd been reading.

"You can have any book you want," I said. "Right now though, you look like you could do with coffee."

She stretched languidly, like a cat, legs and arms uncoordinated. "I told Seph I was going to spend the week being a tourist: it might end up being a tourist of your bookstores."

"That would be lame. Do your legs still work? If not, I'll bring coffee over."

She arched her back and stretched some more and I made a mental note to thank whoever it was who had decided the snuggle chairs would be a good idea for the end of the aisles. "I need to abandon my apartment and move in here. I don't have much stuff. No one would notice."

"I'm not sure the clientele would appreciate the overwhelming smell of your atrocious pizzas." I offered a hand to help her up, not that I thought she needed it, but I wanted to touch her again.

"There's nothing wrong with my pizza, Anders," she said, standing up and bouncing on her heels. "My legs might've gone to sleep though." She bent down to pick up her book, her tight jeans sticking to every curve and I couldn't fail to notice that. I wanted to offer to help wake them up, to tell her that it was nothing that a good massage wouldn't fix but instinct told me to remain in the friend zone.

"Can you walk or shall I send a courtesy mobility scooter for you?" I said, keeping the tone cutting.

"Walking's fine," she said. "This has been lush though. Sitting here and just reading. I can't remember the last time I did this."

"Why?" I said. I got when my friends who had kids couldn't find time, but the rest—skip Netflix, skip a night out or make it a thing to finish work on time, not even early, and go home to pick up a good book to lose yourself in.

"Because. Work," she said. "I'm too exhausted when I get in to focus. Hell, you saw the state of where I live."

"I get that," I said, and I did. "But if you love reading then read a chapter a night to switch off from work."

She walked to me and stretched to reach up to put her fingers in my hair, pulling it sharply. "You don't need to use your sales techniques on me. Now, find me coffee or I'll have an incredible hulk moment right here."

We were sitting near the café for all of two minutes before my mother found us, a bit like a heat-seeking missile but with better seeking powers. "You must be Payton," she said, tucking her long skirt up before trying to climb into one of the high stools I'd wrongly thought would be a deterrent.

"Some days I decide I'm actually She-Ra or Lara Croft, it's just the rest of the world fails to acknowledge me as that," Payton said, her face completely expressionless and her tone flat.

My mother nodded. She was a master of subtleties and unfortunately they were going to get along. Unlike Amber, my ex, Payton had a sense of humour.

"If I cast myself as Lara I'm afraid they'd have me sectioned. However, I can get away with the odd Frasier or Seinfeld character. As long as no one from a medical profession is nearby. How's your niece?"

Payton's face lit up like fireworks on New Year's Eve. "Gorgeous. She'll be home in a couple of days so I get to see her whenever my sister needs a sleep."

"Move in then. The first few weeks are hard because you're terrified they've stopped breathing or they're crying and you can't hear it. I was dreadful with Owen until he was about four, but that was because he was such a good sleeper."

"It was all the herbs you exposed me to, Mum," I said, needing to get some control over the conversation as I knew where she would take this. "I've told Payton about your youth."

My mother rolled her eyes. "He knows nothing. You, however, can sort the mess that my ex has left us in. You look like a pixie, so let's hope you have fairy powers too."

I tried not to physically cringe. Payton, however, looked enamoured, which was the effect my mother had on most people.

"It will be sorted," Payton said. "These sorts of disagreements are unfortunately quite common. I'll have a forensic accountant put forward a suggestion of how much his half of the business is worth and we'll go from there. I doubt your ex will accept the first offer, but it gives us a starting point to head into mediation with."

"What's mediation?" my mother asked. She had worked for Cases since I opened it and was now pretty much a general manger. She had a talent with staff; training them, managing them and disciplining them when necessary.

"Mediation is when two parties try to come to an agreement without going to court. It's more cost-effective and time-effective than getting a judge involved," Payton said, pushing her hair back behind her ears. She didn't look as tired as she did yesterday; her eyes were brighter and her smile was wider. I'd seen the photos on Instagram of her tidied apartment and the celebratory hashtags she'd added.

"Does that mean Owen will have to sit in a room with him?" my mum asked, with a roll of her eyes and a loud sigh. "He will drag this out for as long as possible."

"I'm not bothered by seeing him," I said. "You're the one who's fallen out with him for whatever reason."

"Why did you split up?" Payton asked, accepting a latte that I'd ordered as soon as we'd sat down. "Did he cheat?"

My mother shook her head. "No. It was just time."

"Time for what?" I asked. That was more than she'd given

away before. Neither her nor Dave had said anything other than it was 'complicated'. Wasn't everything fucking complicated?

"Owen told me your niece was born yesterday," my mother said.

I knew there was no chance of any further information. We had a curious relationship. She'd always been there, for whatever I'd needed whether that had been as someone to be angry with for no reason when I was thirteen and hitting puberty like a train, or when I'd needed a quick lesson in contraception at fifteen and my girlfriend (who was older than me) was over and I'd forgotten the essentials, or when I'd needed a good hard kick up the arse when my now-ex had the guts to call it a day on our relationship which was way past its use-by-date. But she'd never given me anything to rebel against. Her hippy principals allowed me the freedom to try, as long as I was safe or knew how to be safe. She had never said no. My requests had been met with 'have you considered what will happen if?' and I learnt how to take a risk.

But now, with her own relationship having ended, I was seeing a side to her that I wasn't sure had existed before. She was closed from me and anyone who asked about Dave. The openness that had defined her previously was now unavailable for that one topic.

"She was. She was two weeks late. I didn't know until later but my sister hadn't felt the baby move for a few hours, so her partner took her to the hospital and they performed an emergency c-section. I probably overreacted when I got the message but Owen was great. He just took me straight there and stayed, putting up with my mad family," Payton said, her phone coming out to show pictures.

My mum waded through them, commenting on the change in the baby and Claire even over one day. More photos seemed to be added to Payton's group chat constantly and her face beamed as she showed off her sister and niece.

"He grew up surrounded by small children and babies for most of the time. Do you remember the birth in Hebrides when you were twelve?" Mum said.

I stifled my wretch. It had almost been enough to put me off ever having sex if a baby could be the result. "Yeah, still trying to forget that, ma," I said, giving her the title she hated most.

She shook her head. "One of the women on the island went into labour during a storm and there was no way to get her off the island to a hospital. I'd assisted at a few births before so I leant a hand and Owen was my gopher. He had a couple of nightmares afterwards."

"It was the noise. No one prepares you for the noises. It was like something from a fucking science-fiction movie," I muttered, trying desperately to put the memories back into the deepest recess of my brain. "If I'd ever needed counselling that would be the reason why."

"It'll be different when it's your own. Plus, you'll know what to do," she said, practical as ever.

I stared at her. "Yes, Dot, I'm sure it will be useful, but as a twelve-year-old whose knowledge of female parts was limited to a couple of dirty mags that was possibly something that could've put me off everything ever."

Payton was laughing quietly, watching me with interest. "He was fine yesterday," she said. "He even held the baby." She flicked through a few photos to the one she'd taken of me holding Elizabeth Rose and my mother's mouth curved into a wide smile. I knew she wouldn't make any embarrassing comments about wanting grandchildren as that wasn't her: she swore that there was a time and a place for everything and rarely tried to force an idea.

"He's good with kids," she said. "Mainly because he's still

one himself. What are you planning to do with yourself for the rest of the day or is that a silly question given that you're in a bookshop?"

Payton smiled, her focus on my mother rather than me which made me want to do something to get her attention, but I pretended I was an adult and stayed quiet, looking at the new couple of books I'd picked up. "I want to buy a couple of guides to London. I have a few days off work as my stupid brothers seem to think I need to take a break, so I've decided to be a tourist."

"We have plenty of guides. How long have you lived here?" my mum said, her eyes narrowing with interest.

Payton shrugged. "We have a house in Oxfordshire and a town house here, so as kids we flipped between the two. I went to UCL for my degree, so I never really moved away, but I haven't seen the sights since I was probably about twelve."

My mum nodded. "We never pay much attention to what's on our own doorstep. That was one of the reasons I liked to move around when Owen was younger: we'd get to a new place and we'd explore it properly. Since I've lived in London I can't remember the last time I went to a museum or an exhibition, unless it was to visit friends who live in different cities." She sighed. "I should make more of an effort, especially now I have more free time without Dave."

"Maybe you should explore some different male sights to then," I said, taking off my glasses. I had a very low prescription and didn't need to wear them as much as I did, but I quite liked the geek look they gave me. "If things have properly ended with you and Dave and you're wanting him to be clear on that, then why don't you start dating again?"

My mother sat up straight, her hands sitting on her lap primly, something I knew my mother wasn't. "I think that's an excellent idea. Where do I start?"

CHAPTER 7
PAYTON

Thursdays were usually when I'd go in work really early and start my time recording, logging down the hours and half hours I'd spent on each case so we could bill the client. If I'd had a reasonably early night, I'd even head to the gym in the basement beforehand and catch up with my brothers or Vanessa, Jackson's wife. This Thursday I woke up late, sunshine already pouring through my windows where I'd forgotten to close the curtains and immediately smelled coffee, glorious coffee, which meant someone was in my apartment.

I pulled on my dressing gown, hearing voices but not recognising who as they were purposely being quiet, and walked barefoot into my lounge. Seph and Owen stood at my breakfast bar, a couple of bags from Amelie's café next to them, completely oblivious to me as they were deep in discussion.

"I've seen Myers Linders play and they're screwed for speed. They've got a property lawyer, Graeme Fitzpatrick, who's fairly quick, but he's usually injured or hungover so we should have a good chance of a decent win," Seph said, his hands flying everywhere as they did when he was enthusiastic.

I tried not to look at Owen. Over the past couple of days, I'd learnt that looking at him was a bad idea, especially if he caught me looking at him and gave me that smile—the one that had probably melted several thousand panties and wrecked a few hundred more pantyhose. His body was the result of running, weights and playing sports: squash, rugby, rowing when he got the chance and anything else that came along, and it had left him sculpted, because there was no other word. When he'd picked me up, it was as if I'd weighed nothing and I had a feeling that should I ever really refuse to move, he would just simply lift me and place me where he wanted me to be. I wanted to lick him all over and find out what it was like to have his weight on top of me, his hands holding my wrists above my head. I wanted to discover if he could do everything well with his body.

At this moment in time however, I wanted to know exactly why he and my brother were in my lounge.

"Lost your job, Seph?" I said, because he was the easier target.

He turned around, surprised to see me and I gave him the glare.

"And good morning Owen." He gave me a sheepish grin. He was dressed in jeans and a T-shirt, his hair still wet. My brother also looked freshly showered so putting two and two together—they'd been exercising.

"If there's anything she can throw nearby, move it quickly," Seph said. "I know that look and she's pissed off."

"And why do you think that might be, brother dear?"

Owen held out a mug of coffee. "Peace offering. Before the war starts. He's sorry."

"But you're not?"

He smiled, dimples appearing, and shook his head. "I

know your schedule today and I thought I'd join you. Besides, I need your help."

"I'm going to shoot. I've borrowed one of your takeout cups, sis," Seph said, grabbing a bag. He was already in one of his usual three-piece suits, no tie. "I'll give it back." He wouldn't. I'd find it in his office in a few weeks, more than likely unwashed. "See you tomorrow evening, Owen." Then he rushed out and left me to my dashing bookstore owner.

Suddenly I became aware that my dressing gown was short and while the faux silky material wasn't see-through it was clingy. My legs were on display up to past mid-thigh and my lack of bra was obvious. The atmosphere in the room became a little thick and Owen's eyes seemed fixed on mine. I put my hands on my hips and tried to pretend that it was just one of my brothers' friends standing there in front of me, not the leading man in a fantasy I may or may not have had the night before.

"Why are you joining me today?" I said. I had a day of sight-seeing planned: The Tower of London, a boat trip down the Thames to Greenwich on the Clipper and possibly a Jack the Ripper tour before finding one of the restaurants I'd listed to try. Yesterday, I'd been north of the Thames to the museums and St Paul's. Obviously, I'd been to one of the Cases bookstores and met Owen for lunch afterwards in a tiny café that served strong Belgium beers in small glasses.

"I've given myself a few days off. And I'm looking for another location for a new store, possibly in Greenwich or in between Greenwich and Borough. And I wanted to see you. Plus, I need a favour." His expression became darker.

"Okay." I pulled my dressing gown tighter around me, aware it was doing nothing to conceal the shape of my breasts. "What's the favour?"

"In brief, my mother has a date and I want to be in the same restaurant while it's going on."

I frowned. He sounded panicked and everything I knew about Owen so far pointed to him being laid back and calm. "Isn't that on the creeper side of normal?"

He sighed and his eyes slipped to my chest. His hand brushed through his hair. "Payton, shit, yeah. It's on the verge of creeper status except it's my mother and I really don't like the guy she's going on a date with. I'll tell you more when you're wearing no clothes... fuck, I mean more clothes. Although I'm totally open to no clothes but we won't just be friends anymore and the only sight I'll be seeing will be you."

His words hummed through me and turned everything inside me inside out and replaced my organs with tissue that was no longer held together. My mouth had dropped open and I was aware I hadn't managed to say anything yet, and I probably needed to sooner rather than later.

"Shit, sorry Payton." He rubbed his face with a hand. "I shouldn't have said that. You want to be friends and that's fine, I respect that. Shit, forget I said anything."

I walked towards him and pulled at his arm so he stopped rubbing his face. "I'm not helping matters by standing here like this, am I?"

He looked down at me, the height difference significant when I was in bare feet. "No. But I can control myself and, yeah. Blood's not in my brain right now."

My smile was victorious although I did try to help it. "Thank you," I said. "It's a compliment. And, you know, I think you're pretty spectacular too. I just don't want to date anyone at the moment. If I did, it'd be you, although you're not enough of a tool to be someone I'd date."

He laughed, a proper belly, body laugh. "I'm not sure if that's a compliment or not, Payts."

"You're too perfect for me," I said. "I've only ever dated wankers. Have my brothers not filled you in on my whole gory dating history?"

He shook his head, his hands by his sides, fixed to the denim of his jeans. "No. They've only told me about you, about how hard you work and how you try to look after all of them, especially Seph and Ava and you forget yourself. I respect that you don't want to date but you standing there like that is really making it difficult to not touch you so please will you go get dressed and then I can tell you about the idiot my mum's fixed herself up with for a date?"

My feet stayed planted and I wanted to stand on my tiptoes, take his face in my hands and kiss him, knowing full well it wouldn't stop at simply being a kiss. I felt warmth and wet between my legs from his stare alone: if he touched me I'd likely combust. "You brought breakfast?" It was a ridiculous thing to say.

"Yes," Owen said, still looking at me, hands still frozen. "You can have it when you're dressed."

"That's blackmail."

"It's saving my sanity."

I forced myself to move and headed to the bathroom, turning the shower on full so the water could heat while I stripped and brushed my teeth. The tension in his body had made his biceps bigger, his jaw had been clenched and I'd noticed the tightness in his jeans. I stepped in the shower, the water hitting my nipples and making them pucker and harden. I pinched them, softly then harder, pretending it was Owen's fingers and not mine, then I slid a hand down between my legs, feeling the smooth skin from where I'd been waxed bare. Using my own wetness, I circled two fingers around my clit, thinking of Owen, imagining him pushing me against the wall and lifting me onto his cock, filling me hard and fast, pumping into me with my legs hooked around his back, the base of his cock banging against my clit, his fingers twisting my nipples and his mouth sucking the skin of my neck. The water pounded and pounded and pounded against my skin, its heavy rhythm pounding loudly, masking my moans as I came, pushing two fingers inside me and imagining it was Owen's hard cock.

I leaned back against the tiles, my heart rate starting to calm and then I heard what was pounding. The door to the bathroom.

A fist on the door to the bathroom.

Holy fecking fucking mother of Mary.

"Payton? Payts?"

I turned the shower down slightly. "Yeah?"

"Are you okay? I thought I heard you…"

I bit my bottom lip before I could tell him the truth. One, because I found it hard to lie at the best of times. Two, because if I told him what I'd just done it would be very easy to invite him in the bathroom and in somewhere else too. "I'm good. You just heard me singing badly. That was all."

There was a laugh. He didn't believe me. He knew damn well what I had been doing, the shit. "I'll make another coffee."

"Thanks." I started to wash as quickly as possible, putting thoughts of Owen out of my head and focusing on trying to look natural as opposed to someone who had just had a rather powerful orgasm.

Skinny jeans, blue sweater, blow-dried hair and barely there make-up made me feel something close to normal. As I stepped into my lounge, I saw Owen sitting on my sofa, reading David Copperfield and drinking a coffee. There was a half-eaten Danish on a plate next to him.

"Feel better?"

I felt the heat rise to my cheeks. "There's nothing wrong with singing in the shower," I said, taking the other coffee and the raspberry and chocolate Danish. "It relieves a lot of stress."

"I know something else that relieves stress," he said, his eyes dancing dangerously.

"I bet you do."

He grinned. "My back massages."

I shook my head. "No way, Anders. Your blood runs south with me in a dressing gown, what would happen if you actually touched my skin? We'd have to amputate your balls."

He winced.

"Apologies. Maybe that was too graphic."

"A little. I can get you to relax without injuring myself though. Let's try it later. After I've stalked my mother on her date."

We started at The Tower of London, taking in the suits of armour on display and the Crown Jewels. It lent itself nicely to selfies and jokes about other sets of crown jewels and what vast amounts of blood could do to them. A tour guide overheard us and assumed that our crown jewels conversation was a sensible one, pointing out that the jewels were stored so that no bloodshed should ever disturb them. Somehow we managed to make it till we were out of earshot before we both burst out laughing.

The tube was packed, as it always was. Owen insisted we go to Borough Market for grilled cheese, and although it was close enough to where I worked for me to go there most days, his enthusiasm was such that I couldn't say no. He then led me down the busy side street to The Shard, its glass sides reflecting the late April sun.

"Cocktails?" he said. "Or do we have to ban any reference to appendages?"

I laughed. "Cocktails are on the list of non-prohibited topics. As long as I can pay. You've got everything so far."

"Fine," he said. "I'm good with being a kept man."

We headed to the Aqua Shard, a restaurant and bar that had natural light pouring in as well as the view of the London skyline. There was no queue, which was a nice surprise, and we managed a table next to the window.

"You're okay with heights?" I asked Owen, who looked a little tentative as we sat down.

He nodded. "I am once I'm used to it."

"The view's spectacular."

"The view I have right now is better."

The blush that was becoming commonplace rose to my cheeks again. "That's corny."

"But true. And besides, the view out there is a bit too high still. I'd rather look at you for a couple of reasons." He lounged back in his chair and studied me. "Have you chosen a cocktail?"

"A Breakfast at Tiffany's," I said. "Vodka and other things along with a bank loan. You?"

The dimples popped out. "A gin and tonic. Probably a double. Wouldn't want to bankrupt you."

A penguin-suited waiter appeared and took our order and I looked out over the city, the scent of Owen's aftershave reminding me who I was with. "Tell me about your mum's date and where it is. I'll probably need to get changed."

"First thing you think of. I'll let you take as many selfies as you want and you can tag me in them," he said, still watching me.

"You have an Instagram account? Is this so you can creep me?"

"I've always had one. Well, not always, but for a couple of years. It's helpful for finding bands and singers to play at

Cases, especially early on. Now they contact us to see if they can perform there."

My phone was out already. "What's your name on there?"

"Owen Anders with an underscore at the end."

I searched quickly and found his account, grinning victoriously. "You liar," I said. "You use this as much as me. You're just more discreet at putting up pictures." There were some from today: me and him taking a selfie with a suit of armour; the view from Tower Bridge and one of me looking over the side of the bridge at the Thames. He'd altered the filter to give the photo a soft tone and had caught the moment when the wind had blown my hair. His caption was simple: beautiful woman.

I clicked follow and set it so I would have a notification whenever he posted. No more stealth photos.

"Are you mad?" he said quietly.

"No."

"Are you freaked out?"

"No."

"Really?"

"Kind of. But not because you're a creeper."

"Why?"

"Because of how I think you see me."

"That picture shows how I see you."

"I'm still not—"

"Dating," he interrupted. "I know."

"Your mother. Tell me about her date."

Our drinks arrived and Owen took a good gulp before he explained. "He's called Trey Buchanan and he owns an accountants three doors down from the Covent Garden store. He buys a lot of books and has chatted to Mum loads which I don't have a problem with. My issue is that I know he's demanding of his dates. He had a short relationship with the aunt of a girl I dated for a few months and at first he was charming, really full on but smarmy with it. After a few weeks he became possessive and started to be controlling: she didn't get to choose where they went out to eat or even what she wore. When she ended it, he kept turning up at her place at all hours, making threats and such. It didn't last very long; I think he'd already picked his next victim but he wasn't pleasant."

"Have you told your mum this?"

"Of course. She's not denied it, but she said she's going to see what he's like for herself. Which I suppose is fair enough, but I feel she's a bit vulnerable at the moment," he said, looking preoccupied.

"Why do you think she ended it with Dave?"

"I think the grass looked greener. They've never lived together and I think he suggested that they finally moved in. She's never lived with another man, apart from me obviously, so I think she panicked." His drink was nearly empty. I gestured to the waiter to bring two more.

"Where are they eating?"

"The Oystermen. We have a reservation at eight and it's definitely my treat. You do like seafood, don't you?" He sat slightly forward, clearly worried that he'd made a faux pas.

"I hate it. Can't stand oysters or especially lobster."

His face dropped. "Shit…"

"I'm kidding. I love seafood. Not sure either of us should have oysters though."

———

We took the Clipper down the Thames to Greenwich, the expanse of the river soaking away my worries and stresses about work, and, for the first time in forever, I lived in the moment. We laughed and teased, taking tons of photos, some artistic and others simply stupid with the sounds of the city surrounding us. I found out Owen could actually sing, when he started humming on the journey back his version of Tom Walker's *Leave A Light On*. I told him about how I would write stories when I couldn't sleep and that I'd never shown them to anyone. He asked to see them and I said he'd have to see my bare boobs first. His response was silence until he assured me he'd have no problem with that.

He didn't ask me on another date. There were touches; he put his arm around me, placed his hand on the small of my back and occasionally took my hand to change our route as we took a self-guided tour around the East End where Jack the Ripper had tormented London, using Google as an assistant.

"There's so much history here. Every step on the pavements has already been taken so many times before," I said, sipping a beer. We'd paused for a drink before heading back to my apartment so I could pick up a change of clothes. Owen lived near to The Oystermen so I'd get changed there.

He scratched the stubble around his jaw. "That's very deep for this time on a Thursday after a couple of cocktails and beers."

I laughed. "I clearly need alcohol to be deep and meaningful."

He didn't laugh back. "I disagree and please don't put yourself down like that." It wasn't a reprimand, instead it was a polite request. "You say lots of things that make me think and consider stuff I haven't thought of before, that's why I like spending time with you."

"You're very honest," I said, unsure as to how to deal with his compliments.

"Yes," he said. "Drink up. Let's go get your outfit. I have a spare room if you want to stay over. If you don't, that's fine— I'll make sure you get back okay," he said, downing the rest of his beer.

"I'm fine at getting across London on my own. I've been doing it long enough," I said, smiling. I knew my limits; I knew where was safe and where wasn't.

"I'm not saying you don't, but you're doing me a favour and I'll be happier knowing that you're home okay or staying with me. I promise I won't try anything," he said, one side of his mouth curving into a smile.

Maybe I want you to. "I'll take a change to stay at yours. Any funny business and I'll call my brothers."

He laughed. "Don't rely on them. They've got me playing Sunday morning for their rugby team. Seph offered to put a good word in for me with you."

I held my head in my hands. "I'm being pimped out so they have more players for the team. Brilliant!"

He walked around to my chair and offered a hand to help me up. "Just to me," he said and I saw something in his expression that I hadn't caught before.

CHAPTER 8
OWEN

I was a bastard. My forehead rested against the floor to ceiling window that looked out towards Covent Garden and I waited for the bolt of lightning to hit me, or at the very least, my mother's voice to come booming through the walls. Payton was getting ready in the bathroom, having grabbed her girly toiletries and whatever else she needed and now my apartment was flooded with the scent of her and the sound of her singing, which was nothing like what I'd heard this morning when she was in the shower. I was pretty sure what I'd heard this morning had been moaning, the sort of moaning I wanted to cause.

I promised her I wouldn't ask her on a date, that I understood she wasn't interested in dating, but that was what I'd spent the day doing: dating her, just covertly. Of course it was a fucking date, and it had been fucking perfect so far. I knew that she wasn't going to end up in my bed by the end of the night, and I could live with that because I wanted her there badly enough and more than once to make sure I didn't rush this. It had been a long time since I'd felt this strongly about a woman, in fact, I wasn't sure I had ever felt this strongly this quickly. Even with Amber it had been more of a slow burn with sex being the main driver and her becoming a good habit. We'd worked well together until we hadn't.

"Hey," Payton said. "You trying to listen to that window's secrets or something?"

"Or something," I said, turning round. She had a towel wrapped round her, hair damp around her face. Her face was bare of any make-up and she looked beautiful. I figured she probably wasn't wearing anything under the towel and tried not to focus on that.

She smiled. "I could do with some water. And no more alcohol tonight. I think I've had enough."

I went to the fridge and passed her a bottle of mineral water. "You feel buzzed?"

"Sleepy," she said. "Nap-like." It was punctuated with a yawn.

"Why don't you grab thirty minutes while I get a shower?" I said, taking a water for myself. "The bed's made up. I'll wake you up. How much time do you need to get ready?"

Her eyes were sleeping, making me think of how she'd look waking up next to me. My jeans felt tight, I just hoped she wouldn't look down. "About half an hour, but I need a good twenty minutes to come around."

"Go grab a nap," I said. "I'm going to shower and check my emails so don't worry about being a good houseguest." I grinned at her. "I'll wake you up in an hour."

"Thanks. I guess everything's catching up with me and it's been a busy day." The sleepy smile was still there.

"If you're not up for The Oystermen…" I said, pushing a hand through my hair. I did need to go as I didn't trust that idiot with my mum for half a second, but I knew Payton needed to relax too.

"I'm really looking forward to going," she said and

headed towards me, the towel wrapped around her coming to just below her arse, leaving most of her legs on display and her shoulders bare.

She put the water bottle down and closed the rest of the gap between us. Her arms stretched up and I imagined the towel dropping, which meant any blood left in my brain headed south.

The towel didn't drop, but her arms went around my neck and she hugged me, her body pressing against mine. My hands went around her lower back, with my hands managing not to land on her ass. "Thank you," she breathed into me. "Today's been amazing." There was no way she wouldn't have noticed my erection.

"I've had a great time too. Go get your nap." I loosened my hold, not sure I could have her that closely and not touch her elsewhere.

"Sure." She gave me another beaming smile, picked up her water and I watched her arse as she went to my spare bedroom, biting my lips in pain as my jeans were doing a good impression of strangled my cock.

I hit the shower, stripping off my clothes and getting straight under the hard stream of water. The icy cold turned hot soon enough and I faced the tiles, placing my palms on them and let the water hit me. She was becoming my fantasy, this little lawyer who was full of sass and sensitivity and tried not to stop. With her curves and her deep blue eyes, I wanted nothing more than to lose myself in her. The towel that had been covering her hadn't hidden much—nothing that my imagination couldn't fill in—and as I thought about what was underneath (tits that were just a bit more than a handful, a flat soft belly and how tight her pussy would be and how I could make her come, make her tighter) my dick became excruciatingly hard. Leaving one palm against the tiles, I used the other to grasp my cock and started to stroke, the hot water providing the lube. I imagined my hand was hers and thought about how she'd grip me, gently or firmly; how fast she'd stroke, how she might taste the head with her tongue. I imagined her mouth on me, stretching round my girth, taking me towards my throat and I imagined my mouth on her tits, tasting her pussy and then being inside her. My heart rate quickened as I thought about fucking her, watching her eyes as I made her come all over my cock and then pulling out, my semen coating her tits and owning them.

My orgasm was hard and fast taking over my body and leaving me breathing heavily. I rested both palms back on the tiles and looked down, my heart beating fasting than a hummingbird's wings. I washed off, decided not to shave and tried to focus on my mother's date rather than the woman in the bedroom next to mine. I didn't know what the world record for the most boners in one day was, but I was pretty sure I could give it a good shot if my obsession with Payton got any stronger.

―――

Emails had been hitting my inbox all day. Most I could answer tomorrow as they weren't urgent, but there was one from my dad, inviting me to join him in buying a gallery that was struggling. He'd included a business plan and although he didn't need help with the financial side, he thought it was a venture that would appeal to me as there was enough space in the building to accommodate live music and a pop-up bar. I was interested. Cases could almost run itself and having a new business to work on was something I was keen for at the moment. I made arrangements to meet him in the morning for breakfast and started to feel more in control.

Payton was sleeping when I opened the door to the spare bedroom. She was on her side, facing the window, just a sheet over her, seemingly naked underneath. I stepped closer, seeing her hands next to her face on the pillow, her expression peaceful. I looked up to the ceiling and prayed to the god of self-control to stop me getting in bed with her.

"Hey, sleeping beauty," I said, feeling like a shit for waking her.

She moaned and shifted onto her back, the sheet pulling tightly across her chest, the dark of her nipples visible through the thin sheets.

Tomorrow I'd buy new bedding with a higher thread count in order to stop this torture.

I stepped back towards the door, not wanting her to open her eyes and see me staring at her tits. "Payton, it's time to wake up."

She stirred again, turning onto her side to face me and this time the sheet slipped slightly, more of her breast exposed. I looked up to the ceiling again, *you're not fucking helping here*, I thought to whichever god of self-control should've been on duty.

"Payts!" My voice was louder and shorter, probably out of frustration.

Her eyes fluttered open. "Hey," she said, unware of how she looked, of where the sheet was. "Is it time to get up?"

I nodded. "We've about forty minutes until we need to head out. Do you want me to make you a drink? Tea? Coffee?" *And how would you feel about an orgasm and some hot sex to go with that?*

"Tea would be great," she said, rearranging the sheet so she could sit up. Her back was exposed and I knew I needed to get out of the room fast. "This bed is really comfortable. Much better than mine. I might have to move into your spare room."

Please do. But not the spare. Mine.

"You should try my bed some time." And I knew exactly what I was saying.

"With you in it?" she said, laughing so that her tits moved, the friction from the sheet making her nipples stand out. I didn't try to keep my eyes off them as I figured she knew full well how she looked. If she didn't want me looking, she would've pulled the blankets over her too.

"Anytime. I'll go make you a mug of tea." I backed out before we could have the no-dating-just-friends conversation again and decided that tonight I had to find out why she was so against dating at the moment.

She appeared fifteen minutes later, her hair dry and the small dressing gown tied round her, legs bare. "Thank you," she said, taking the tea. "I'm always thanking you."

"You don't need to. I don't do anything I don't want to do. I'm not doing anything for your thanks," I said. It was true. I'd grown up helping people, because that was what my mother did, but she did it because she wanted to, not because of what she'd gain from it or to have someone's gratitude.

"I'll stop saying it then. A dress is okay for tonight, isn't it? I brought a couple of things if it's not." She sipped the tea.

I'd never understood the whole girl and clothes thing, so I wasn't entirely sure of what to say. "I don't know what's fashionable for a crashing your friend's mother's date-scenario, to be honest."

Payton rolled her eyes. "Will there be other girls in there wearing dresses on a Thursday night or will everyone have jeans on?" she said, her tone impatient.

"It's Covent Garden. There will probably be someone wearing a ball gown and someone else in a whole punk get up." I said, looking down at my trousers and blue shirt. I felt her eyes on my chest and caught her eye, grinning and enjoying the victory. "I assume I look all right?"

"You know what assume did?" she said, referring to the

old joke, then turned around and looked at me from over her shoulder. "I'll be ready in fifteen."

That was all it took her. She appeared in a tight blue dress and skin coloured heels. The dress left her legs pretty much exposed and her arms were also bare. She looked at me, clearly weighing something up. "Can I borrow a jacket? I haven't brought one and it's not the warmest night."

"Cupboard next to the bathroom." She shot me a smile and headed there.

A minute later and she had my old leather jacket slung over her shoulders, the worn material adding a little bad to her pretty look. "I need a compliment here, big guy," she said.

"Do friends give compliments?"

She hit me with her sassy glare. "All the time."

"You look all right," I said. "I don't mind people knowing you're with me." She looked fucking edible and it was taking every single fucking drop of restraint that I possessed not to put her on my sofa, push that tight dress up, see what she was wearing underneath and put my mouth on her pussy. I did not want to take her out looking like that because I was going to punch out the lights of any guy who looked at her and it was not my place to. Because we were just friends. Because she wasn't mine.

"You look all right too," she said. "Your blue shirt means we almost match."

"Shall I change?"

"You don't want to match?"

"You said it like it was a bad thing."

Her blonde hair shook as she giggled. "It's fine, Owen. Let's go. She tucked her arm into mine and I caught the scent of her perfume. I tried to inhale as much of it as I could while

I sent another prayer to the seemingly absent god of self-restraint because tonight was going to be a long one.

"What's she doing?" I asked, watching Payton knock back an oyster, her eyes closed.

"Hmmm. That's so nice." She blinked and licked her lips. "She looks quiet and the waiter has just taken away her plate. Trey looks uncomfortable."

"Good," I said, taking an oyster for myself and trying not to be grumpy. "Has she seen us?"

"Oh, yes," Payton said. "She's looked over a couple of times and did not look impressed. They're getting the bill." She paused. "Looks like she's paying."

"He won't like that."

"She's waving his hand away and he's pulling a face."

"Is she okay?"

Payton stared and then smiled. "She's fine. She's just given him a peck on the cheek and he's leaving." She took a sip of her water. "And now she's coming over here."

I heard the rhythmic sound of my mother's footsteps, slightly weirded out that she'd worn a pair of high heels. I only remembered her wearing flats when she went out with Dave.

"I really did not need two chaperones," she hissed as she came close enough.

I saw Payton colour and look embarrassed.

"Don't worry, honey, I know this wasn't your idea. It's was shit–for–brains here. Owen, if I had any concerns I'd have phoned you. As it is, he only wanted to talk about himself and thought the sun shone out of his arsehole, so I paid and got rid of him, but having you sitting here in your judgemental corner was not helpful to my self-esteem. I have another date with someone else lined up for in a couple of weeks and I don't want an appearance from you. Now, have a good night and I'll see you tomorrow." She bent down and kissed the side of my cheek, then stepped round to Payton and did the same. "You look lovely together by the way."

I expected Payton to remind her that we were just friends, but instead she simply smiled.

"See you tomorrow, Mum," I said. "Get home safely." I felt the glare burn through my skull. At least she hadn't slapped me.

We chatted through the rest of the meal, Payton asking questions about the places I'd lived as a kid and telling me stories about her brothers and sisters. Claire was due home tomorrow with the baby, so Payton was going to see her before meeting everyone apart from Claire and her parents at a bar near the Callaghan Green offices. I was due there too, although I had plans to meet a friend from college just beforehand for a beer.

I paid the bill, ignoring Payton's frowns, and guided her out of the restaurant, managing to not hit a bloke in a suit who couldn't take his eyes off her, despite him being with his wife or girlfriend.

"Are you sure you don't mind me staying at yours?" she said once we got outside, my old jacket back round her shoulders.

"It's fine. I'm leaving early in the morning, so I'll try not to wake you. Help yourself to whatever you want, I think there's a few edible things in the fridge. There's definitely orange juice."

She looked up at me and smiled, her arm linking mine again. "I'll make sure I leave everything tidy. I'm going to head straight from yours to Claire and Killian's so I might leave some stuff with you. Is that all right? I don't want it to be in the way if you're planning on bringing any women back to your place this weekend."

I knew she was goading me. "I'll make sure it stays in the spare bedroom," I said. "Then they won't ask any awkward questions."

I expected a sarcastic reply but instead got silence.

"Why aren't you dating?" I said, filling the void with the subject I needed to learn about.

"Honestly? I keep picking idiots. Men who mess me around or I think we're getting serious and it turns out they're on a completely different page to me. I had two boyfriends that were kind of long term and both of them ended up being idiots. Since then, I've just had casual relationships but I'm not even very good at that." She sounded wistful.

I stopped walking, jerking her towards me and wrapped my arms around her. We were blocking the pavement but I didn't care. "Those two men who hurt you—they were dicks for not realising what they had but that's a good thing because you're not stuck with them. You can do better." *Like me.*

She pressed her forehead into my chest, her small hands in my stomach, fingers playing with the buttons on my shirt. This wasn't friends. We couldn't be just friends. I'd pretend for as long as it took for her to see that, but this, the way we fit together, the way she felt in my arms, was sex and love and Sunday mornings in bed and Monday evenings on the couch. It was longevity and friendship and a good hard fuck followed by a long slow afternoon of making love.

"With who? I'm high maintenance. I stress and work all hours. I fuss people and make demands and have this wacky full-on family who I love. I'm messy and I have habits."

"Like what?"

"Like eating pastries in bed and drinking coffee, too much coffee. And books. Too many books."

"There's no such things as too much coffee and too many books. Anyone who tells you otherwise is a liar." My hands ran up and down her back, soothing. "And what you've just listed is what makes you who you are."

"One of my exes told me I was too much. That he could never relax around me."

"Then that was his problem, not yours. I've been relaxed around you all day."

"The other told me I worked too much and spent too much time with my family, so he couldn't imagine a future together."

"Clearly you weren't that into him because you would've made more time for him and wanted him more involved with your family."

"You're not going to let me win this debate, are you?"

"What debate?"

She laughed, the sound vibrating through me. "I think you're the perfect man."

I turned around, keeping one hand on the small of her back.

"You have no reply to that?"

"No," I said. "My reply would've been to kiss you and that wouldn't have been friend-like."

"I've kissed you. Maybe you're allowed one pass."

We got to my apartment without me saying or doing anything that would've caused my balls to be any bluer than they already were. I was pretty sure the colour of them matched her dress. Heading straight to the fridge I tried not to look at her; my resolve as thin as ice on a puddle. "Have a bottle of water for the night," I said, passing one to her.

She accepted it and put it straight down on the table. "Owen," she said, now a foot shorter than me in her bare feet. "I've had such a great day."

Her eyes were wide and contained a pool of emotion that I couldn't untangle enough to decipher. "Me too," I said. "I'm going to get it in the neck from my mother tomorrow though."

She shrugged, stepping closer. "You probably deserve it, although I'm glad we went to that restaurant. It was amazing. And entertaining. Although you were quite growly."

"There was the idiot my mother was with and some tosser who couldn't take his eyes off you. I'm sorry if I was growly."

Her smile lit the room. "Growly suits you sometimes."

Then she was in front of me, close enough to touch. "Do you want me to kiss you?" I said, needing her to have the power.

"Yes," she said, almost too quietly to hear. "Just a kiss. That would make it the most perfect day ever."

"Just a kiss," I said, closing the distance between us and then pressing my lips to hers. It was sweet and innocent and although the need to deepen it and allow myself to be consumed by her was there, I held back.

She pulled away, her lips already swollen and her eyes dark with lust. "Goodnight, Owen. I'll see you in the evening."

"Goodnight," I said, watching her head into the spare room, the wrong room, once again. I wondered what she would do when she got in bed and it was that thought I took with me as I stripped and got between my own sheets, cock in hand for the second time in just a few hours.

CHAPTER 9
PAYTON

Sleep had been cool sheets and a peaceful room, dreamless and restful and I woke naturally with the spring sun streaming in through the window. I could taste Owen on my lips, the memory of his touch on my arms and back still vibrant and warm, his words when he told me I was worth something still in my head. But I still didn't feel worthwhile enough and it was only me who could change that. I was a brilliant lawyer, a good daughter and sister and I knew I looked okay, yet there was a barrier there and I couldn't identify what it was.

Owen's spare room was neat and tidy: grey curtains and a blind with geometric yellow and green designs were at the window. The furniture was Scandinavian in design and the carpet plush and grey. The walls had a greyish tinge to them, with one wall covered in feature wallpaper. If I'd seen this room before getting to know him, I'd have argued his mother or an interior designer had put it together, but knowing him better, I figured he'd done it himself.

Having grown up with a ton of elder siblings, I was nosy by nature and had a strong survival instinct. The more secrets you knew, the easier it was to bribe someone, so when I thought about having a good look around Owen's apartment, my conscience didn't let off alarm bells. The bad fairy sat back happily while the good one was locked away in a cupboard and I set off to explore, starting with the lounge.

There were photos in the drawers of the coffee table, some in photobooks that had been put together online and some that had been printed. A reoccurring woman was in them, tall with long red hair and pretty features. There were several of her and Owen together when he looked a few years younger and I figured that this was the ex he'd mentioned. There were no names on the backs of the pictures or the dates so I was no clearer factually.

He was tidy and neat, which made it easier to rummage. His bedroom was clean, no dirty clothes on the floor or used condoms under the bed—and yes, I looked. There were no women's clothes in his closet, just a pile of books instead, some historical fiction, some crime and some erotica. The erotica caught my attention and I'd ask him about them later. I did not keep my rummaging secret. That would be wrong.

Bedside table drawers I knew for a fact were where the secrets were kept. I opened the one on the unmade side, figuring that was where Owen slept. The pillow smelled of his aftershave and I'd be lying if I said I didn't bury my head in it for a moment. My chest pulsated and my stomach twisted in anticipation, of what I wasn't sure, but I felt like I was fifteen again and was waiting for my first proper kiss. The drawer contained condoms, lube and a set of handcuffs. A bit more digging around and I found a butt plug, still in its virgin box. My pussy clenched tightly and I bit my lips together. There was a cupboard beneath the drawer, but I didn't want to go there yet, some things needed to be kept as secrets until the right time, if that ever came.

I headed into the lounge and made a coffee. My phone

was on the kitchen worktop, left there from the night before. I didn't want to be disturbed in the early morning with the light of the screen illuminating the room as my siblings messaged me or any emails came in from work.

Sitting down, I sipped the coffee and started to check my messages. There were the usual ones from my brothers and Ava, planning the night out tonight and whose turn it was to look after Seph when he got too drunk. Allegedly it was Callum's, but that could've been because he was the last to deny all knowledge. Then there were a couple debating what I was doing and if I'd taken over a small Caribbean country yet. I didn't respond: a picture of my niece dressed up to come home had been sent, then a selfie of her with Claire and Killian holding her. My heart burst and I knew that if anyone could see they'd wonder why I was grinning so hard.

I started to text Claire, knowing that if they were still on their way home and Killian would be driving.

> Me: She looks beautiful. I'll be at yours in an hour or so. Is that okay?

> Claire: Just got home now. K's making us all breakfast—so sick of fucking hospital food.

> Me: How are you feeling? I hope K's looking after you.

> Claire: He's driving me mad. He won't even let me pick up my handbag. Or rather, let me carry it. All I'm apparently allowed to do is sit or lie down, eat and feed the baby. I'm going to fucking kill him. How's Owen?

> Me: Why?

Claire: Because according to my sources, you've been spending a lot of time with him.

Me: Seph's filling your brain with shit. We're friends. He's a client.

Claire: You're stupid if you don't tap that. I may have been under the influence of a shit load of drugs, but he was hot.

Me: Have you shared those thoughts with Killian?

Claire: Of course. His reaction was exactly what you would predict but at least I got to carry my own handbag.

Me: I'll be round in an hour or so.

Claire: Where are you exactly?

Me: Owen's. I stayed in his spare room last night. We went to The Oystermen in Covent Garden to stalk his mum and her date.

Claire: This is good. Tell me more when you get here. Need to go, Killian is trying to change Eliza and it looks like he's about to cover himself in shit. Love you.

I started to raid Owen's kitchen for something breakfast-like when I noticed a paper bag on the side. There was a note by it and I swore it hadn't been there when I first woke up.

The handwriting was neat and cursive, probably as presentable as it had been when he was in school. *Payton*, it said. *Realised I had no pastries in and didn't want the world to face you when you hadn't had your morning fix. Not sure why you were in my bedroom, but your brothers did warn me that you liked to look in other people's stuff. Hope you found the butt plugs. Owen x*

I opened the paper bag and decided to eat my embarrassment away.

———

Just over an hour later I was at Claire and Killian's house, a four-storey monstrosity that Killian had bought a couple of years previously. There was the usual amount of security before I entered: a camera at the door which I was pretty sure scanned faces and an odd ornament in the porch which I was convinced was a metal detector.

Killian ran a security firm, one that had been started by his elder brother and he'd joined when he'd left the marines. He didn't talk about his work, nor did he usually ask permission to add a bit of extra security to our lives. The only person who complained on a regular basis was Claire, and that was because she'd spent the past five years complaining about him.

The house was military tidy as usual. There were few ornaments about, neither Killian nor my sister being the type to have tons of crap. Already the place was baby proofed, which knowing Killian, had been a military procedure.

He was Maxwell's best friend and partner in crime before he became my brother-in-law, meaning I'd known him since I was nine; he'd always been another brother to me. When we found out he'd been seeing Claire at college and they'd somehow resurrected their romance a year ago, I'd been thrilled.

"Morning," I said to him, fighting back a laugh at the muslin on his shoulder that was covered in spitted up milk. "New accessory?"

"You are so much like your sister," he said, holding the

door open. She's upstairs. Please don't let her do too much. She's meant to be resting as much as she can.

"Noted," I said. "K?"

"Payton."

"What do you think of Owen?"

"He's a good player by the looks of things. Strong and surprisingly quick given his size." I tipped my head to one side and inhaled deeply. "That wasn't what you meant, was it?"

"Not really."

"Do I need to have 'the talk' with him?"

I knew exactly what he meant. He was offering to threaten to stuff his testicles down his throat and peel them out of his arse if he so much as let me open a door for myself.

"No. I'm not dating anyone at the moment."

"Then why are you asking?"

I shrugged. "I just wondered what you thought of him. No hidden agenda."

Killian considered this for a moment before he said, "He's a good guy. Honest, can take a joke, straightforward. There's nothing not to like. We'll see how he handles his beer tonight. You're coming, aren't you?"

"That's interesting. You know for sure someone you met a few days ago is coming out to celebrate the birth of your daughter but you're not sure about your sister-in-law." My hands went to my hips and I sassed like the world was ending.

Killian laughed, completely unmoved. "You're not in our group chat. Neither's Ava, so don't get your pants in a twist."

Footsteps on the stairs made us both look up and my older sister made her way down. She looked tiny still, her short bobbed hair framing her delicate face, her brown eyes looking huge. "Do not say one word about me coming downstairs, either of you. I've had a baby. Women do it every day and then carry water on their heads for five miles."

If any of our brothers had been present they'd have run for the hills with Claire being in permanent hormonal bitch mode. Killian simply looked at her.

"That's fine. No lifting. Unless it's Eliza. I'll make coffee for you both." He disappeared as if into thin air.

"And it will be decaffeinated. He thinks I haven't noticed," she said, heading into the lounge. "Mum and Dad will be here in an hour or so. They're staying for a couple of nights."

I sat down on the couch where I'd slept off a horrific hangover, both alcohol and man induced, a few weeks ago. "Mum will be useful. She'll help you get some sleep."

Claire nodded. "She will. To be honest, Killian is more than pulling his weight. I'm glad he's going out tonight though. He'll probably have a timer set on his phone to check I'm okay every half an hour."

"Just keep sending him pictures of Eliza."

"Then he'll come home. He's absolutely smitten with her. God knows how much trouble I'll have to help her stay out of when she's a teenager. He'll probably do security checks on every kid in her class. That's if he decides not to home school." Claire sighed, sitting down with a groan and fidgeting to get comfy. "Right, spill the details about the hot bookstore owner."

"He's really… *fuck*. He's just like this living example of a perfect man. We should shoot him, stuff him and create an exhibition on just how perfect he is." I twisted my hair round, something I did when I felt uncomfortable.

"No one's perfect, Payton. Don't tell Killian, but I think he's as close to perfection as they come. That's why I had his baby and I'm going to marry him, even though he drives me mad most of the time," Claire said.

"You realise he'll have this room bugged and will be listening to our conversation?"

She shook her head. "He's more interested in the neighbours. He's convinced they're spies. I think he's imagining things so he doesn't catch baby brain from me. Back to Owen. Why's he so perfect? He's gorgeous in a geeky, body builder way and he seems pretty decent."

"He is. He's interesting and intelligent and he calls me on shit but defends me too. He says he's happy being friends but he's made it clear he'd like more if I was interested," I said, knowing that my sister would pick straight up on the tone in my voice.

"And you've told him you're not dating?"

"Yeah. I know."

"So the first decent guy in forever comes along and you're not dating because you think he's too good for you?"

"Hole in one, Claire."

She shook her head. Killian came in with a French press of coffee, cups and warm milk. Eliza was strapped to his chest, looking tiny against the hugeness of him. "I'll come back with her in a bit," he said. "Drink your coffee first."

Claire rolled her eyes at his retreating back and waited until he'd cleared the room before saying, "I know. Overprotective daddy. It is very sweet though. He looks gorgeous with her."

I raised my eyebrows. "You're planning more?"

"Yes. Not right now, obviously, but there won't be too big a gap between her and the next." She smiled. "I am coming back to work though. At some point."

"Good to know. I can't wait to hold her."

"Wait till she's sick on you for the first time. Holding her will lose its novelty then. So what are you going to do about Owen?" Claire said, shifting forward so she could pour the coffee. I went to do it for her but she gestured me away. "I'm not a fucking invalid."

"I don't know. We've kissed. But…" I shrugged.

"Is there no chemistry?"

There was more chemistry than a fecking high school lab. "There's plenty of chemistry." I told her about the previous day, about how easy it had been, how we'd just clicked.

"I don't understand why you're not sleeping with him. It's ages since you've had sex, Payts. Get it out of your system. It might be shit and you just stay friends or it might be a life changing event and that's you off the dating scene forever, making happy with Owen Anders. Right, let's discuss Ava. Something's going on there which she's not taking about. Thoughts."

Friday nights out after work were something of a habit. More often than not, someone from the office was celebrating or commiserating something and an email would fly round about three to see who was interested in a couple of after work drinks. Some weekends most of us Callaghans would head over to Oxfordshire to see our parents, but Whisky Ginger—a cocktail bar near Tower Bridge—was generally populated by at least half a dozen people from our firm.

I sat with Ava and Victoria, Maxwell's girlfriend, and nursed a glass of prosecco. Killian was on his first drink and had already checked his phone three times and called Claire once, which had resulted in his beer being spiked by Seph with a shot of vodka. Given that Killian rivalled Owen for size, I didn't see it making much difference.

"How've you enjoyed your week off?" Ava said, looking like she'd just stepped out of Vogue in black leather trousers and a blouse that would've looked terrible on anyone that wasn't her. Claire and I had come to the conclusion that she was seeing someone, someone we wouldn't approve of, although we had no idea as to who it could be.

I smiled and looked at my drink; I wasn't in the mood for drinking much and I wanted to avoid a hangover tomorrow. "It's been better than I thought it would be. I actually haven't missed work that much."

"Good," Ava said. "You need to take time out and get some balance and then the rest of us can stop worrying about you working yourself into oblivion. How's Owen? I hear you've spent a lot of time with him this week. In fact, I heard you woke up in his house this morning."

"But not his bed. We're just friends." Saying it made disappointment rise up into my chest and squeeze my heart. I was definitely interested, just afraid. I'd made bad choices in the past, ones that had worried my family and I didn't want another.

"Good friends," a voice behind me said. "As in a friend who goes through their friend's drawers and cupboards."

I turned around and gave Owen a huge megawatt smile, ignoring Ava and Victoria laughing. "It's a really good way to get to know someone. You're more than welcome to do the same at mine."

"And what would I find, Payton Marie?" he said, his eyes twinkling behind his glasses. He was wearing slacks and a shirt, which was untucked and the top couple of buttons were open. The sleeves were also rolled up, showing strong forearms and I remembered what it was like to be held by them.

"Photos. Books. Toys…" I said. "You had quite the collection." Ava and Victoria were distracted by Max and Jackson who had just turned up.

He shrugged. "My favourite flavour has never been vanilla. What can I get you to drink?"

I looked at the half-full glass of prosecco. "This is sitting well. Maybe something fruity and sweet. Or a margarita?"

"On it." He grinned and headed to the bar and I noticed a couple of the women from work looking in his direction. It disturbed me. He was single and there was no reason why he wouldn't go home with one of my colleagues or someone else tonight and take them to bed. We were friends and that was it.

I headed over to where my brothers were. There was some girl hanging off Callum; Seph looked like he was drinking lime and soda, which was an interested turn of events, while Max and Jackson were nursing whisky. There was no plan for the evening. I suspected the Callaghan Green crew who were out would drop off to go elsewhere, while my brothers and a couple of their friends would head to the whisky bars and restaurants they favoured. Killian's brother was out too with his girlfriend who was heavily pregnant herself, as were a couple of friends of Vanessa's, Jackson's wife.

"Here," Owen said, passing me a margarita. "Congratulations on becoming an auntie." He lifted his whisky to clink my glass.

"Cheers," I said. "To nearly a week of knowing each other."

He laughed. "Is that all it's been? It feels like I've known you forever. And that's a good thing." His free arm slipped around my waist, his hand on my hip and I let him shift me closer into his side. The bar was busy enough for no one to really pick up on it and I enjoyed the feeling of him being close far more than I wanted to admit.

"Are you mad I hunted through your stuff?" I said.

"No. I have nothing to hide. If I did, I'd hide it better. My mother has no concept of privacy. Any questions on what you found?" he said, taking a drink of the golden liquid.

"Plenty," I said. "You have a kinky side?"

"I'm not sure a butt plug and handcuffs are kinky."

"Do you use the butt plug or..."

He laughed, his arm tightening around my waist. "I've used them on a couple of girlfriends. The ones in the drawer are new though. I take it you haven't used one?"

I shook my head. "No. Not something that's been in my repertoire. And I think we should leave that conversation here."

Maxwell headed over and the conversation turned to rugby, Elijah joining in. Another round of whisky arrived with a couple of jugs of margaritas for me, Ava, Victoria and Vanessa and the night slipped into a happy dance of drunkenness and conversation and eventually—for everyone except Jackson and Max—dancing.

For the first time in forever I felt relaxed, comfortable in my own skin. I wasn't looking at the men in the room or thinking about what I should be doing, instead I was liking being who I was.

Owen had a drinking competition with Callum and took Seph outside to throw up. That was when we found out his lime soda had vodka in also. Killian managed to check his phone just twice an hour and only had one conversation with Claire where she told him to 'fuck off and leave her alone for a few hours.' That caused another round of shots and by midnight only a few of us were still standing. Seph was asleep in a corner; Ava had long since disappeared; Jackson and Vanessa had slipped off and Eli had disappeared around the same time as Ava.

I sat down next to Victoria who was watching Max with interest. "I haven't seen him this drunk for a long time," she said. "This means he'll spend most of the day in bed so I can go shopping without him."

"Does he usually go with you?"

"Most the time. He says it's to keep me company, but we

always end up in Victoria's Secret and he insists I get a basket and he slips things in. Then asks me to model them when we get home to 'check they fit.'" She smiled as he swayed a little.

"I wouldn't have thought he had it in him."

"You'd be surprised. I'll spare you the details though. Owen's lovely. He says you're just friends though."

"Yeah. I'm thinking that was a stupid idea now," I said. I liked Victoria. She was feisty and argumentative and very clever: everything my eldest brother needed.

"There's still time to change your mind," she said. "I'd best get Max home. No chance of getting him up the stairs."

"Good luck with that." I stood up with her and looked about the bar for Owen, aware I hadn't seen him for some time. I had no messages on my phone to say he'd headed home or gone to meet up with other friends.

Then I saw him in a corner with a tall, slim dark haired girl. Her hand was on his chest and they were chatting intently. I watched, unable to take my eyes away, a bit like passing a car crash. I had known him less than a week and seeing him chat, flirt, with someone else was cutting me up.

"I'm going to head home," I said to Victoria. "I'll see you later."

"You sure you're okay?" she said, looking concerned. Max was starting to look a little nauseous.

"I'm fine. Just tired. I'll see you a week on Sunday at yours, if not before," I said. She nodded and started to coax Max outside into the fresh air. I looked up one more time to where I had seen Owen. This time he saw me and caught my eye. He gave me a grin and started to untangle himself but I pretended not to notice and instead slipped out of the bar onto the street.

My head pounded with the alcohol and the pictures in my head from the night. Tears pricked at the back of my eyes. I was half way home and determined not to cry when my phone rang. Owen's name flashed up, a picture of the two of us on London Bridge from yesterday.

"Hello," I said, hoping I sounded bright and happy.

"Where did you go?" he said, slightly slurred.

"I didn't want to cramp your style. It looked like you had company for the night." There was no point in trying to cover it up as it was fucking obvious why I had hotfooted it out of the bar.

There was a roar of laughter. "You're jealous!"

"I'm not jealous! I just didn't want to cockblock you."

"You are! You're jealous. That's hilarious, isn't it Jessamyn?"

"Jessamyn? Who the fuck's Jessamyn?" I sounded like a fishwife bellowing across the River.

There was more laughter. "I've no idea who Jessamyn is. I'm on my own and heading somewhere to sleep. In fact, I can see your brother so I'm going to find out if he has a spare bath I can use."

"You're not going home with that girl?" I said, my brain slowly catching up with his words. "I thought…"

"We were talking and she was drunk and a bit handsy, but that was it. I wasn't interested. She wouldn't have been interested in my handcuffs and butt plugs," he said, sounding slightly soberer. "So you don't need to be jealous."

"I'm not jealous!"

"The lady doth protest too much. I'll speak to you tomorrow, princess. I'm going to catch up with Callum. Sleep well." He hung up just after I heard a big booming voice shout Cal.

Home felt strange after not sleeping there the previous night. It felt quiet on my own, the buzz of the bar and the sound of my siblings now a memory away. I settled into bed with a book, another Lucy Score that I was rereading again and a mug of tea, hoping that the oddness I'd felt at Owen possibly going home with another woman would fade.

My phone pinged just as I was about to go to sleep. It was a text with a photo. A selfie of Owen, his glasses still on, his hair mussed and stubble almost a beard. *See, I'm in bed on my own,* he'd put. *I liked you being jealous though x*

I put my phone down. I'd reply in the morning, when I'd thought of something suitably witty.

CHAPTER 10
OWEN

Hangovers were the opposite of whisky: they did not get better with age. I ran down the left flank, dodging Seph who I was pretty sure should not be alive, and ran straight into Killian.

"Fuck!" I said as I was floored. "I'm too old for this."

"No, we're just too old for drinking beer, shots and whisky," Max said, barely having broken a sweat. The man was made of steel or some other banned material. "Let's call it a day and grab something greasy to eat."

I'd woken up in Callum's spare bed, Seph having been left in the recovery position in the bathroom. It had taken the two of us to carry him upstairs and had resembled two grown men trying to move an adult-sized toddler having a tantrum. I was pretty sure that was the reason why my back was aching slightly today and not the drills we'd been doing on the field.

At least my head had stopped pounding and I was started to feel more resemblance to something human; a greasy fry up sounded like heaven, and possibly a gallon of coffee.

"Have you got that acoustic set on tonight?" Callum said,

grabbing a bottle of water. He'd looked like something dug up at nine-thirty this morning. "Not sure which one of your shops it's at."

I nodded, accepting a bottle he passed to me. "Two on tonight: Covent Garden and Soho. You want to go?"

"If you've still got tickets. One of the keepers at work has had a shit week so I promised to cheer her up."

"Does she happen to be five-ten and blonde?" Seph said, his hair still perfectly styled.

Callum slapped him across the back of the head. "No, she's five-three, ginger and had a girlfriend until Wednesday. It is possible for people from the opposite sex to be friends without trying to bone each other. Look at Owen and Payton." His grin became broader.

"Fuck off," I said, heading to the showers. Once we got Seph upstairs and out of danger from choking on his own vomit, I'd drunkenly word vomited over Callum who found it hilarious I'd been friend zoned by his little sister.

Seph laughed loudly. I liked the Callaghans; they reminded me of the communal houses I'd lived in as a kid where everyone tolerated each other with a side of humour and and a shit ton of kindness.

"Payton's hiding this morning," Seph said, catching up with me. He reminded me of Tigger from Winnie the Pooh: overly enthusiastic and happy, continually looking for the next happy thing to go to, but that made him vulnerable. Payton told me how the split with his long term girlfriend had ruined him, to the extent where she'd come home early from working at the Manchester office.

"What do you mean, she's hiding?" I said, panic stabbing me. I knew it was irrational. If any one of them had been worried about where Payton was, they'd have started a fucking search party.

Seph gave me shit-eating grin which let me know my

panic had been duly noted and would be used against me later. "She's reading our messages but not saying anything. Ava's spoken to her though; she is okay before you go postal."

"What are the messages about?" I said suspiciously.

"There are lots of friends references—not the programme. She's fine though, probably in a better state than us after that," Seph said, pulling off his top, his hair staying perfectly styled.

"How much fucking hairspray do you use on that?"

He shrugged. "Fuck knows. Ask Victoria. It's hers."

Max's eyes fell on his brother. "Does she know you use it?"

Seph pulled a face. "I'd assume so. It's either that or she thinks you've got a hairspray fetish. I'll replace it, don't get your jockstrap in a twist."

There was a grumble from Max that was mostly unintelligible.

Once everyone smelt better than stale beer and sweat, we headed for a late breakfast at a chain pub near to the field where we'd trained. A rugby game was being shown on the large TV screens and a few of my new teammates had already hit the Guinness. I was in work later, so more alcohol wasn't on my menu. The stores were well managed enough that I rarely had to get involved in the day to day running of them, but when we had gigs on, particularly with well-known singers and groups, I tried to be available. Tonight, there was a singer-songwriter on at the Covent Garden store and a band doing an acoustic set in Soho. I knew the band well and on a couple of occasions I'd subbed in when they needed a lead guitarist. It was also the band that my ex, Amber, would join if she had nothing better to do and they wanted something different, not that she was there tonight. Amber was in L.A. at a coding conference as one of the speakers; I'd had an email from her a couple of days ago with a picture of the view from her room, another man's feet included in the picture. They were probably her new boyfriend's, Gregson's, if I'd listened properly and she didn't mean anything by including them. It had been three years since we'd been over officially and more since we'd been over. We were friends and much better that way.

"Which gig are there tickets available for?" Callum said, pinching food off Seph's plate while he wasn't looking. They were on their second full breakfast, and to be fair, so was I.

"I can get you in either. If your friend needs something a bit happier, go for the band in Soho. I'll be around there as well so just give me a call when you arrive. Doors open at eight," I said. The all-day-breakfast was doing its medicinal job.

My phone chimed. I checked it, hoping it was Payton. She hadn't responded to the drunken selfie I'd sent her last night when I'd finally got in bed and the room had stopped spinning.

It was her.

My chest felt like someone was whacking it from the inside. There was nothing detailed, just a message to check her Instagram.

Her feed had a picture of her sitting on a snuggle seat in the Soho branch of Cases, her feet tucked under her with the caption 'My favourite store' and a load of hashtags. It already had over fifty likes and had only been posted for five minutes.

My response was immediate and easy. *My favourite girl.* I knew as soon as any of her brothers saw it I would be ripped to pieces, possibly online.

I opened my camera app up and elbowed Callum in the ribs. "Try to look pretty," I said. Seph saw what was happening and pushed his way in. From the looks of it, someone had bought him a pint of Guinness. A couple of the others stood behind us and I ended up with a series of photos with various faces being pulled and hand gestures. I picked the one least likely to get me put in Instagram prison and posted it without a filter, although Seph was trying to talk me into airbrushing his hair which Max had managed to mess up properly.

It took about fifteen minutes for Payton to comment on the photo with *some of my favourite people.* Then my phone pinged with a text.

Payton: I see Seph's liver survived.

Me: Just. Callum made him clean the bathroom first thing this morning. I can no longer tolerate the smell of bleach.

Payton: How's your head?

Me: Fine although I had a lump from where I ran into Max. I swear your brother is made of stone.

Payton: According to Victoria, parts of him are. I didn't ask which.

Me: That's too much information. Are you still in Cases?

Payton: I'm surrounded by books. I think I may be on the way to bankrupting myself.

Me: Leave them behind the main till and I'll get them for you.

> Payton: Seriously, I can afford a few, err, dozen books. Might need a bigger house though. Your mum said hi and told me she'll give me the staff discount. Check my Instagram again.

I switched to her Instagram account, ignoring the heckling I was getting from her brothers, Eli and Killian. There was a picture of her with piles of books; she was hugging several of them and she'd inserted a heart. I liked the picture and went back to my messages.

> Owen: Are you trying to make me jealous?

> Me: Yes.

I saw more of Payton's brothers than her over the next few days. Callum turned up at Cases, Soho for the band with his colleague and Sunday was spent getting our arses kicked at rugby by a rival law firm. That led to a marathon drinking session and a huge Sunday lunch at a pub by the river, where all the Callaghans were present, including Payton and her new niece.

I smoothed down the collar of my shirt and checked my tie: Wednesday had come around quickly, which meant mediation had arrived. Dave disagreed with the sum the forensic accountant had suggested and had his own accountant look through the finances. Today would be the start of the fight to come to sort some kind of fair agreement as to what I'd buy him out for.

"You ready?" Payton said, coming into the room. "Enough coffee?" She was wearing a navy blue suit, the trousers showing off every curve on her arse and I'd been trying not to stare when I'd seen her earlier. Full business mode had been engaged and I was in the client zone—nowhere near the friend zone.

"I'm good." I was, just slightly apprehensive. I'd known Dave for years and genuinely liked the man. As to why my mother had called it off, I was still not just in the dark but blindfolded. Today would be the first time I'd seen him since they'd broken up and I was bracing myself for an awkward exchange.

"Okay. We're going to go into the conference room where the mediator will go over the facts and outline what we're trying to do here. Then she'll speak individually to you and Dave to find out what your bottom lines are and hopefully we'll get an agreement." She sat down next to me and put her hand on my arm. "Hey, you look worried."

I shrugged and pushed my glasses back up my nose. "I really like the guy. I don't want to be in this situation and ideally I'd like him to stay on as my business partner."

"Has your mum said anything else about it?"

"No. She has another date on Saturday. I was hoping you would be free so we could date-stalk again."

Payton laughed, both hands wrapped around my arm now. I felt better with her there although I hoped she didn't offer the same attention to all her clients. "I don't think your mum will appreciate that."

"She won't. But before Dave you should've seen who she dated. It was a parade of ex-cons. Dave was the first person I knew apart from my father who was verging on normal," I said, pouring more coffee.

"Maybe that's the reason she ended it."

"What's that?"

"She's wondering whether there's something more exciting out there."

"Maybe you're right. It's a good restaurant anyway: Padella," I knew what her response would be as we'd talked about Padella a few times. It was her favourite, so I'd already booked a table for the two of us.

She tried to bite back a grin. "And you know I won't turn that down. You have an invite for Sunday lunch at Max and Victoria's the day after. The whole family and extras are going so earplugs are recommended, or tranquillisers."

"Noted."

"Come on, let's go get this started."

Six hours later and we were nowhere near to a conclusion. Bee Jeffries, the mediator, was frustrated as every suggestion I agreed to was turned down by Dave. Once we hit seven o'clock we'd all started to wilt. Payton had told me that mediation would go on as late as it needed if there were signs that it could be resolved but she was now coming to the conclusion that we were going nowhere except court.

"Right," she said, closing the door to our room. "We're done. Bee's recommended to Dave that he goes back to his lawyer and seriously thinks about what he wants from this. His lawyer is banging his head against the wall, and I mean that quite literary, as anything reasonable that's been suggested to Dave, he's shot down like a pheasant on the Glorious fourth. He doesn't want to sell, Owen. He wants your mum back."

I cursed under my breath and stretched my back against the chair, hearing it click. "That's not the best place to be in," I said.

She looked confused.

"The middle. Do we need to see Bee?"

Payton shook her head. "I think she's left already. She's working in Birmingham tomorrow and didn't anticipate this going on so long. Dave and his lawyer were heading out too. You want to grab something to eat?"

"Always," I said. "Where can I take you?"

"My treat. Let's find something we can eat with our fingers or a plastic fork."

We stopped at Al Masar, a Lebanese restaurant that did hot and cold mezze to take away and ate it in silence as we headed down to the river. It was still fairly light and neither of us wanted to sit down and eat inside; there had been enough of being encased in four walls during the day. The food was good and once we'd got to the river and found a bench to sit on, most of it was gone.

"I feel sorry for Dave," Payton said, pinching the last stuffed vine leaf from my box. "I'm not sorry for taking that though. They're divine."

I stared into her box to see what she had left: a couple of falafels and hummus. Fair game. "I'm sorry for him too," I said. "But if he's that upset about my mum splitting up with him, why doesn't he try to get her back? As far as I know, the only thing he's done is go legal to get me to buy him out."

"Maybe he doesn't know what to do?" she said, looking at a piece of falafel in the same way I'd seen her twin eye bacon on my plate a few days before.

I dived in and took the last falafel, ignoring her telling off. "How can he not know what to do?"

"Well, what would you do? If your relationship had ended and you wanted her back, what would you do?" she said between mouthfuls. "And how would you make it work?"

"It would depend on what she'd like. No point doing the whole flowers and romance and shit if she's not into romance. How would a guy get you back?" I said, dipping the falafel into what was left of her hummus.

"I don't know. No one's ever tried." Her tone was sad and I felt like a bastard for bringing it up. "When any relationship's ended that's been it. I haven't chased them down and vice versa. I like flowers. And books. But I don't know what a successful apology would be like because there's never been one."

"What's your favourite flower?" I said, taking her now empty carton and putting it with mine. The sun had set, leaving us with a crescent moon that was pinned above the Thames. Lights from the boats and the bridges glinted in the water and the sound of seagulls muddied the air.

She smiled. "Are you going to turn up with a huge bunch of them tomorrow?"

"No. Because that would be something I'd do before taking you out on a date. I'm just interested, that's all." And I wanted that piece of information for future reference.

"Roses. I know it's a cliché, but I love roses. Not red ones; I prefer the pastel colours that look slightly faded." Her face lit up as she described them and I wondered if anyone had ever bought her a dozen roses.

"Is that why Eliza has the middle name rose?" I said.

"You don't miss much, do you? Yes. The middle name couldn't ever have been Payton or Ava as that wouldn't be fair on the other, but all of us love roses, so Claire chose Elizabeth Rose. We've talked about having a rose tattooed on us in a few weeks. Killian already has one, I think." She sat forward, her elbows on her knees and cupped her face, looking over the river.

"It's on his chest," I said. "He showed us last night." Two training sessions a week had seemed a bit much when Max had told me, but you weren't expected to make both and they were an excuse for food and beers in a female-free zone.

She turned her head to eye me judgementally. "That all sounds very cosy. Has he shown you the rest of his tattoos? Do I need to warn Claire that she has competition?"

I put my arm round her shoulder and pulled her into me roughly. "It's not some ancient Greek re-enactment, so she doesn't have to be concerned."

She leaned into me, her body heat merging with mine and for a few minutes neither of us said anything, just watched the boats on the Thames as they bobbed up and down, a late clipper passing through the water.

I felt different when I was with her, different in a really good way. She made me see things from a new perspective without having to work to get me to do so and she brought energy to any room she walked into which made me feel awake and alive. I liked being with her in a way I hadn't with Amber. Whereas Amber was demanding in her quest for life, Payton simply bloomed and gave everything around her more colour. The few days away from work had strengthened her; Seph had told me that Monday and Tuesday this week she'd left work on time to go and see her niece and go to the gym, rather than trying to find more work to do. I knew that when she was in the middle of a big case, early finishes weren't possible, but it was good to hear that she was making the most of it now.

"What would you change?" I said. "If you could change anything right now, what would it be?"

"My shoes," she said. "They've been killing my feet all day and I know I have blisters. You were expecting something deep and philosophical, weren't you?"

I laughed. "I wasn't expecting that. I can carry you back though if you want."

"Haven't you already worked out today?" she said,

stretching her legs out in front of her. "What would you change?"

"Honestly?" I looked down at her head that was resting on my shoulder. "I'd change your mind about dating."

I felt her laugh but didn't hear it. "Give me time, Owen. Let's just have this for the moment."

I walked her back to her apartment, despite her insistence that she could manage to get home safely on her own. Before she went in her shared entrance I enveloped her in a huge hug, breathing her in. "Have a good evening with your books," I said.

Her arms were around me, hands sliding underneath my suit jacket. She looked up at me and I just about managed to not drown in her eyes. "I'll have a very good time with my books," she said. "Does that make you jealous?"

CHAPTER 11
PAYTON

From what I had seen so far of Dot, she'd have no issue with causing a scene if something irritated her enough. Like Owen, she could manipulate a conversation and knew exactly how to avoid talking about something she wanted to avoid, but unlike Owen, she had a temper. I'd seen it once already this week when he'd told her we were going to Padella also, to which she'd had a small, but contained, verbal explosion. Luckily, we were in Owen's office, so no one else had the pleasure of her informing Owen of what exactly he could do with his Saturday night, which involved him sticking it where potentially only a very long butt plug could reach.

Padella was its usual busy self for a Saturday night and the manager greeted me with a grin. I've known him for a few years and seen him on various dates, so I figured he was going to assume I was on yet another time waster with some indeterminate male. I wanted to say to him that this was different; that Owen wasn't my usual egocentric shallow non-conquest. Instead, he was intelligent and interesting and interested.

And as freaking hot as Venus in a heat wave.

He was wearing trousers that looked like they'd been cut with the sole purpose of displaying his ass, his button-down shirt tapered in at the waist and tight around his biceps. His grin was broad and cheeky as soon as he saw me, as if he knew I was checking him out and he was perfectly happy with that because it meant he had won some battle.

"Hey," he said, leaning over to kiss my cheek.

I wanted to lean up and take his lips with mine, but I remembered I was staying single because it was simpler while I sorted my life out. "You look gorgeous."

"You're not so bad yourself," I said quietly. "I don't mind people thinking we're on a date with you looking like that."

"Just say the words and this can be a date," he said. "Anytime. You know that."

"Maybe at some point. If you've not got bored of hanging around by then," I said, cold gripping at my chest.

He gave me that smile, the one that said he knew everything and there was no need to worry. "Shall we have a bottle of wine or are you in the mood for something else?" he dodged responding to my comment.

"Wine. A malbec or rioja, but you can pick."

That smile again.

Jake, one of the managers, came over and said hello, taking the drinks order and talking to Owen. They knew each other from a business forum and I figured this was how Owen had managed to get a reservation, as usual it was first-come first-served.

"How's your mum managed to get a reservation here?" I said, once Jake had moved on.

"She knows Jake too. Used to babysit him when we lived near Glastonbury," he said. "Don't worry about her date, unless we need to intervene—and that might be more for his sake than hers. How was your spa day?"

He'd remembered, although I wasn't surprised. Vanessa's best friend, Sophie, owned a chain of beauticians and spas across London, including a men-only one that had been really successful. Every so often she'd give us a huge deal on a spa day if we reported back as secret shoppers and had certain treatments. Five of us had spent the day having massages, being waxed and generally managing to chill the fuck out. The waxing part wasn't quite as relaxing as the other aspects, but the beautician had done a very good job. "It was good. Claire enjoyed it—I'm not sure Killian found looking after the baby as easy as he thought. He rang her three times in the last hour and a half."

Owen laughed. "He was telling us this morning how easy it all was. I'll remind him of that tomorrow. What was the problem?"

"I think he wasn't sure how hot the milk needed to be. Then it was what she'd puked up and at the end she wouldn't stop crying. Claire texted me when she got home to say Eliza stopped crying as soon as she got home, which really pissed off K," I said. "How were your friends?" I knew he'd met up with some of his friends from university for a couple of hours as they were stopping over in London before catching a flight out to the U.S.

Owen nodded. "Good. It was really easy to catch up and it felt like we'd seen each other last week rather than over a year ago. We said the usual: we should meet up more frequently, but time fucking flies by, so it'll probably be another year—unless anyone gets married."

The conversation drifted easily from topic to topic: friends, family, work, politics, travel and books. Lots of books. We briefly looked up from each other when Dot arrived with her date, a balding guy with a thin, straggly ponytail.

"I'm not passing comment," Owen said quietly. "Other

than her taste has regressed to what it was twenty years ago, just with less hair."

"Hopefully she'll see that and reflect a bit on what she does want."

"What about you? What do you want?"

"To be with someone who makes being happy easy. I know that's a big ask because a relationship's far more complicated than that and takes work, but my dad and mum—they row and fight but ultimately they make each other happy and want to do that for each other. What about you?"

"Something similar, I guess. I want the family bit. My upbringing was weird, and I wished I'd had a brother or sister, so I know I want the kids plural at some point and a base. I don't want to be a nomad like I was when I was growing up," he said. "Don't get me wrong, I've no hang ups or issues that haven't been therapied out of me. Unlike down there." His gaze went over to the window seat where Dot was sitting with her date. She was talking animatedly, her hands moving wildly and in danger of knocking something over. I braced myself for it to be the bottle of red. "This isn't going to end well."

It didn't. Forty-five minutes later and we were now a table for three, with the remainders of the wine and two shots of decent tequila.

"Who turns up a date stoned?" Dot said for the sixth or seventh time.

"Aged hippies who still think it's nineteen-seventy-two," Owen said, looking the most irritated I've ever seen him. "Who dates aged hippies who still think it's nineteen-seventy-two?" He glared at her.

Dot huffed and glared back, the father-mother resemblance uncanny. "You know, it is okay to try to have a good time when you're older, Owen Anders. There's nothing wrong with dating someone who reminds you of a good time in your life."

Owen squinted at her. "Maybe I'm missing something, mum, but I'm pretty sure you've been having a good time for the past seventeen years or so. Maybe aged hippies no longer do it for you because you're a different person."

Dot raised her glass and a took a large mouthful of wine. "Maybe that's true. But you can't judge all people the same just because of one bad egg." Her eyes fell on me. "I'm sorry, Payton. As you can see, Owen and I have a very open and honest relationship and have no issue in telling each other what we really think."

I glanced at Owen, knowing full well he hadn't asked his mother why she had ended a long relationship with David. He was too busy staring at his glass as he topped it up to catch my eye so I decided to go for it. "Owen hasn't told me why you and David split up," I said, Owen looking up immediately and frowning.

Dot gave an irritated sigh. "That's because he hasn't asked because he thinks he knows the answer. He thinks I'm having a midlife crisis and that I'm bored, and do you know what? Maybe I am. Maybe I want a bit of excitement in my life and for a man to sit up and take some notice, make me feel special. Seventeen years we've been together and he's never asked me to move in with him. Or bought me a bunch of flowers." She knocked back the rest of the wine. "Maggie has invited me to hers to test her home brew, so I'm going to go there for the night. If you don't hear from me tomorrow, it's because I'll be sleeping off a hangover. Have fun and use protection." She leaned across and kissed his cheek. "See you soon, Payton. Look after my boy, even if he is a humongous pain in the arse." She popped a kiss on the top of my head as she passed.

Owen looked at me as he took another long gulp of his wine. "Apologies."

"None needed," I said. "You know that compared to my family, she's completely sane."

He walked me home after we'd finished drinking; we talked about Dot and David and I saw the upset he was feeling that their relationship had ended. I tucked my arm into his, taking his warmth and giving him mine. I simply enjoyed the conversation, trying to lend him some balance, make him smile again.

"You're playing rugby with my brothers in the morning, aren't you?" I said as we stopped outside my apartment.

He nodded. "Then having Sunday lunch at Max's. You're sure you're okay with me spending so much time with your family?"

I reached up and touched his face gently with one hand, cupping his jaw. "Why wouldn't I be? You seem to have adopted each other."

He pressed his hand on top of mine. "It's been good hanging out with people without it being work related. With setting up the shops and the music venues, everything I've done for years has been related to work or contacts or, God, even coding. Not that I wasn't happy."

"Are you ever not happy?" I said, the words barely audible.

"I have my moments. But there's always something to be thankful for and someone worse off than you. I want to carry on talking, Payts, but here on the street isn't doing it for me. I'll see you tomorrow," he said, his hand pushing through his hair. He looked frustrated.

"Do you want to come up for coffee?"

This time two hands pulled at his hair. "You know, yes, but then I won't want to leave."

Maybe I don't want you to leave. I felt inexplicably lonely at the idea of him going home, leaving us both alone. "Okay. We've got tomorrow. Max's house is huge so we can escape the madness and hide away somewhere."

"Why don't you come watch the game before?"

The idea of him wearing shorts and a rugby top, sweating as he tackled someone to the floor was enough to make me hope my vibrator was still charged. "I'll see if Ava wants to come. In fact, I think Claire's going to watch and she's taking Eliza so I'll see you there." I stood on my tiptoes and kissed his cheek, my lips lingering there for longer than necessary.

Owen wrapped his arms around me and I felt muscles tense as he gathered me into his chest. "I want to kiss you goodnight but friends don't do that. Thank you for coming with me tonight and for putting up with my mum. And for looking beautiful."

"I'm not beautiful," I said, looking at him. The expression he wore told me I was wrong.

"I think you're beautiful." He kissed the top of my head and let go. "I'll see you tomorrow at the game. I expect my name on the back of your shirt."

I laughed. "I'll bring a banner too. 'Night." He started to move away, backwards, watching me enter my apartment block. It was getting harder and harder to leave him.

I didn't have his name on the back of my shirt, but I may as well have. Both Claire and Ava made not so subtle comments about my inability to keep my eyes off Owen as he ran down the wings, throwing himself onto the ground or at opposing players. His hair was mussed, he was covered in grass stains and sweat and he looked like sex personified. If I had any doubt as to how much I was attracted to him, it had been melted away by midday.

"You need to experience that hotness," Ava said quietly, making sure that no one overheard, which was unusually subtle of her. "Never mind about Sunday lunch: take him home and ride him like a pony. Do you think his cock's proportionate to the rest of him?"

I didn't answer because I didn't want her to know that this was something I'd already considered. "We're just friends. And he's still my client."

Ava shrugged. "Honestly, I think you need to get his case sorted as soon as you can and have a friends with benefits type relationship and then you can still be friends, experience his cock and be satisfied without dating a jerk. Not that Owen's a jerk. He's nothing like your exes. Nothing." She gave a little smile, one that I recognised as a sign that she was planning something.

"Ava," I said, trying not to sound too panicked. "Please don't get involved in me and Owen. We're friends and yes, he's gorgeous, but we're just friends and it needs to stay like that."

She shrugged. "I don't see why it has, but I'm not planning anything. I have my own life to deal with." There was a toss of blonde hair and she strode off in vintage Doc Martens, looking ridiculously gorgeous as always.

"She's up to something," Claire said quietly. Eliza was secured in a sling across her front and she'd slept through the entire game. "She was coming here today before I asked her and she's been around far more than normal, but she's hiding something. Do you remember when she applied to her college courses without telling anyone so no one could try to give her any advice?"

I twisted to face Claire, immediately getting what she was saying. "Yes. She'd accepted a course while we were all thinking she was taking a year out. She's been around loads but she's hiding something. Something in plain sight."

"Business? Boyfriend? Maybe she's heading to New York like she kept threatening. She hasn't said anything about that for a while," Claire said, a sweaty and muddy Killian heading towards us, Owen following behind with Elijah.

"Could be New York. I know she's heard from the cousins over there a few times recently. I saw something on her Facebook from Marc saying 'it was good to talk'. Shall we confront her?" I said, trying desperately not to look at Owen.

Claire shook her head. "Not yet. Let me do some digging. She's taken to coming over in the evening to see Eliza and she talks to her as if she really can understand. I'll keep the baby monitor on me to see if she gives something away."

"Isn't that a bit underhanded and sneaky?"

Claire's look suggested I had not only lost the plot but my mind also. "She's our sister. It's our job to be underhanded and sneaky."

Killian stood in front of his fiancée and kissed his daughter's head. "What did Eliza think of Daddy's try?"

"She thought it was sleep inducing," Claire said. "Mummy found it quite hot though. Can you get a lift to Max's and I can go straight there? She's going to want feeding soon and I'd rather not do it on a rugby field. I have some standards."

"I can give you a lift," Owen said. "As long as you shower first. You smell like a dog that's rolled in fox shit."

Killian lifted his shirt and sniffed a large brown stain. "I think you're probably right. This isn't just mud." He looked utterly disgusted.

Owen choked back a laugh. "I'm pretty sure it's not as bad as baby shit." His eyes fixed on me. "Where's the banner you promised?"

"I didn't want you to get any unnecessary teasing from my brothers," I said. "I was protecting you." He looked huge in front of me, muscles pumped and shirt tight over his arms.

"I think I could've handled it. Do you want a lift too?"

"How long will you be preening yourselves for? I think Seph's record for getting ready is about ninety minutes, so longer than the actual game," I said warily. I had waited for my twin a few times to get ready and each time had been torturous.

"Seph's getting a lift with Callum, so I'll be about twenty minutes. Wait for me."

I nodded, because there was nothing else I could do.

Max's girlfriend, Victoria, and Jackson's wife, Vanessa, had joined forces to create a Sunday buffet. There were roast meats, veggies, salad, roast potatoes and Yorkshire puddings, which I dived into before my siblings could eat my share. My parents had driven over that morning and the wine was already open.

"Couldn't wait, Payts?" Seph said, pinching a roasted parsnip from my plate.

Max had set up the large antique dining table, but this wasn't a formal occasion and my family and friends were scattered around the room, most of them tucking in to food. The atmosphere was celebratory: since Callum had returned like the prodigal son from some remote country in Africa family gatherings had become more frequent but it was unusual for everyone to be able to make it. This was the first Sunday lunch since Eliza was born and she, plus the victory today, added to the feel.

I was happy. My world was around me and all was well.

Owen stood next to the beers, deep in discussion with Jackson, plate in hand. I watched him for a moment. His hair was still damp, his face unshaven, and he wearing his usual jeans and T-shirt. From behind his glasses blue eyes shone.

"He's going to see you staring at him like that, you know," the most familiar voice in the world whispered over my shoulder.

"Mum," I said. "Don't sneak up on me!"

"If you weren't paying attention to only one thing you'd have noticed me there." She nestled her chin on my shoulder, and I smelled her perfume, the same scent she'd always worn for the day time. It was childhood and comfort, my every safe place. "He is rather attractive; I have to say. And he seems to really like you."

"We're just friends."

"Ah," she said, and then fell silent.

"What does that mean?" I asked when she offered no further explanation.

"Baby, the way you look at each other makes it seem like you want to eat each other up. He's itching to come over to you. You might be just friends now and think that's all you want because you're scared, but what happens when he gets a girlfriend? How will you feel about being just friends then?"

Fucking mortified.

"I'll give that some thought," I said.

"See that you do."

―――

Eventually, we found each other. Owen brought a plate over to me that was filled with yet more food; cold cuts and cheese had magically appeared from Max's fridge.

"Can you show me round the house?" he said quietly, not that there was much chance of being heard given the racket Seph and Callum were making.

"Sure," I said, picking up a slice of Parma ham. Max and Victoria had been living here together for only a couple of months, but it had been Victoria's grandparents' house and she'd done most of her growing up here. As a historian, she tended towards the old and antiquated furnishings so there were lots of pieces of unique chests of drawers and unusual tables, many repainted. Ava helped Max to remodel the property, taking it from an old fashioned, rather dark building to something that was open plan and warm. My little sister was talented for sure.

"It makes me want a house instead of an apartment," Owen said as we headed into the large sitting room with bi-fold doors that opened onto the garden. It was turning out to be a warm spring day, so the breeze drifting in was pleasant.

My father was watching Killian cuddle Eliza, whose big baby blues were fixed on her daddy. Claire was gossiping with Mum about one of their neighbours back in Oxfordshire and Ava was talking to Eli about whatever it was they had in common. I sat down on a wing back chair, Owen perching on the arm, close enough so I could feel his body heat.

"We're looking at the tailor's cottage on Saturday," Killian said to my father. "It needs some modernisation but it'd be a great place to spend long weekends and for me and Claire to escape to."

My father's face lit up. He missed working in London, I knew, but he loved being in the village. Having Claire and his first grandbaby would be amazing for him and my mum. "That goo."

I sat up and looked at my father, unsure of what he said.

"Do you know the people selling it?" Killian said, sitting forward, and I knew he had noticed it too.

"Peter Mike. He an guy…" My father looked puzzled and tired.

"How much has Dad had to drink?" I said, trying to smile, make a joke of it and fighting the build-up of panic that was bubbling in my stomach.

Killian ignored me. "Grant, can you lift your arms?"

My dad nodded and put his arms out, his right lifting higher than the left. "See. I'm fine."

Killian looked at Owen whose expression was concerned. "Claire, take Eliza into the kitchen." He passed his daughter over, his concentration focused on my dad.

"Why? What's happening?" Claire said, the gossiping stopping immediately, the atmosphere thickening with fear.

"What's happened to you mouth, Grant?" my mum said, calmness in her voice that told me she was anything but calm.

Killian stepped over to my dad and knelt down beside him. "Claire, take Eliza elsewhere please."

"You're scaring me." This was my fearless sister, the one who would take on the world and win.

"No need to be scared. I'm going to call an ambulance as I think your dad's had a TIA," Killian said. "We need to get him to hospital and get him checked out. Grant, do you have a headache?"

My dad nodded, his colour now pale and his eyes worried. I had never seen my father scared. I bit my lip from going into panic mode, the mode that would do no one any good.

"Shall I call an ambulance?" Claire asked.

"I will. Payton, talk to your dad. Keep him calm."

I swapped places with Killian and took my dad's hand, half listening to Killian making the emergency phone call. I talked to him about the restaurant last night and Dot's date, praying Owen wouldn't mind. My dad seemed to be listening but didn't speak, just nodded. Max and Jackson were now in the room, watching and speaking to Killian. I heard Owen telling Callum and Seph what was happening and helping them come to the conclusion to give my dad some space.

"The ambulance is on its way, Dad," Max said, standing behind me and putting a hand on my shoulder. "You don't need to listen to this one rabbiting on for much longer." I stood up and stepped away, letting Max talk about rugby.

"Is he okay?" Seph said, looking at me urgently from around the door into the hallway.

I nodded, stepping towards him, knowing how my brother needed us strong around him. "Killian mentioned a TIA. But he's focused and aware. We're just trying to keep him calm."

Seph nodded. "That's a mini-stroke, isn't it?"

"I think so. Look, can you see to Claire and make sure she's okay. I can hear Eliza crying." I said. Redirection would help him right now. "She's probably picking up on everyone's worry."

"I can do. Are you going to the hospital?"

"Someone needs to go but not all of us." I stopped speaking as two paramedics walked down the hallway. "Go see Claire. I'll text you if I end up going. Just keep everyone, and yourself calm."

Killian spoke to the paramedics, giving a factual account of what we'd observed. They were reassuring and kind, checking the basics.

"Payton, can you and Owen follow in Owen's car? Mum's going to go in the ambulance with Dad and Jackson's gone to get his bike so he'll meet you there," Killian said. "I'd go but I'm going to need to stay with Claire and the baby. I don't want Eliza in a hospital."

"Sure," I said, tightening in all the pieces that wanted to crumble. "We'll keep everyone informed."

Killian gave me a half-smile and I felt arms encompass me from behind, my back resting into a rock solid person.

"I've got you," Owen muttered and I felt tears pricking at my eyes.

"Stay strong and do what you need to do, but I've got you."

Lips brushed the top of my head and I didn't care who saw or what they thought. My world was imploding, my centre splitting and I didn't know how to fix it. At this moment, right now, I needed this, I needed his strength, his arms.

I needed him.

CHAPTER 12
OWEN

Payton was pale-faced and wide-eyed in the waiting room. She'd fetched coffees for us all: Jackson, Ava and Eli, who had driven Ava. She had then gone in search of her mother to find out where they had taken her father. Payton had been reassuring and steady, promoting the hospital staff and their work, reiterating comments about the stroke unit and how strong their statistics were. There was no sign of panic or any uncertainty in her body language or expression. She rationalised what had happened and talked about treatments and preventative measures should it be a TIA like we all suspected.

"I've seen Mum," she said, bringing in five bottles of water. "And Dad very briefly. We'll be able to all see him in another twenty minutes or so, the doctors are just finishing off their initial assessments."

"What did Marie say?" Jackson said. He'd looked like the world was about to end since we'd left Max's house.

Payton sat down after passing out the water. "It's a TIA—transient ischemic attack—and they're going to do an angiogram and a couple of other tests tomorrow so he is staying in overnight. His blood pressure is high."

"A TIA is a warning isn't it?" Ava said. She was standing next to Eli, who'd looked almost as worried. He'd been at Callaghan Green for a couple of years and had worked closely with Grant before he'd retired, and by the look on his face, he'd fucking liked the man.

"It's the proper name for a mini-stroke," I said. "There's unlikely to be any lasting effects but it's a sign that a stroke may happen. My uncle had one last year. He takes warfarin and has lost weight but that seems to have lessened the risk of a full-blown one."

The door to the waiting room opened and Marie came in, more colour in her face than earlier. "So your dad is going to have to go on a bit of diet, do more exercise and drink less alcohol. All the things I've been telling him since he's retired. You lot," she glared around the room, "need to help him and not encourage him."

Ava went to Marie and put her arms around her, her shoulders shaking slightly. "He's going to be okay?"

"He's going to be fine, you silly girl." Marie pulled her into a hug. "Why don't you go and see him? Then you can all go back to Max's and give everyone an update?"

Jackson nodded, putting his phone back in his pocket. "What tests are they doing?" he said.

"Angiogram, the usual blood tests, an echocardiograph and possibly an MRA. He's scheduled for all those at some point tomorrow. He's asked if someone can bring him his iPad from Max's as he wants to Google everything and find out what they're poking him with. Those are his words not mine," Marie said, pushing Ava away from her gently. "There's no need to be upset. I know everyone's had a shock, but honestly, it's a good thing this has happened as it gives us a warning that we need to change things. I'll need earplugs to cope with all your father's moaning. And maybe ask Simone for some healthy recipes or even to do those cookery classes she was thinking of."

I glanced at Payton, unsure of who Simone was. "She's a chef," Payton said. "Owns the Mount Street Social. And she's a friend of Vanessa's. I'll make us a reservation there." Her hand slid onto my arm and I was aware of Marie watching us.

"I've seen it. Not eaten there though, so that would be good. How's Grant feeling?" I said, the last to Marie. I could feel Payton's exhaustion just from her touch.

Marie smiled. "He's okay. A little shocked and embarrassed. I think it's been a bit of blur but now he says he feels fine apart from being tired. He's told me a couple of times to 'stop fucking fussing', so his mood is back to normal. They did say he could go home overnight and come back tomorrow, but he's agreed to stay."

"In other words, you told him he's staying." Jackson had just typed another message again, probably to his other siblings. "Less worry for you because if he goes home you'll stay up all night to check he's breathing."

"Absolutely. Besides, we'd have to go back to Max and Victoria's and while I know they won't mind, Seph will be there and I can do without his meltdown and how he'll fuss your father," Marie said. "I'll get a taxi back there when he's settled. Why don't you go see him, Ava? Then you and Elijah can get back to Max's for a bit. Payton, you need sugar else you'll start going dizzy. Owen, can you take her for some cake and a coffee?"

"Come on then," I said, taking her hand and pulling her up. "Food before you hangry out on everyone." I saw Jackson raise his brows and smile briefly.

"I'll head up with Ava and Eli to see Dad then I'll head off. Max is going to drop Dad's iPad off and bring Seph and

Callum for half an hour," Jackson said. "Claire's staying with Eliza. She says she'll see you tomorrow and can you send her a photo of Dad so she's knows he's okay?"

"I'll send her one of Dad if she sends me one of Eliza. Then I get the better end of the deal. Right, let's get you up to see him. Payton, it's room three on Ward C-Four. Come up after you've had food." Marie patted her arm and led the way out of the room, leaving me and Payton alone.

She leaned against my shoulder and closed her eyes. "I feel sick," she muttered.

"You probably do need something to eat. Did you have much at Max's?"

She shook her head. "A bit but not enough. I could just do with a sandwich and hot tea maybe."

"You know he'll be fine, Payts," I said. "They'll find out what's caused it and treat it. He'll have to change some of his lifestyle like your mum said, but he'll be fine."

"I know. It's just the first time I've had to think about anything happening to my parents. It's a shock," she said, keeping her head on my arm.

I moved in closer, picking her up and pulling her onto my lap, knowing that this was over and beyond the friend zone. "It is, but he will be okay. You and Killian did a great job back there."

"So did you," she whispered, looking up at me, a couple of tears slipping from her eyes and down her cheeks. "I saw you reassuring everyone and keeping Seph out of the way. And then talking to Claire."

I pressed my lips to her hair then resting my chin on her head. "Food, drink, see your dad and then home?"

"Yes. All of that."

———

We grabbed tea and a couple of slices of something just labelled 'cake' in a small volunteer run café, sitting next to each other instead of opposite. Our phones continually dinged with messages from the Callaghans and others in a group that I had been added to. There were explanations of angiograms and MRA's and jokes about how mad Grant would be when his drinking was limited and he had to exercise, plus various cartoons and GIFs Seph and Callum found and distributed that poked fun at their father's expense.

"I'm nervous about seeing him," Payton said after several minutes of staring into her mug.

"Why?" I asked.

"I'm scared he won't look like my dad. When I was little I visited my dad's uncle in hospital after he'd had a big heart attack and he looked all in on himself and tiny and old. Before the ambulance came, my dad looked different, not like him. I'm scared of what my reaction will be like if he doesn't look like my dad," she said, speaking it all in one breath.

I slipped my arm round her. "Let's go see him. Because if he looked anything like you're worrying about, Marie would've warned you. You know that." I stood up and offered her my hand, knowing she thrived from physical contact, the reassurance of touch. We walked through the hospital corridors, passing other visitors and patients in wheelchairs or walking up to Ward C-Four. Marie was talking animatedly to the nurses and waved at us, pointing in the direction of Grant's room.

The door was slightly ajar, her father sitting up in bed, watching a replay of a rugby match on a sports channel. He looked tired, but other than that, he seemed healthy.

"Ava said you'd be up to see me," he said, muting the TV. "She was having a complete fluster about how she'd never been so scared and listing all the things she'd thought. Basically, she talked non-stop at me so me, Eli and Jacks ignored her for ten minutes and watched the rugby. It was a good game."

"Your words make sense," Payton said. "Thank fuck for that."

"Swearing is not lady-like," Grant said smiling at her. "Come here and give me a hug and then we don't have to talk about what happened."

She laughed and went to him, landing in his arms. He kissed her hair and muttered something to her, making her giggle again.

"How do you feel?" she said, sitting down on a chair. I leaned against the arm, watching him carefully.

"Tired. I can't wait to go to sleep and for your mother to clear off and stop talking about healthy recipes and going to some stupid cookery course. Do you remember the last time she tried to follow a recipe?"

"I think you suggested a good divorce lawyer to her," Payton said. "We can discuss your eating habits after you've seen the doctor tomorrow." She was trying to sound firm but I knew if he'd asked her right now to smuggle several donuts in, she'd agree. That was going to be the problem.

Grant nodded and looked at me. "Thank you for looking after this one," he said and I felt my body go rigid. I'd met a few of my exes' fathers and I'd had the 'don't fuck with my daughter' conversation on a couple of occasions. Thankfully, Amber's father had been more of a 'would you like to share a joint' type guy and I honestly didn't think he'd felt the need to protect his little girl from any bad boys. And really, Amber had balls of steel bigger than mine, so she hadn't needed her father to defend her.

"She's more than capable of looking after herself," I said. "But it was good to be able to help."

Grant smiled at me. "Ten points for the correct answer.

She's more than capable, but that doesn't mean she has to look after herself all of the time."

"You can stop talking about me as if I'm not here now," Payton said. Our phones chimed and she checked hers. "Max is on the way with some of your stuff. He's bringing sweat pants and T-shirts so you don't scare the nurses in that hospital gown."

Grant glared at her and straightened the blanket that he was using to hide what he was wearing. "Lovely. As long as I have some access to the internet so I can find out what they're going to prod me with tomorrow. Go home now, Payts. You look worse that I do."

"Thanks!" She looked to me. "I'll just drag Mum away from nagging the nurses and let her know we're going."

She scarpered, leaving me with her father who looked at me through eyes the same as Payton's. "Just friends, my ass," he said.

"That's all she wants," I said. "I'm happy for it to be more and I wouldn't mess her about."

He nodded. "Thank you for looking after her. As much as Payts looks after everyone else, she forgets to look after herself, just like her mother did until she learnt better. The rest is up to you. Jackson said you played a good game today?"

And the conversation stayed on the safer topic of rugby until Payton returned with Marie, looking brighter, happier.

I took her home via Max's to pass on how her father was and grab some leftovers from dinner. It was close to eight in the evening and it felt like a different day than the one where she'd watched me play rugby. She was quiet on the way home, although with her siblings she had been talkative, explaining how he was and how their mum was doing.

"Do you want me to come up with you?" I asked as I pulled into the parking space for her apartment. I wasn't sure how to read her right now; she was locked in her mind and nothing was spilling out through her eyes.

"Come up, please. I don't need to talk but I don't want to be on my own. Unless you need to go?" she said, eyes on me, wide and questioning.

"I've nowhere I need to be. My mum's staying at her friend's again tonight so she's not expecting me to call in or anything." I grabbed my phone and wallet from the car. "Let's watch some crap on Netflix or something. Max was going on about some new series him and Victoria are addicted to."

"Sounds good," she said and I followed her to the elevator which she never usually took.

"You need me to carry you?"

She stared at me before laughing loudly. "Do I look that tired?"

"Yes, but you're still beautiful."

"How do you say that without it sounding corny?"

"Because it's genuine." The elevator stopped and I followed her out, my hand on the small of her back.

Her apartment was tidy. There were throws and cushions that looked new on her sofa and a pile of magazines on the coffee table. She disappeared to her bedroom and returned five minutes later wearing the short, silky dressing gown I'd seen her in before. Her legs were bare as was her neck. I was in fucking trouble if I thought too much about what was underneath.

"I've made tea," I said, holding up a mug.

She walked into the kitchen and picked up hers, her hair

mussed and face bare. "Sorry I look a mess. And don't say I look beautiful again because I know I don't."

"It's a matter of opinion. I don't think you look a mess; I think you look fucking gorgeous." I didn't let her eyes drop from mine, holding her gaze. The air in the room felt thick with her unspoken words. I didn't question her or probe; I didn't need to know what she was thinking.

Her hand went to my arm. "Sit with me on the sofa?"

I followed her—I would've followed her fucking anywhere—and sat down, shifting cushions. She sat next to me, flicking on the TV and sipping her tea. "I think this is it," she said. "I'm not sure how much I'll take in."

"I'll give you the cliff notes later."

There was a soft laugh and we both grew quiet. Her head began to lean on my shoulder, her leg pressed to mine. The stool was at the other side of the room so I took her empty mug from her hands and shuffled on the seat so my legs stretched out, manipulating one behind her, then moved her in between, so her back rested on my chest. It was not the sitting position of friends and I knew that the feel of her heat against mine and the slip of skin I could see down her dressing gown would mean it wasn't just my back she'd be pressing against.

"Comfy?" I said as I tucked my chin against her neck. She leaned back further into me, taking one of my arms and putting it around her waist like a seat belt.

"Yes," she said and I felt her relax, one of her hands resting on the outside of my thigh. We watched another episode, but I couldn't tell what happened. I was too hyper aware of the woman I was holding, how she felt against me, the softness of her, her scent.

The episode ended and she turned her face and body so it was easier for her to see me. "Owen," she said, her lids heavy. One hand went to my shoulder and she placed her hand on me and twisted, bringing her to her knees in between my legs.

"Payton," I said, trying to lighten the atmosphere which was starting to crackle.

"Will you stay? I don't want to be on my own."

"Sure," I said. "Course I'll stay."

She smiled, looked shy, awkward. "Will you stay with me? In my bed?"

"Payton…" This time her name was a groan. "I only have so much fucking willpower. And you want to just be friends."

She bit her bottom lip and made me want to suck it better. "How about with benefits? Shit, this isn't going like I thought it would."

My cock begged to differ. He thought it was going exactly like it should. "Payts, I'm a guy, you might be noticing that right now and I'm really, really good with the idea of being friends with benefits but what's led to this suggestion?"

Her eyes dropped to my crotch and she smiled, grinning wider as she caught my eyes. "Definitely male. Sorry. Filters aren't at their best."

"Payton. Tell me why?" I pressed. I was more than happy to spend the night in her bed, in her as well, but I needed to have an idea of how to handle the aftermath, which meant knowing what had brought her here."

"Because I need to not think about today. I need to feel grounded again and you do that just by touching me. Because I want to know what's it's like to have you inside me and on top of me. I want to know what it's like to let someone else take care of me," she said, her hand tracing under my T-shirt. "But I need us to be friends again in the morning."

My hands were on her hips, holding tightly because I didn't want them to wander elsewhere. "Okay. But I sleep in your bed and we remain friends with benefits in the morning too. I won't let things be awkward so if you think you're going to regret this, I'll go home now."

"Am I using you?" she said, worry ripping through her. "I don't want you to think I'm using you."

"No. Let's watch another episode." I guided her back around, but this time didn't try to keep my hands in friend prison. One rested on her thigh, stroking the skin, slowing creeping higher up her leg. The other I kept at her waist, pulling her close so she could feel my hard cock.

She rested her head on my chest, her hands touching, slowly exploring. Neither of us were taking in any of the episode but I didn't care. Going straight to her room after her request would've made things false and awkward; this way gave us time. I kissed the smooth skin of her shoulder where her dressing gown had fallen away and felt her shudder. Her head turned and she found my lips with hers and this time the kiss lacked the barriers, there was nothing kept reserved.

Her lips parted for me and I tasted her mouth, my hands moving upward, over her tits, realising she was probably naked underneath. Her fingers ran through my hair pulling me closer and I untied her robe.

"You sure?" I said, freeing her mouth.

"Yes. Definitely." She slipped off the dressing gown, leaving her naked in my lap. Pretty tits with hard erect pink nipples, a soft stomach that was toned enough and a bare pussy.

And my self-control, my good friend resolve, snapped like a stretched spring. I possessed her mouth, my hands cupping her tits and roughly pinching her nipples, eliciting a moan. She pushed her hands up my T-shirt and left them there, responding to my touches, my mouth, as I licked and bit her neck, down to her breasts, sucking on one nipple and then the other. She lay on her back, her legs spreading to give me space. I wanted in her, wanted my cock in that wet pussy, making her come on me, making her scream my name.

"Tell me what you want, Payton," I demanded, needing her words. I could see her arousal; her hardened nipples, the wetness between her legs, on her pussy lips and thighs. "What do you want me to do to you?"

"Fuck me," she said. "I want you to fuck me and make me come. And I want you naked. Preferably two minutes ago."

I grinned and lost my T-shirt, liking the way her eyes ate me up and her hands went to touch. For a minute I let her have free range, fingertips running over my abs, palms over my pecs and then back down to my cock where it pressed against my jeans, itching to get inside her. She bucked as I ran two fingers down the centre of her body, over her stomach and then lifting before I could touch her where she really wanted my fingers.

Leaning over her, I kissed her deeply, feeling her respond, touching softly. She was giving me control and I had to reign in my urgency, knowing that she needed me to be controlled, to forget today and what tomorrow would bring and just be here now.

I pulled her into me and stood with her in my arms. "First time will be in your bed. Then maybe your bed again because you'll be too fucked to move."

"Is that a promise?" She wrapped her legs around my hips and one hand went to her ass, my fingers grazing over her soaking pussy.

"More than a promise," I said. "You're so fucking wet. Is that all for me?"

"All of it. I need you to make me come, Owen," she said and I nearly ploughed right into her then.

I placed her on the bed and undid my belt, trying to take off my jeans without looking desperate. There was a sharp intake of air as I pushed my underwear off with my jeans and I tried not to look cocky.

"Shit," she said, using her arms to push her up to see me. It also pushed her tits forward and I needed to spend more time with them, getting to know them better.

"Come here," I told her. She moved to her knees and towards me. I used one hand to cup her breast, teasing the nipple. With the other I began to finger her, moving along her slit, slightly dipping into her wetness and gently over her clit. "I need you wet enough to take me but I'll make you wet enough. Trust me?"

She nodded. I pinched her clit.

"Good girl. Condoms? Where are they?"

She shook her head. "I'm on the pill. I'm clean. I don't want you to use anything."

My cock hardened so it was comparable with diamonds. "I'm clean. Squeaky. Why don't you want me to use a condom?"

"I want you to come in me."

I flicked her clit again and heard her whimper. Her reward was a finger in her pussy, deep and slow and I felt her start to contract, but I didn't want her to come with any part of me in her yet. "Lie back, Payts. Spread your legs for me."

She complied, her eyes pooled with desire, lips parted. It took just two fingers circling her clit twice before she broke apart, her hips thrusting, legs contracted. I pushed two fingers inside her before she'd come back down and found her pussy tight and swollen. Tasting her would've been high on my list, but right now, all I could think about was my dick being inside her.

"Spread your legs again. You're really wet and I want inside you. Are you ready?" I said, surprised I still had words.

Her legs moved apart, her wetness gleaming like pearls in the lamp light. "Go slow."

"Relax, think about my cock filling that tight pussy," I said, leaning over her, using one hand to move one of her legs to my waist, widening her for me. My dick was proportionate to my height and build and I'd had one girlfriend when I younger change her mind about sex when she saw the size of me. Since then, I'd learned more about foreplay, how to use words, how to appear to take control.

I moved my cock up and down her slit, her wetness coating the head and settled at her entrance and started to ease in. She gasped as I entered and I stilled, giving her time to relax and adjust, her hands on my arse.

"Fuck," she said. "That feels…"

"Tell me how it feels," I said quietly, kissing her neck, her jaw.

"Tight. A pinch, but good. More. I want more of you."

I bent over and nipped her nipple, pulling another moan and slid in deeper, her hands on my arse, nails digging in, encouraging me to go deeper until I filled her.

"You good?" I said.

She pushed her chest up, her other leg now around my waist too. "I feel like you're splitting me in two and it's so good."

"Put your hands over your head."

She didn't ask, just stretched out. I took her wrists with one hand, holding them gently down and then I started to move out and in, her wetness and warmth tight around me, her heavy-lidded eyes on mine. She was gloriously exposed, tits bouncing as I moved in her, faster and slower, watching her responses. Her chest was flushed, nipples hard tipped, her moans breathless and begging. I angled my hips to add pressure on her clit which caused her legs to brace around me. Two more quick thrusts and she cried out loudly, my name on her lips and her pussy clenched my cock, pulling my own release.

"I'm going to come in you," I said, almost stuttering the words. "Is that still good?"

"Fuck yes," she said. "Do it."

I thrust a little faster, a little harder, her moans and whimpers becoming louder again. "Can I make you come again?"

"Just come in me," she said and then I saw stars and heard angels singing as I felt my balls pump deep into her, filling her up over and over as she clenched around me again.

Her released hands reached around my back, her lips seeking mine. I kissed her lightly, gently, my cock still inside her and not wanting to leave. Recovery time was usually fairly speedy, but it had been a couple of months since I'd had sex and I hadn't orgasmed like that for as long as I could remember.

"How do you feel?" I said, needing to check in with her, to hear her words.

"Well fucked," she said. "Words aren't quite there yet. Full."

I shifted us, managing to stay inside her, so we were on our sides and facing. I wanted her close, but my weight was too much to stay as we were.

She laughed. "Wet."

"Sorry," I said. "I'll take the wet patch."

"Such a gentleman. The bed's big enough for us both to avoid it."

"Does that mean you don't want space while you sleep?" I stroked her hair off her face, feeling her heat. She looked sated, happy, relaxed.

"No. I want to sleep wrapped up in you. Maybe I should nip to the bathroom first."

I chuckled, my cock soft now. She slipped off the bed and I heard her laugh. Looking up I saw her biting her lip and cupping underneath her pussy. "You were insistent on no condom," I said, loving the idea of my come still being in her tomorrow. I knew it was caveman of me and possessive, but there was something about it that made me want to beat my chest and declare her as mine.

"Be quiet, else you will sleep in the wet patch," she shouted from the bathroom.

Once she was finished cleaning up, she returned to the bedroom and slipped in between the covers with me, curling up with her ass against my cock. I put an arm around her, cupping her breasts because I'd never be able to feel them enough and kissed her neck. "No weirdness. If this is just one night and one morning let's enjoy it."

"Hmmm," she muttered, half asleep already. "Thank you. Feels so good."

I kissed her shoulder and closed my eyes, unsure of how I felt but knowing that this couldn't be our only night.

CHAPTER 13
PAYTON

A finger slowly circled around my nipple. At first I thought I was dreaming, that the sensation and the response of my body were the result of some fantastical dream, but then the fingers gently pinched and my eyes fluttered open. Another hand had crept under my side and was stroking the soft mound between my legs. I became more aware of the warm body behind me and the hard cock pressed against my ass, the wetness between my legs.

Somehow Owen had turned me into a needy puddle of want and desire while I had been sleeping. He sucked and bit my neck, one nimble finger finding my clit and lightly rubbing it. I pushed back against his cock and urged my brain to catch up. We'd had sex, amazing, orgasm filled sex and he used the biggest cock I'd ever been acquainted with to fill me to the hilt. My head should've been riddled with questions about what would happen next and how we'd be friends, but instead it was letting my body take over. And my body had only one request: sex.

"Are you awake?" he said, a whisper against my neck.

"I think so," I said, only cognizant of his fingers on my nipple and finger on my clit.

"I want to make you come and then fuck you. Can I do that? Do you want me to fuck you?"

His words, those quietly spoken, dirty words, brought me closer to the edge. I managed to nod, my legs going rigid which was my tell that I was about to come.

"Need your words, Payts. If you want me in you, tell me," he said. His fingers left my nipple and slipped between him and my ass, one pressing at my pussy. "You're so tight and swollen. Your cunt feels incredible around my dick."

"In me," I said, a finger pushing inside to that spot I'd once considered a myth until I learned more about the use of vibrators. "I want your dick in me."

"You have to come for me first. Are you going to come on my hand?" He pressed down on my clit and I started to spasm, my pussy pulsating, my hips jerking.

He pulled his finger out and started to push his cock inside, moving my top leg back and over him. There was a pinch of pain as he moved inside me, stretching me around him. I touched my tits and found my nipples like diamonds.

"How do I feel?" I said as he sunk deeper. He was going slowly, lazily, holding my hip so he could manoeuvre me and I felt wanton, needed.

"Like fucking heaven," he said. "You're soaked. When I woke up I had my hands on your tits and my cock was almost in you already. I don't think my body's going to want to give you up. You were already wet." He pulled out and I keened at the loss of him and then he began to move my hips and his into a rhythm, shallow gentle strokes that teased the sweetest spot inside me. "Can I come in you again?"

"Yes," I said, barely able to breathe, let alone speak. He moved a little harder, his body tensing and stretching longer.

My legs were spread wider, one backwards over his so he could go deeper. "I want you to fill me up."

He kept moving inside me, moving my hips to suit his rhythm and I felt as if I was being thoroughly fucked. I cared about nothing else at this point, just the pleasure between my legs, the man behind me giving me his cock and his dirty words, telling me what he was feeling, what else he wanted to do to me, how my pussy was his and no one else's and I didn't want to argue or disagree.

When I came it crept up on me, slight tremors that became an earthquake and my body became vulnerability portrayed. My breasts thrust out and my movements were for the convenience of the man behind me. His cock grew harder and I felt it pulse as he began to come, hot jets of semen shooting up, saturating me. I felt his teeth on my shoulder as he stilled and a hand moved onto my breast, cupping it.

My heart rate hadn't come down any: it still stabbed my chest, my breaths deep and hard. "I want to fall asleep with you in me," I said. "But I should get up and use the bathroom."

"Wait a few minutes," he said, tucking me in closer, kissing my neck. "This doesn't count as morning. It's not light yet."

I laughed quietly, holding his arms so he held me harder. "I don't want it to be morning. This feels too good."

"That's the idea," Owen said, his words whispers in the silence of the night. "I make you feel good."

"I want you to feel good too."

"I think the evidence of that is about to spill out of you."

My laugh this time was louder, which did create more wetness on my thighs. He had softened inside me and I knew I had to move.

When I returned from the bathroom, feeling sore and wondering if I was walking like I'd been riding a large stallion for a week straight, he was lying on the bed, eyes open, sheets mussed around his middle and his chest exposed. We hadn't closed the curtains because there was really no need and I liked being able to see the city lights in the distance, reminding me that someone was always awake in the world.

"You're awake still," I said softly, taking in my fill of him in case this was the last time I saw him in my bed. "I thought you'd have fallen asleep."

"I wanted you here first." He moved the sheets back so I could slip in next to him, exposing more of his body. His abs were defined, strong, and his chest was sculpted. Muscles contoured his thighs and his cock was still long and thick as it rested next to his thigh. His chuckle was proud and boastful as he caught me staring. "If you take photos, I'll charge."

I shot round to the bed, remembering that I was naked too, every unwanted bump and bulge on display. He kept the covers down as I tried to pull them back up and hide.

"Payton, you're gorgeous."

"I'm not perfect."

"No one is."

"You are." I moved into his arms, my head on his chest, my arm across his stomach.

He pulled the sheets over us. "That's how you see me. I see you in the same way."

My eyes started to close and I felt Owen's breathing deepen and slow. His heat seeped through to me and I felt my muscles relax, any thoughts that would've intruded on my sleep barricaded by the big man lying next to me. For the first time in I didn't know how long I felt steady, peaceful.

Happy.

———

My phone rang as it was becoming light, the ring tone the one I'd assigned my mother. I fumbled for it on my nightstand, knocking off my lip balm. "Mum," I said. "Is Dad okay? Are you at the hospital?"

"Stop," she said. "Quick phone call. Dad's fine, he's had a settled night. He's having his angiogram first thing. I'm fine —slept amazingly in a big bed on my own. Max is cancelling your meeting this afternoon so you and Seph can pick up your dad and bring him back here as I'm going to one of Sophie's salons for a massage."

"What about Dad?" I said, confused by her lack of worry.

"Payton, this isn't the end of the world, sweetie. It's all investigatory and preventative. He's okay in himself and isn't worried. If he was, I'd be there but I think I'm irritating him." Her voice had the firm, no nonsense tone to it that I knew too well from my childhood when I'd been an insane worrier.

"So you want Seph to irritate him instead?" I said. Owen had sat up and had his arms around me, kissing and nibbling my back. Any awkwardness that I'd thought there might be was absent.

"Seph irritating him will keep his brain from turning to mush and keep his wit sharp."

"And possibly his fists fresh," I said, knowing full well how Seph could annoy our father. Owen had pulled me back into bed and was doing his best not to distract me by holding me as still as he could. "I've got to go, Mum. I need to get ready."

"How's Owen? Are you seeing him today?"

I was seeing, and feeling, rather a lot of him but she didn't need to know that. "Yeah, I'm meeting him for breakfast. Talk to you later."

"Sure. Love you."

"Love you back." I hung up and turned around, curling

up next to the man I was just having breakfast with. "I had to lie to my mum."

"No you didn't. We can have breakfast and then it'll be true. And if you want to tell her the rest, that's fine with me." His chin landed heavily on my shoulder.

"That I had sex with my friend."

"Several times."

"Several times is true. That's the reason I'm going to be walking funny."

"How about a hot shower to help ease you into your morning?" His hands were now on my breasts, playing with my nipples which was sending electricity straight to my pussy.

My back arched of its own accord. "I do need a good wash. I got a little dirty in the night."

His laugh was deep and reverberated through my body. "I'm happy to clean you up as long as I can get you dirty again first."

―――

"I think it's the right way to approach it, though, don't you?" Seph had his elbows on his thighs and was looking intently at our father. "If I take the more traditional view, there's the potential the opposing lawyer will use the precedent set in eighty-six, Morris versus Taylor."

Our dad nodded. "I think it's a good idea. Now get your backside out there and see where the doctor is. I want to get out of here and go annoy your mother."

Seph grinned, looking much happier than he had done when he'd picked me up to come to the hospital. He'd panicked last night, his mind creating impossible scenarios of unlikely events. Max ended up huffing off in a sulk and Jackson made a quick exit with Vanessa, leaving me and

Owen to talk some sense into him, seeing as Callum was quite happy to find Seph's verbal mania amusing. "I'll go see how long they'll be."

"You have all your medication?" I said, knowing that he had.

"Yes, I just need to sign the forms. Are you seeing Owen tonight?" His look was entirely too innocent.

"No, I'm going for a Chinese with Seph. Owen and I are just friends, Dad," I said, not believing that at all.

He smiled. "Bullshit and you know it. He's in love with you for a start."

"We've not known each other long enough," I said, debating whether I needed to be admitted given how fast my heart was now beating.

"I knew your mother a few days before I knew how I felt about her. There's no contract that love follows, kiddo. And that man's in love with you. It was written all over his face last night when I was talking to him about you," my dad said, his attention turning to the door where a doctor was. "Am I allowed to go home?"

She laughed. "Yes. All your results are back and the consultant will get in touch with your doctor tomorrow or the day after. You know the schedule for your meds. Start exercising more, healthier meals and less alcohol. No stress." She eyed Seph. "Family need to keep it stress free for a while."

"No chance. I've seven kids. Stress came with the label of '*dad*.' Thank you for your help; where do I need to sign?" He was itching to leave, which I supposed was good.

We took him back to Max's, briefly seeing Mum who looked unsurprisingly relaxed after her time at the spa. It wasn't often she did anything like that, so I supposed she'd needed to find that head space.

Seph's conversation distracted me from what my father had said about Owen. It had made me nervous and I wasn't entirely sure why. I didn't want to distance myself from him; instead, I was anxious to see him again, to see if I could spot the signs my father had seen.

"You're quiet, Payts," Seph said when we were seated in Lin's, one of his favourite restaurants in Southwark.

I smiled, looking at him from above the menu, which was pointless as I had pretty much memorised it some years ago. "It's been a busy couple of days. I'm just catching up."

He put his menu down. "But you've been quieter since we dropped Dad off. What did he say to you when I went to get the doctor? He didn't tell you that something was wrong, really wrong, and not to tell the rest of us, did he?"

I sat my menu down. "Joseph, Dad is going to be fine as long as he does what the specialists have advised. He'll be fitter than you in about three weeks."

"Then what did he say to you? Are you okay? I know we were worried about you a couple of weeks ago because you were so burnt out after finishing that case, but you've seemed more like your old self since then," Seph said and took off the glasses that I knew he didn't need. My twin was an enigma. He was beautiful and looked like a Greek god, probably the cleverest and most brilliant out of all of us but a complete and utter klutz when it came to relationships and friendships as he had no filter and cared too much. He was currently living with Max and Victoria, a temporary arrangement he'd managed to wrangle, as he hated living on his own. It hadn't occurred to him that they might've wanted some privacy, because Seph was Tigger from Winnie the Pooh and didn't understand the need for being private.

"I feel much better," I said. "Obviously Dad being poorly has thrown me like the rest of us, but I know he'll be okay. He did say something though."

Seph's eyebrows raised. My twin was my best friend. We had always leaned on each other, stuck up for one another and I could trust him to tell me the truth even when it would hurt, if he had to.

"Dad told me that Owen was in love with me," I said as the waitress came over to take our order.

Seph remained quiet after asking for his usual soup, dim sums and crispy beef. He hadn't needed a menu for years.

"You disagree? I mean, it has only been a couple of weeks and we barely know each other. He's a really good guy, not a jerk like my usual type. He's successful, personable, kind—"

"Payton," Seph interrupted. "What are you asking? And can I have an indication as to what you want the answer to be, please?"

God, I loved my brother. "Do you think he likes me as more than a friend? Start with that one. And I want the truth."

He laughed loudly, loud enough for the waitress to look at us in some concern. "For fuck's sake, Payts. If you think he just wants to be friends you need to go back to dating girls again, because you clearly can't read men."

"Straight answers, Joseph." I rapped my knuckles on the table.

He folded his arms and I wondered how much time he'd been spending in the gym because my twin looked huge. "He wants to be a lot more than friends, otherwise he wouldn't be spending this much time with you or looking at you the way he does."

"How do you know that and how does he look at me? And can you confirm you're not taking anything you shouldn't to help you in the gym?" My filters were never on when I was talking to Seph. There was no point.

Seph's eyes glinted. "I'm not taking steroids. I am taking supplements and pre and post work out drinks, but nothing that could cause harm. I've researched it. You don't need to worry."

"Are you getting obsessed with training?" Seph had a tendency to throw himself into something with determination and a hell of a lot of motivation.

"Kind of. I'm following a plan, but no more than that. I have rest days. The exercise is keeping me level and happy. Back to Owen," he said as the waitress dropped off some prawn crackers.

I bit one noisily.

"He looks at you like he wants to eat you and he's nearly always watching you. Not in a creepy stalker way, but like he can't take his eyes from you. When did you sleep with him?"

I sat up straight and stared at my brother, then shook my head. "How do you know these things?"

"The same way you always do. It's a different vibe you give off."

"Last night and this morning."

"I thought you were walking weird. I thought you didn't want to get involved with anyone? Although saying that usually means you'll meet someone great because you're not looking."

"I know. I really like him but I don't want to get hurt. I've had enough of men who don't live up to my expectations and I keep giving them chances thinking they'll end up being great and they don't," I said, eating my way through another cracker. I hadn't been to the gym in four days and I could feel the calories gathering on my hips and having a party.

"He's the first friend of yours—and by friend I mean fuck buddy—that I like and even if he wasn't hanging out with you, he would be with us. No one's perfect, though, Payts. He will have his faults. I know you think Max is amazing, but Vic puts up with a hell of a lot of shit from him. He's moody and obsessively tidy and really does snap when he can't find the words he needs to say how he feels," Seph said. "I keep out of their way and I am looking for somewhere else to live, but I do notice their relationship."

"Is Vic happy?"

Seph smiled. "Crazily so. She doesn't mind living with a huge grump and she sees straight through his moods. They make each other smile. I went downstairs last night to get a hot drink and they were in her snug: Max was sitting down and Vic was holding his head in to her belly with her hands in his hair. I think he was upset about Dad. I didn't hang around to spy or anything, but they're such a team and I never thought Max would have that."

My eyes welled up. Our oldest brother was a workaholic, gruff and determined. He'd had plenty of relationships with women who had been besotted with him, but no one had ever captivated him enough to tear him away from his practice as a clinical negligence specialist until Victoria. Max had been our idol growing up: he would often look after us and was more of an uncle than big brother, especially because he was quite a bit older. He'd also looked after Claire and Callum after their mum died and before Dad married our mum, Marie.

"I'm so glad he has. He's so much happier now he's with Victoria."

"Why did you sleep with Owen?"

Seph was the only one of my brothers who would ask that question. "Because I needed someone last night."

"Was that fair? You know he likes you a lot. Have you led him on?"

"He was happy when I suggested we should be friends with benefits for the night. He just made sure we wouldn't be awkward today," I said, aware that I hadn't replied to his last message.

"Has it been awkward? You know, he's a good guy, Payts. I don't want you to piss him off because you'll be mortified if you do," Seph said as his hot and sour soup was put in front of him.

I shook my head. "It's not been awkward. We've spoken a couple of times…"

"What about?"

"What's this? Seph the relationship guru?" He pulled his face at me. "Just how Dad was, what we were doing, nothing in particular."

"So not the sort of conversation you'd have with Ava or one of your friends?"

He had a point. "No. Nothing like it." Especially when I'd mentioned that I was sore today because of his cock. That led to an entirely different conversation.

"You're not just friends then. You're in a relationship."

"No. We've said we're friends and that I don't want to get involved…"

"Fuck off, Payts. Just because you won't label it as a relationship doesn't mean it isn't one. Are you going to sleep with him again?"

"When did these conversations about our sex lives stop becoming uncomfortable?"

"Probably about the time when we were sixteen and you were going out with Tom Gaffney and I was messing around with Lila Towers and I ran out of condoms that evening our parents were out with Ava and ran into your room," Seph said, dipping a cracker into his soup. "There's nothing like seeing your sister issuing very specific directions to your desperate to please teammate with both of them naked."

I shrugged. "You should've knocked."

"I didn't know you were in your room. I had music on. Lila was loud. Back to Owen."

"Why don't I want to be in a relationship with him?"

"Because you're scared you're either going to get hurt or

he's not going to live up to your expectations. Or you don't really like him like that. Can we eat?"

I nodded and we changed the topic of conversation to other things: friends, a date Seph had on Wednesday, Callum and his mysterious ways and Ava and how she was pretending to be single. I checked my phone when Seph went to the bathroom, responding to Owen's message about not being able to put a book down by a new author he'd discovered. I responded by taking a selfie and it continued from there. Seph became increasingly irritated at the amount my phone vibrated, which only added to my amusement. I was going home to the bed I'd shared with Owen the night before, to sheets that needed washing and pillows that smelled of him and me combined. I wasn't sure how I'd feel, sleeping by myself and I knew I needed to consider that maybe my brother was right: we weren't just friends and maybe I could be happy with that.

CHAPTER 14
OWEN

Payton had told me in a text that my body wasn't what she would've expected of a book store owner.

If she'd seen me this morning, she would've known straight away I was either a librarian or had some form of nerdy profession as I was rocking the whole geek look. My glasses were thick rimmed and prominent; I wore chinos, a light blue shirt and a brown tank top. Had I still been at school there was a good chance I would've had my head pushed down a toilet while it was being flushed—that was the action this look would've inspired, had I not also been six foot four and built like a redwood tree.

It was early morning, but London was its usual busy self with plenty of people in suits looking tired and rushed. One of things I loved about what I did was that I was able to set my own agenda. I decided what time I started work and what happened during the course of my day. Sure, there were emergencies where I had to get up at three in the morning because one of the stores had been broken into or there was a staffing issue and I needed to resolve it, but Cases was my baby and my main livelihood so I rarely minded.

Today was different. It was a Friday, so the busiest part of my week had ended: Fridays were usually quieter and more relaxed, but today I felt apprehensive.

I hadn't seen Dave since the mediation, and even then I hadn't seen him to talk to. He'd been a constant in my life since I was a teenager and although I was aware relationships ended—mine and Amber's being the prime example—I had expected him to be in touch before now. He'd messaged me on Wednesday during an acoustic set from a band I was pretty sure would be selling out arenas in a couple of years, and asked if I wanted to meet him for breakfast on Friday. Breakfast seemed to be the go to meal for social occasions as you were guaranteed to make it on time, mostly.

We met in a small café down a side street near St Paul's Cathedral that specialised in Fairtrade coffee and gluten free everything. Dave had celiac disease, so places that did gluten free were well known to me.

He looked tired and lean, as if he'd lost weight in the past couple of months but his grin was still the same.

"Morning," he said, folding his paper and putting it to one side. "You look like a librarian."

"I tried," I said, sitting down opposite. "You look like shit."

He eyed me. "Yeah. Not been sleeping that well."

"Or eating."

"That too."

"Why?" I knew the answer, or at least I thought I did.

"I've screwed up." He looked majorly pissed off with himself. "Order your coffee, then I'll start by apologising."

I headed to the counter, needing a strong black and a something filling as I'd barely eaten the night before; I'd left rugby practice to go to an event at one of the publishing houses. There had been canapés and other silly dickwad pieces of food but nothing substantial, so a full English breakfast was definitely on my list of things to eat. And maybe a lemon muffin. And possibly waffles.

"What do you need to apologise for?" I said, sitting back down with a large mug of caffeine.

"Fuck, Owen, you can try to make this easy for me."

I laughed quietly, adding a drop of cream.

"Fine. I'm sorry about going legal on you. The store and all. I don't want to sell my share; I've no reason to," he said, shaking his head. "I just needed a way to keep in touch with your mum."

"I figured as much and so did she," I said, nearly burning my mouth with the coffee.

"It didn't work. I left her at least a dozen voicemails asking her to meet so we could talk but she didn't respond or return any of my calls.," He looked downcast and genuinely sad. I thought about how I would feel if Payton stopped speaking to me and realised that not much else would matter anymore. That was a thought to continue with later. "What's she told you?"

"Nothing," I said. "Absolutely jack fucking shit apart from something about not living together. It all sounds like a bit of a mid-life crisis."

"It's my fault."

"I doubt it." I gestured to the girl at the counter for more coffee for both of us. "But tell me why you think it is."

Dave pushed a hand through his hair and looked pained. He was a good man, a busy, successful one, but a good man. Between him and my father, I had decent role models growing up, particularly when it came to treating women. "I should've asked her to move it with me. I should've been more romantic. You know the books she reads—the modern romance stuff…"

"Mum reads that?" I was surprised. I'd only ever seen her

with classics or literary fiction, although I knew Payton liked romance novels.

Dave nodded. "She started to read paragraphs out, you can imagine which sections, and I think it gave her ideas."

"Do I need to know anymore?"

"Probably not, but I should've realised she wanted more attention. Flowers, dates, gestures. I hadn't been putting the effort in and we were just a habit. But she's a habit I'd like back," he said, looking up at me hopefully.

I shook my head. "I can't get involved. Not because I don't want to help you—I'd be the happiest person if you two got back together—but because she's more stubborn than a mule with oppositional defiance disorder and me trying to persuade her to get back together with you would just push her the other way."

"So do the opposite," Dave said. "Tell her you're glad we've finished and we were never right for each other. Set her up with someone else."

"What are you going to do?"

He smiled, taking the coffee gratefully. "Wait. And if she does want to see me again, I'll make her feel like the leading lady in one of her romance books."

"As long as you never give me details," I said, deadly serious. I never, ever want details of my mother's personal life. Ever.

Dave looked slightly better than he had when I first saw him; there was a glimmer of hope where there'd been nothing but loss before. I felt a pang in my chest, possibly hunger, possibly something to do with the tiny blonde I had only seen once since I'd left her bed on Monday. We'd both been busy; she with work and her dad, me with the stores, the gallery that my dad was investing in and various work events in the evenings. We'd grabbed a quick lunch together on Wednesday and it hadn't been weird; we'd talked like we usually did and before we parted, I'd held her and given her a quick kiss, one that didn't know what it was meant to be.

"I promise never to disclose anything," Dave said. "I'll also tell my lawyer that I'm no longer interested in selling my part of Cases. Is that okay with you? Unless you do actually want to buy me out and then I'll agree to the price the mediator suggested."

"No," I said, shaking my head. My breakfast arrived and I wondered whether I was actually drooling. "You can pay my legal fees though."

"Happy to. Your lawyer was a bit of a talent, wasn't she? Richard said she pretty much tore what he wrote to pieces, word for word." Dave's eyebrows were raised in alarm and he looked genuinely impressed.

Payton would love to know what he'd said. "She's incredible," I said and knew I hadn't managed to stop the goofy grin appearing on my face. "She's bright and quick and funny."

"And you're completely in over your head with her," Dave said, leaning over and pinching a mushroom. "That looks good."

"Get your own then," I said. "Appetite coming back?"

"I feel better now I've spoken to you. If you'd have been against me trying to get your mum back, I'd have sold," he said, then shouted over to the waitress for another breakfast. "I am sorry you got caught up in this."

I shrugged, devouring a rasher of bacon. "I'm thirty-two; it's the first time it's happened so I think I've done pretty well."

"Tell me about your lawyer."

I sat back, chewing, unsure where to start. I hadn't really talked to anyone about Payton. The friends I'd seen since I'd met her hadn't been the ones I'd confide in, if I was going to do that at all. I usually sorted out my own shit, not that this was shit. She felt like the best thing that had happened to me, but I wasn't sure if I was the best thing that had happened to her.

"I walked into her at Cases in Soho. She was taking a picture and we argued. I needed a lawyer so I called her and we became friends. I was with her when they took her sister in for an emergency caesarean and we just kind of clicked."

"What's the issue?"

"A relationship isn't on her agenda. She wants to be friends. With benefits."

"Why doesn't she want a relationship?"

"She's been hurt in the past because she's always gone out with wankers and she's been run down with work," I said, keeping it factual to what she'd told me rather than psycho-analysing her. "It feels like we're in a relationship with how much we talk and how we are with each other."

"Romance her. Maybe you need to do what I should've done."

I nodded. "I do. But not yet. I need to get her to agree to go on a date first and she has to decide that for herself."

———

A tall redhead was sitting at the coffee bar in the Soho branch of Cases when I finally arrived there. A tall, familiar redhead. She was sipping a cappuccino and laughing with my mother who was next to her, a stack of book on the bar. Their heads turned to me like sheep, as if they were one and I paused, folding my arms. I knew an ambush when I saw one.

"Owen," Amber said, rushing towards me. She looked like she always did: model tall, almost model thin and beautifully put together. Today must've been a down day from work as she wasn't wearing a suit. I used to tell Amber she was born wearing a trouser suit she was in them that much.

"You look amazing. Your mum said you're playing rugby again."

"Yep," I said, arms still folded. I still had a good seven inches on her height wise and I planned to make the most of them. "What can I do for you?"

"You always assume I'm after something."

"Because you usually are."

She narrowed her eyes and then grinned. "I suppose you're right. How's business? It looks like it's booming."

"It is," I said, my voice softening. It had been years since we'd split and we had never fallen out. Just woken up one morning when neither of us had any work commitments and headed out to the seaside. It was painfully awkward and we realised that we had nothing left to talk about. We rarely had sex and our lives had begun to differ when I stopped developing apps and coding, which was what Amber had built her life around. She was a geek who happened to be gorgeous, but right now, I couldn't remember why I'd been so attracted to her.

We'd never been in love. There'd never been any passion, just friends with benefits who got on, which was another reason why I knew Payton and I weren't just fucking friends, no matter how hard she was trying to keep it in that box.

"Okay. You have the Blue Lines playing in a couple of weeks," she said, giving me a beaming smile.

"I have. Dean, Vinny and Jon. Acoustic set."

"This is awkward."

"Hit me with it."

"I'm kind of seeing Vinny." This was unusual. Amber liked men and since we'd split she'd had a number that she toyed with, a bit like a cat would play with a catnip toy before destroying it. She'd never directly told me about anyone specific.

"Is it serious?"

She moved her head from side to side and held her hands up to show she didn't know. "It's been a couple of months. He'd asked if I'd play and sing when they're here. Just for shits and giggles. I'd really like to but I just wanted to make sure you'd be okay with it. I know we tend to keep our distance."

I kept my distance. Amber had come back to me occasionally to remember the good times we'd had, which inevitably led to sex, which led to me doing yet another post-mortem to work out where we'd gone wrong. If I was in a relationship, I gave it my all and I hated to fail. I saw what happened with me and Amber as a failure, even though it had been anything but. "It's fine," I said. "There's no reason why you shouldn't."

"Would you play too? When's the last time you were on stage with your guitar?" she sounded excited, like a little girl on Christmas day, which was Amber all over. Payton had the same enthusiasm and love of life, but hers was more mellow, more consistent. More me.

"I'm not playing."

She squinted at me. "One song. Play one song. I'll harmonise with you. Dean and Vinny won't mind, in fact Dean asked me the other day if you still did the odd session with your guitar."

Years ago, when I was developing apps and running the dating one, I'd spent time at gigs, filling in for bands who were missing a guitarist and helping out a couple of mates here and there. I'd met Amber through my Master's degree, but we got to know each other through music and being at the same venues.

Her hand touched my arm and she squeezed my bicep. Before there would've been a reaction, even if it was just by association—Amber touching me had usually lead to sex in the past—but now there was nothing. I wanted the small blonde tornado who made me feel like I'd come home.

"One song. And it's my choice."

She rolled her eyes dramatically. "Folk-rock here we come. You're such a contradiction. The body of a god, chiselled cheekbones and you like folk-rock. Where's your beard and sandals. Don't forget the socks."

"Agree or there's no deal."

She shook her head. "You drive a mean bargain, Owen Anders. I'll see you then."

I raised an eyebrow.

"What?"

"How do you know you'll still be involved with Vinny by that time? Or is this just in case you are?"

Her smile was one I recognised from myself. She was smitten. "I just know," she said. "I hope you're good with that. Your mum told me you'd met a girl."

Trust my mother to tell my ex I'd met someone. It showed she liked Payton though; my mum was making sure Amber couldn't sabotage whatever we had, whatever it was. "Yeah," I nodded.

Amber smiled. "You really like her."

"I think so." I thought it was turning into more than like. "We're taking it slow though."

"Whisk her off her feet, Owen. Do what we didn't and put the romance in there. Otherwise you become companions and without that spark you're just friends with benefits." Her smile was genuine. "See you in a couple of weeks. Look after yourself and your girl." She swung round to wave to my mum and then stepped away, this time leaving me without a mystery.

Amber and I had been friends with benefits and as fond of her as I'd been, it hadn't been an epic love story, just mutually convenient.

Payton was different: she made me want to take days off work just to stay in bed and forget about meetings and deals and contracts. I wanted her body wrapped around mine, her laugh filling the air around me and her words, all her words.

I needed a plan, which shouldn't be a big deal given I ran a very successful business and had interests in several other venture too. But first, I had to set another plan into action. "Mum," I called when she was in earshot. "What are you doing tonight?"

CHAPTER 15
PAYTON

At least once a month, most of us would try to get over to Mum and Dad's to spend some time there, see our parents and catch up with each other. We were close as far as siblings went; I guess we got lucky that way, but we could go a while without seeing each other properly with work getting in the way and the other commitments we all had. We were like worker bees: busy things but ultimately we all centred back to the hive, which for us, was each other and our parents.

Most of us had something already scheduled for this weekend. Ava's friend from university was coming to stay with her; Max and Vic had a meal booked somewhere uber posh and I expected he was going to propose; Jackson and Vanessa had her gran over for the weekend—although her gran was still coming, being a rather formidable lady who ate balls for breakfast; and Callum had a date. Claire and Killian were already there so Marie could help with Eliza.

Dad's TIA had given us a scare. He was still young at fifty-eight— at which point nowadays was someone described as old?—and we'd thought he was healthy, so last Sunday had taken us all back.

I unpacked my suitcase which was neater than usual. Since tidying my apartment I'd kept it that way: clothes folded, accessories organised, so my case took minutes to put together and less time to put away when I got to my room at my parents'.

They'd had the house modernised a year ago, pretty much gutting everything and redesigning it. Ava had a lot to do with it structurally—her favourite thing was to see what a house could be like with walls in different places and I'd seen her in action knocking a wall down shortly after she'd caught a boyfriend cheating. Marie had overseen the interior design, finally having rooms that were meant for adults rather than teenagers or children.

I loved it here. It was my childhood home and held all those memories like a jar filled with fireflies. The room I was in had been Seph's when we were younger and one day he tried to be Spiderman and climbed out of the window. Sticking to walls hadn't been something he was made for, and he'd tumbled down to the garden, picking up various cuts and scrapes and a broken arm. It shouldn't be a favourite memory, but he'd truly believed he was Spiderman and had been bit by some insect, despite me and Ava yelling at him that it was just fiction. I remembered him sitting on the grass with me and Ava looking down at him through the open window and him shouting at us that it *hadn't worked and he didn't know why*. I truly loved my brother and all the crazy things he does on a semi-regular basis.

"Payton." There was a knock at my door and my mother's voice rang through the wood. "Payton, can I come in?"

"Shit, yeah, you usually don't ask," I said, quickly putting my underwear in a drawer. I'd packed some pretties, although I didn't know why. The only person who'd be seeing them was me, which was more than enough, I knew.

I hadn't seen Owen since Monday morning although we'd spoken and texted and chatted plenty. We'd had a long conversation about his breakfast with Dave this morning and he told me who he'd set his mother up with for a date tonight. I was officially no longer his lawyer, which was one less barrier in our way to something more than friends, if that was what we wanted.

"I have been asking since you were eighteen, Payton Marie, but you're usually wearing headphones or engrossed in social media so you don't hear," Mum said, pushing the door open. "It's tidy in here."

I frowned. "What else did you expect?"

"Something akin to a clothes shop at the end of the first day of the sale." She sat down on the bed. "How's work been?"

"Good," I said. "I've been making more of an effort to stop work at a certain time and do something during the week other than work, sleep and eat."

Marie smiled. "What's made you make that change?"

I knew what she was fishing for. "Knowing that everyone was worried about me burning out."

"And Owen? Or is it just coincidence that he's been around since you started to get your shit together?" Marie said, unfolding and refolding a pair of jeans that I was planning to change into.

Owen. I'd check my phone to see if he'd sent a text or if I had a missed call from him, and when I hadn't, I'd debate messaging him with something fun or interesting or about the book I was reading. "I don't think it's all coincidence. He runs this successful business and is involved in others, yet he manages his time to do other things and he's so calm with everything. Apart from the first time we met. Then he was a bit stressed."

"You smile when you talk about him. Are you sure you're just friends?" My mother had three gifts. The first was being a shit hot family lawyer. The second was being able to tell my father what to do and get him to do it. The third was that she could read any of her children like a basic story book. There was no point trying to act confused.

"It's not just friends. But I don't know what I want," I said. "We get along so well and he's really, really hot. He likes this lot of weirdos enough to see them three times a week and even Seph being annoying drunk hasn't scared him away. He's successful and gorgeous and clever and all that and he likes me. And I think he likes me a lot."

"So why aren't you more than friends, Payton? It seems like you know you should be. Is there no chemistry there?" my mother said as loud music blasted out from the room next door.

"Thanks for putting me next to Seph," I muttered. That meant he'd be waking me up at stupid o'clock for a midnight feast because we had the tendency to turn into seven-year-olds when we came back home. "There is chemistry. It's me. I'm scared because everyone I've ever dated has turned out to be a jerk and then I've got hurt. He's too perfect so there has to be a fault there and I'm worried that when I find that fault I'll end up getting my heartbroken again. Which then upsets everyone else because they worry about me."

My mother had the audacity to laugh. The Blossoms latest album pulsed through the walls and my memories of being a teenager weren't so sweet, with Seph's inability to do anything quietly. "Payton, our job is to worry about you. Like you worry about your brothers and Claire and Ava. If you tried it with Owen and it doesn't work out, we'd be here to pick you up and dust you down. Same with if it does work out: we'd celebrate with you and make sure he knows he's got a foot in the grave already if he messes with you."

I nodded, not knowing what else to say. There was no point in arguing because she was right, I just had trouble accepting it and that people being concerned and caring about me was not a sign of my failure. "Did you want me for something specific?"

"Just to tell you to hurry up as we're opening Champagne. I think everyone's here. There was just Ava left to arrive—she was running late but she might be here now," Mum said. "I'd best go startle Seph."

When my parents had the house renovated, they'd had three rooms knocked together to create a large kitchen come dining room come lounge and it was this room that we took over when we were all here. We'd eaten, somehow all squashed around the long table my parents had acquired from a monastery of all places, and gone through several bottles of wine, apart from Claire who was breastfeeding and whose only pleasure was to glare at Killian as he took sips of wine with a look of bliss on his face.

"I hate you," she said. "I give you your daughter, decide to breastfeed her and in repayment you drink in front of me. Where's your sense of decency?"

"Lost in the large pile of crap I scraped from up her back earlier. You're doing brilliantly, dear. Keep a tab and those are all nights out where I have to stay in and babysit," Killian said calmly. He'd thrown in the 'dear' specially to rile her, and judging by her blazing eyes he was about to have his daughter launched at him.

"Your daddy is a nasty man to Mummy," Claire muttered in a sweet tone. "When Daddy next changes your bottom, make sure you save him your biggest poo for right after he's cleaned you all up."

I wasn't concerned. My older sister had always had an extra couple of mad frogs in her box. She also adored Killian and vice versa; they just liked to bicker, or rather she did and he liked to ignore her because he knew it irritated the shit out of her.

"What she produces is nothing compared to what I've dealt with today," Callum said. He was sprawled out on the floor opposite Seph with a game of four in a row between them.

"You'd be surprised," Killian said in the quiet way he had. "I hope none of you suffer it though because it is fucking ugly."

"Elephant with a stomach upset today," Callum said. He was a vet and not the type to be limited to small pets and animals. He'd spent the past couple of years working abroad on sanctuaries and in the wild at times, mainly in Africa. He was now back home permanently, working at London Zoo which was better for all of us as we'd seen him far too infrequently while he was away. "That was bigger and smellier than anything my niece could produce, trust me."

"Be interesting to know proportionally who would win that battle," Killian said. "And if Seph could compete in terms of vomit after a night out."

"I can't help it if I'm drunkenly challenged," Seph said, denying nothing. There would be no point: at one time or another all of us had carried or dragged him back to ours, lost a toilet for the night and put him in the recovery position covered with towels.

"If you get any heavier we'll need to start taking a wheelchair out with us. It took both me and Owen to get you upstairs the other week," Callum said. "Or you could just stop drinking shots. Then you'd at least be able to crawl."

"Is Owen coming this weekend, Payts?" Jackson said. He had Vanessa sat on his lap and I don't think anyone had noticed that she wasn't drinking anything alcoholic.

I shrugged, feeling my neck flush hot. "He's meeting a friend tonight. I didn't ask him. I wasn't sure who else was coming besides us."

"Amelie and Simone are coming tomorrow and bunking in the coach house. There's another room available there if he wants to come over. I think we're barbecuing tomorrow. With a lot of salad and lean chicken," my mother said, eyeing my father.

He rolled his eyes. "Barbecuing the healthy way. She'll have a recipe book written before you know it. Didn't you just say that Simone was coming? She'll have some ideas of how to still make things tasty then, won't she?" He sounded desperate. My father liked good food and even better wine. He wouldn't be bothered about the thought of more exercise, it would be the idea of having to restrict his food and wine intake.

"It's not a busman's holiday for her," Mum said. "She's not coming here to cook you ten course tasting menus."

"I didn't say that. Just that she might have some ideas…" He stopped as Mum glowered at him.

I knew before too long someone would suggest poker and the night would take a turn that way, with plenty of ribbing and joking and accusations, mainly from Seph and directed at Callum. I loved my nights here with my family, where no one had to worry about getting home or sleeping on a sofa. We had wondered if our parents would downsize once Ava moved out, but they'd insisted on keeping the property so there was somewhere for us all to be together. Both of them came from families that owned law firms for generations and we had been lucky growing up to never have to worry about money. That hadn't meant we were spoiled. Marie's mother had come from a family that had been poor in the sense they'd barely had enough to eat, so despite marrying into wealth, she'd saved as opposed to spent and taught her multiple children the same. Marie had us well trained with money from the time we left school.

Our childhood home had changed considerably over the years, but the pictures and ornaments had remained the same to a certain extent. And the voices hadn't altered: I could hear my siblings yelling and teasing, Seph insulting Max so he had no comeback and Victoria laughing. But it felt odd with Owen.

The room felt empty. Owen was meeting a friend tonight, as well as arranging his mum's blind date. He'd set her up with an acquaintance who was a few years younger than Dot and a serial dater. He'd told me about his impulsive lunch with her where he'd mentioned that he was really happy she'd ended it with Dave and gave a list of reasons as to why he hadn't thought it would work forever. She'd reacted like he thought she would; defensive of Dave and challenging his opinion.

My phone vibrated in my pocket, making me smile because I knew who it would be.

> Owen: Operation horrendous date successful. She hated him and he bored her to death.

> Me: Did she say anything about Dave?

> Owen: No, just that dating was turning out to be a waste of time. I didn't stalk her either. She came and found me afterwards.

> Me: Are you still out? I've just eaten enough to fill a small country for a week.

Owen: Just got home. My friend's wife just had a baby so he needed to get back. I'm in bed actually, about to read.

Me: What are you reading?

Owen: Your texts! No, I'm going to start American Fire. It's true crime. What are you up to?

Me: Watching my brothers set up to play poker. I think I'll head off to bed soon too.

Owen: You're not joining in?

Me: No. I'm rubbish at poker. I'm going to get an early night, maybe read in bed for a bit. Claire's going to bed soon and Mum's got one of her friends over. Ava hasn't made it—she's coming tomorrow instead.

Owen: I thought I saw Ava tonight. Her double was in the Wickentree when I met Ste.

Me: Who was she with? It could've been Ava. She likes it in there. Though according to her, a friend was having a meltdown so she was helping her.

Owen: I didn't get a proper look at said friend but if they were tall, male and dark haired then that was who she was with.

Me: Interesting. If it was my sister, then she's up to something.

Owen: It could've been a male friend who was having issues. She'll tell you when she needs to.

> Me: Unlike my brothers, you're too nice. I'll phone you in a bit. Just need to fail miserably at poker before they let me go to bed. Looks like I haven't gotten out of playing.

> Owen: Okay. Speak soon x

I knew I wasn't texting any of my other friends at this time on a Friday evening, just Owen. There wasn't any one I was going to call before I went to sleep, just Owen, and it wouldn't be the first time this week either.

And I knew I missed him.

"Texting lover boy?" Callum said, dealing the cards. I'd been coerced into playing, which happened whenever I was the last woman standing.

"I thought you were just friends?" Killian said. Eliza was strapped to his chest in a sling. He'd been allowed to stay up as long as he was on baby duty.

"We are," I said. "It is possible for a man and woman to be just friends."

"I agree," Callum said. "I just don't think it's possible for you and Owen. You look at each other like Jackson and Van do and we all know she's adding to the niece and nephew collection in less than nine months."

Jackson glared hard. Vanessa and Victoria had driven out to the twenty-four-hour supermarket to pick up some bits for tomorrow that Mum hadn't had chance to get. I missed the opportunity to go with them, which was unfortunate as I now had to put up with Callum's input into my love life.

"Just because she's not drinking doesn't mean she's pregnant," Jackson said. He looked at his card and his expression changed. He was a decent poker player so I figured it had nothing to do with his cards. "Okay, she's pregnant. I've been dying to tell you but please don't say anything apart from to Claire and Vic." He eyed me. "And Owen. We only found out this week so it's really early days and she's nervous."

"Congratulations, Jacks," Max said, putting his cards down and pulling Jackson out of his seat into a huge hug.

My eyes filled up as my brothers, Killian and my dad hugged Jackson. Seph looked ridiculously joyful.

"You told them, didn't you?" Vanessa stood in the doorway, Victoria just behind her and smiling broadly.

Jackson walked over to her. "They guessed. You weren't drinking so Cal put two and two together and managed to make four, which is good considering he needed a math tutor when he was at school." He wrapped his arms around her and I felt a pang of happiness and an ache that it wasn't me who had that connection with someone else who was here to hold me. "Let's hope the baby inherits my math skills and not his."

Vanessa shook her head. "Go make me a cup of tea. I've bought decaffeinated, and then you need to tell your mother before she finds out from Seph."

"Why does everyone always blame me?" Seph called loudly. By this time Eliza had woken up and was starting to cry.

Marie walked rapidly through the doors into the kitchen side, looking annoyed. "Joseph, do you need reminding to use your inside voice? You've woken the baby," she said, pointing which meant she was really cross at him.

"Yeah, but only one of them," Seph said. Jackson looked murderous.

Mum looked round the room from person to person, her eyes finally landing on Jackson and Vanessa. "Is he telling me something about you two?"

Jackson looked at Vanessa, his expression one of absolute

awe. "He is, Mum. It's very very early days though. We've only just been to the doctors."

Marie opened her arms and filled them with Jackson and Van and I heard another bottle of Champagne open.

"Oh fuck, more stuff I can't drink," Claire said, dragging herself into the room, looking like she'd just woken up. Her bed-hair was worth risking a photo for prosperity's sake.

"You're going to be an auntie," Jackson said before she'd even looked at him.

"I'm what?"

"I'm pregnant," Vanessa said.

Claire shrieked louder than Seph had shouted. My eardrums bled a little.

"Fuck it. I've expressed enough for more than twelve hours so I can have a glass to celebrate," Claire said, her eyes on Killian who nodded. Eliza was completely awake and staring at her daddy. I started to take a few photos, ignoring the glares some of my siblings sent over and accepted a glass of Champagne.

It was nearly two hours later when I finally got in bed, my latest read on my lap as I checked through my phone. It was still before midnight so I doubted it was too late to call Owen, but this late on a Friday night was definitely stepping out of friends' territory.

There'd been various references tonight to Owen made by my siblings and Vanessa and Victoria, and it seemed as if they already thought of us as being, well, an *us*. And I wanted him to be here. I felt empty without him, as if something had been removed from deep within me.

I clicked on my recent calls and touched his name. There were only a couple of rings before he answered.

"Hello, gorgeous," he said, his voice low and melodious. "How was poker."

"An announcement saved me from an ass-kicking," I said, tucking myself under the sheets. "Guess what it was."

He laughed quietly. "Seph's moving out of Max's?"

"No, don't be ridiculous. He'd only do that to move in with me."

"You've only got one bedroom."

"Seph's good with a sofa. But it's not that anyway."

"Tell me."

"Vanessa's pregnant," I said. "I'm going to be an aunt again. Hopefully this one won't have such a dramatic entrance. She's only just though—Jackson couldn't keep it to himself."

"I'm not surprised. He looked happier than normal on Thursday and got to practice a bit late because of an appointment. It all fits together now," Owen said. "You sound happy."

"I am. It's been an amazing evening." It had, but every couple of minutes I'd thought about him. He was filling me up with his words and his calmness and his Owen-ness. "I haven't phoned too late, have I?"

"No. It's good to speak to you. And I was reading. I'll pass it to you once I'm done. You'll enjoy it." His voice was full of sleep. I stretched out and felt the coolness of sheets.

"What are you doing tomorrow?"

"Meeting with one of the managers to go through some summer reading promotions and discussing a couple of author signings we have lined up, then I'm free. A couple of mates are meeting up in Brixton to watch a band so I might join them. What about you?"

My chest felt tight, my breath squashed. "I think we're just staying here. There's a barbecue planned for late afternoon. A couple of friends are coming over from London—Simone and

Amelie. Simone's the one with the restaurant. Do you want to join us? You don't have to if you don't want; I know you mentioned the other plans."

"Yes."

"Yes you don't want to join us?"

"Yes I'll join you. Will it be okay with your parents?"

I had been lying down in bed but now I was sitting up, feeling nervous, feeling as if I was about to go on a date. "Yes, they'd love to have you here."

"Shall I get to you about two? Will that work? I don't want you staying in all day waiting for me," Owen said. "And what gift should I bring your mum?"

I giggled, a noise I hadn't made since I was about sixteen. "Two's fine. I'm staying here tomorrow for the day—no plans to go anywhere unless we go to the Maker's Market in Oxford early on. You don't need to bring anything. You will be enough."

"That's not how Dot brought me up. Books? Would Marie like a book?"

My chest felt full and my eyes had moistened. "Yes. She loves books."

"Sorted. I'm going to go to sleep and if I don't go now, I'll end up talking to you all night."

"Same here. See you tomorrow."

"See you tomorrow. I'm glad we can say that."

I closed my eyes and tried not to think. If I started to hyper-analyse everything I'd end up not sleeping. Instead, I wanted to just look forward to him being here and getting to spend precious time knowing him more. That was all. That was all it needed to be. Especially if we had separate rooms.

I slept late, not just because I was tired after a busy week and the house was so quiet in the countryside away from the continual roar of traffic, but also because I was woken by my twin trying to turf me out of bed at two am, thinking I was in his room. Whoever had let him near the tequila—probably Callum—needed electrocuting, something I'd threatened to do quite happily.

After that, I'd slept soundly, missing breakfast and brunch. I also completely missed Simone and Amelie's arrivals. Even the noisy neighbouring rooster hadn't raised me from the sleep that was usually reserved for the newly dead. I slipped downstairs just after midday to find a glorious late spring day. The sun was full in a blue sky that was cloudless and full of promise and I felt the same sort of excited anticipation as I had when I was younger and felt that something special was going to happen.

Seph was mowing the lawn directly behind the kitchen and Callum was on the sit-on mower, going over the expansive grassy area that surrounded the house. My parents had a gardener who came regularly, but there were always jobs saved for Callum and Seph, especially when Marie knew we were coming.

My mother was weeding the herb garden she kept but rarely used to actually cook with. She smiled as she caught sight of me, a smear of dirt across her cheek. I decided not to tell her about it.

"You look well rested," she said, stretching.

"Is that another way of saying I've slept late?" I said, raising my brows. As kids, my dad had been fastidious at waking us before nine on a Saturday. I still didn't understand why.

She shook her head. "Not at all. You look much healthier than you did a few weeks ago. Your skin's clearer and your eyes are brighter. It's good you're looking after yourself."

"I haven't slept this late in years," I said. "I spoke to Owen last night. You're still okay with him staying?" I watched her face closely for her reaction.

She gave away nothing. "Totally. There's a room in the coach house that's made up already unless he's staying with you?"

"The coach house is fine. Where are Claire and the baby?"

"Gone with your father to see the house in the village that's for sale. Can you start lunch? There's a pot of soup on the go that needs blending slightly, not so that it becomes pureed. And there are cold cuts to put out and salad. Simone's just getting settled then she'll come and help too," she said, picking up her trowel. "I like Simone. It's a shame she's had such a bad time of it with men. Maybe if you're not interested in Owen, you could set them up on a date?" She smiled beautifully at me.

"Absolutely no way. And don't be telling anyone that I've said that. Give me time to get myself ready, mother." I picked a basil leaf and rubbed it between my fingers, the smell making me think of food.

This time her smile was gentle. "I won't say anything. But please don't keep the boy hanging on by a thread. It's not fair and there are other women out there who are good enough for him too," she said, smacking my hand. "And don't pick my basil leaves. Now, go help with lunch."

Simone was already in the kitchen, bustling around with balsamic vinegar and sea salt, and eyeing up a rather large knife which was disconcerting. She'd met us through Vanessa, whose marketing company she'd engaged to help with her newest restaurant and had since become part of our shared circle of friends.

"Hiya, Payts," she said, barely looking up.

"You sure you don't mind helping out? You do this all the time." I looked under near the lid to a large pot where it looked like Marie had made her summer vegetable soup that really only needed a little blending.

Simone shook her head. Her make-up was perfectly applied and her long dark hair was shining.

As the owner of two fine dining restaurants in London, Simone was obsessed with food, just not necessarily eating all of it. I already knew I couldn't be a chef. Any restaurant I had would run at a loss as I would literally eat all the profits.

"I really enjoy working with food and nowadays, other than creating the menu and designing the dishes, I rarely get to cook, unless I don't have a chef, and that doesn't happen anymore."

"Then feel free to knock yourself out. No one here will complain, least of all my dad," I said, finding the hand blender.

"Here," Simone said, taking the blender straight from me. "You don't need to use that. I'll sort the soup; can you chop the onions?"

And just like that I became the sous chef.

———

Owen arrived just as everyone was migrating inside for lunch. I found him next to the platter of Parma ham and prosciutto, creating some form of behemoth sandwich that was almost as attractive as him. "Nothing like coming over and saying hi," I said, creeping up behind him. He wasn't surprised, simply turning around and biting into the mouth-watering creation. My eyes were fixed on the food rather than him.

"I'd usually tell someone to get a room if they looked like you do," Victoria said, watching us. "But I think the phrase should be to get some food instead. You need feeding Payts, before you actually eat a person." I acted on the advice and filled my plate with far more than I knew I could eat.

My mother had already set her sights on Owen, commandeering him before he'd even manged to get half way through his sandwich. Her talk was the usual, asking how the journey was and what he'd done this morning, before launching into a discussion about books and what she was currently reading.

I left them to it, discovering the cheesecake that Simone had brought with her. It became partway through the afternoon before I had a chance to speak to Owen as he was dragged off by Seph and Callum to help with the mowing and then Max grabbed him to look at something mildly irritating on YouTube that they found hilarious.

"I think I've seen everyone but you," he said, sitting down next to me on the blanket I'd laid out the lawn so I could sprawl out and read in the sun. "It was like your family were doing their best to make sure we couldn't talk."

I put my book face down and turned to look at him. He was slightly sweaty and I figured he'd probably been participating in some stupid stunt given he had grass stains up his T-shirt. "What idiotic things have my brothers had you doing?"

He grinned wickedly. "We might have created an obstacle course. Your dad might not be happy with what's happened to the spare tyres for the sit-on mower."

"Do you never grow up?" I prodded his chest, hitting the solid muscle beneath the material and I felt a clench deep within me.

He lay down on his stomach next to me, stretching out. "It's such a warm day. I hear we're barbecuing later."

"Simone is. Or she's going to try to tell my dad and Maxwell what to do. That will also be the entertainment. You can't be hungry already though." I eyed him suspiciously.

"That was some obstacle course and I didn't have breakfast. I can wait though. What are you reading?" He picked up my book and started to have a look. "Did you buy this the other day?"

I nodded, closing my eyes and enjoying the sun. "It was from Cases. I haven't been cheating on you with other book stores, don't worry."

There was a chuckle and some rustling of material. I had a feeling that if I opened my eyes, I'd see a semi-naked man and I wasn't quite sure how I would deal with that without needing to lick him.

"I get the feeling you're a little more loyal than that."

"Stupidly so. I use the same brand of make-up even when there's a better deal on another type." My eyes were still closed.

"There's nothing wrong with that. Good choice of book, by the way. Not your usual read?"

I picked up a copy of *The World Broke in Two*, a non-fiction biopic about Virginia Woolf, T. S. Eliot and a couple of other authors.

"Occasionally I read something other than romance and crime. I read a lot of Virginia Woolf back in school and Eliot as part of my course, so this was something I was interested in. Have you read it?" I asked, finally opening my eyes and seeing him sitting cross legged and bare chested. I bit my lips together hard to stop myself from saying something inappropriate, given that most of my family were nearby.

"Not yet. It's on the to be read pile though, which is bigger than the Empire State at this point," he said. "I need a holiday. Somewhere hot where I can sit by a pool and read all day and have someone bring me bottles of beer with little umbrellas in them."

I spluttered at the picture. "Why beer and not cocktails?"

He flexed his pecs so the muscles moved. "Not manly enough."

"I'm not sure you have any trouble needing to be more manly."

"Is that a compliment, Ms Callaghan? I'm man enough for you?" His eyes danced and his grin was pure smoulder.

"Stop it. Else they'll think we're more than friends," I said quietly, noticing that the eyes of most of my brothers and Ava (who had just arrived) were on us.

His smile this time was knowing. "Payton, there's nothing about this that's *just* friends. You know that, right?"

I turned onto my back and shielded my eyes from the sun, my glasses out of reach. "I know."

"Thank God for that," he said, watching me like I was food that had already been marinated and barbecued. "But I get you don't want to go full on into one of those sickeningly sweet relationships like you read about in your favourite genre."

My twin decided now was a brilliant time to come over with a couple of beers. "Mum's making pitchers of margaritas for those who are allowed alcohol. Safety warning: don't go near Claire." He pointed towards our eldest sister who was clearly trying to instigate a law about no one else being able to drink if she couldn't and not getting a great deal of support. "Killian has threatened to lock her in the snug if she carries on. Apparently, she can't get out of there. I didn't ask how he knew. That was something I didn't want to have therapy for." He sat down next to me and yet again I wondered how he'd ended up with no idea how to read people. "That looks like a proper book you're reading, Payts. Not your usual sexfests."

I shook my head. "You could learn a lot from what's in those books, Joseph. You'd pick up some tips."

"Don't need any. I'm such a sex god I have a waiting list of women."

"A waiting list of women to do what? Castrate you, to save the disappointment of the next?"

He glared, stood up and gave me the finger. "You're not worth my time. Jackson!" And then he bounced, Tigger-like, over to the barbecue where Jacks was standing, beer in hand, inspecting the huge metal thing that was allegedly being used to ensure we didn't receive food poisoning.

"Back to what we were saying," Owen leaned back, his chest looking golden from the sun already.

I figured that the obstacle course had been done shirtless and was now sorry I'd missed it.

"Your favourite genre," Owen clarified.

I took a swig of beer. "I read romance books. And? I don't have anything lacking from my life. I have a wonderful family, good friends and a fulfilling career. I don't need Mr Romance to sweep me off my feet and into bed."

"Okay."

"I have a very good vibrator."

He choked on his beer.

"You prefer that to Sunday night? If so, can I have some feedback so I can improve my technique for next time?" He recovered quickly.

"Next time?" I smiled arrogantly. "Who said there will be a next time?"

"There'll be a next time. You've not turned me off sex completely, so there will be a next time. Might not be with you though."

I put my beer down before I dropped it. "That was... cold, Owen. Such rejection."

He started laughing, resting on his forearms, head up to the sun. The light caught the gold flecks in his hair and I wondered if I was staring too much. "I'm hoping the next time will be with you, if that stops you from feeling rejected." One hand took his weight and he used the other to move a strand of hair from my face.

I prayed my family weren't watching right now else they'd be shortening the odds on when we were going to officially be a couple, and that was pressure I didn't need. Not yet. "We can arrange some more benefits. I forgot to pack my vibrator anyway."

"I've got something you can use," Owen wriggled an eyebrow at me which made me begin to giggle. He could go from being Mr Sexy McDroolsome to a complete goofball in under two seconds and pull it off. "If you want a repeat performance, that is. And you didn't find it too unsatisfactory."

"You know I found it very satisfying. Shall I show you where my room is? You can sneak up there later if you need to prove that you're better for the task than the Purple Penis," I said, desperately trying to keep my hands to myself.

"I'm sure I can find your room. Just tell me which one it is," he said, his expression cocky.

I shook my head. "Seph has the one next to me. You really don't want to pay him a night time visit. He'd have a lot of questions…"

"Show me your room then. Although this is making me feel like I'm fifteen again."

We headed in, picking up another couple of bottles of beer on the way. Everyone was too busy to notice us for once as we slipped into the kitchen, through the huge open plan room to the stairs. I made a point of telling Owen who was in each room as we passed, until we got to mine. "This one," I said, tapping the door. "The one facing the Keeley Farmer painting." I pointed to the picture facing my door. "That's the sign for your booty call."

Then he turned suddenly, powerful arms capturing me

between him and the wall. "And what's my prize for following you here so you can show me the door of your room?"

I kept my hands by my sides and tried to ignore the heat I felt between my legs. "Certain benefits later."

"Can I preview one of those benefits now?"

My eyes dropped to his jeans. He was hard. I hadn't even touched him.

He took one hand and used a finger to lift my chin so I looked at him. "You were telling me about your Purple Penis, Payts. Where do you think that took my imagination?"

"I would've thought you might've started questioning your technique?" I said, digging a finger in his chest.

"It made me think about you lying on your bed with your legs spread, playing with that tight pussy and all I now want to do is be the only one who's playing with it. Every night this week I've lay in bed and jacked off remembering how it felt when you came around my cock." His words were a whisper. No one but me would be able to hear them, even if they were standing two feet away.

The finger that had poked him in the chest was now palm-flat on him, the other hand joining it, running over the contours of his muscles. He hadn't put his t-shirt back on and I didn't have the vocabulary to complain. Then lips pressed against mine and he took my mouth with his, probing with his tongue, demanding of me what he needed. My kind, sometimes geeky, bookseller was a pure alpha when he was on his own with me and I liked it.

His hands went to my hips and steadied me while his stepped closer, close enough that he could press his body against mine. "Every night, I've been this hard because of you. When I've made myself come, I've been thinking of how your tits feel in my hands; how your pussy feels when I'm fingering you; how my name sounds when you come around my dick. That's how hard you keep making me." He took one of my hands and squeezed it between us, pressing my fingers against his cock. I became wetter at the feel of its size, my body remembering how he'd stretched me so I fit all of him in.

"Now," I whispered. "We have time before dinner. I need you to fuck me."

He let go of me and took a step back, giving me that big dirty grin. "You'll have to wait, gorgeous. Maybe use your Purple Penis seeing as it's so good."

"Bastard," I said to his back as he walked off. "I'll lock my door later. I'll use that Purple Penis then instead of having you."

He turned around grinning. "You so won't. Friends don't lock each other out. And you know I'm better."

I bit my lips together and opened my bedroom door, needing to look less like I was on the verge of an orgasm before I joined my parents for dinner, cursing the man who had brought me to this state and wondering exactly what would happen when he did sneak into my room later.

CHAPTER 16
OWEN

Ignoring the woman you're desperate to be inside of is not the easiest task when she's sitting in front of you looking ripe for eating.

Payton had changed into a strappy blue dress that was fitted around her chest and barely made mid-thigh. She looked pretty and happy and so damn fuckable I spent the evening with an erection that was damn right painful. I cursed myself for not going with her into her bedroom because all evening all my fucking head kept going back to was how it felt to be in her, to have her pussy wrapped around my cock. I wanted to pound her deep until she called my name again. She had deliberately annoyed me, riling both of us and I only hoped she was as on the edge as I was because there was no way I wasn't going to her room when the house was quiet. Although that was possibly to apologise given I'd been nothing but friendly to her all evening, talking to her family and Simone, who was debating writing her own cookery book.

"Shall I get set up for poker?" Grant said. He'd already been told in no uncertain terms that if he wanted more wine, he wasn't allowed any more food. The look he'd received from Marie reminded me of Payton: feisty and fierce. I'd glanced at her then and found her looking at me, lips slightly parted and I knew she was thinking of earlier, outside her room.

"Not for me tonight," Jackson said. "We're heading for an early night." He leant over and kissed his wife who hadn't stopped smiling since I'd been here.

Max picked up another beer. "I'll have a couple of games. Owen?"

"Sure," I said, ignoring the eyes boring into my head. "As long as you accept books as payment."

"If they're antique, Vic would be more than happy," Max said, taking a seat round the small table in the corner that had been set up for the purpose of poker. Seph and Killian joined us, Grant staying next to his wife and shaking his head, muttering something about needing more alcohol in order to play. Callum had headed back early as an elephant was in labour and he'd been called back to the zoo, which he'd anticipated.

"I'll play," Simone said and I thought I saw Payton glare at her. Simone was classically beautiful. She reminded me of Amber to a certain extent, except she was less flighty and easier to talk to. We had spoken about using her restaurant as a venue for an author whose novel was based around food on a Monday evening when the restaurant was usually closed and that had led to a conversation around venues in general and how she was looking for a third premises. I'd caught Payton watching me then too, and figured that the whole being friends for her came with a large dolloping of being fucking jealous, which did my ego no harm.

"I'll join in too," Payton said, taking seat next to me.

She was terrible at poker; she didn't have the patience for it or the skills to keep her excitement hidden. After the third game she'd given up and announced that she was heading to bed. I played till the end, somehow managing to win a couple of rounds even though my mind was preoccupied by what she might be doing in her room, whether or not she was waiting for me, or whether I had pissed her off enough with my friends only routine.

"I'm heading to bed," Seph said, handing over the winnings to Killian, who'd had a successful night.

Killian stood up, grinning at Seph who he'd just creamed in the last round. "Thank you for your cash, Joseph," he said. "I've no doubt it will be spent on diapers or formula or muslins."

I laughed. "The joys of fatherhood."

"Wouldn't change it," he muttered. "Best thing ever, especially since I've had the night off. Night, fellas."

"Night," Seph said, following him to the door. "Try and keep the noise down with my sister."

"What?" I said, piling up the cards that had been left on the table. The rest of the place was immaculate. We'd been told to leave the cards and empty bottles till later. "I'm in a different room."

Seph laughed. "She's been giving you the eye all night. Even though you've been ignoring her. Thanks for that, by the way, best entertainment I've had for ages."

"Fucking idiot," I said to him. "Don't say anything to her."

"Why?"

"Because she wants to just be friends."

"And you don't?"

I stood up, headed towards the door. "No. I really like her. And not just as a friend."

He nodded. "Good. Just keep the noise down."

I hung on a few minutes so I wasn't walking with Payton's twin on the way to her room because that would've been just weird. The house was quiet, the open windows letting in some of the night time noises as foxes called and an owl screeched. I heard Killian talking to his baby daughter as I passed their room and became painfully aware of how quiet we'd have to be. If Payton wasn't really mad with me.

I didn't knock on her door, not wanting to wake anyone else up. If it was locked, she was pissed with me and I'd head back to the coach house. I twisted the handle and pushed slightly, opening the door to find my girl sitting at the window in her dress, reading. This time it was a romance, judging by the man on the cover.

"Took you long enough," she said. "Thought you might have gone back to your room."

I stayed near the doorway, hands in pockets and smiled at her. She was fiery and cross and absolutely fuckable. "You thought I'd forget about you?"

She shrugged. "You spent a lot of time talking to Simone."

"And I'm fickle enough to have you pressed up against a wall telling you how hard you make me then make a play for another woman?"

"Some men would."

"I'm not some men. I'm sorry if I've upset you but I knew you wanted us to just be friends in front of your family."

"I know. You seemed to be enjoying how it made me feel and that was a shitty thing to do."

I nodded. "It was. You're right. I knew you were jealous of me talking to Simone."

"So why did you keep talking to her?" she said then looked down. "Shit, that's not what I wanted to say."

"Come for a walk with me."

"What?"

"Let's go for a walk outside. To the stream. Your twin

knows I was coming to your room and knowing him he's got a cup to the wall."

"You know him so well already." She grabbed a jacket from the back of a chair. "Let's go."

We walked through the house in silence, ignoring the soft sounds that came from different rooms: laughter, a baby's cry. We were half way across the grass before I had my arm around her waist and felt her start to relax.

"Let's sit here," I said as we reached the flattened grass where me and her brothers had been acting like teenagers a few hours before. "I'm not interested in Simone. You know I'm interested in you and I'm not a dick who has more than one woman on the go at once. My mother would've shot me if I was like that."

She sat down in between my legs, her back to my chest. The dress she was wearing gave me full access to her tits and I was pretty sure she wasn't wearing a bra, but I tried not to focus on that right now.

"I'm so used to the guys I date being like that, Owen."

"Your brothers aren't. Killian isn't. I'm pretty sure you have male friends who know how to treat a woman."

She rested her head back against me. "You're right. My father isn't like that either so I've been brought up knowing what to expect from a man. I have high standards but all the men I've picked so far haven't lived up to them."

"Maybe I'm different." I so needed her to know that I was.

"Maybe you are. But I need to keep you at arm's length until I believe that you are."

I used a thumb to stroke her cheek, seeing her look up at me with those huge blue eyes. "Do I get a chance?"

"You're actually asking me something rather than telling me?" She laughed. "I bet that killed you!"

"I can let you be in control sometimes."

"Really?" She turned around and straddled me, fire

burning in her eyes. Near to us, the owl screeched again, another answering back. My hands went to her waist, steadying her. "Would you let me be in control right now."

"Right now, I'd probably let you control everything." I liked to dominate in bed, with words, actions, but I needed her to see I could let her share, that she had power too.

I watched, fascinated, as she slipped the thin straps from her shoulders, pushing them down and sliding her arms out, exposing her breasts to me and the air outside. We were far enough away from the house that no one would see us and I doubted anyone else was around, but there was still the risk of being caught.

"Can I touch you?"

"I'd be disappointed if you didn't."

My hands left her waist and cupped her tits, feeling their weight, teasing her nipples. "Can I taste them?"

She nodded and my head went to the right, teeth nipping and pulling gently, making her whimper. I used a hand to play with the left, stroking and pinching in time with the other and then I switched. Her hands were in my hair, pulling and gripping. I'd discovered on Sunday she liked to have her tits played with and I had wondered if she could come just from my doing that, but not outside, not right now. There were other things to discover.

"Can I touch your pussy?" I said, pulling back to see her face flushed, nipples hard and red.

"Where are your manners?"

I grinned. "Please can I touch your pussy?"

She knelt and pulled the dress up to her waist. She was bare underneath, no panties, no hair, just her arousal glistening.

"Does that mean I can, or am I just allowed to look?"

"You can touch. But you have to make me come. Do you know how to do that?"

I wanted to flip her on her back and push my cock straight into her, make her orgasm around me and I was pretty sure she wouldn't complain if I did. "I do. Will you take your dress off for me?"

She pulled it over her head and tossed it to the side leaving her naked in my lap. I didn't touch for a moment, just looked and looked. "You're fucking gorgeous. I think you're the most beautiful thing I've ever seen."

For the first time, she didn't argue or contradict me. Instead, she took one of my hands and guided it between her legs, putting my fingers at the opening of her slit. She was dripping wet and the very thought of pushing a finger in there was almost enough to make me come like a teenager. I teased, more to try to control myself than anything. "I can smell you," I told her, looking in her eyes, needing that connection. "Can I taste you?"

I flicked her clit with a finger and felt her shudder. "Yes."

Not something I needed permission for twice. I lay down and shuffled until her hot centre was above my face, guiding her pussy down on to my mouth, holding her hips. Her head was dropped to watch me as I started by sucking on her clit, then licking from back to front, one of my hands clutching her ass, my little finger nearing her puckered hole. I touched there and felt her jerk, but she said nothing, nor did she try to move, other than to encourage my tongue to roam again. "You taste like salted caramel," I said and she laughed. I licked again, harder and then sucked, repeating the action until it became a rhythm, her hips shifting in time and my little finger pressing slightly into her ass, her own wetness lubrication.

Looking up, I could see her playing with her tits, pinching her nipples and my mind went to the nipple clamps she hadn't found when she was rummaging through my stuff. I was pretty sure she'd like them. I sucked hard on her clit and she broke about me, my face flooded with her juices, her moans loud in the still air.

"Fuck," she said as she stilled, her breathing erratic. "Your face…"

I shifted up and sat, her hands going to my jeans and undoing them, pushing them down. I hitched my hips so she could free my cock, which by now had swollen hard. "What about my face?" I kissed her tits.

"It's got me all over it." She relaxed her legs so my cock brushed the entrance to her pussy.

"Do you want you to be all over something else?" I said, pinching her nipples a little harder than I had before.

"I want to fuck you," she said. "And I want you to come in me. Like you did on Sunday and Monday morning. I still had your semen coming out of me on Wednesday."

And damn if that didn't make me even harder.

"You going to sit on my cock, Payton?"

She grasped its base and guided it into her, inch by inch. I watched as I disappeared inside her, how she stretched to accommodate me, how her nipples went harder.

"Am I filling you, baby?"

She nodded, her mouth open in a tight circle. I wanted to fuck her mouth soon and then come on her, mark her as mine in some way at least.

"How does my cock feel? Is it good?" I was all the way in now and even in the moonlight I could see her flush, the redness of her chest and cheeks.

"It feels amazing," she said, breathless. "Help me move."

I grinned and held her hips, pulling her up and starting to move my hips. She was almost immobile, clutching onto my shoulders, arching her back so I could suckle a nipple. I felt her muscles contract around me and I bit sharply. She screamed my name as she came and I really hoped that her parents had their window closed.

"Can I fuck you now, Payton?" I slowed my rhythm, about to fill her with my come and wanting to make it last as long as possible.

She nodded, her hands gripping my shoulders. I lifted her onto her back, keeping my cock inside her still pulsing pussy and moved her legs over my shoulders. "Does this feel good? It needs to feel good. I'm deep in you."

"Feels. Like. Heaven." Her eyes stayed locked on mine and I began to move, deep in and then almost all the way out, slowly at first. I wasn't going to last long and I wanted to try and make her come again before I did, although I knew I was pretty much going to have to carry her back to the house. I changed my angle to hit the spot just inside her and upped the rhythm, her moans becoming deeper.

"I'm going to... I don't know what I'm going to... Fuck..." She started to spasm and jerk and I thrust in her harder and deeper, feeling my balls tighten. My hands went to hers, our fingers intertwining as I came deep and hard, filling her up, groaning her name.

I held her against me, the grass cool against my skin, my jeans and underwear somewhere around my ankles but I didn't care. She clung onto me as if I was life raft and she was drowning. "You okay?" I said, kissing her softly. "I've not hurt you?"

She shook her head slightly. "No. I'll be sore again. You're on the big side and I'm not used to you yet."

I liked the *yet*. It meant there would be more.

"How do you feel?"

"Like I don't want to let you go. Three orgasms have made me shaky. And emotionally needy," she said, her eyes on mine.

"I'm sleeping with you tonight," I said. "I'll sneak out in the morning if you want, but we don't have sex like that and not wake up together after. I'm needy too."

"Good. And you don't have to sneak out."

"Then I won't. Do I need to stay in the friend zone tomorrow?"

Her hand cupped my face. She looked fragile and soft and I needed her touch more than I could admit. "No. Please don't."

"I don't think I can be with you like this at night if I can't at least hold you in the day."

"You do hold me," she said. "Just not in the way you think. But, yes, I understand that."

We headed back to the house, her dress pulled over her untidily, my jeans hitched up. She kept giggling about my come dripping down the side of her thigh and I tried to be sympathetic when actually I was proud. Back in her room, I cleaned her up with warm water and a flannel and wrapped my arms around her waist as she brushed her teeth and washed her face.

Her bed was big and wide, but we took up just one side, as we entangled ourselves around each other, both still spent. I fell asleep wondering if I'd found the thing I had never realised I didn't have, but desperately wanted.

I woke with the bed covers pushed back and my dick in Payton's mouth, her hand around the base. I had no idea how long she'd been there, but I did know I wasn't that far off coming right down her throat. Her tits we there for the touching and behind her was a mirror, which meant I had an amazing view of her ass and pussy with the way she had positioned herself. I grabbed her head as gently as I could and pulled her from me, her lips puffy.

"Good morning," she said, keeping her hand on my cock and rising up on her knees. My eyes drank her in, as my hand went straight to her nipples, brushing them with my thumbs.

"Are you wet?" I asked, not stupid enough to think that giving a blow job was as much of a turn on for her as it was for me.

She nodded. "I woke up with your cock almost in me. It was the way we were sleeping."

"Turn around. I want to fuck you from behind."

I saw her pupils dilate and her nipples hardened into tight nubs. I grinned greedily; my girl liked being told what to do in bed as much as she liked being asked for it. She shifted onto all fours in front of me and I bent down to lick her pussy and around her ass. She was wet and slick and hadn't come yet, so I knew I'd have to go slow, especially in this position.

"Has anyone ever been here?" I asked, touching her puckered hole, pressing against it with a finger.

She gasped. "No. Never. And you're too big."

"Doesn't have to be my cock, beautiful. Lots of things we can use to give you more pleasure. You'll know that from your books." I moved my tongue so I could lick her clit and felt her quiver.

"Do you like it? You know, going there…"

"Yes," I said. "I'm male. But I like this too." I positioned my cock at her pussy and started to breach her entrance, hearing a long moan come from her mouth, watching her eyes close in the mirror. She looked fucking good with my cock in her.

Neither of us lasted long, even after last night. I sat back against the headboard, Payton between my legs, her legs spread, her arms wide. It was a carnal position as she hid nothing from me, not with the mirror there.

Looking at her, a post-coital flush across her body, my arms around her, I wasn't sure how I was going to go back to sleeping alone.

"Last night you were okay with us being more than friends. Is that still okay?" I said, kissing her neck.

She moved my hands onto her stomach, round her waist. "Given how noisy we've just been I think the people on either side of us are pretty clear we're a lot more than friends. I do need some space though, I don't want to panic and do something that hurts you… hurts us."

"I get that. I won't be full on."

She turned her head so we could kiss and my cock started to get ideas, ideas that weren't going to come to fruition given the banging at the door.

"We know you're awake, Payton, because we heard you. Does Owen want go to rugby practice?" It was Ava's voice that blasted through the door. "They're doing bacon sandwiches in the kitchen now too."

"I apologise for my family. You have no idea how much I wish I was an only child right now," she said as she buried her head in my chest. "Next Sunday, we'll have a morning where there are no interruptions."

I brushed my fingers through her hair. "There's no need to apologise, Payts."

"Are you alive in there or have you died from over-orgasming?"

"For fuck's sake!" Payton slid out of bed, pulling her robe around her. "Keep covered. She's probably got her phone out to get evidence." She pulled the door open and Ava practically fell through into the room, phone in hand. "Were you actually listening in?"

"Kind of. Not for the whole 'oh my, I'm coming so hard' thing. I didn't need to listen closely for that. The neighbours half a mile away heard you," she said and I wondered if I needed to apologise or at least look sheepish. Or if her brothers were going to use me as the rugby ball. "Morning,

Owen. There's coffee downstairs although I recommend a shower and clothes beforehand."

"Who heard us?" Payton said, biting her bottom lip. The gesture made her look adorable.

Ava laughed. "Just me and Seph. Claire, Mum, Vic and Vanessa have gone to look at that house again with the baby. And see another one because Jackson had one of his bright ideas at about six-thirty this morning. Dad and the others were outside doing something with the tyres that you lot used yesterday when you were at the height of your loudness." Payton glared at me. I grinned.

"We'll be down in twenty minutes," Payton said, pulling her gown tighter around her.

Ava smirked. "If you don't get distracted again."

"You're just jealous because you're not getting any," Payton said and I put a pillow over my mouth to try and stifle the laughter. It was like watching two teenage sisters.

"Who says I'm not getting any? You're just assuming that I haven't got someone secret tucked away." Ava strutted out of the room with Payton following, a dozen questions shooting from her.

Still laughing, I grabbed my jeans and T-shirt and headed out of Payton's room to mine, where all my clothes were. I didn't need space from her, but she needed the normality of her sister and family, and not just a new strangeness with me being there. Last night had been different. I liked sex; it was part of who I was and generally I didn't have any issues finding a partner. Short relationships, with an unspoken mutual agreement that it would indeed be short, had been my norm. Until now, until Payton; I hadn't met anyone where I didn't want it to be short term and last night had been more than just sex, for me at least and I thought for her too. And I hoped so; I really hoped so.

CHAPTER 17
PAYTON

In a previous life within this one, Wednesday mornings were usually reserved for my college friend, Aiden. We'd meet for a run round Burgess Park in Southwark, managing to get together at least every two weeks out of four, but since the visit to see my parents after my dad's TIA, it had become a more sporadic arrangement. A lot depended on where I was sleeping the night before and if her relationship was on or off, which very much depended on Saturn's alignment with the moon or something equally ridiculous.

It had been just over a month since the visit where Owen had joined us and things had changed. At breakfast that morning, he'd put an arm around my waist, kissed my cheek and made me coffee the way I liked it, the significance of which was wasted on no one. He didn't crowd me, didn't need to be in every conversation that I was and he gave me space, honesty and the hottest sex I'd had in my life.

Life had become easier somehow and I'd tried not to analyse how or why, just knowing that his presence seemed to help things fit: he was the shoe horn for a pair of shoes that were perfect in every way, just difficult to get on.

My dad's health had improved, work was simmering nicely although Eli was acting slightly weird and I was worried he was looking for a job elsewhere. He was a brilliant lawyer and if he was to get an offer we'd have to better it as I didn't know how my department would manage without him. I'd spoken to Jackson about offering a pay rise or even the opportunity to buy into the business and expanding what we did, although anyone who wanted to join our particular brand of insanity needed to be certified first.

And Max still hadn't proposed to Victoria, although we all knew it was coming.

My Wednesday morning run had been changed to Thursday as Aiden was staying at her current boyfriend's, although they had been having emergency talks when she messaged me last night.

As a treat, I stopped in Amelie's café near to the Callaghan Green offices for a pastry and coffee. My pastry addiction had been replaced with a sex one, or more specifically with Owen's cock, fingers and mouth as I found I craved less sugar. That was a scientific study for the future.

Amelie had been a family friend since I was a little girl, although she'd had little to do with them since she'd been eighteen and her father tried to arrange a marriage to enhance his business connections. Her family were old money, the sort that Jane Austen might have written about, or even Dickens. Amy, as Max called her, had been semi-adopted by us and at one point, I'd thought she and Max might had got together but she had more sense than to take on my grumpiest brother.

A familiar figure was sitting at one of the tables, one that made me smile and head towards the spare seat facing him.

"Morning, Dave," I said, sitting down. "I didn't realise you came in here."

"I've a meeting at the Shard in about half an hour. I

remembered you and Owen talking about this place so thought I'd give it a try."

I'd met Dave a few times over the last few weeks, including dinner one evening when Owen had needed to go through some business details with him. Dot hadn't been on any more dates recently, seemingly happier to see friends and run evening reader groups at Cases on a more frequent basis. Owen had a theory that she was writing a book herself but he hadn't asked, instead offering to help set her up more dates, which she'd declined.

"It's good," I said as Amelie brought my latte over. "How are you?"

"Busy with work. How's Dot? I still haven't heard from her." He looked sad.

"She's okay. She's busy with the shops and her book clubs."

"Any more dates?"

I shook my head. "No. Owen's suggested a few people but she's outright refused and she's got rid of the dating apps she was using. Have you been on any?" He was an attractive older man, with an excellent job. He was interesting when he wasn't looking so down.

He shook his head. "No. I'm miserable, to be honest. I've sent her a couple of messages but she hasn't replied. I think she's moved on."

"Maybe," I said honestly. "You haven't seen each other for a while." I had an idea, a glimmer of one, one that could also go horrendously wrong. "Are you busy Friday night?"

"Why?" he said, which was exactly the question I would've asked.

"There's a gig on at Cases in Soho, some band Owen's friends with, and Dot's going as a guest rather than working. How about I set you up on a blind date?" The pastry I'd ordered landed in front of me, delivered with a beaming smile from Amelie.

"How can it be a blind date if I know who I'm meeting?"

I rolled my eyes. I knew him well enough by now to not need my filters. "Blind for Dot. Let me work on her. She'll agree. At least that'll give you chance to talk, which it seems you've not been able to do."

He nodded. "I get it. What if she storms out and won't talk?"

"Then that's over to you. But you'll be in a big area with people that she knows, so she's unlikely to cause a scene." Which I knew she was perfectly capable of doing. I'd seen her in action once when Owen had pushed it a bit too far with how he'd criticised Dave. Dot was no longer talking about Dave and wouldn't entertain any criticism of him either, which was interesting and I had a feeling that if we could just get the two of them together, she might reconsider their relationship.

He nodded. "I'll try anything. And I'd just like to see her again, you know? Let me know if she refuses."

"She won't," I said. "I'm still new enough and she's trying to be as nice as she can to her son's new girlfriend, that if I ask her she won't say no."

"That's very manipulative."

"I'm a lawyer."

He laughed. "True. How well are you doing with manipulating Owen?"

It was my turn to laugh. Owen wasn't someone who could be manipulated. He could be persuaded and was keen to always try to understand my feelings but the moment I tried to sway him through some deceptive means, he would fold his arms and raise his right eyebrow. He was my safe space. "Not very. The man knows his own mind too well. Something I wouldn't change."

"He's a good man," Dave said. "I was worried he'd stay with his ex when she clearly wasn't right for him. They were really good friends but were together because it was easy and they looked the part."

"Amber?" I said. I'd heard bits about her, seen the odd photo of a beautiful woman with him on holiday and at a formal dinner. They'd been together since Owen had done his Master's degree, both studying business and computer programming. She'd become some high-tech app developer acting as a consultant and they could've been a power couple, but Owen said it just wasn't there. She'd come home from work one day and told him she'd met someone else and they were better off as friends. He'd agreed. No argument. No row. And they'd parted ways.

"Amber," he said. "She was a nice girl but she didn't make his eyes light up like they do when he's with you. When you met us at that restaurant last week, his whole face beamed when you came over. It was good to see."

I smiled, feeling reassured.

My day at work was fairly light, which was a relief given how busy Monday and Tuesday had been. Monday had involved a full day in court while Tuesday had been a mediation that had gone on for over fourteen hours. Fortunately, the resolution was favourable to us, so that sweetened the fatigue I'd felt going home. I hadn't seen Owen since Monday morning and it felt like too long already. I swung by Amelie's and picked up the biggest sub she made and headed over to Cases at St Paul's, knowing he was using the office there to answer emails and deal with an issue caused by one of the distributors.

It was June and warm, which seemed to make everyone

more relaxed and less impatient to get where they were meant to be. Around the St Paul's area were businesses, with fewer tourist attractions other than the bijoux shops and stores. I loved my city when it was like this, relaxed with that hint of a buzz of excitement.

Cases had its doors open, the scent of coffee wafting down as soon as I entered. I mooched about, looking at the just released and bestsellers, debating picking something up to read this weekend as for once, my diary wasn't packed, and then I saw Owen.

Spending four or five nights a week together had become the norm. We stayed in, watched Netflix and binge-watched different box sets, took trips out to see parts of London neither of us had explored and ate out. We saw my siblings and his friends and we'd found what was our happy place. But neither of us had put a label on it. In bed, he was dominant, playing my body like he played his guitar; he knew exactly what to press, to pluck, how hard or how soft and he'd tell me I was his, using all his dirty words and sometimes toys.

But we'd not called ourselves anything. No one had declared exclusivity and we hadn't been out on what either of us had termed a 'date'.

So when I saw him sitting at a table with a brunette with long curly hair and legs that looked like they went on for months, never mind days, my chest exploded into my mouth. He was leaning across towards her, talking animatedly and smiling in broadly. It was what I'd termed 'full charm mode' but the brunette was interpreting it as flirting. She toyed with her hair then reached for his arm, her finger sliding up his forearm.

My lips began to throb from biting them that hard. Owen hadn't noticed me and I'd slunk behind a bookcase so I could watch without being noticed. I felt like I was about to have a heart attack; the blood was pumping around my body so hard my ears were throbbing. I didn't know what to do. Had I seen any of my exes like this I'd have walked away and said nothing, calling the end there and then, but I couldn't read this. I pulled my phone out of my purse and snapped a photo, sending it to Ava. Apart from being flighty and sometimes downright weird, she was practical and level-headed when it came to men and relationships.

My phone rang twenty seconds later. "Okay, is he still with her?"

"Yes," I said. "I don't know what to do."

"But you haven't walked out of there so you must want to do something. Is he touching her at all?"

"No, and when she tried to touch his arm he moved away. Not quickly but subtly. Ava, what do I do?" I said, hearing desperation in my voice.

"How does it feel to be jealous?" she said and I heard the laughter in her voice. "You don't know who she is. She could be an author, or a singer, or a publisher. Go over there. Go say hi. If it's business, he'll say. If it's personal, you'll be able to tell. But there's no point in speculating because you don't have a clue when you're hiding behind a bookcase."

"I'm not jealous!"

"Yes you are and that's healthy as long as it doesn't become problematic. Go speak to him. Put your big girl boots on and get over there. I'll see you this evening." She hung up and I knew she wouldn't answer if I rung back.

Still holding the book I'd picked up, I moved into the section where there were tables of promotions just before the coffee shop. Owen almost immediately looked up and stood, leaving the brunette mid-sentence. She glowered at me briefly, diverting her eyes when he walked towards me.

"Payton," he said, immediately bending down to kiss me as he became close enough. His lips were gentle on my cheek, lingering just long enough so it was obvious that he wasn't kissing a friend. His voice dropped to a whisper and he stayed close. "I'm really glad you're here. I think she's trying to eat me alive."

"Who is she?"

"An author. Apparently she's written the next big thing in literary fiction. Mum's not here else I'd have switched with her. Come sit with us. Please." He touched my waist, gently and discreetly because he'd kept his word about giving me space, especially when we were in public.

'She won't mind?"

"I hope she does." He took my hand and led me over, the brunette's stare becoming stronger and harder.

"Livi, this is Payton, my girlfriend," he said, pulling out a chair for me and glancing at me with the word girlfriend. "She's a partner over at Callaghan Green, if you've heard of them."

Livi smiled falsely. "It's good to meet you. I wasn't aware Owen was seeing someone."

Owen's expression was its usual serene self. "Maybe you didn't hear when I said my girlfriend was a reader and she'd be interested in your book. I don't want to keep you too long, Livi. Is there anything else you're concerned about before the book launch?"

"Will you be arranging it?" she said. "My publisher said that the owner would be overseeing everything."

Owen shook his head. "I'm away that evening. Dot Anders will be overseeing everything but the manager, Cal Griffiths is more than capable."

Her head swung round to me. "Callaghan Green—isn't that the firm where some of the partners are brothers? They were in a magazine last year? Three really attractive men in suits?"

I wasn't sure whether she was trying to make Owen jealous or find a way in to meet the 'really attractive brothers'.

"Yep," I said simply with a smile that I tried to make seem friendly. Owen's hand brushed my legs under the table. I knocked my knee against his and saw him smile.

"How do you work with that amount of hotness around you all the time. They're what fantasies are made of," she said full of enthusiasm. "And so rich too."

I could sense Owen struggling to keep from laughing.

"I have no issue working with them as they're my brothers," I said, digging my nails into my hands. "And even if they weren't, I'm a professional and try to act that way, so I wouldn't be entertaining a work place fling just because someone was hot or rich. It could be too damaging."

She looked at me blankly and I wondered whether I'd just responded to her in Spanish.

"Well, maybe you could bring them with you to the launch party. I'd love to meet them," she said, casting her eyes back to Owen, as if I had been dismissed.

"We'll make sure invites are sent out to the right people," Owen said, leaning forward over the table slightly. "Your publisher has already given us a list and we've agreed on the catering, so everything should be taken care of." He stood up and offered his hand. "It's been good to meet you."

"You too. Should I take your mobile number, just in case…"

Owen shook his head. "You're best contacting me via email as I'm not always able to answer."

"Sure, no problem," she shook his hand limply and gave me a watery smile. "See you soon."

We watched her go, Owen's hand on my leg under the table. "You were jealous, weren't you?"

"No, I didn't even spot you until you called my name…"

He laughed loudly. "Bullshit, Payts, I saw you as soon as

you came in and waited for you to come over, but you went and hid behind the crime books."

I strummed my fingers on the table. "I brought you a sandwich." I reached for the paper bag and passed it him. "Thought it'd make a change from work food."

"Thank you," he said. "You were so jealous."

"You sound very pleased at my jealousy." I decided not to argue.

"It's made my day," he said, then took a large bite into the sub.

I looked at him, worried, anxious and utterly confused. "I thought a girl being jealous is a big turn off?"

"Who told you that?" he said, swallowing what had been a hug bite.

"An ex. I asked him once what he'd been doing with another girl and he accused me of being jealous, then told me how much of a turn off it was."

Owen put the sandwich down and grabbed my hand, pulling it under the table and onto his crotch where his cock was hard. "Now do you think I'm turned off?"

I gave a quick grab and moved my hand back to the table before anyone became suspicious. "That's because I was jealous."

"So you admit it?"

"If you want me to ever touch your dick again with any part of my anatomy move on from revelling in me being jealous."

He laughed, his sandwich back in hand. "Because it means you're invested and I want you to want this as much as I do. If I'd come into your offices and seen someone pawing at you like Livi was with me, I'd have used them for rugby practice."

"Oh, okay. I get it." I felt warm from my toes to the top of my head and was aware I'd probably flushed pink. "You really want this."

"I really want you. And not just for the nights. I want you for the days as well." His arms moved around my shoulders and I leaned into him. Affection between us in front of my family or his mum hadn't been an issue, but we tended—or rather I tended—to be more reserved at his work or while we were out. He kissed the side of my head and for a moment we just sat there, two people, a couple. "Are you busy tonight?"

"I'm going to Ava's. It's mine and Seph's birthdays at the end of June and she wants to plan something. I made her swear that this year she'd let me get involved rather than it being a total surprise," I said. "Maybe we could have it in one of your stores." I wanted to take the words back as it was a presumptuous thing to say.

But Owen just gave me his perennial grin. "I like that idea. Would she mind me coming with you?"

"Not at all. Do you want to meet me there or…"

"I'll see you there. I should get back to work. I need to ring Livi's agent about the details and I might just mention how tactile she was. It's not a good thing to be in this industry."

"Okay, I'll see you at Ava's."

He took the book I'd chosen from me and promised to bring it later, wandering off and leaving me with a smile on my face and feeling both ease and excitement. Everything was going to be more than okay.

"Just a sec!" The voice was unquestionably Ava's, her yell louder than most church bells and seemingly coming from just as high up. She was currently living in a townhouse in Southwark that she had renovated and redecorated. It would be going on the market sooner rather than later, as being typical Ava, she was bored of living somewhere she'd finished and she wanted to live in a dump again.

"Have you been napping?"

"Totally. You were late so I made the most of it." I heard crashing and decided not to ask, instead trying the door and finding it open. Ava was being security conscious, as usual.

There was swearing and another loud bang and then a voice that sounded familiar but I couldn't place. "Ava? Are you okay?" My imagination ran to the place where Ava was actually being held hostage in her own home and I started to climb the stairs.

"I'm fine, Payts, don't come up. It looks like a bomb's gone off up here." Something else banged.

"Are you sure you don't want any help?"

"Absolutely."

"Why's it so untidy?"

Ava emerged at the top of the stairs, wearing a robe, her hair piled up on top of her head. "I'm starting to pack."

"The house isn't on the market yet," I said, surprised. I knew she was planning on moving soon, but not quite this quickly.

"Had an offer that was too good to refuse." She smiled and pointed to the living room. "Let's talk in there. What happened with Owen? You're smiling, so I'm assuming everything was cool."

I gave her a brief rundown of what happened, including Livi's suggestive comments about our brothers, which made Ava laugh. "Where are you staying between houses then?"

"With a friend. Let's talk birthdays. I was thinking about something at Cases…"

"Which friend?"

"Oh, just someone you don't know that well—"

"Is it a man?"

"Yeah, but—"

"Are you moving in with someone?"

Her face paled and her mouth froze into an 'O'. "It's just a friend, Payts and we need to leave it at that. If you ever find out you'll understand why I'm being cagey about it. But you won't find out because it's not going anywhere."

"You want me to drop it?"

"Please. Everything is more than fine and I'm happy, but I really need you to not say anything about this. Please." She looked more desperate that I'd ever seen her.

"Is he treating you well?" I'd seen her in relationships before where she'd let men get away with a little more than she should.

"Too well." Her eyes shone. "Birthdays. Let's plan."

Owen arrived shortly after seven pm with a bottle of Champagne and two pizzas. He was wearing the same outfit as before and looked tired.

"Busy day?" I leaned into him to kiss him. He responded with surprise as it was usually him who would greet me this way.

"Too busy," he said, sitting down on Ava's velvet Chesterfield that she had reupholstered herself. "Livi Mason's got form for trying to grab people by the privates. I spent about an hour on the phone to her agent and publisher. She's a liability if she acts like that with someone from the media."

"Don't you think she'd have more sense?" I said, hearing the pop of a cork as Ava opened the Champagne in the kitchen.

Owen shrugged. "What've you planned so far?"

"Are you okay about using Cases?"

He nodded. "How many people?"

"Around fifty," I said. "It really is family and close friends. You won't need extra insurance."

"How about catering?"

"Simone," Ava said. Her back door slammed shut. I raised my eyebrows, suspicious of exactly why the door had just banged. "That was nothing. Just the wind."

Owen looked at me frowning. I shrugged.

"Simone's doing the catering, or rather, one of her underlings is in charge of making sure everyone's stomach's lined. Do you know a singer who we could hire?" Ava said, as if there hadn't been any strange signs that someone else had been in the house at all.

"I can find someone. You want background music?"

I nodded. "Nothing expensive or famous or anything like that."

"Do you celebrate everyone's birthdays like this?" Owen looked between us, curiosity in his expression.

"No," I said. "Mine and Seph's was the first birthday when everyone was home from university so our parents tended to use it as an excuse to get everyone together. It's just stayed like that. When we were younger, people would go on holiday during July and August and we'd not have chance to all meet up until Christmas. And now it's tradition."

"It's a good tradition," he said softly.

I saw Ava roll her eyes. "If you two are going to eat each other can you pass me the pizza first?"

CHAPTER 18
PAYTON

"You look..." Seph looked at me with narrowed eyes. "Rested."

"I'm not sure that's what you actually mean," I said, walking behind where he was sitting at his desk. "Be more direct."

"When's the last time you stayed at your apartment?" He quickly changed the tab on his browser and I became automatically suspicious. This was him trying to deflect from what he was actually doing, because Seph had never kept tabs on where I was sleeping, unless he was concerned.

"Why? It was Tuesday night and it's only Friday. Are you concerned about Owen?" I needed to ask the question else I'd be worrying about it all day.

He swivelled round on his chair and I glanced at the tabs at the top of his screen. "No. I like him. He was at training last night and he was on good form. He said you were going out for dinner."

"We went to Simone's. Finally. What's your concern?"

Seph shook his head. "I'm happy for you. He's a good

guy. I'm not sure he deserves you entirely, but then again I don't know what he needs punishing for."

I smacked the back of his head. "Arsehole. Why've you got a dating website up?" He thought he'd got away without me noticing. Apart from work, where no one got one past Seph, he was notorious for thinking he'd fooled people when actually he'd still been blatantly obvious. "I can see the tab, Seph. Struggling to fool ladies into going home with you?"

He reddened, the same tone I coloured when I was embarrassed or turned on. "Actually, I'm fed up of meeting girls in bars and it just being one night. Family gatherings are getting a bit weird, given that only me and Cal are single. Everyone else has a plus one and you all look so fucking happy," he said, swearing which was unusual for Seph unless he was drunk, which wasn't unusual.

"Ava. Ava's not properly dating anyone." I pulled up his other office chair and sat down. "What do you know? She's up to something, I just don't know what."

He pushed his chair away from his desk. "Not much. She's become secretive. The other weekend when we were all at Mum and Dad's and she came on the Saturday because her friend was having a bad time—I don't think that was true."

"Owen thinks he saw her out that night with a dark haired man," I said. "And she came over later in the afternoon and left early, which is unlike her. She's selling the townhouse."

"I know. I'm buying it."

My hands clutched the sides of the chair. "What? I didn't know this. Why?"

He shrugged. "Only Ava knows. It's an investment. I'll rent it to professionals. I've told her there's no rush for her to move out though."

"When I was there on Wednesday she was already packing. And someone else was in the house with her. He sneaked out the back. She told me she was seeing someone, but it wasn't serious and we couldn't know about him. She said if I knew who it was, I'd understand why. She's moving in with him too, although she says it's temporarily."

"It is. She's found her next flip, or the one she'll live in for a bit. It's uninhabitable at the moment, so there will be a delay before she can shift in there. Why's she not telling us who he is?" Seph said. He looked hurt and I remembered that as much as he was a hot shot lawyer who had a reputation already, he was the most sensitive of all of my siblings.

"It's someone she knows we won't approve of. Either someone we know, or he's older or he's a troublemaker. We have to trust her though, Seph. She'll tell us when she's ready. Or when she needs us." I stepped over to him and batted a hand at his perfectly groomed hair.

"Oi! Stop it!" He tried to grab my hand, but I just added my other and managed to disturb the well-glued style he'd groomed his hair in to. "I might have a date after!"

"Let's see then. Who's made the shortlist?"

He clicked on the tab and we started to look through the photos and bios of various twenty to thirty somethings who had made it through my twin's filters, laughing at some of the comments and pictures, several of which had been through too many filters.

"She looks like your ex," I said, pointing to the picture of a pretty dark haired girl with large green eyes.

"Yeah, don't need to relive that."

"Do you miss her?" I asked. They'd been together from when they were twenty to last year and although none of us were ever convinced she was right for Seph, she'd kept him level and calm. My brother was best when he was in a relationship; it made him feel secure and he liked having someone to care for. I had suggested a pet, but seeing as he struggled to feed himself some mornings, my idea was vetoed.

"I miss the idea of her, but not what she actually was. I'm fed up of one night stands though. I don't know how Callum does it. Three different girls last weekend. He's probably diseased." Seph looked repulsed. "At some point Cal's going to meet someone and fall hard. I can't wait. Hopefully, she'll walk all over him and he'll get a taste of his own medicine."

"That was very bitter for you."

Seph shrugged. "It's living with Max and Vic. They make each other happy."

"Even when she loses her temper at him and he goes into bear mode?"

"I think they enjoy that. I am looking to move out, you know?" he said. "I know everyone thinks I crashed their party, but I really couldn't stay living on my own anymore."

My heart broke a little.

"You could've stayed with me," I said. "I know it's only one bedroom but we could've managed it somehow."

Seph smiled and hugged me into him. "I know. But Max and Vic own a six bedroomed monstrosity. You've got a one bed apartment with a kitchen-diner and one bathroom. It was never going to work."

"You want to live on your own now though? What's changed?" I said gently. He was a thinker, my twin, sometimes too much of one.

"I'm going to buy something that needs a bit doing to it. Not one of Ava's demo jobs, but something that needs redecorating, a new kitchen, bathroom—that sort of thing. Then I've got something to focus on and it'll be mine." His face was bright and I could see the genuine excitement.

"When did you decide this?"

"When you were being swept off your feet. I've been thinking about what to do for ages. Max's was temporary. This feels like the right thing to do. Speaking of which—

haven't you got work to be doing or has love addled your brain so you don't know how to lawyer anymore?"

"I'm not in love with him. It's not that serious," I said, laughing.

Seph shook his head and closed his browser. "You're in denial."

"No."

"Yes. And don't forget, the last time we had a yes/no argument we were eight and I won, so give up now."

"There's absolutely no logic to what you've just said."

"That's fine. But you're in love with Owen and denying it won't make it any less true," he said, pulling a file out of his desk drawer.

I really did have work to do, but right now I needed to put my brother right on how I felt.

"I can't be in love with him. I haven't known him long enough."

"Because that matters? Look at Mum and Dad and how long they knew each other before she came back to England with him. You're just scared."

I didn't respond. "I'll see you later. I need to get onto Paul Janelle about the Scriver case."

"Chicken!" he called to my back as I left the room.

I didn't think I was in love. How do you describe an emotion? Poets and novelists and songwriters had been trying to describe love for centuries, maybe longer, and clearly no one had succeeded because they were still trying to do it. I thought I felt more for Owen than friendship and lust, that the bubbles in my stomach before I met him for dinner or coffee were more than just indigestion, but love?

Confirmation of this would not come from a legal document or Google, so instead I phoned Claire. My elder sister would give me a straight to the point answer with no bullshit. She answered on the third ring, a gurgling baby in the background.

"Claire, how did you know you were in love with Killian?"

There was a sharp intake of breath. "Oh holy fuck. You're having a moment, let me sit down." I heard rustling and a muttering of some sorts to the baby. "Right, what did you say?"

"How did you know you were in love with Killian?"

"That's what I thought you said and wished you hadn't. It's a really difficult question and if you're looking for a precedent, it might not happen."

"Why?"

"I knew I was in love with Killian the first time when we were at college because he was the centre of everything. I wanted to be with him, I thought about him all the time, he made me happy," she said. "The second time, I knew I was in love with him because I didn't want to murder him anymore."

"That doesn't help."

"Didn't think it would. Do you think you're in love with Owen?"

"I don't know. Seph thinks I am."

"Seph's probably right. You shared a womb. He knows everything about you. Tell me your symptoms."

I inhaled deeply and closed my eyes. Saying the things I thought aloud made them real, factual and not something I could as easily dismiss.

"I look forward to seeing him and if I'm not seeing him I miss him. I feel lonely if I'm not with him in the evenings, even if I'm with a friend. I feel happy and settled when we're together. I don't want him to be with anyone else, and I don't think I want to be with anyone else either."

"Tell me about his faults."

"He's quietly bossy and can manipulate anyone. He's obsessively tidy. He's a workaholic although he'd never admit it. He's a mummy's boy. Shall I carry on?"

"Do his faults bother you?"

"No. Do K's bother you?"

Claire laughed. "Only when I need them to. Love's a strong emotion. It knocks you over and pulls you by the hair into a ditch where it stamps on your face with unicorn shoes. It makes your heart centred around one person and gives them the power to determine your happiness. Yes, I know happiness is a choice and all that crap, but sometimes you meet someone and you let them have a little bit of control because they're worth it. They make your world worth living in."

"He does."

"Does what?"

"What you've just said. He makes my world worth living in." I remembered I was talking to my sister, who was just as sensitive as Seph in her own way. "As does my family, but he compliments that."

"Tell him."

"What?"

"Tell him how you feel. See how it is to say the words." A loud roar almost deafened me. "Got to go. The sleeping banshee of London has awoken."

I had planned what I was going to say. Kind of. I had never told anyone I loved them, even the couple of boyfriends I'd been serious about and I was more nervous about this than the first time I'd been in court. That had been successful; this I wasn't one hundred percent confident about. I thought I knew what his response would be, but I couldn't predict it based on precedents and previous cases.

I wore a floral print dress and cowboy boots, aiming for the boho look and wishing I'd called Ava over to help me get ready, or at least give me a decent confidence boost. Every possible response to what I wanted to tell him had gone through my head and I was greatly considering retreating back to my almost single forever mode.

We were meeting at Cases in Soho for the acoustic set that one of Owen's friends was playing. Dave was meeting Dot there at eight pm, and I was interested to see how they got along and whether she'd speak to him or storm off to the offices in the back. Dot was already there when I arrived, sitting at the bar with a glass of red wine and a suspicious look on her face.

I approached with some caution, having spent enough time with Owen's mum that she was no longer on her best behaviour with me. She eyed me accusingly. "This had better be good, Payton. I've worn my best shoes."

I glanced down. She wore a pair of Irregular Choice heels that were red with hearts decorated them. They were eye-catching, while the rest of her outfit was fairly casual—skinny jeans and a tuck in blue shirt. She didn't look like she could be Owen's mum, but the one time I'd mentioned that I'd been treated to a lecture in feminism, the media and expectations. Owen had sat there and looked amused while eating a bag of popcorn. I'd retaliated by delaying his orgasm significantly later on.

"If you aren't enjoying yourself, you know enough people here to turn it into a gathering rather than a date."

"Hmmmm," she said. "We'll see. The fact you suggested it after Owen's series of disasters gives me hope."

I shuddered slightly, knowing exactly who was going to be on the other side of the lecture when she found out who her blind date actually was. "I just hope you have a good evening." *And you don't kill me afterwards.* "Have you seen Owen?"

"He was sorting something out with Vinny. I think he's going to play guitar for him for a couple of songs, which means you can chaperone me and my date. You both have got so good at it, you know?" Dot's lips pursed in a knowing smile.

"I'll have a glass of wine." I caught the eye of Amanda who was manning the bar with Ped. I'd met them a few times over the past few weeks. "A large one."

I was about three sips in when I saw Dave approaching. There were already a few people in for the gig, which was due to start at eight-thirty, but he was early. I sensed a change in Dot's demeanour and felt a finger dig my side, hard enough so that I nearly spluttered my wine.

"What did you say the name of my date was?"

"I didn't. I just described him."

"Tall. Dark haired with flecks of grey and an athletic build. Business man and entrepreneur. Brown eyes, cheekbones. I remember. What you didn't say was that his name was Dave and he's my ex," Dot said, through gritted teeth. "Does he know he's meeting me?"

"He does. He really wanted to see you."

"Does he think it's a date?"

"That was how I described it. And given what he's wearing, he's dressed for a date," I said, turning to watch her expression.

"Well, I never," she said, eyes identical to Owen's fixed on the poor man coming straight towards us. "He's not wearing a suit. This must be the first time I've seen him in public without a suit on for about ten years."

"He looks good," I said, meaning it. Dave was older, but he was attractive and Dot seemed to have remembered this.

"He does. I'll speak to him. Then I'll speak to you. And my son because I assume he had something to do with this."

Dave finally reached us, fiddling with with his collar and looking apprehensive. "I'll leave you to it," I said, picking up my wine and slipping off the bar stool. "Hi, Dave." I gave him an encouraging smile.

"It's good to see you, Payton. And it's good to see you too, Dot," he said. "You look great. I like the shoes."

I saw her preen from the corner of my eye and slipped away towards the area near the makeshift stage. The usual Chesterfield sofas and tables had been moved, and a microphone had been placed in the centre with a few old school benches for people to sit on if they wished. The lighting had been altered, becoming dimmer, more atmospheric and a large number of people had filtered past the doormen, the chess pieces set for the evening.

"Hey," a very familiar voice rang from behind me. "Mum's not killed Dave yet. I've just seen them talking."

I turned around and felt something burst inside me, trickling through every fibre and into every vein. "Hey," I said, reaching a hand out to touch Owen, needing to feel his warmth on my skin.

He grinned his trademark smile and pulled me into his chest. "Do I get to take you home tonight?"

"I hope so," I said, wrapping my arms around him as he bent down to kiss me.

"Good," he said. "I wanted that to be the answer. Or just 'yes'. I'm going to get drinks for Vinny and Amber. Don't pay for anything at the bar."

Blood left my head and arms, pumping too fast for it to actually feel like it was staying anywhere. The only Amber he'd mentioned had been his ex. I knew there was a chance that this Amber was a friend, or someone he knew through Vinny or Vinny's band, but rationalising anything wasn't working. I wanted to run, to turn around and head to my brothers who were at Simone's restaurant or to Ava, who I was pretty sure was at a nearby bar, but my feet remained planted.

So what if it was his ex—she was his ex. But why hadn't he told me she'd be here?

Because he's a man and if it doesn't matter to him, he won't realise it will matter to you.

I remained frozen, feeling warm with all the thoughts that were bouncing around my skull like captured flies. The lights dimmed further and there was noise from the crowd, the doors now closed and the set about to begin.

Owen was back near the mic, talking to Vinny and warming up a guitar. He'd mentioned he might play a couple of songs and I'd been keen to hear him. I tried to forget he'd mentioned Amber and concentrated on the music that was starting, acoustic versions of songs I'd heard on the radio from local stations and when I'd been at Owen's. It was folk rock; Vinny had a gravelly voice that he could turn smooth and he sung about relationships that weren't working out and the loss of the girl of his dreams.

Then another voice joined, a strong female tone that complemented Vinny's. At first I didn't see her, the lighting was dim and she was out of the spotlight, then I noticed the long red hair, the beautiful smiling woman from Owen's photographs. It was her. It was Amber. Owen's ex.

Reducing every insecurity I felt wasn't curbing my anxieties. I didn't understand why he hadn't told me that she would be performing on his stage, potentially with him. The omission equated to a lie and already I could feel my shoulders sinking and the need to run out and find the nearest bottle of whisky almost like a pair of hands pushing my back.

The song finished to a large round of applause. Vinny started to speak and introduced Amber as an amazing woman and I wondered if they were together. The way he looked at her suggested they were.

"Thank you," Amber said, stepping forward into the light. She looked a little nervous which I took pleasure in and then felt a bitch, "It's good to be able to sing sometimes. I'd just like to thank the owner and brilliant mind behind Cases, Owen, who just happens to be my ex-husband…"

I didn't hear the rest, instead my feet began to move, blood hitting my ears like a tsunami and I started to shift from the crowd. This was a lie. He'd been married and hadn't told me; what else was there? I doubted he had a child—we'd spent too much time together for that to be a possibility—but there was too much doubt lingering now like a bad smell from a disused fish stand.

"Payton!" I heard my name as I reached the emergency exit. "Payton, stop. Please."

The music was still carrying on, the crowd receptive to the set so far and no one had noticed me, except Owen.

"Why didn't you tell me?" Thankfully my voice came out calm rather than whiny.

He looked beautiful: black jeans and a dark blue shirt that was tight around his arms as usual. His eyes were blazing and his jaw was tense. "Because we were never really married. I understand why you're mad right now because I haven't told you something that should be massive. Can I have a chance to explain?"

The teenager that lived inside me wanted to tell him no and stomp off, but then I knew I'd be left wondering and I didn't want that. I'd had that before. Owen and what I felt for him was worth more than sitting at home moping around and torturing myself with all the reasons why he might've lied. "Yes," I said. "I think I deserve an explanation."

"You do. Follow me to the office?" He reached for my hand but I pulled it away, following him a few footsteps behind as we pushed through the people. There was a double door at the bottom of the cookery aisle. He pressed the keypad and held the door open for me, the sound of Vinny and Amber's voices dimming into the background completely.

"Which room?"

"I have an office on the left."

He led the way, the corridor dotted with rolled up posters for displays and the odd pile of books. If it had been under different circumstances, I would've stopped to have looked more closely.

"This room here," Owen said, unlocking a door with his key. He pushed the door open for me to go in first. I took two steps inside and stopped dead, Owen walking straight into the back of me.

"For the love of all things that are holy and sacred…" he said, surprising me at how he managed to get so many words out given the scene that was in front of us, over what was probably his desk.

Dot and Dave had clearly resolved their differences and were making up for lost time. She was laid back on the desk and Dave was over her, naked from the waist down. The rest I didn't take notice of, backing out of the room back into the corridor, where Owen was resting against the wall, covering his face with his hands.

I wanted to touch him, to reassure him and then laugh with him, because given everything we'd done over the last few weeks; the blind dates, the criticism of Dave which Owen had hated, the mediation—all of this had ended in what he'd wanted, his mum and Dave reconciling.

He moved his hands and looked at me. "Let's use this room instead and never think about what we've just seen."

CHAPTER 19
OWEN

I had seen Payton already, standing in the crowd like she had a spotlight on her. She was beautiful and she was all mine. The last few weeks had been a whirlwind of getting to know each other, taking chances and changing routines; I hadn't experienced this before and she'd become a drug I wanted to stay addicted to. Tonight had a special feel to it. Even though it was the first time Amber had been back around London for weeks, it didn't feel as if it was going to be about her.

Amber. I hadn't explained to Payton about Amber. It hadn't been needed as there wasn't anything to say. I watched Payton's face as Amber walked onto the stage, her eyes questioning, her expression unsure and I realised I might've just fucked a lot up.

"It's good to be able to sing sometimes. I'd just like to thank the owner and brilliant mind behind Cases, Owen, who just happens to be my ex-husband, although we were better friends than anything else. Here's to your future happiness, Owen." Amber said, smiling around at me and Vinny. Vinny started to play a familiar riff and the crowd started to applaud and call, but my attention was on Payton and the hurt that had painted her face.

Shit. Shit. *Shit*

I'd never told her Amber and I had been married. It was the one thing she didn't know and this would kill her.

The crowd parted as I walked after her, speeding up my steps so I could get to the door at the same time as her and stop her from leaving.

"Payton!" I said as she reached the emergency exit. "Payton, stop. Please."

She turned around to face me, disappointment in her eyes and I felt like the biggest bastard the world had ever created. "Why didn't you tell me?" Her voice was level, as if she'd expected this all along, because the men she picked were always let-downs.

"Because we were never really married. I understand why you're mad right now because I haven't told you something that should be massive. Can I have a chance to explain?" I knew there was no point begging and my reasons for not having told her were genuine: it didn't matter that Amber and I had signed a bit of paper in front of two witnesses we'd pulled off the street. I shouldn't have been so stupid. It would matter to Payton that she knew.

"Yes," she said. "I think I deserve an explanation."

"You do. Follow me to the office?" I said, reaching for her hand but she didn't take it. My chest felt as if a nest of wasps had erupted inside me and stung. She followed me to the door that led to the back rooms we used for stock, meetings and as staff rooms. There was an office that was used by the manager and my mum when needed, as well as myself, but it was kept locked. I fumbled with the key, my hands shaking with sheer panic at the possibility of this being the end of us, of me and Payton, and more than anything, I didn't want that to happen.

I opened the door, letting Payton in first and then saw a scene that I had managed to avoid of all of my thirty-two years so far: my mum and Dave on my desk and they weren't working. I backed out into the corridor and covered my face, hoping that a few seconds of seeing nothing would forever erase the image from my memory.

The door closed and I was aware of Payton standing facing me. All I wanted at that moment was her in my arms and to hear her laughing at what we'd just seen. I moved my hands away and saw her, her beautiful face sad and hurt and all the things I never wanted to make her feel. "Let's use this room instead and never think about what we've just seen," I said, opening the door to a stock room.

She followed me in, sitting down on one of the piles of boxes. "Why didn't you tell me you have an ex-wife?"

"Because I never thought to," I said. She looked at me disbelievingly. "Amber and I were together for three years. We were students together, our relationship worked because we were both so busy we didn't have time to date and neither of us questioned the other about having to cancel dates or being home late as we were both in the same position. We got married on a whim without telling anyone. I think at that point we knew there was no future as we were just friends who lived together but there was a sense of loyalty. The day after we got married Amber flew to America to attend a conference for a week. When she got back she told me she'd had an affair and getting married wasn't the right thing to do."

Payton looked white, her hands clenched together. "So what did you do?"

I shrugged, leaning against the shelves we kept stock. "I agreed. I wasn't in love with her. I think I knew that before we got married. We got an annulment rather than a divorce. So yes, Amber is my ex-wife but we didn't ever live together as husband and wife. When she got home from America and told me, she moved out immediately."

"How often do you see her?"

"Rarely. We did hook up a few times after we split because it was easy and convenient to scratch an itch that way. That's me being honest with you, Payts, but that hasn't happened for about eighteen months. And the only person I want to hook up with is you," I said, my eyes fixed, trying to read her expression. "More than hook up and you can't understand how much I'm kicking myself right now for not having told you about Amber."

There was a knock at the door before it opened and Amber stood there, looking panicked and worried.

"I saw you leave—one of the staff told me where you were and let me through. Shit, I'm so sorry." She looked at Payton. "I'm guessing this idiot hadn't told you we were married for all of about three minutes?"

Payton nodded, regarding Amber with complete confusion. "I knew you'd been together for a while, but he didn't say you were married."

Amber nodded. "I'll have to be quick because I promised it was just a quick break. We got married, I went away, came back and we had it annulled. Not because Owen would've been a bad husband or father or anything like that. He's amazing and I was probably stupid, but we were friends with benefits. There wasn't any chemistry and we were never in love. It was just convenient. I had a fling in America and I realised that friends with benefits wasn't enough for forever." She paused, pointing at me. "He's told me so much about you and it's clear he's head over heels in love. Please don't judge him by one instance of being a dick. I have to go. I'm sorry I said what I did. I didn't mean to cause any trouble."

"Are you dating Vinny?" Payton said just as Amber opened the door.

Amber's expression softened. "Yeah. I think it might be a bit more than dating."

"Good luck. I really hope it works out if that's what you want," Payton said. "And thanks for coming back to explain."

"No problem. Everything's fine out there although I haven't seen your mum for a while," Amber said, closing the door and leaving us alone again.

"Is there anything else you haven't told me?" Payton said, her arms crossed over her chest.

"No," I said. "You know everything else except I haven't told you I love you yet but I wanted to say it when it would be memorable in a good way and I knew that you were ready to hear it. Please don't let this one thing stop us from having something really good."

Her eyes were bursting with tears and she looked away from me. "I need to go. I need to think. Can you let me out without having to go through the crowds?"

I nodded and followed her out of the room, disappointment and anger at myself filling my chest. "What do you need, Payton? What can I do?"

She turned around when she reached the door that led onto the side street. "I need to think. There's nothing you can do. I believe you about your marriage and I get why you didn't tell me. But I need to think because I know no one's perfect but I thought you were close and this makes me worry."

I nodded, wishing I could touch her but knowing it was the worst thing I could do. "I understand. I can keep explaining and telling you how I feel but I know that's just going to make me sound like an idiot."

She moved towards me and pressed her lips to mine, surprising me. "Let me think," she said. "I need to think and not overreact."

I watched her leave, heading down the side street towards

the main road and itched to follow her, but sense somehow kept my feet from moving.

"What's happened?" My mum stood a few feet away, watching, Dave behind her.

"I might've just blown it with Payton," I said. "I never told her I was married. Amber mentioned it during the set."

"Oh," my mother said. "I can kind of see both sides. What are you going to do?"

"Give her some space," I said. "Then show her how I feel."

Her brothers, at least, didn't try to kill me during rugby practice on Saturday. She'd headed to Claire and Killian's after leaving Cases the day before and had told them factually what had happened. There were a few piss-taking jokes made at my expense and reassurance mainly from Seph that Payton would be rational and realise that this didn't mean we had to be over.

During the course of the ten days or so since it happened, we exchanged a few messages, general day-to-day comments about the weather, which had been torrentially wet, and books, plus a couple of things that had made me think of her. She responded every time but didn't take the call I made on Wednesday, instead sending me a message that said she wasn't ready to talk to me right now. I didn't try to persuade her otherwise. She was stubborn and argumentative and I needed, to a certain extent, her to come back to me so she'd made the decision. That didn't mean I wasn't going to show her in other ways how I felt.

My apartment felt empty without her. In the nights leading up to Friday, we'd spent very little time apart and she'd left a collection of her stuff at mine. My bathroom had been taken over with make-up and toiletries and my sheets still smelt of her perfume and the body stuff that she used. I should've changed them already but I couldn't bring myself to lose the smell, something I didn't admit to anyone other than myself.

I didn't need anyone to tell me what I was feeling; I understood it too well. This was completely different from what I'd had with Amber: we'd been friends who were really good at tolerating each other and compatible in bed. Payton made me want to wake up in the mornings just because she was there. I wanted to read her body with my fingers, my mouth and my cock so I had every word of her committed to memory and then I wanted revision sessions. I wanted to be the one who made her smile, who helped fix her problems, who she could lean on, and I wanted her to be the same for me.

Luckily, my father's offer to the gallery he was interested in was accepted, so I had something to throw myself into. I was busy looking at development plans and attending a couple of meetings with London-based artists, as well as starting to interview for a couple of positions on my management team. I'd made the decision to step back from Cases on a day-to-day basis and concentrate on expanding into other areas. Only every thought led back to Payton. I wanted to call her and tell her about the gallery and get her thoughts on its focus; I wanted to have her look through the applications I'd received; I wanted her with me.

It was a week and half since I'd seen her when Ava and Claire strode into Cases with Eliza. I had seen plenty of Payton's brothers, but Ava and Claire, as I'd have expected, had been absent. They didn't play rugby so it was unlikely that our paths would cross unless they wanted to seek me out for something. Like now, it seemed.

"Owen!" Ava called, waving from the bar at the café in her usual exuberant manner. "Come join us. We need to talk."

I wondered what my chances were of escaping without them grabbing hold of me first but then Claire made eye contact and I understood why Killian was half way to being scared of her.

There was a spare seat a bit further down from them, so I dragged it over and braced myself for the verbal onslaught I figured I was about to receive.

"She's miserable," Ava said, accepting the cappuccino placed in front of her. "She's working all hours again and has just taken on a ridiculous case that Eli says is going to be a nightmare. What are your plans?"

"You need to up your game. None of her previous boyfriends have fought for her. The relationships simply ended and then that was it," Claire said, Eliza sleeping soundly in her arms.

I asked Katie behind the bar for a coffee and looked from one sister to the other. "I don't want to push her. She asked for me to give her time."

"She's had time," Ava said. "She's had a week and a half of moping around and discussing it with us *infinitely* because all of us are saying we get why you forgot to tell her and it wasn't a deliberate omission. Now she doesn't know what to do because she's proud."

"Are you still coming to her birthday party?" Claire said. "She's not said anything about changing the venue or anything like that."

"I'd like to still be there." It was on Saturday, three days away, although her actual birthday was Friday. I considered head butting the nearest wall to knock the sense into me that I needed a few weeks ago when I should've told her about my very brief marriage.

Ava sipped her coffee while watching me. "What've you bought her?"

I felt more nervous now than I had before I took my driving test. Or any other test. I was about to be judged. "Earrings. And a necklace."

"No ring?"

I sputtered and just about managed to put my cup down before I dropped it. "I think it's too soon and given she's only just found out that I've been married before. I have a lot more to prove to her before she'd even consider accepting and I don't want to ask and there be a chance she'd turn me down."

Claire looked up from Eliza whose eyes were now wide open. "But you've not said you don't want to get married again or you can't see a long term future with her?"

I shook my head. "I want everything with her, if she'll have me."

"Then that's what you need to tell her," Claire said.

"But she won't pick up the phone to me."

Ava smiled, looking as devious as a small child with plans to raid the cookie jar. "Then you need another way to get her undivided attention."

CHAPTER 20
PAYTON

"What his lawyer's claimed here is completely unfounded. He's got absolutely no evidence to suggest this. He's trying it on."

"Payton…"

"Why do they resort to this? Instead of fabricating a pile of absolute shit, why not just try to negotiate and use what they've got. This is what gives lawyers a bad name for trying to just cash in—"

"Payton. Stop."

I looked up from the pile of papers on my desk into deep brown eyes set in a tanned face. Elijah was looking at me as if he was about to grab hold of my shoulders and shake.

"What?"

"It's past four. You've been here since before six this morning and you haven't eaten." He sighed and stepped back. "We're all worried about you. Again. You're working too hard. Again. This is how people burn out. And there's someone waiting in reception to take you for a late lunch."

"Who? Is it Owen?" My heart started to pound so fast I figured it was trying to bust its way out through my ears.

Eli shook his head. "It's his mum. And you're going to go with her, eat and not come back to work, else Jackson is putting you on leave."

I gripped my fists tightly and waited for the anger to bubble. It didn't. Not that I was surprised. I didn't have the emotion left in me. For the past week and a half, I'd thrown myself into work, my safest place, and spent the nights trying to methodically decide what I wanted to do about my relationship with Owen.

He'd sent me messages and I'd replied, but the thought of seeing him scared me, even speaking to him worried me, because I knew that as soon as I heard his voice or saw him, I'd let his secret he'd kept become history. I didn't want to take a chance; I wanted a certainty. But nothing was certain. Even the cases I knew I should win were never certain.

"She's going to persuade me to get back with Owen, isn't she?" I said to Eli.

"I don't know," Eli said. "She might be here to tell you never to speak to her son again because you've broken his heart. You'll just have to go, eat and listen."

Eli had spent most of the past ten days ignoring my moods and purely talking to me about work, which had been helpful, but clearly he was now getting annoyed with the wallowing in self-pity. This was hardly surprising given I was now at Olympic standard. "Do you think him forgetting to tell me he was married is a justifiable reason to end our…" I couldn't say the word relationship. We'd never labelled it and I didn't know quite what to call it.

"You want my opinion or a breakdown of pros and cons?" Eli said, taking a seat.

"Opinion, please."

He raised his brow as if to ask if I was sure. "You've dated some absolute penises since I've known you and I know the couple of guys you saw seriously were deadbeats according to your brothers." He paused, watching my reaction. "Everyone has a past, Payts. Whether that's an ex, an ex-wife or kids or really shitty parents, we all have one and that's what makes us who we are. Owen forgot to tell you because he was married for two point four seconds and then it was annulled—it didn't even need a divorce. He's not a penis and he's not a deadbeat. If you let this one thing he forgot stop you from giving him another chance then you're a fool. If something else comes out that he's not told you, then that's different. You re-evaluate it then. That's my opinion. Do with it what you wish." He stood up and pulled the file from under me. "I'm having this. You can advise."

"That's…" I went to grab it.

"No longer your case. It's been reassigned until you can find that balance between work and not work again. Owen's mum's waiting. Go eat." He walked out of my office and I swore I heard him chuckle.

I nipped into the bathroom and checked my appearance. I'd not been sleeping well. My bed felt too big and I was purposely working late so I could immerse myself in work rather than make a decision. My eyes had dark circles under them that were visible even through my concealer and my lips were dry. Right now, I did not look like a catch.

I did what I could with the make-up that I had in my handbag and headed into reception. Dot was talking animatedly to Carol who was working on the phones this afternoon. She looked over and smiled. "You look like something that was dug up and forgot to be put in the freezer."

"I know. I just scared myself when I looked in the mirror."

"We're going for an early dinner. Alcohol not included. Come on."

We wandered down through Borough towards Southwark and Bermondsey, discussing everything other than Owen. She and Dave had met up several times and things were going well. He was trying to impress her rather than just assuming she would be impressed. I wondered if she knew how we'd walked in on them in Cases, but decided not to mention it. Owen had been mortified, but there was a possibility Dot would be even more so, although I doubted it. She didn't have an ounce of prudishness in her.

The Jose Tapas bar was a pretty restaurant in Bermondsey. I'd been a couple of times before although not recently, but the food had always been heavenly and I suddenly realised how hungry I actually was.

"This suits you?" Dot said, sitting down. "I haven't brought you to a tapas bar for a Spanish Inquisition though. I've brought you here because I fancied tapas and a chat."

"It suits me fine," I said. The waiter brought over the menus. "Thank you for dragging me out of the office."

She shrugged. "Your brother, I forget which one, told Owen you weren't eating and Owen told me. I think he'd have dragged you out himself but he wasn't sure if that would be what you wanted. Not that I'm prying. How's your niece?"

My face fractured into a smile. "She's amazing. She's managed to get into a sleeping pattern now, so Claire and Killian are in better moods. And she's smiling loads, although Claire thinks it's just wind."

"Tell your sister to make the most of her being a baby. That stage doesn't last long. You wish it away because it's hard, harder than anything you've ever done, but when you look back you realise you should have appreciated those moments more," Dot said as she browsed the menu. "Tapas is good on an empty stomach. Stops you guzzling too much in one go and feeling poorly. You've lost weight, Payton."

I nodded. It didn't take much as I had my mother's metabolism. I figured I'd lost half a stone in the past few days and I knew that wasn't healthy. "I need to take better care of myself."

"So what's stopping you?"

"I don't like making big decisions in case it's the wrong one," I said, honestly. The waiter came over with a carafe of water and olives. I picked one and felt its flavour ooze out as I bit into it. I loved olives; their savoury bite was one of my favourite tastes.

Dot regarded me as if studying an animal that was potentially about to pounce. "Then how else do you learn? Payton, my dear, Owen's dad was my biggest mistake and my best. He broke my heart into more pieces than I've ever found, but because of him I knew what it was like to be in love and experience the exhilaration that brings. And it gave me Owen. I was hurt when our relationship didn't work out, but that opened the doors to me having what has been a wonderful life so far."

"How's Dave?" I asked, diverting the subject completely and aware she wouldn't have missed the side step.

"He's good and thank you for doing what you did. I've already thanked Owen. Sometimes you need to take a step back and see the bigger picture. Both of us needed to do that. I also needed to apologise for having nabbed the office when you and Owen were looking for somewhere to talk the other Friday," she spoke with a shit-eating grin on her face that told me she was anything but sorry.

"Owen was mortified," I said, then couldn't help the laughter that fell. "I don't think he's ever seen Dave arse before, let alone…"

Dot started to giggle. "Dave was mortified too when Owen told us. He's thirty-two; he can deal with the fact that his mother has a sex life. I coped walking in on him several times."

I sat back and folded my arms, enjoying talking about Owen, hearing about his life. "Do tell."

"He was sixteen and he assumed I was out. I assumed he was studying with the music up loud and went in to tell him to turn it down. Turns out the muffling was drowning out the moaning of his older girlfriend who seemed to think she was a cowgirl." Dot said. "Then we had him trying to be romantic in front of the open fire, although to be fair, he did think I was away for the night with Dave."

I started to laugh, feeling desperately sorry for Owen but wanting to tease him at the same time. "He must've been so embarrassed."

Dot shook her head. "He chose not to be. He was brought up in communities where self-exploration was encouraged and other than the 'be safe and don't hurt others' there were no boundaries around sex so there was no embarrassment after the initial, 'Oh shit; my mum copped me.'"

"What did you think of Amber?" The words were out before I'd considered them and I wished I could pull them back. I didn't want to be the type of person who needed a character study on someone they might pursue something with. I wanted to be easy going and carefree, that girl who just gets on with things and has a good time and doesn't worry herself into pacing up and down at three am because she might've forgotten to lock a door.

Dot smiled. "Amber was always a nice girl. She was bright and mischievous and constantly on the go. In all the time they were together I saw her maybe two dozen times. They didn't spend a lot of time together as she was working as a consultant and would be away for weeks at a time. Ask away. I'm not going to tell Owen that you're asking twenty questions, especially if it helps you make your decision."

"Were you surprised when they got married?"

"Yes. They didn't get engaged and as far as I knew, they

hadn't even talked about it. Amber was very impulsive and I suspect it was a total spur of the moment decision. I know they both had doubts about their relationship as I could see it. They didn't know what they were and because they didn't row they didn't have cause to end it. It was a make or break decision," Dot said, catching the waiter's eye. "I need food and so do you. Once you've eaten at least enough to feed two of your brothers you can think about a small glass of wine."

I felt my shoulders relax as Dot ordered enough tapas to sustain me for a couple of days. She asked if I wanted to add anything else to the order, but other than the chorizo bites, she'd ordered everything and more.

"Why didn't he tell me?" I said as the waiter moved away. "I could've dealt with the whole past marriage thing, especially how it happened. But why didn't he say?"

"Honestly," Dot said, picking up an olive. "I think he's moved on from Amber far enough he's forgotten it happened. She cheated straight away and I suspect that was because she'd then have a reason to finish it, to give Owen a reason to not want to be with her and to prove to herself that their relationship was not a long term one. When she told him, they didn't fall out and I don't think it bothered him. He's never been hung up since about girlfriends or fidelity, so the experience hasn't scarred him."

I nodded, processing the information. "I can understand that. I just have to get over myself."

"Things aren't always black and white, Payton. A relationship with anyone, and not just a romantic one, is filled with every shade of every colour. You have times when you pull and you push and times when you're close and when you're far apart. It's always a work in progress. When it stops being, like with Owen and Amber, that's when it needs evaluating, because people change and a relationship has to change to grow with them," she said, finishing as two bowls of Padron peppers landed in front of us.

"What happened with you and Dave?" I said, biting into a pepper that turned out to be one of the spicy ones.

Dot thought for a moment, her teeth resting in the flesh of a pepper. "We were stagnant. We'd changed and moved on but our relationship had paused. I wish now we'd been more serious early on and I'd moved in and we'd had a child, maybe. That ship's sailed across several oceans by now, but we were still having the same routine and I needed more. Instead of asking him for it, I wanted to look elsewhere."

"But you didn't find it?"

She shook her head. "No. Because I love Dave and that hadn't stopped. We're working on it. I think we'll look to buy somewhere together in the next few weeks and make a commitment. Maybe we'll get married. Who knows?"

We carried on eating, the tapas reminding me why food was good and the conversation reminding me of why I didn't live simply to work. I was well aware of my head in my ass tendencies and my use of work as a shield. I could carry on like that forever, not risking being hurt and staying safe, but that would leave me as the delightfully weird maiden aunt probably surrounded by a gazillion giant bunnies, as I wasn't a cat person.

I managed to get home around eight pm, having had the best night I'd had since that Friday. Dot hadn't talked about how Owen was getting on, except casually mentioning him, nor had I asked. I did know he hadn't met anyone else or started seeing Amber again; both situations had crossed my mind and I had dwelled on them, usually at around three o'clock in the morning.

The only person I was fighting with at present was myself.

Owen had done one thing wrong, and not deliberately. I got that. He wasn't a twat like the men who had fucked me over in the past. But letting this go and giving it that chance was leaving me even wider open to be crucified should this relationship not work. My instincts were to run for the hills – or in London's case the depths of the Thames – and not get involved with a man who could have the power to crush my heart.

Only one key was needed to get into my apartment. I stopped, paused, wondering who the hell was inside or if I'd left it unlocked this morning or if I'd been broken in to and the thief was still there.

"Only me, Payts!" The dulcet tones of my twin hit my ears like cymbals—irritating and loud.

"For the love of all things holy, why are you here and how did you get in?"

"Claire gave me your key. I've come to hang."

"Why?"

"Because." He eyed me and I noticed he'd opened a bottle of malbec and was currently half way through a glass. "Two reasons really: the first, I figured you needed company and I've no intention of talking about Owen, unless you want to, and you might because I had beers with him before; the second, I walked in on Max and Vic doing it in the kitchen and I think I'm going to need more therapy. I can't go back there tonight."

I frowned, ignoring the comment about Owen for now. "It's Max. The kitchen will have been vacated by now. You'll be safe."

He shook his head. "Nope. I think he's proposed. The hallway was full of flowers and I could smell dinner. I think they'll be going at it all night."

"Did he not give you the head's up? Tell you to keep out

of the way?" I said, surprised. Maxwell was generally quite thorough.

"I had an email from him that I didn't opened. I thought it was probably reminding me about a meeting with one of his clients. Then I got distracted by a message from a potential date. so yeah, he gave me the head's up, but I didn't get it in time," Seph said, rambling on as per usual. "What are we watching?"

"Do I need to feed you too?"

"No. I grabbed pizza with Owen. Where've you been? I know you weren't at work. Eli said you'd gone already," Seph said, putting his feet up on my coffee table, that was still tidy. I hadn't slipped back into my messy mode which I was proud of.

I grabbed a glass and sat down next to him, picking the bottle up from the floor. "I met Owen's mum for tapas and a talk."

Seph nodded. "Did she tell you anything you didn't know?"

"She told me more about Owen and Amber's relationship. And we talked in general about things, family, work and such." I sipped the malbec and enjoyed its taste on my tongue.

"Did she say how Owen was?" Seph asked and I knew right then he was enjoying having information that I didn't.

"No, and I didn't ask. I know he's not seeing Amber again or anyone else," I said. "And I'm not in the playground at school, needing to know what he said."

My twin flicked on the TV and turned on Netflix. He started to scroll through, looking with feigned interest at the possible options.

"Okay, Seph, tell me how Owen is."

"No. You said weren't interested and were pretty much calling me immature, so I'm saying nothing. You could always call Claire or Ava; they saw him this afternoon too," Seph said, smirking. I vowed revenge.

"For fuck's sake, tell me." I elbowed him in the ribs. "In fact, decide on what you're going to tell me while I get changed and if you're not going to say anything then go and stay with Callum."

I left my wine on the coffee table, praying my brother didn't knock it off with his huge feet, and went to throw on something old and comfy, which happened to be a pair of pyjama bottoms and one of Owen's Cases T-shirts that he'd left. I'd slept in it most nights since.

Seph pointed and laughed when he saw what I was wearing. "You're so not going to get over him any time soon."

"Fuck off," I told my brother, sitting back down and rescuing my wine, inspecting it for anything he might've dropped into it while I was gone. "How's Owen?"

"He's okay," Seph said. "He's steady and resilient. He hasn't become a workaholic, although he's got some interesting business opportunities at the moment. He misses you. I don't know how else to explain it without losing my man card."

"Try." I didn't want to enjoy Owen's discomfort, but I was glad to hear he hadn't moved on. That might make me a bitch in some people's eyes but it made me feel better.

Seph winced. "Really? How else do I describe it apart from he misses you?" He picked up his phone.

"You're not messaging him, are you?"

"Give me some credit, Payts. I'm not that emotionally stunted."

My phone chirped ten seconds later.

Seph: Payts is worried Owen's forgotten about her.

Claire: No. Anything but. Is she seeing sense yet?

Me: I am included in this group message.

Ava: Good. I'm in a bar and my date is talking too much to someone else.

Me: When are we going to meet him?

Ava: Never, unless he remembers shortly that I exist.

Seph: Who's on Ava duty this week?

Jackson: We stopped taking duties when you started to get your shit together, Joseph. Owen's game is much better when you're together, so for the sake of the rugby team can you please sort it out.

Ava: It's okay. He's back with food. You're still not meeting him though.

Claire: These things will be discovered. Payts, Owen misses you. But he's a man. He doesn't know how to put these things right and the obvious things like flowers and chocolate don't seem thoughtful.

Me: But I'd quite like flowers and chocolate. And I'm not sure he needs to put things right. It's not that simple.

Killian: For fuck's sake, Claire.

Seph: Popcorn ready, folks.

Claire: What?

Killian: I've apologised. I bought you flowers and chocolate because that's what you told me to do last time. What else do you want?

Ava: What's he done?

Claire: Long story. But short version, he might've missed an appointment.

Me: She's good with flowers, chocolate and public humiliation, K. Go back to your computer games.

Killian: Too fucking right. I'll make it up to you later, babes. 8=======>

Claire: We should have a criminal defence lawyer in our practice for when I kill him. Payton, put the poor man out of his misery. If he ever hurts you, we'll be there to pick up the pieces like you've done for most of us at some time or another. Seph, stick your popcorn up your arse. Good night all.

Ava: I second what Claire's said. Give things a chance, Payts. You deserve good sex.

Jackson: Anyone heard from Max this evening? I realise I'm changing the subject completely away from Payton's sex life, because fuck knows, we've not heard enough about that over the years.

Seph: Trust me. I had a bedroom next to hers. I've heard more than you. You won't hear from Max.

Jackson: Why's that? Has he lost his phone again?

Seph: I had the bad timing to walk into the kitchen while they were 'celebrating'. I'm scarred.

> Claire: This really isn't about you right now, Seph. Finally! Max put a ring on it! They can celebrate as much as they want!
>
> Callum: If Vic said yes, then there's hope for us all. Maybe not Seph…
>
> Seph: Fucker.
>
> Ava: Do you think she's pregnant?
>
> Payton: No. They'll have a timeline of events to follow. Marriage will be first. Shall we turn our birthday into an engagement party as well? They haven't had one.
>
> Ava: Good plan. I'll sort out the additional requirements.

"See," Seph said, topping up his wine glass. "Everyone's in agreement. Give it a proper go this time with Owen. If Max can get someone normal and intelligent to marry him, you should have no problem."

CHAPTER 21
OWEN

I stood back and looked at the setting. It had taken an hour and a half to get things right, which was a lot less than I would've given. She'd messaged me on Thursday, nothing in-depth, just a sentence to say she was looking forward to seeing me on Saturday and she hoped I'd still be there.

Of course I was still going to fucking be there.

I'd set up a table, some candles in a glass thing in the middle, every bunch of flowers I could get my hands on from the florist I knew and chocolate. Red wine. And books. Plus one very special book.

I wiped my hands on my trousers and cursed, causing Ava to turn around and laugh. "Stop it, Owen," she said. "She'll come. My sister can't turn down the chance to come to my rescue. Do you know what you're going to say to her?"

"Kind of." It was pretty much all I'd thought about all day. And most of yesterday. Ava and Claire had offered to arrange it so that Payton had to speak to me, saying that she would just dodge having to make a decision until it was made for her. I'd gone along with it because I knew if I suggested meeting up, as I already had done a couple of times, she'd find excuses. What I was going to say and how I was going to explain to her the deception I wasn't sure. In fact, I was fucking clueless, but I wasn't going to admit that to Ava.

"It looks amazing," Ava said, admiring what was mainly her handiwork. "She'll love it. She'll probably cry because no one's ever made this much of an effort over her."

"Why? She's gorgeous and brilliant."

Ava laughed. "Because she's always gone out with dicks who are afraid of her and end up doing something stupid like cheating. Because she's that amazing she scares men, and she chooses the ones she can scare because she knows they'll fuck up before she can get too attached then she can't get hurt."

I looked at Ava. "I'm not going to hurt her."

"I know. I wouldn't be doing this otherwise." She flashed me a huge grin. "I'll call her."

I opened the wine while I listened to Ava talking to Payton on the phone, her voice hysterical as she gave her some story about being at the shop and knocking over the huge display of books at the front of the store. "Please, Payton," I heard her say. "I haven't got a clue what to do and I know you're only at Claire's. Please come and help." There was a pause. "Thank you. I know it's your birthday. Thank you. I don't want Owen to be angry."

She put her phone away in her jeans pocket and gave me a beaming smile. "She's on her way. It over to you now, hot shot."

"Thanks for helping out."

She nodded. "It's no problem and you never know when I'll need the favour returning. I'll see you tomorrow about six to get everything set up for the party."

"Are you off anywhere nice now?" She wasn't dressed up but her face looked more made up than for a night in.

Ava tossed her hair back. "Yup. Not out, just in. With the secret boyfriend."

"Who you're living with?"

"Temporarily, yes. And no, I'm not telling you who it is. I don't think you keeping secrets from my sister is a good idea," she said. "Now, try and relax and I'll see you tomorrow." She took off at speed, unlocking the door to get out and almost running down the street.

Her brothers had mentioned she was seeing someone yesterday at training, but none of them had any idea who it was. There were a few comments about having to probably pick up the pieces when it went wrong, but that wasn't the Ava I'd seen. The girl managed construction teams and builders whilst taking absolutely no shit whatsoever. She also knew exactly how to manipulate her four older brothers. I kept my mouth shut, not needing to draw any attention to my own relationship with the other younger sister.

I checked everything one more time, straightening books, making sure the wine was good, smoothing down my shirt. It would take about half an hour for her to get here and I had to kill that time by not thinking about Payton and what I was going to say to her and how I hoped the night would end.

My mum had offered to come in early on Saturday with Dave and tidy up. I suspected she was hoping I'd be needing a lie in. She'd told me about her dinner with Payton, but hadn't given me any details which I expected. All she'd said was that she hoped we worked it out and that Payton wasn't opposed to the idea of a relationship with me.

Marriages weren't black and white. You didn't necessarily marry someone because you were madly in love with them. I hadn't been madly in love with Amber and by that point, I hadn't been madly in lust with her either. She was a baggy sweater that I was comfortable wearing and found easy to put on, but she didn't make my dick go hard and my pulse strum a beat like for a HIIT workout as Payton did. Getting married was us trying to persuade ourselves that the past three years hadn't been wasted, but they had. They'd also taught me what I didn't need from a relationship.

Half a glass of wine had somehow slipped down my neck —although I'd managed to avoid the whisky—when the door pushed open and I saw blonde hair in the shadows.

"Ava?" she shouted. She wore tight fitted jeans and a tank top, her hair tied back. "Ava! Where the fuck are you? The display's fine…"

"She didn't knock it over," I said, standing in the back of the store that was lit with a range of antique brass lamps that Ava had managed to discover from somewhere. They cast a warm shine over the room, creating shadows. "She just wanted to get you here."

Payton wandered through towards the back, to the section we cleared for events. It was now decorated for her. Her expression was that of Alice in Wonderland, eyes everywhere and looking at everything curiously. Bunches of flowers: hydrangeas, peonies and sunflowers, were in tall vases. A trail of petals ran from the door to the table where two glasses of wine sat, waiting. Hopefully waiting.

"This is for me?"

"For you," I said. "It's an apology."

"I don't need an apology."

"I want to give one anyway. I'm sorry I upset you."

She put her hands in her back pockets. "I know you didn't mean to. I'm sorry I've avoided speaking to you."

"I've missed you," I said, my voice gruff. I wanted to touch her, to claim her as mine once and for all, because that was what she was meant to be. As well as amazing and successful and a sister and everything else she wanted to be, she was mine.

She nodded. "I missed you too."

We stood, metres apart, watching each other.

"Do you want some wine?" I said, gesturing to the glasses.

"No," she said, stepping towards me. "I just want you. Let me have you."

I caught her in my arms. "You can have me. As long as I get you in return."

CHAPTER 22
PAYTON

"**K**illian!" Claire hollered up the stairs, holding a now awake baby in her arms. "Can you get milk?"

My soon to be brother-in-law walked down the stairs wearing his leather jacket and jeans, grinning at my sister. "Me and Eliza can manage with what milk you've got."

"You're disgusting," Claire said. "Bring back milk. And chocolate. In less than five minutes, else baby number two will never happen, nor will any practice for it."

He gave her a wicked look and left me with my no longer grumpy sister.

"You don't mean that," I said. "After everything you've said about the sex, there's no way you'd cut off any appendage to spite your face."

Claire snorted. "True. And he knows it. He just knows which buttons to press. Do you want anything else to eat?" We'd just polished off steak and sides, cooked by Killian as my sister couldn't be let anywhere near a kitchen unless it only contained a microwave.

"I'm stuffed. I have a dress I need to get in tomorrow as well."

She looked me up and down and shook her head. "Payts, you've lost weight. You didn't need to lose it in the first place. Get some fucking curves back else you'll start to fall through gaps. How about a glass of something red and alcoholic?"

"I'd feel mean," I said. She was still breastfeeding and her alcohol intake was limited.

"I wouldn't if it was the other way around but I'm not going to persuade you too hard. What's the dress like for tomorrow? I'm still wearing mums-r-us."

I prepared myself for another diatribe on designs for breastfeeding mothers, but my phone began to ring, the tone Ava's. I frowned. She'd said she was out on a date so she wouldn't be able to join us at Claire's. I hadn't made a big deal of my actual birthday. Seph was on a date and my parents were having a meal with one of my father's ex-colleagues, my other brothers were with their partners except Callum, who was travelling from the back of beyond where he'd been doing something vet-like with a tiger.

"You okay?" I said, my sister-sense tingling.

"I'm at Cases bringing stuff in for tomorrow and I've done something really stupid." She sounded a cross between mortified and amused.

"What is it? Is Owen there?"

"I've knocked over the book display as you walk in, you know the one that's made of piled up books? It's everywhere, Payts. You have a photo of it—can you come and help me sort it?"

I groaned. This wasn't how I wanted to spend my birthday, especially if there was a chance Owen was there. I didn't know what to say to him still or how to go about starting something I was so scared of. I didn't know why I was scared though and that was part of my conflict. Owen was like the sea, he ebbed and flowed consistently, he was passionate and calm and made me feel alive but safe at the same time. I was still undecided and at the same time my indecision was leaving him out to dry. He deserved another chance. I deserved another chance. But my fear was providing a boundary bigger than a full-on national security road block to trying a relationship with him.

"Please, Payton," Ava said. "I haven't got a clue what to do and I know you're only at Claire's. Please come and help."

I closed my eyes and prayed for the patience to not kill my sister. It wasn't the first time I'd sent the same prayer and so far I hadn't been arrested for murder. "Okay. I'll come. But then you're buying me a margarita at the Cellar Bar." I wasn't dressed for anything else and I had no intention of getting changed.

"Thank you. I know it's your birthday. Thank you. I don't want Owen to be angry." She was laying it on a little thick and I wondered what else she was after me to do.

"Owen's never angry," I said, then remembered how we first met. I'd enraged him then and had mentioned it several times since, loving his uncomfortable reaction. "Be there in about thirty."

Claire hovered nearby, murmuring to Eliza about silly aunts and crazy uncles. "What's Ava done?"

"Knocked over a display. I'm going to help her sort it out. Sorry to bail," I said, scraping my hair back and pulling a hair tie from my pocket. "I'll see you tomorrow evening. Are you sure you don't fancy some retail therapy tomorrow afternoon?"

She shook her head. "I promised Killian I'd go to lunch with his brother and Katie. They can't make tomorrow night as they haven't got a sitter."

"I forgive you," I said, kissing my niece and hugging my sister. There was something about her excuse that sounded hollow, but for all I knew her and Killian had an afternoon of kinky sex planned. Unlikely with a two-month-old, but you never knew. "See you tomorrow."

The walk to Cases in Covent Garden was about half an hour from Claire's and it was a fine evening so I didn't bother with the tube. My head was plugged with thoughts of Owen and what to do, as I'd be seeing him tomorrow, with my family as a shield. I didn't have to be on my own with him or have the conversation that I knew we needed to have.

I wanted him. I wanted his heat and his touch. I wanted his words and his laughter. I wanted all of him and I could deal with his omission. It didn't show him to be an idiot; it just proved that none of us were perfect. There had been no bullshitting or trying to talk his way out of it, just the truth and that I could live with.

Missing him wasn't something I'd accounted for. Not just the sex, but being able to talk to him and knowing I had someone to speak to other than my family who was primarily concerned about me and was interested in me. I missed having someone to just talk rubbish with or laugh at stupid things like daft greetings cards and random jokes. And I did miss his body; the feel of his skin against mine, his heat next to me in bed and how he'd wake me in the middle of the night, driving me mad with want and need.

Cases' front lights were off; the display I thought Ava had been referring to still standing neatly near the door. I tapped on the glass and saw movement, but it wasn't my little sister, it was a six foot four, broad shouldered, rugby playing bookstore owner.

"Ava?" I shouted, knowing exactly what was happening here and trying not to believe it was. "Ava! Where the fuck are you? The display's fine…"

"She didn't knock it over," Owen said, standing in the back of the store that was lit with the lamps Ava had acquired from some sale. She was using them for the party tomorrow but had clearly set them up already. Owen should probably consider keeping them as they suited the décor in the store, making it look slightly gothic and mysterious. "She just wanted to get you here."

I looked around at the flowers, the bunches of hydrangeas and sunflowers in tall vases and urns, staged near the cases of books. I saw candles flickering and managed not to worry about them setting the store alight, knowing that Owen at least would have risk assessed everything. Then my eyes came to him. There he stood in front of me, arms folded, looking tense and expectant.

"This is for me?"

"For you," he said. "It's an apology."

"I don't need an apology."

"I want to give one anyway. I'm sorry I upset you."

I put my hands in my back pockets and felt vulnerable, as if he could read everything I had to tell even if I didn't have the words. "I know you didn't mean to. I'm sorry I've avoided speaking to you."

"I've missed you," he said, his voice was gruff and tender, his honesty palpable. I realised he was scared that I'd reject him, that I'd tell him he'd blown it and I couldn't let us try again, but that wasn't my decision. I may get hurt in the future, things might not work out, but equally I trusted that this man would never intentionally hurt me and I wanted him. All of him, including his past.

I nodded. "I missed you too." He needed to know, although I was aware my siblings had probably already informed him of this fact. And I had to let go of my fears and trust him not to crush my tender heart.

We stood, metres apart, watching each other.

"Do you want some wine?" He gestured to the glasses.

"No," I said, stepping towards him. "I just want you. Let me have you."

He caught me in his arms. "You can have me. As long as I get you in return." I stilled for a second, letting his glorious heat seep through my clothes and under my skin, inhaling his scent, oaky and musty and male and then I moved back enough so I could start to undo the buttons of his shirt.

Owen groaned and held my hands to his chest. "Slow down, Payts," he said, his voice muted and low. "Talk first."

I raised my brows. "Really?"

He nodded. "I know I'm male but I have some degree of control. Unlike you," he said, his chuckle echoing in the empty store. "It's your birthday. I have presents for you. And words."

He guided me over to the table and pulled out a chair, gesturing to the wine. I sipped at it, recognising it as one of the ones I'd pointed out as a favourite when we'd been at mine. He'd remembered, but that was him. He had no expectations for anyone other than himself, and remembering someone's favourite wine was just the way he was made.

"You didn't have to do all this," I said, slightly overwhelmed.

"Why not?"

"Because it's me and…"

"I did it because it's you and I want to make you feel special and do something to shows you that, although Ava and Claire did help. They knew you wouldn't meet with me because you'd be too worried," he said, putting three clumsily wrapped parcels in front of me and sitting down opposite.

"Claire was in on it too?"

Owen nodded. "Yeah. I wanted to cook you a meal but the logistics were a bit complicated, so we figured we'd get rid of the hangry first. Ava helped with the lamps and setting up. Claire was the folly. Will you open your presents?"

I looked up at him nervously. I felt uncomfortable opening

gifts in front of the person who'd given them. My expression would give me away if I didn't like them and I hated to hurt feelings.

"Payton, open them. I know you'll like them." His eyes were smiling and he held my gaze.

"Did my sisters help?'

"No. This is all me. Top one first."

It was a simple white gold chain with a solid small coffee bean in the centre, easy to wear all the time. I went to put it on straight away, smiling, but not knowing what to say.

"Here, let me," Owen said, stepping behind me and taking the ends of the chain with fingers I noticed weren't steady. He was nervous. I was making this hulking, gorgeous man nervous.

Thumbs brushed the back of my neck, before hands rested on my shoulders, pressing down slightly and weighting me. I dipped my head to my left to softly headbutt his arm, then twisted to skim his skin. "Do you like it?"

"I do. I'll wear it all the time."

"That was what I wanted."

I took the next gift, a smaller, rectangular affair that was just as badly wrapped. Inside was a jewellery case, an old fashioned one and a pair of small sapphire studs. "These are perfect," I said, looking up at him. I wasn't wearing earrings, having lost my cheap silver pair a couple of weeks ago.

"I noticed you don't wear dangly earrings. And the blue reminded me of your eyes," he said.

"You didn't need to get me so much," I said. "I wasn't expecting anything."

"I know," he said, his voice quiet. "But it's your birthday and I wanted to treat you. I didn't know if you'd accept them or throw them back in my face. I hoped you'd accept them. There's one more."

I had a feeling this was the one he was most nervous

about. It was book-shaped and better wrapped than either of the other two.

Carefully I opened the gift, figuring it was something delicate, precious. And it was.

"You remembered," I said, and the tears left my eyes. "Jane Eyre." My favourite book. It was a nineteen-ten edition, hardback obviously and with a dust wrapper that had seen better days. The pages were yellowing and dotted with age and it smelt right. "I think this is the most thoughtful gift I've ever received." I placed it down carefully and moved the wine glasses far away in case disaster struck. Now all I wanted was him, to wipe away the absence I'd enforced over the past two weeks and have him, all of him.

"Good," he said. "I'm not trying to buy you back, Payton. I genuinely wanted to help you have a happy birthday. And try to mend things. But I do want you and not as a friends with benefits arrangement. I've never wanted that. I want you to be mine because," he mussed his hair with his hand, searching for words. "I've fallen in love with you." His fists clenched and I started to laugh, loudly, until the tears that had been there from being overcome were tears of laughter. "What? Why is it funny? Have I said something completely stupid? I have, haven't I? I'm such a geek." He turned away in frustration and I moved to him, wrapping my arms around his waist, pulling myself close.

"No, what you said was perfect. You looked as if you were about to go into a fight with your fists clenched."

His hands moved onto my back and down to my ass, moving me closer. "I was trying not to touch you. I figured you might need your space."

I shook my head. "I don't space any more. Because I love you too. And not just because you've bought me the best gifts I've ever had, but because you're genuine and clever and geeky and fucking hotter than sin. And I'm better with you."

"Then why are you crying?"

"Because I'm not running away scared."

"I'll try to never hurt you, Payts."

I looked up at him and saw the determination in his eyes. "I know. Are you going to kiss me now?"

He nodded, bringing his head to mine. "As much and as often as you like. Can I tell people that you're my girlfriend?"

"Totally."

And then his mouth was on mine, his kiss slow and full and deep, repeating promises. My hands went to his shirt, undoing the buttons, then tracing my fingers over skin and muscle, memorising every rise and fall. I pushed my palms up to the top of his chest and moved his shirt off his shoulders. He pulled his arms away and shucked it off, leaving him gloriously bare chested, golden skin with a dusting of brown hair that thickened as it led further south to the button of his jeans.

"You're wearing too many clothes," he said, his hands back on me, pulling my vest over my head. His eyes were greedy as they looked at my bra, a simple blue lace through which my nipples were erect and visible. His hands went to pinch them, making me gasp and causing wet heat to pool between my legs. Then he'd flicked my bra open in a swift move I didn't want to know how he'd learned and I was bare from the waist up. His mouth was on my nipple, the other ensconced in his left hand, while his right hand was undoing my jeans and pushing them down.

Clever fingers pushed past the matching panties and fingered my wetness, never quite sinking in, simply teasing. "I love how wet you get for me," he said, standing up and pulling away his hands. His gaze went to my tits, smirking at the response he'd elicited and then he sucked the fingers that had toyed with my pussy. "You taste so sweet."

I pushed my jeans and panties completely off and then

attacked his jeans, undoing the fly, feeling the hardness of his cock against my hand. Owen took pity on my fumbling fingers, helping me to loosen his jeans and let them fall to the ground. I dropped to my knees and took his cock in my mouth, my tongue dipping into the slit and tasting his salty pre-come. He groaned, a hand going into my hair, guiding my movements. Looking up, I saw him watching me, my mouth stretched around his cock, a hand on his shaft and my other hand between my legs, toying with my clit and seeking release of my own.

I heard a growl and he moved my head away. "Up," he said, hands on the side of my shoulders, guiding me up until he could kiss me. His cock pushed against my stomach as I stood on my tiptoes, trying to climb him so I could sink his erection deep into me and ride him hard. Then I was lifted up and carried towards the Chesterfield sofa, my legs around his hips, my clit pressing against his dick.

He was inside me before my back hit the cool leather, his entry causing me to cry out as my body sought to stretch to accommodate him. Quickly, the pinch became pleasure. I moved my legs around his waist and he tipped my hips towards him so he could go deeper, hitting my clit with each thrust.

"I'll fuck you slow and sweet when I get you home," he said. "Then I'll put you on top and let you ride me hard so I can play with those sweet tits. But right now, I just need to be in you because two weeks has been too long, Payts." He stroked the side of my face with his hand, the tenderness in contrast to the power of his thrusts.

I couldn't say anything, my breath pumped out of me as he moved inside, my orgasm close. My vision was wobbly and I was about to come, my pussy giving his cock one hard, long clench before I let out a noise that sounded more like a wild animal. Then I started to spasm around him, my hips moving wildly with the power. He held onto me, smiling, watching my eyes. "Love it when you come on my dick. Love filling you up." His back arched and he called as he started to come, his hot seed pouring deep into my pussy and I couldn't help but be thankful that we were on leather that was easily cleaned.

"Shit," he said, half collapsing onto me. "Every time it gets better." He lifted me so I was sat on his lap, his cock still hard and inside me. The feeling of being so full was delicious, my pussy still having aftershocks, still pulsing.

My hands roamed through his hair and I pushed my lips to his, the kiss soft and not as needy as before. His hands perched on my waist, just holding and the kiss merged into small touches of our lips, our eyes transfixed on each other.

"Will you stay with me tonight?" Owen said. "And tomorrow night?"

"Yes," I murmured, still needing to touch him. "We have two weeks to catch up on."

"Good," he said. "Let's clean up and go home."

It felt warm and familiar when I woke up on Saturday. Snippets of early morning sunlight gentled the room, casting a light that seemed brighter than previous days. My bed felt right, no longer empty and when I shifted from the arms that held me, a soft snore emptied the silence from the room.

Owen had a sheet loosely across his torso, exposing his chest and abs and I debated waking him in a way I knew he would enjoy. He had no qualms about accepting blow jobs as long as he'd already come inside me that day. That seemed to be his rule and I hadn't managed to break it.

As soon as we'd arrived back at his after leaving Cases, he'd stripped me of my clothing and proceeded to trace every inch of me with his tongue and then we'd made love rather than fucked, taking our time over it rather than simply rushing to the finish line. It felt different: like we'd found our way through some invisible barrier that had been preventing us from finding out who were were together.

"Are you just going to watch me sleep all day or are we going to make use of not having to get out of bed this morning?" Owen's eyes remained shut and his voice was sleepy.

"How might we make use of the morning then?"

His smile turned wicked. I'd already noticed the morning wood he sported.

"I think I'm too spent after last night. I'll go make some coffee."

I giggled as arms brought me back down on to the mattress and he moved on top of me, boxing me in. "I can unspend you," he said, kissing my neck and giving me a quick bite.

"No, I think I'm good…"

"I know you're good. Let me show you how good." His mouth started to trail down to my collarbone to a spot he'd found that made my toes curl.

"It's not working," I totally lied.

His mouth moved to my breasts, taking one nipple between his teeth. I suppressed a moan and resisted the urge to grip his hair. His cock was huge and heavy against my leg and my core throbbed, needing to have him inside, to feel him stretch my pussy.

"Still not working?" he asked as he switched to the other side.

"No. You must've lost your touch." I was rewarded with a sharp suck and then two fingers pushed into my pussy. I heard the wetness as he fingered me and felt his body vibrate as he laughed, his mouth still on my nipple.

"Are you telling me you're not wet enough for me to fuck

you right now?" he said, his fingers moving inside me, his thumb petting my clit. He sat up, on his knees, still continuing his ministrations. I stayed still, trying to stop my body from belying my state apart from the obvious wetness. I was close to coming and he knew it.

"Nowhere near wet enough for your cock."

"I'll stop then. Take care of myself in the shower."

He started to move his hand, so I clamped it still with my thighs.

"Really, Payton?" He raised a brow.

"Make me come," I whimpered, jutting my hips to encourage him to move his hand.

He stayed still. "Turn over," he said, moving his hand away.

I followed his instruction and shifted onto my front, spreading my legs unashamedly and sticking my ass in the air. His hand made contact with my butt cheek, a soft sharp slap that automatically sent jolts of electricity to my pussy. He did the same to the other cheek and then I felt warm breath near my entrance.

His tongue hit my clit, licking as if I was an ice cream on a hot day. One hand held my wrist, the other palming my tits. The long licks became short fast ones and I broke apart quickly, as I came with his name on my lips. I had no other coherent thoughts except I needed him inside me.

"Are you wet enough now?" he said, pushing one finger inside, slowly in and then slowly out. "I'm not sure. Maybe we should try again later."

"Owen, just fuck me please."

He laughed quietly, then I felt his cock at my entrance, his hands holding my hips and bringing me back, impaling me.

"This is amazing," he said.

I wondered yet again how he managed to string words together when I was incapable of even seeing straight.

"You're amazing."

His dirty talk faded and instead it became just us, the contact and the physicality. I felt him moving inside me, how his body changed as he came closer to coming. His grip became tighter and then he pulled out and turned me over.

He pulled a pillow under my ass, lifting my hips higher to an angle that suited both of us. Then he pushed inside me again, his eyes drifting between my face and my tits as his cock moved in and out of me. I started to come without warning, my body almost betraying me. He seemed to know how to make me feel electrified and alive and free.

"Love it when you come," he said and I could tell he was close. "Can I come on you?"

I nodded and he pulled out of me, his semen hitting my stomach and chest in hot lengths. His expression was greedy and victorious. "Mine," he said. "You're mine."

And I was. Hopelessly.

EPILOGUE
OWEN

There were at least fifty people in Cases, but I only had eyes for one of them. Everyone else was welcome to go the fuck home whenever they pleased, because the only person I wanted to be with right now was wearing a tightly fitted dress that dipped enough at the front to have kept me hard for most of the evening. This was an uncomfortable situation to be in, given that the room contained her father and four brothers.

Payton looked happy. Her face lit up whenever she spoke to someone, whether it be one of her friends or a family member who had come for the occasion. I'd stopped trying to remember exactly who I'd been introduced to, instead shaking hands and making small talk that had never been a problem for me. She'd introduced me as her boyfriend, her arm around me, stealing kisses when she could, all of which had made me stupidly happy.

"If you keep grinning like a fucking idiot I'll have to call a doctor," Seph said to me, pouring whisky into our glasses. "You almost look happier than Maxwell."

The party had been combined into a celebration of Max

and Victoria's engagement, although they'd been too busy finding quiet corners to notice anyone else. "Yeah, well," I said, clinking his glass with mine. "Your sister makes me happy."

Seph grinned, genuinely happy. "As long as you make her happy. I'm glad you got it sorted. You've got a good woman. I know I've got to say that because she's my twin and if I didn't she'd refuse me a kidney or something, but I really mean it. And she's not picked a complete dickhead either."

"I'll take that as a compliment."

"Good. Now let's get this whisky drunk."

Seph continued to circulate, charming everyone, including a couple of Ava's friends who looked particularly interested in him. I stayed out of the way, watching the scene playing out. Her dad was much better and had lost over a stone already. He looked proud, especially when Claire handed him Eliza so she could knock back a couple of glasses of Champagne.

"Who are you watching?" Soft arms wrapped around me from behind. I turned and brought her into my arms, knowing I'd never be tired of the feel of her.

"Everyone. I haven't seen much of Ava," I said. She was the only sibling I hadn't spoken to at length.

"That's because she's been talking to Eli. You know, Eli my colleague, who I run the department with," Payton said, her tone suggesting that what they were doing was more than 'talking'.

"Is that a problem?"

She shook her head. "Eli's great. He's nine years older than Ava. They're friends. Friends who have gone missing together at quite a few events, such as Vanessa and Jackson's wedding. It's just clicked now."

"Again, is that a problem?"

She turned around in my arms and I remembered how

fucking lucky I was. The singer strummed through some indie-folk tune and we shifted to the music. "Right now, nothing's a problem. I'm right where I want to be. With all my family around me, and the man I love."

I knew I was grinning like an idiot again. "Say that again."

She smiled, widely, taking hold of my shirt in her small hands. "I love you, Owen Anders. Even if you get crabby when I take photos of your bookcases."

I kissed her, aware that there were several pairs of eyes on us. "I love you, Payton Callaghan because you take photos of bookcases and everything else."

The End

Want an extra specially long bonus epilogue to see what Payton and Owen get up to? Clicky here - you'll need to subscribe to my newsletter but that's amazing anyway!
https://dl.bookfunnel.com/3dj0s6bvme

READY FOR YOUR NEXT BOOK BOYFRIEND?

Want some more time with the Callaghans? Let me help you make your mind up with where to go next.

Love a best friend's younger sister romance? Meet Eli, partner in the Callaghan Green law firm and Ava's Callaghan's steamy one-night stand that she just can't seem to keep as just one night. Independent, strong-willed and intelligent, can Eli be the man Ava wants? Find out in Changing Spaces .

Want to find out more about the Green side of the family? Check out Imogen Green's fake wedding in The Wedding Agreement.

Or, do you fancy a change of scenery and want to take a

trip to a small town? Visit Severton, in Sleighed; this friends-to-lovers romantic suspense will capture your heart as much as Sorrell Slater steals Zack Maynard's.

Still not sure? Then turn the page and find a little peak into each!

NEXT IN THE SERIES.

Callaghan
GREEN

She said one night. He said more. She should've known better than to argue with a lawyer.

Ava Callaghan was never going to be just one night. She was going to be more, much more. She just didn't know it yet.

Hotshot lawyer Elijah Ward can't be interested in his friends' and colleagues' little sister. With his long-term relationship over, he isn't looking for anyone, including off-limits Ava Callaghan with her long blonde hair and zest for life that eclipses everyone around her. She's the daughter of his old boss and the sister of his new one – not a good career move.

She and Elijah can be for one steamy night only. Settling down isn't on Ava's agenda: the only thing she's planning on settling is the foundations to another refurbishment project.

But one night is never going to be enough, not when Eli has as much mastery in the bedroom as the courtroom, and Ava has to decide whether it's worth changing the space around her so there's room for him.

A life-changing incident, family shenanigans and a persistent ex-girlfriend are enough to persuade anyone to close the door and walk away. But Eli isn't the type to let what he wants walk off with his heart.

Eli Ward argues a good case for making their space a joint one. The question is will she let him win?
Carry on reading for a quick peak.

CHANGING SPACES

Callaghan GREEN

CHAPTER ONE – APRIL

Ava

"Sorry, was that your toe?"

I shook my head and bit back the words that hung like sharpened knives on the tip of my tongue. It was a wedding, a big celebratory family occasion and as much as I have enjoyed, and maybe shed a few tears, seeing my brother say his vows to his bride, my tolerance for fuckwits who were trying to cop a feel was wearing low.

"I'm a much better dancer if you turn round."

Yes, so you can grind your cock into my ass mistakenly thinking it's going to spellbind me into sleeping with you. "I think I'm going to take a break. These shoes are a nightmare." I tried to flash a smile at some son of my parents' friend who'd been brought at their plus one. His mother had smiled desperately when he'd offered me a drink and I'd heard the warning bells in my head that she was hoping she'd found her son – Bradley, I think - a potential wife.

"I'll come sit with you. I'd like to get your thoughts on

what area I should be looking at to buy a rental." His hand was now on my hip.

If I had been in a bar or a club, or even at a function where my brother had not just committed himself to the most perfect woman for him, I'd have removed the hand from my hip and potentially from Bradley's wrist too. But violence, so my mother had told me, was not on tonight's agenda.

Another hand, this one firmer, touched my shoulder, causing my head to snap round. "Ava, I think your sister was looking for you."

My smile this time was wider than the Cheshire cat from Alice in Wonderland and my sigh of relief nearly blew my saviour away. I knew for a fact that neither Payton nor Claire would be looking for me. Claire, my eldest sister, was heavily pregnant and had gone for a 'lie down' with her fiancé in their hotel room; Payton was currently having a drinking competition with her twin brother. "Thanks, Eli," I said, my hand automatically moving to his arm. "Sorry, Bradley, I need to check on Claire."

"No problem. Catch you later? I'd like to buy you a drink – maybe see if you're free one evening next week." Bradley's eyes were too far south for anyone's liking, apart from his. At least I'd got his name right.

I looked at Eli, hoping he could somehow read my mind and help me out of a situation that could end up being persistently irritating for the rest of the evening. The firm hand that had been on my shoulder transferred to my waist and I was pulled into his side. A possessive move. I let myself lean in a little and gave him a thankful look with a little extra eyelash fluttering for good measure.

Elijah Ward was a partner in my family's law firm, Callaghan Green. He was the senior partner in my sister, Payton's, commercial something department and was good friends with my three brothers who also worked there, one being today's groom, Jackson. I was one of two Callaghan siblings who weren't lawyers: instead I flipped houses and made them pretty, hence I had no idea about the department Eli worked in.

"I think we're busy most nights this week. We have that meal with my sister on Wednesday." He gave me an amused glance.

He was tall, almost a foot more than I was, which wasn't difficult given that the women in my family were tiny.

"But thank you for the offer."

Bradley's jaw dropped. The urge to laugh was strong, but instead I focused on Eli, his dark pools of chocolate eyes and the six o'clock shadow that was grazing it. "I'd forgotten about that. I'd better find out what Claire wants. Do you know where she is?"

We walked away from the dance floor, his hand on the small of my back, guiding me towards the courtyard outside that had been decorated with fairy lights and flowers.

"Thank you for saving me," I said, the quietness outside almost unsettling with the party that was still going on.

"You mean you're not coming to dinner with my sister on Wednesday?" Eli raised his hands in mock horror. "Damn."

I laughed, sitting down on the bench, my feet genuinely aching. I would've abandoned the shoes by now, but my bridesmaid's dress was long and I needed the extra height they gave my short-assed self.

Eli sat down next to me. "I would've 'saved' you sooner, but I wasn't sure if it was needed."

I wondered how long he'd been watching me for and why. I'd met him several times after work with my brothers and sisters when we'd gone for drinks. He was around my eldest brother's age, nine or ten years older than me, and as far as I knew he was in a relationship, albeit a long distance one. His girlfriend had been out with us once or twice. She'd been pleasant, again - older than me, maybe older than him and very sensible. Payton and I had been on our fourth round of shots when she'd ordered water, giving us a knowing look that we'd thoroughly ignored.

"It was needed. He was about to get handsy," I said, my own hands moving around, gesturing, which was how I usually knocked things over. "He's the son of a friend of my parents and I think his mum was hoping he'd get lucky and find a rich wife. Or maybe even just a wife. Although I suspect he'd have been happy with a lay." I winced. "I'd have dispatched him but I didn't want to cause a scene."

Eli chuckled, his face breaking out into a broad smile. "I almost feel sorry for him. He was looking at you as if you were all his Christmases rolled into one with a couple of Hanukahs too. Want to wait out here for a bit to give him time to move on? I could do with some fresh air."

"You mean you want to get away from the madness inside?" I said, understanding how he felt. It had ended up being a big wedding reception after a smaller, more intimate service. Jackson and my brothers had looked horrendously handsome and Vanessa, my new sister, had been beautiful and excruciatingly happy. The day had been perfect - except for Bradley and his adventurous hands. But it had also been busy, the room now packed with colleagues, friends, old school chums and family connections such as Bradley and his mother, so I understood Eli's desire to sit outside in the spring evening sun.

His laughter was deep and vibrated through me, waking up sense that had been dulled by alcohol.

"I could do with a break. How about I get us some drinks so you don't have to fend off any more Bradleys?"

"Sounds perfect," I stretched out my legs and figured I could get rid of the heels from hell. The bride and groom were too wrapped up in each other to notice that I'd disappeared, and given that alcohol was as plentiful as blood in most Callaghan veins right now, there was a good chance my siblings wouldn't notice either.

The flash of a smile brightened his usual serious expression and I found myself genuinely smiling back. It wasn't that I didn't like weddings, or social gatherings. I did. I enjoyed the chat and the music and the fun that was there to be had and the day had been perfect. But it had also been exhausting. We'd been up early to have our hair done and then make up, manicures, pedicures and every other cure Vanessa had thought of. It hadn't been painful or tedious and I hadn't needed to keep my filters on as I was with my sisters and two other women I was close to.

Watching my brother see his bride and say his vows had been hard. I rarely bothered to control myself: my tears fell as easily as I usually issued my smiles, but today I'd finally, at the age of twenty-seven felt grown up. Jackson managed the law firm; he carried his responsibility well but had, like the rest of us, avoided serious relationships. For all of us, our loyalty was to our jobs and we'd learned that from our father. But Vanessa had changed something in him, something for the better, something that made him contently happy.

A bottle of champagne and a jug of what looked like margarita appeared before me like an offering to a god. Not that I was a god, at the moment I was a tired and slightly dishevelled bridesmaid. It was however the first alcohol I'd had apart from a glass of champagne with the speeches and I was feeling the need to catch up. "Thank you, thank you, thank you," I said, looking up at Eli.

"It's not all for you, you know," he said, sitting down next to me. "Shift up and share the seat. And the champagne."

I moved, aware of his size and his scent, which reminded me of the woods and forests, clean and musky. His leg brushed against mine and I remembered watching him playing rugby with my brothers: he was strong with cut, lean, defined muscle. "I'm happy to share. I have six siblings. If I couldn't share I was doomed to start with."

There was that chuckle again. "Eldest of four. I had no chance but to share, otherwise it got taken from me. You're the youngest – everyone had to share with you." He uncorked the champagne quietly and poured. "I guarantee you that if you drink your champagne before me, someone will come over and say, 'let Ava have the rest of yours because she's younger!' Seriously, it happened all the fucking time." He glanced up at me with a tiny smile that belied the humour beyond his annoyance.

"Eldest of four," I said, surprised I didn't know this already, but then why would I? "Brothers? Sisters?"

"Three sisters," he said. "I was serious about Wednesday. I'm meeting the eldest of them, Izzy, for dinner." He looked cranky.

"Does she live in London?"

Eli nodded and was about to speak but a loud whoop came from inside the function room that sounded suspiciously like one of my brothers.

"She lives in Highbury." He rolled his eyes at the noise. In all likelihood, it was Seph, providing extra entertainment.

I prodded his thigh with my finger. "I'm assuming from your decided lack of enthusiasm that this isn't going to be a highlight of your week?"

He reached to the tray and passed me a glass of champagne. "You assume right."

We knocked the glasses together and sipped liquid, the burn and bubbles familiar as the drink slipped down my throat. It had been a steady stream of alcohol and the hit of the shot gave me a pleasant buzz. I was staying over at the venue, so I wasn't overly concerned about having a couple of drinks. "So tell, why's seeing Izzy not on your list of Top Ten Things to do in London this week?"

He sipped the champagne. "Because she's going to ask me thirty dozen questions, none of which I'll have the right answer to."

"What's the theme of the questions?"

He shook his head, finishing his glass and then topping up both of our glasses. "Let's not go there. I saw Bradley at the bar. He came over and apologised."

I frowned. "What for?"

"For assuming you were single. He then congratulated me on finding such a 'good catch' who was also 'hot as fuck'." He was deadpan as he said it.

I let my forehead hit the table, not quite enough to hurt, but dramatically enough to make Eli laugh. "Seriously? Why? Why do men still think it's okay to talk about women like they're some sort of trophy?" I muffled my rather loud groan with my hands.

Footsteps thudding made me look up to see two of my brothers head into the courtyard, two blondes with them. I quietened and watched as they displayed the mating rituals of peacocks; Seph trying to flex his bicep subtly and failing; Callum, running fingers through his hair like a C-list movie star. I shook my head and downed another shot. "I can't watch this," I muttered to Eli. "It's like a bad soap opera."

His hand touched the small of my back, a soft pressure applying warmth through the thin material of my dress. "You should watch. It's comedy gold."

Pulling my head up and setting sight on the scene in front of us took a lot of effort. I'd been witness to many attempt by my brothers to entice some poor pretty girl into their beds for the night and it never became less cringe-worthy to watch. "Seph's using his reel-them-in-with-his-physique-technique,"

I said in an undertone. "The poor things usually fall for it too."

"Maybe I should take some tips from him," Eli said.

I frowned. "What would your girlfriend say about that?" I hated cheating. If you were interested in someone else, then your current relationship wasn't working and you needed to get out of it.

"I don't have a girlfriend anymore."

"Oh."

I wasn't sure what else to say. None of my brothers had mentioned it, but why would they? Callum chose that moment to thread his arms around his girl's waist and pull her into him with his hands cupping her ass; Seph had slid over to a darker corner of the courtyard.

"I really can't watch."

There was that short laugh again. "Do you want to move back inside so you can't see?"

The night was one of those that should've belonged at the end of a heady summer's day with a bonfire on a field and vats of moonshine, cut off shorts and no fucking worries in the world. And the courtyard was gorgeous, full of spring flowers and fairy lights. Plus, two too many members of my family. I stood up suddenly, almost rocking the table. "No. Why don't we go to my room?" I wasn't entirely sure where the words had come from, all I knew was that I needed a break from the constant parade of dramas that were unfolding throughout the venue. Then I thought about my words and laughed. "I didn't mean it like *that*. I'd just like some quiet for an hour or so."

Eli stood up and started to put our glasses on the tray with the remainder of the bottle of champagne. "Same here. Lead the way."

My brothers were oblivious to me being anywhere nearby. Had it been Max and Jackson, the eldest, they'd have had some weird sixth sense about me being there with Eli and on our own which would've made them look concerned and perturbed, probably more about Eli's wellbeing than mine. We slipped away, through the hallways of the building to the small hotel where family and a couple of close friends were staying. "Are you staying here?" I said to Eli, slipping my hand into my bra for the key card to my room.

His brows raised at what I was doing. "That's one place to keep it safe," he said. "No, I'm heading home. It isn't that far."

I sensed there was more of story there, probably one about his ex-girlfriend and them meant to be making a weekend of the wedding, especially as she hadn't lived in London. My door clicked open, exposing a room that was thankfully tidy given that the getting ready had been done in the bridal suite. Had it been used for me getting ready it would've been a case of the room being coated in outfits and makeup and probably underwear, although pretty underwear in all fairness. There was a small table and two chairs near to the large windows that overlooked a small park. Eli headed over there without asking or waiting for me. Decisive.

I closed the door behind us and studied the man in front of me. Eli was broad and built, a long drink of something hard but smooth, served without ice because there was no way any woman would want to cool that heat. His ex must've had her reasons for ending it and I'd have been lying if I said I didn't want to know what they were.

"It's a nice room." He added more bubbles to our glasses and passed me mine. "I know Max is staying here. Are the rest of your family?"

His tie was slightly askew and as I sat down opposite him at the table I resisted the temptation to straighten it, to see my fingers against the plaid pattern and feel its silk. "We're all here. My mother's beside herself. And Claire's managed not to give birth yet, so it looks like we're all staying." My eldest sister was pregnant with her first child. Very pregnant. And very irritable. "Are you close with your family?"

He looked preoccupied, as if a ton of something prickly was sat on his shoulders. "Not as close as you Callaghans," he said. "But we're close. I'm only wanting to avoid Izzy because she'll feel sorry for me about breaking up with Andrea. And ask lots of questions."

"Why did you break up with Andrea?" I said, the words tumbling out before I had time to clamp my jaw shut. I chugged back some champagne.

His smile was genuine but knowing. "I heard from your brothers that you said exactly what you thought."

"Shit, they warned you about me?"

He laughed, the sound warm and full. "They've mentioned you a couple of times."

"I didn't mean to pry," I said. "Well, I did, but not in a gossipy way."

He folded his arms and grinned, saying nothing. His eyes were hazel, flecks of gold brightening them and his features were chiselled. He looked nothing but masculine and for a nano-second I felt like the geeky girl in the corner. A nano-second. No longer than that, because I wasn't the type to do shy or retiring. Elijah Ward was hotter than a kitchen fire.

"So tell Aunty Ava exactly why you're now single and about to Tinder." I folded my arms too.

"I'm not going on Tinder," Eli said. "Ever." He passed another shot glass over to me. "Drink."

I obliged, downing the liquid in one and feeling the alcohol hit me, feeling how it soothed the busyness that I'd been swimming in all day. "There's nothing wrong with Tinder," I said. "Depending on what you want."

"Ava, I'm thirty-five. I've swiped right in real time enough in bars and clubs."

I opened the door that led onto the small veranda outside, the sounds of the party downstairs flying up to us. The cooler air was pleasant and fresher, the evening starting to dumb-down the unusual April heat. "So why did you split up?"

"Persistent, aren't you?" His eyes meeting mine - those chocolate eyes. "She ended it. The long distance wasn't working for her and she'd ended up meeting someone else who had just started working for the same company."

I nodded, holding his gaze and not wanting to let it go. "Long distance is hard."

He nodded. "The plan was for her to relocate and move here, but it never happened. She got a promotion and she had friends and a base there. We grew apart."

"Relationships are difficult," I said. "And I know you're going to roll your eyes and question whether I've ever been in one and the answer is yes, but none for any duration. A year was the longest when I was at college, but that ended before I came back to England."

"I wouldn't patronise you."

He didn't smile when he said it and for a second I didn't see my brothers' colleague and friend, I saw someone else. I just wasn't sure who.

"Yes, relationships are difficult."

I put my non-drinking hand over his that was resting face down on the table. My hand was tiny compared, pale against his darker skin. I didn't want to move it, and he seemed quite happy to keep it there. "You know what they say: the best way to get over a woman is to get under another one." There was a hitch to my voice and I bit my lips together, realising what I was suggesting. My heart had started to tap out a dance and my head started to risk assess my current situation.

Sex was fun and I enjoyed it. Eli was attractive and not a douche, but he was also hugely connected to my family. But he wasn't twenty-five and he wasn't a bit of kid. If he was interested.

He moved his hand away.

"Maybe you're right. I saw it coming and now I'm pissed that even though we were seeing each other for two years I'm not that bothered we're done."

"You're angry you wasted time when you could've been meeting someone else. Or several someone elses?" I said, eyeing the tequila and deciding it was a bad idea.

Eli's eyes danced and he picked up a shot glass. "I'm not Callum. Sticking my dick in anything half way to being pretty has never been my thing."

"You've summed Callum up well." My brother was the definition of a manwhore, especially since he'd come back from saving animals in India or somewhere. "Honestly, you just have to move on. The more time you spend thinking about what you should've done; the more time you're wasting."

The rest of the champagne was drained into our glasses and I debated phoning reception to have another bottle sent up, them remembered the bottle I'd been storing for late night drinks. We Callaghans were nothing if not prepared if there was a possibility that the bar would close. Although, I was trying to maintain a degree of being drink-aware and keep an eye on my liver.

"Whisky?" I felt suddenly nervous. "Or we have another bottle of decent fizz." I jumped up again, grateful to move.

"Are you trying to get me drunk?" His eyes following me as I moved across the room. I was off kilter; Eli appeared to have some strange device that threw me off my usual confident trajectory, like an invisible space force field. "If so, go ahead."

I turned to look at him and took a step back with a smile.

"How do you take your hangovers?"

"With a full breakfast, a shot of whisky and a long run. How do you take yours?"

"I'm immune," I said. "I don't get them." I'd learned to drink water, lots of it and to ease off a couple of hours before I went to bed. I was also my mother's daughter and could handle a few drinks."

"Bring the champagne," he said. "Let's start there."

THE WEDDING AGREEMENT

CHAPTER 1 - NOAH

"I completely disagree with the colour for the bridesmaids' dresses."

My mother's voice tore through the dusty peace of the salon. We were seated in her favourite room in Wastham Hall, our family's country home in Norfolk. The room hadn't changed since I was a child; the chair I'd been sitting in when she administered a scolding about my English grades was still proudly placed next to the window that overlooked the lawn, recovered in exactly the same material as it had been back then. The settee was a new leather chesterfield, but exactly the same as the one that had been there when I received my first lecture on what a suitable girlfriend looked like. And there was, of course, the small, walnut side table on which my mother's latest notebook was placed.

I had no idea what was in those notebooks; I never did have the urge to take a look, but I was pretty sure it was a list of all my failings and misdemeanours. Lady Soames-

Harrington was not one to overlook an error, no matter how small.

"I think it's too late now to change." I glanced out of the window where my niece was dancing around the lawn, and hoped my mother didn't notice. If she did, she'd complain that the child was ruining her grass.

The lawn, one should note, was key to her ladyship's happiness. This was something myself and my brothers had never fully understood. Football, rugby, cricket and setting fire to the delicate blades of grass had been strictly forbidden and punishable in many, many ways. To be fair, the setting fire I could understand – that had been problematic – but the rest... when I had children, they'd be able to play on the lawn as much as they wanted.

Just as long as that lawn was not Lady Soames'.

"It's never too late to change. I can have a seamstress to your fiancée's apartment tomorrow to take measurements, and they'll be ready with plenty of time for any alterations, although I can assure you that the people I would arrange wouldn't need to make any alternations." She picked up her notebook and studied her pen.

I sat a little further back into my seat and glanced over at my father. He was studying the paper he always placed in the salon, knowing that Lady S didn't approve of technology in there. He didn't look up, fully immersed in the crossword and paying no attention whatsoever to the conversation.

"Carla is pretty set on what she's chosen." My wife-to-be would certainly not humour my mother in any way, shape, or form. Both were as stubborn as hell, and both were extremely happy to use me as their go-between.

"Why is Carla not here? I had assumed she'd be with you this weekend." Her Ladyship sat up a little straighter, those finishing school lessons on deportment never having quite left her.

Jeanne Soames-Harrington, neé Buchanan, had been a Lady from birth, the second child and oldest daughter of my maternal grandfather. She married my father, who was also a Lord, at nearly thirty, had my brothers when she was thirty-two and thirty-five, then I arrived, rather a surprise, when she was forty-two.

She was now seventy-four, her father ninety-eight and still one of my favourite people, living in his Scottish home that was from the stuff fairy-tales were made of. Physically, Grandfa was in the finest of health, but dementia had relieved him of some of his faculties a few years ago. I visited him as often as I could, which wasn't as often as I liked, given work and the various engagements I had to attend.

"Carla's having a girls' weekend to prepare for her hen events." I tried to bite back the irritation I was feeling. We were due to get married in six weeks. In that time, she had three hen parties: this weekend in London with meals at the top restaurants, a spa day, and 'secret' events that I'd seen the invoice for. It was enough to buy a top of the range Maserati. Another was a five-day trip to Monte Carlo; the third a sedate afternoon tea with her mother and older guests.

Lady Soames' nose wrinkled briefly. "How very modern." There was a brief shake of her head. "I have informed her that I find her bridesmaids' dresses more than distasteful. I understand she's a modern woman, but she has been brought up to have some dignity. Also, I raised the issue with her mother."

I nodded and glanced back outside. My niece – the daughter of my eldest brother, Angus, was still running on the grass. I really hoped my mother didn't spot her. Luckily for Catherine, Lady S's attention was all on me.

"Her mother understood, of course. I think she's most disconcerted by Carla's behaviours."

She wasn't the only one.

"Apparently, Carla's dress is rather undignified also."

"I wouldn't know, mother. Tradition is that the groom doesn't see the dress until the wedding day." I sighed and folded my arms, trying to conjure up some form of excitement at seeing my bride walk down the aisle towards me, and failing miserably, just as I had for most of the last six months since we'd become engaged.

Don't get me wrong, Carla was gorgeous, in a way that social media expected her to be. She was the daughter of the owner and CEO of a company that developed software, and her father was ambitious for her to step into the upper classes of society, hence the reason for part of the marriage.

Or possibly most of the marriage.

"Of course, and this will be a very traditional wedding. I was hoping she'd be with you this weekend. I had the Hollyhock room specially prepared." There was another shake of the head. "Such an inconvenience."

My mother was under no illusion I was a virgin, but she had every hope that Carla was. She wasn't. I had first-hand experience that her V-card had been well and truly stamped, and not by me. Not as much experience as you might've expected given we'd been engaged six months and 'dated' for two, but we'd managed a few nights together in between dates on her hectic social schedule.

"I'm sure Carla didn't mean it to be an inconvenience, mother." I was pretty sure Carla hadn't even thought what preparations might occur for in case she stayed. This wasn't what you could call a love match. Complicated match was definitely a better description.

There was a shout from outside, my nephew, Catherine's slightly older brother rugby tackled her from behind, slamming them both onto the ground. I watched, ready to run outside if Catherine was injured, but instead she wriggled free and punched him in the face.

The sound had caught Lady Soames' attention, her usually pale skin flushing pink. Not with concern for her grandchildren, but instead for her lawn.

"I'll go and ask them to play elsewhere." My father put his paper down and stood up. "You continue with your conversation. That's far more important."

My father was one of the few people who could play her like a fiddle, completely ignoring the glare she gave him, folding his paper and strolling out of the room, knowing full well she wouldn't argue with him in front of me.

That would be uncouth.

"Have you arranged for movers to pack and transport Carla's belongings to your home while you're on your honeymoon?" Lady Soames clasped both hands in her lap. "You shouldn't return to different houses after your honeymoon."

I didn't let the wince show. I wasn't sure I was ready to live with Carla. She stayed over a couple of times a week, usually after we'd been out to dinner with some of her society friends or business acquaintances of mine. I lived in West Brompton, in between Chelsea and Fulham, in a house that had been in our family since it was built.

Carla had an apartment in Chelsea that she shared with her friend, a friend who'd made appearances on a long running reality TV show, something I figured my mother was unaware of. If she was, she'd been remarkably calm about it, and I had a feeling that if she knew what Carla's friends were like, she'd be terminating this engagement with immediate effect.

"I have a team booked." This wasn't quite true. I had the number of a team to book when I got round to it. And when I'd discussed it with Carla. She'd hinted at moving in already, but we'd decided that we were better waiting until after we were married – which seemed to please both sets of parents, at least. Carla had mentioned that she wanted to make a big deal of it when she moved in, having a housewarming or something so she could show her new friends where she now lived, which seemed to be the theme of our relationship so far.

The door opened, my eldest brother, Angus, burst through it. Angus should've been the one to carry on the family business of property management and looking after the investment portfolios that my father had inherited from his father, but he'd avoided that by becoming a surgeon. A pretty good one, or at least good enough for Lady Soames to not be too displeased by his decision to flee the family shackles – sorry, business.

"Afternoon all." He grinned as he walked in, sitting heavily on the sofa. "How's the groom to be?"

I flipped him the bird.

Her ladyship looked displeased.

"It's not that bad. Just learn when to nod without actually listening. That's how our dad survived for so long." He put his feet up on the coffee table.

"Angus, you are not at your home now. No need to act as if you are feral."

"Sorry, Ma." He put his feet down and grinned, the dimple that we'd all inherited on display. "Looking forward to your stag do?"

I grunted, trying to drum up some enthusiasm. Truth be told, I wasn't looking forward to anything.

The wedding ticked boxes. A society wedding that met Lady Soames' approval; a bride whose family were old-new money and she therefore wasn't after any of our fortune – although I suspected she was hoping she'd have more to spend than what she got from her father; a future wife who understood etiquette and presented nicely, which equalled the youngest son married and settled.

And it meant my grandfather would see the one thing he seemed to remember wanting.

Alister Buchanan had been my favourite person when I was a kid. I spent summers with him, and most Christmases too. He taught me to ride, to shoot, to fish. He taught me the rules of rugby and exactly how to camp with nothing other than a tent and a running river.

He was my boyhood hero, and when his daughter was being unnecessarily strict, he stuck up for me.

Four years ago, he was diagnosed with dementia but remained physically fit. He still recognised me now, he'd phone me, and we'd have a conversation about the next time we'd go wild camping, or about the rugby, and then he'd ask me when I was getting married.

He wanted to see me married. He'd ask about my girl, then want details about the wedding. I knew we probably didn't have that much time before attending a wedding would be beyond him, or how much longer we'd have him around.

That was why I was marrying Carla so quickly, or maybe even at all. She ticked boxes. She was attractive, she could hold a conversation and maybe we would fall in love, eventually.

Just excuse me if I wasn't that enthusiastic.

"It's a weekend of drinking." I shrugged. My stag do would have to happen. After it, we'd be closer to the wedding.

"There's nothing wrong with a weekend of drinking. Make the most of it, because once that ring's on her finger, you no longer belong to you. You'll just be some sort of lackey with the title of 'husband'." He grinned, rubbing his hands together. "I'm looking forward to watching every minute of it."

"That does not sound pervy at all." I glared at him. He was basking in the idea of me getting married.

Gus had married his wife when he was twenty-four and still in med school. His wife was not the socialite Lady S had wanted for him, but the doctor who'd been there while he recovered from some near-fatal virus he caught from a patient he'd been treating.

Vivi was great; no nonsense, practical, organised and completely ruled his roost. My brother loved every minute of it, and he'd told me on at least three occasions when he'd had too many whiskies how glad he was that he found her when they were young.

I hadn't envied him. Our mother had been half-pissed off that he married someone she hadn't decided for him, him being the first born and all that, but she begrudgingly liked Vivi, she just hadn't been the one to 'pick' her as a wife and future Lady. And unlike me, Gus hadn't been pictured in far too many gossip columns with a different woman on his arm each time.

That *had* been me.

"I don't mean watching *that* bit." He laughed, glancing at Lady S.

She looked even more disgruntled. "Do you have to be so uncouth?"

Angus laughed. "Boys will be boys, mother."

She shook her head. "You need to speak to Vivienne about letting the children play on the lawn, Angus."

"No, I don't." He sat back. Angus did not take any telling off from Lady S, he never had. "They're children and playing outside is good for them."

"But they flatten my lawn."

"Which will repair and be as good as new, unlike children's spirits if you quash their enjoyment out of them." He raised a brow at her.

"I didn't let you destroy my lawn and you turned out…" She stopped and shook her head. "Never mind. I have to go and prepare for my call with Jane Bebbington." She stood up, more slowly than she had in the past, but still with the same grace I knew she'd wanted to pass onto a daughter. She sometimes tried with Catherine, who was more tomboy than future socialite, and never in the mood to listen to what her grandmother had to say.

Angus seemed to be studying me as Lady S left the room, his arms folded over his chest.

"What?" I stood up and went to the bay window, looking at the lawn that was definitely flattened.

"If she's not right for you, don't, for fuck's sake, marry her." His voice was low, quiet. "You might look pretty together, but you have no chemistry and I'm not sure you even like her, never mind be in love with her."

"Being in love with someone isn't necessary for a wedding."

"This isn't just a wedding, Noah, it's a marriage. One of those commitments that's meant to last a lifetime."

I didn't say anything, because part of me knew he was right. Marrying Carla was a way to cover a lot of bases, the biggest being my grandfather getting to see me married. I had no idea what would happen six months, twelve months, hell, even two months, after we were married. Neither of us had thought that far ahead.

"If she's not your Vivi, you shouldn't marry her. Even for Grandfa." His expression wasn't full of laughter now. He looked serious. "I know why you're going through with this, Noah, and it's noble of you, but Grandfa wouldn't want you to marry just to so he could see your wedding."

I sighed and watched the river that ran through the garden, far enough away that it looked like more of a stream.

"I know. But for how much longer is he going to be aware

of anything that's actually happening? If Carla and I end up separated after six months, he's not going to know. But at least I'll know he saw me get married. I'll have those memories." I turned back around, my father chasing Catherine and my nephew, Jimmy, across the lawn now my mother wasn't around to watch.

"What's her motivation for marrying you? Apart from the obvious." Gus rubbed his chin.

"She has enough money of her own. Her parents are pissed at her for how she's been behaving the last couple of years and they're on at her to settle down. And I think she's pretty into me." I felt a total tool saying that last bit, but I kind of got the impression that she did. She'd told me once that I was 'good arm candy', and how much the camera loved me. I'd put her words down to the margaritas she'd been drinking and hoped there was more to it than that.

Gus shook his head. "Whatever. Vivi doesn't like her. And she doesn't like what you're doing either. She thinks this is just going to end in disaster."

"Not everyone can fall madly in love with the right person at the right time. And you know I don't subscribe to this whole madly in love with someone fairy tale any way. You and Vivi are an exception." I'd already known two of my friends go through divorces, one engagement end sourly and seen one of my best friends from university get severely fucked up when the girl he'd lost his mind over ended their relationship. Carla was a lot of things I wasn't sure of, but I was sure that I wasn't going have my heart broken by her.

"What about Robbie? Does he not count?" Gus grinned when he mentioned our other brother.

"He counts double. You think Her Ladyship will ever actually say she's happy for him?" Robbie lived in Manchester with his husband. When he came out to our parents, Lady S had refused to speak to him for three months.

It was awful and difficult for us all, especially Robbie and Connor. Dad wasn't surprised or bothered, and Robbie had told me and Gus a couple of years before that he was gay, although it wasn't like we hadn't suspected it.

Lady S was always going to take it badly. She actually asked what she'd done wrong, something that made Gus lose the plot completely and Dad walk out. But, to her credit, she attended Robbie and Connor's wedding, and made Connor feel welcome when they visited. But we all saw that she was struggling with Robbie not being 'society perfect' even if he was the happiest he'd ever been. Now she'd worked through it, and her relationship with her son-in-law was one we all knew she treasured. Thankfully. Else we'd have had to disown her.

"I think she just pretends to not be impressed. She's far worse with Carla. Robbie said they've started to look into a surrogate." Gus stretched and the rubbed his shoulder.

"That's good. They'll make excellent parents."

Gus laughed. "No one makes excellent parents, but they'll give it their best shot. Have you sorted the pre-nup?"

I pushed a hand through my hair. "Her solicitor has sent it to mine. I'm meeting her on Monday."

"Callaghan Green?"

I nodded. We'd been using Callaghan Green for years. My father and Grant Callaghan went way back, and I'd continued to use the same firm when I took over the reins. "I need to go into their offices anyway to sort out this boundary dispute."

Gus didn't even try to look interested at that. "Before you sign the pre-nup, can I look through it? I know you're desperate to get married so Grandfa can be there, but that's not worth a momentous fuck up that'll hang over the rest of your life."

I nodded. "Meet for drinks on Monday?"

"Can do. I finish at four, so I'll see you at five. The kids have a party to go to and it's Vivi's turn to sit through hell." His grin was wicked. "Never, ever go to a children's party. It's a level of pain that you've never experienced before."

I nodded. There wasn't much chance of that at the moment.

SLEIGHED

Annie Dyer
SLEIGHED

SEVERTON SEARCH & RESCUE BOOK 1

Take a trip to Severton, with this small town, romantic suspense - you'll never want to leave!

Zack Maynard rubbed at the thick stubble that had accumulated since that morning and debated which incompetence he should yell about first. He was spoilt for choice given that one of his staff had failed to lock a door that should be kept locked and bolted at all times, and a resident had gone exploring. His cousin, Jake, had delivered a truck full of alpacas to the field next to Severton Sunlight Care and Nursing Home and had neglected to tell his farmhand to ensure the gate was shut. And the world's slowest builders had seemingly been employed to take as much time as possible to erect the extension to the dementia care unit and entertainment hall, and the words coming out of the site manager's mouth were not the ones he wanted to hear.

"We're looking at mid-January."

Zack stuffed his hands in his coat pockets. "I'm sorry. Can you repeat that?"

"It's unlikely to be finished before mid-Jan. I realise that's a bit of a pain…"

His accent was broad, thickly Northern and Zack knew he needed to be careful not to mimic it.

"You realise there's a clause in the contract if the building wasn't fit for purpose on December twentieth so we can use it for Christmas dinner?" He managed to ignore an alpaca that was lingering nearby. He was going to kill his fucking cousin.

Jez Hammond, site manager non-extraordinaire, nodded and made a noise that could be interpreted as an agreement. "I realise that, as does the company. However, there was some issues with laying the foundations that's slowed us down and we've encountered a problem with labour."

Zack looked at the site, the half-finished shell of a building and the surrounding rubble. "What's the issue with labour?" He could see maybe four men at work and even though he wasn't an expert on construction, even he knew that this wasn't enough.

"The usual shortage. Contractors, you know?"

The alpaca made an odd snorting noise and edged closer, its mouth slightly hung open, displaying large teeth.

Jake was going to die.

And then possibly be used as alpaca food.

"I don't know. I manage a care home for the elderly. Working with builders, electricians, plasterers, plumbers —*that* isn't my speciality. It's what I'm paying *you* for. And right now, I can count the number of people working on this project on *one* hand."

The alpaca came closer. It nudged Jez's arm and made a strange sound again. A rather excited sound. One Zack was wary of. He was going to fucking kill Jake, even if it would upset his aunt.

"I'm doing what I can, son. We were running behind, but we should've been done in time for Christmas so you could use the hall for your do, but the lass at the hotel on the hill has paid over the odds for labourers so we're down. If these bloody schools would stop encouraging kids to go to university to study bleeding Harry Potter and get them in proper work instead, we wouldn't be so far behind." Jez patted his shapely beer belly.

Zack's words froze in his mouth. Not because the temperature was skating lower than normal for this time of year, but because the alpaca's expression had turned to one of sheer delight as it started to sink its teeth into the thick fleece of the site manager's coat. It was an action Zack could only attribute to fate.

"Holy fuck!" Jez yelled, yanking his arm away. But the alpaca's teeth were firmly sunk into the material. "Get this bastard animal off my bleeding arm? I thought this was a care home, not a freaking petting zoo with sadistic fucking beasts." He carried on pulling his arm away from the set jaws of the alpaca.

"I'm going to feed Jake limb by limb to his new fucking pets," Zack muttered under his breath, trying to entice the alpaca away.

He saw Lee Barnes, Jake's farmhand trying to round up the rest of the escaped animals and shouted him over. Lee strode over, taking his own sweet time. He was dressed in just a T-shirt and ripped jeans, oblivious to the cold.

"We have a situation." Zack pointed at the animal. "Please let my cousin know he's going to be in a situation later. Where the hell have these creatures come from? And why?"

Lee shrugged. He was a man of few words at the best of times, preferring to communicate through the set of drums he hit most weekends. He leaned over to the creature and blew at its nose. The alpaca gave a gentle snort and released its death chomp.

"Sorry about that." Lee didn't look that sorry. "I'll get rounding them up."

"Make sure you do." Zack turned back towards Jez. "Why can't you stop your contractors from working on the hotel and get them back down here?"

Jez rubbed at his arm. "We don't have the budget to pay them what the lass up there has agreed to. And they'll only be a couple of weeks, then they'll come back down here and finish off. I'm sorry, Zack, but there ain't much more I can do."

"I'll see about upping the budget." Zack rubbed his face. He hadn't slept well the night before, which wasn't unusual, but he could do with climbing into bed in one of the unoccupied rooms—or hell, even May Pearson's room because she didn't move from her sofa in front of the TV—and collapsing for an hour or six. "Find out how much more she's paying them and let me know."

Jez shook his head. "But then you'll be stuck paying that rate until the job's done. It's not just extra cash over two weeks, you'll end up going right over. If I were you, I'd hang on till the lass has had her work done. It's only an extension and from what I hear it's pretty straightforward." He looked to where Lee was herding the alpacas, apparently turning into the animal whisperer. "How do you think those animals taste?"

"Not as good as revenge will when I get hold of Jake."

ALSO BY ANNIE DYER

The Callaghan Green Series
In Suggested Reading order (can be read as stand-alones)
Engagement Rate

What happens when a hook up leaves you hooked? Jackson Callaghan is the broody workaholic who isn't looking for love until he meets his new marketing executive? Meet the Callaghans in this first-in-series, steamy office romance.

White Knight

If you're in the mood for a second chance romance with an older brother's best friend twist, then look no further. Claire Callaghan guards her heart as well as her secrets, but Killian O'Hara may just be the man to take her heart for himself.

Compromising Agreements

Grumpy, bossy Maxwell Callaghan meets his match in this steamy enemies-lovers story. Mistaking Victoria Davies as being a quiet secretary is only Max's first mistake, but can she be the one to make this brooding Callaghan brother smile?

Between Cases

Could there be anything better than a book boyfriend who owns a bookstore? Payton Callaghan isn't sure; although giving up relationships when she might've just met The One is a dilemma she's facing in BETWEEN CASES, a meet-cute that'll have you swooning over Owen Anders.

Changing Spaces

Love a best friend's younger sister romance? Meet Eli, partner in the Callaghan Green law firm and Ava's Callaghan's steamy one-night stand that she just can't seem to keep as just one night. Independent, strong-willed and intelligent, can Eli be the man Ava wants?

Heat

Feeling hungry? Get a taste of this single dad, hot chef romance in HEAT. Simone Wood is a restaurant owner who loves to dance, she's just never found the right partner until her head chef Jack starts to teach her his rhythm. Problem is, someone's not happy with Simone, and their dance could be over before they've learned the steps.

Mythical Creatures

The enigmatic Callum Callaghan heads to Africa with the only woman who came close to taming his heart, in this steamy second-chance romance. Contains a beautifully broken alpha and some divinely gorgeous scenery in this tale that will make you both cry and laugh. HEA guaranteed.

Melted Hearts

Hot rock star? Enemies to lovers? Fake engagement? All of these ingredients are in this Callaghan Green novel. Sophie Slater is a businesswoman through and through but makes a pact with the devil – also known as Liam Rossi, newly retired Rockstar – to get the property she wants - one that just happens to be in Iceland. Northern lights, a Callaghan bachelor party, and a quickly picked engagement ring are key notes in this hot springs heated romance.

Evergreen

Christmas wouldn't be Christmas without any presents, and that's what's going to happen if Seph Callaghan doesn't get his act together. The Callaghan clan are together for Christmas, along with a positive pregnancy test from someone and several more surprises!

The Partnership

Seph Callaghan finally gets his HEA in this office romance. Babies, exes and a whole lot of smoulder!

The English Gent Romances

The Wedding Agreement

Imogen Green doesn't do anything without thinking it through, and that includes offering to marry her old - very attractive - school friend, Noah Soames, who needs a wedding. The only problem is, their fauxmance might not be so fake, after all…

The Atelier Assignment

Dealing with musty paintings is Catrin Green's job. Dealing with a hot Lord who happens to be grumpy AF isn't. But that's what she's stuck with for three months. Zeke's daughter is the only light in her days, until she finds a way to make Zeke smile. Only this wasn't part of the assignment.

The Romance Rehearsal

Maven Green has managed to avoid her childhood sweetheart for more than a decade, but now he's cast as her leading man in the play she's directing. Anthony was the boy who had all her firsts; will he be her last as well?

The Imperfect Proposal

Shay Green doesn't expect his new colleague to walk in on him when he's mid-kiss in a stockroom. He also doesn't expect his new colleague to be his wife. The wife he married over a decade ago in Vegas and hasn't seen since

Puffin Bay Series

Puffin Bay

Amelie started a new life on a small Welsh island, finding peace and new beginnings. What wasn't in the plan was the man buying the building over the road. She was used to dealing with arrogant tourists, but this city boy was enough to have her want to put her hands around his neck, on his chest, and maybe somewhere else too...

Wild Tides

Being a runaway bride and escaping her wedding wasn't what Fleur intended when she said yes to the dress. That dress is now sodden in the water of the Menai Strait and she needs saving - by none other than lighthouse keeper Thane. She needs a man to get under to get over the one she left at the altar - but that might come with a little surprise in a few months time…

Lovers Heights

Serious gin distiller Finn Holland needs a distraction from what he's trying to leave behind in the city. That distraction comes in the form of Ruby, who's moved to the island to escape drama of her own.

Neither planned on a fake relationship, especially one that led to a marriage that might not be that fake at all...

Manchester Athletic FC
Penalty Kiss

Manchester Athletic's bad boy needs taming, else his football career could be on the line. Pitched with women's football's role model pin up, he has pre-season to sort out his game - on and off the field.

Hollywood Ball

One night. It didn't matter who she was, or who he was, because tomorrow they'd both go back to their lives. Only hers wasn't that ordinary.

What she didn't know, was neither was his.

Heart Keeper

Single dad. Recent widow. Star goal keeper.

Manchester Athletic's physio should keep her hands to herself outside of her treatment room, but that's proving tough. What else is tough is finding two lines on that pregnancy test...

Target Man

Jesse Sullivan is Manchester Athletic's Captain Marvel. He keeps his private life handcuffed to his bed, locked behind a non-disclosure agreement. Jesse doesn't do relationships – not until he meets his teammate's – and best friend's – sister.

Red Heart Card

She wants a baby. He's offering. The trouble is, he's soccer's golden boy and he's ten years younger. The last time they tried this, she broke is heart. Will hearts be left intact this time around?

Severton Search and Rescue
Sleighed

Have a change of scenery and take a trip to a small town. Visit Severton, in Sleighed; this friends-to-lovers romantic suspense will capture your heart as much as Sorrell Slater steals Zack Maynard's.

Stirred

If enemies-to-lovers is your manna, then you'll want to stay in Severton for Stirred. Keren Leigh and Scott Maynard have been at daggers drawn for years, until their one-night ceasefire changes the course of their lives forever.

Smoldered

Want to be saved by a hot firefighter? Rayah Maynard's lusted over Jonny Graham ever since she came back to town. Jonny's prioritised his three children over his own love life since his wife died, but now Rayah's teaching more than just his daughter – she's teaching him just how hot their flames can burn.

Shaken

Abby Walker doesn't exist. Hiding from a gang she suspects is involved in the disappearance of her sister, Severton is where she's taken refuge. Along with her secrets, she's hiding her huge crush on local cop, Alex Maynard. But she isn't the only one with secrets. Alex can keep her safe, but can he also take care of her heart?

Sweetened

Enemies? Friends? Could be lovers? All Jake Maynard knows is that Lainey Green is driving him mad, and he really doesn't like that she managed to buy the farm he coveted from under his nose. All's fair in love and war, until events in Severton take a sinister turn.

Standalone Romance

Love Rises

Two broken souls, one hot summer. Anya returns to her childhood island home after experiencing a painful loss. Gabe escapes to the same place, needing to leave his life behind, drowning in guilt. Neither are planning on meeting the other, but when they do, from their grief, love rises. Only can it be more than a summer long?

Bartender

The White Island, home of hedonism, heat and holidays. Jameson returns to her family's holiday home on Ibiza, but doesn't expect to charmed by a a bartender, a man with an agenda other than just seduction.

Tarnished Crowns Trilogy

Lovers. Liars. Traitors. Thieves. We were all of these. Political intrigue, suspense and seduction mingle together in this intricate and steamy royal romance trilogy.

Chandelier

Grenade

Emeralds

Crime Fiction

We Were Never Alone

How Far Away the Stars (Novella)

Printed in Great Britain
by Amazon